P9-DXR-649

Extraordinary Praise for

NEVER HAVE I EVER

"A master of domestic suspense." —*Entertainment Weekly*

"Bestselling author Jackson packs in dramatic reveals about the women's complex histories." —*Time*

"Its several plot twists are surprising and effective. . . . Many books claim to be the perfect beach read. This one . . . certainly fits the bill." —*Wall Street Journal*

"A smart, original thriller with real, compelling characters and a chilling reveal. I couldn't turn the pages fast enough."
—Clare Mackintosh, *New York Times* bestselling author of *I Let You Go*

"Jackson is a master of timing, meting out tension and detail impeccably. By the time of the explosive, entirely unexpected climax, I was clinging to the edge of my seat."
—Sara Gruen, *New York Times* bestselling author of *Water for Elephants*

"A heart-pounding tale of cat and mouse with twists you won't see coming. Just when you think you couldn't be more shocked, Jackson delivers a mind-blowing ending. Riveting!"
—Liv Constantine, internationally bestselling author of *The Last Mrs. Parrish*

Also by Joshilyn Jackson

MOTHER MAY I
THE ALMOST SISTERS
THE OPPOSITE OF EVERYONE
SOMEONE ELSE'S LOVE STORY
A GROWN-UP KIND OF PRETTY
BACKSEAT SAINTS
THE GIRL WHO STOPPED SWIMMING
BETWEEN, GEORGIA
GODS IN ALABAMA

Short Story
"MY OWN MIRACULOUS"

NEVER HAVE I EVER

A NOVEL

JOSHILYN JACKSON

WILLIAM MORROW
An Imprint of HarperCollins*Publishers*

Excerpt from *Mother May I* copyright © 2021 by Joshilyn Jackson.

First William Morrow mass market printing: March 2021
First William Morrow paperback printing: April 2020
First William Morrow hardcover printing: July 2019

Print Edition ISBN: 978-0-06-307368-5
Digital Edition ISBN: 978-0-06-285533-6

Cover design by Ploy Siripant
Cover photograph © jhorrocks/iStock/Getty Images

For three of my favorite girls, in order of height:

Taylor Myers
Olivia Browning
Tiamat Garber

NEVER HAVE I EVER

I

THE GAME WAS ROUX'S idea. More than an idea.
A plan. She made it up herself, this shotgun of a game.
She packed it tight with salt and metal, counting on col-
lateral damage, too, but she aimed it straight at me. She
said it was like Never Have I Ever, but not any version
I'd ever played. It began innocently enough, with everyone confessing the worst thing they'd done that day.

None of us had ever heard of Roux's rules, so it was
possible she invented them that night, for us. For me.
Or perhaps she'd played this way before, spreading it,
so that her game now cropped up at slumber parties
when Truth or Dare or Two Truths and a Lie had lost
their shine. Only middle-school girls could safely play
it, children whose worst thing was, *I showed my bra to
that boy I like,* or *I called my sister the b-word.*

We should have known better.

We were grown-up women, so we packed our worsts
away in hidden boxes. We were mothers, so we sank
those boxes under jobs and mortgages and meal plans.
Mothers have to sink those boxes deep.

Roux announced herself with the knocker, three
sharp raps, though of course we had a doorbell. It was

at least twenty minutes after every other neighbor who
was coming had arrived.

Charlotte, her arms full of refill snacks, paused by
the stairs and asked, "Now, who on earth could that
be?" We already had a large turnout. All the regulars
were here, and then some.

"I'll get it. Go on down to the basement."

I opened the door to a stranger, standing easy with
the fat moon rising behind her, practically perched on
her shoulder. That moon had drenched my neighborhood in silver light, soft and wavery, so she looked like
she'd climbed up the steps from an underwater world
into the egg-yolk glow of my porch light.

I knew from the hair, dead straight and dead black,
falling past her shoulder blades, that she was the latest
tenant in the Airbnb house that was the bane of Charlotte's cul-de-sac. It was a saggy-roofed eyesore that my
husband, Davis, called "the Sprite House" for its peeling green-and-yellow paint job. Char kept up a running
commentary on the house's ongoing decay and the tran-
sients and tourists who passed through it; she'd christened this latest one "Cher Hair."

Charlotte had also said she was pretty, but she was
more than that. She was the pretty that's on television:
symmetrical features, matte skin, and that kind of long,
slim, yoga body that still made me feel self-conscious
about my own. I hadn't been seriously overweight since
I was a teenager, but looking at her I was instantly
aware of the little roll of baby weight still clinging to
my middle.

No purse, no book, no bottle of wine or snack to share.
No bra either. She had on a loose, long sundress, deep

blue, patterned in silver flowers, and a tattooed flock of tiny birds soared in silhouette across her collarbone.

She smiled, and I had no premonition as I smiled back. She didn't look like my own destruction to me. She looked . . . the word was "cool."

An odd thing to think. I was forty-two years old, and "cool" was a concept I had ceded to my teenage step-daughter. Still, it was the word I thought, and if I felt anything, it was a stir, a rise. Here was something interesting.

Oliver was eating solid foods now, and I was emerging from a sedative cloud of nursing hormones a little restless, ready for a break in my routine. I looked at the loaded gun on my doorstep, and, stupid me, I hoped she had the right house.

She said, "Is this where the book club meets?"

"Yep, you found us. Amy Whey." I stuck my hand out to shake hers. Her grip was firm, and she pumped twice in a way that felt weirdly businesslike.

She said, "I'm Angelica, but everybody calls me Roux."

"Roo? As in Kanga?" I asked.

"I'm no Kanga, Christopher Robin," she said, chuckling. Her lips were full and very pale. No blush, no lipstick, but the glossy orbs of her eyes were striped with liquid liner. Her oil-black hair, middle-parted, framed the perfect oval of her face. "It's just my last name. French. With an *x* at the end?"

I knew the word. Butter and flour. A thickener.

"Did you get a chance to read *The House of Mirth*?" I asked, swinging wide the door.

"Sure," Roux said, and came inside.

It was almost eight o'clock. We usually spent an hour chatting, an hour on the book, and by nine-fifteen, nine-thirty everyone was walking home feeling a little buzzed, a little smarter, a little more bonded with the other moms in our neighborhood.

"You're in the green-and-yellow house?" I asked, to be sure I had her right. Charlotte had told me Cher Hair was a single mom with a son who was old enough to drive. Inside, under the lights, she looked to be in her mid-thirties. Awfully young to have a high-school kid.

"That's me," she said.

I led her back through the house to the basement stairs. "I'm glad you came. That place is such a short-term rental, we don't usually get the residents at book club."

"I'm here on business, and I'm not sure how long it's going to take. I could be here quite a while. Might as well meet some people," she said.

We were on the stairs now. "Oh, what do you do?"

She was looking down the stairs and didn't answer. "What's up with . . . what's her name? My neighbor?"

Charlotte was hand-wringing at the foot, giving me emergency eyebrows.

"Charlotte," I reminded her. "I don't know. Let me find someone to introduce you around."

"No need," Roux said. She sailed past me, directly into the crowd, off to introduce herself.

As soon as she was out of earshot, Char said, "Cher Hair came? Now there's twenty-one people here, not counting us, and no one seems to realize we do not have enough chairs. I should not move chairs!" She kept tucking her hair back. She looked like a nervous brown mousey, cleaning its ears.

"Her name is Roux, and of course you can't move chairs, preggo. Relax! I'll get them," I told her.

She still looked worried, because she was Charlotte. Plus, this was her book club. She'd started it when Ruby began crawling and she realized she hadn't read a book since giving birth.

"It's like the baby ate my brain!" she'd said. "Forget reading. I can't remember the last time I washed my hair."

It looked like it had been a good while, but I'd kept that to myself. Instead I'd babysat while Char designed some flyers, and then we'd tucked them into every neighborhood mailbox. She'd called it the Brain-Dead Mommies Book Club, which I thought was bad, but at least I'd talked her out of Zombie-Mombies. It turned out her AA in marketing was wiser than I was. The flyer, the name, attracted the crowd she wanted. Almost everyone here was around her age, all with babies and preschoolers and littlies still in elementary. I was the oldest mommy in the room, in most cases by a good decade.

Before Oliver was born, I'd been on the fringes of this group, knowing them mostly via gossip I got from Charlotte on our daily power walk. Back then I'd played bunco with the middle-aged mothers who had retired from caring about diapers and breast-feeding. That set rolled dice, drank hard liquor, and talked serious about puberty and pot, birth control and college applications. As the stepmom of an adolescent, I'd needed them. These days I fit in better here, and my rare Florida base-ment space and my chair-moving muscles were forever at Char's service.

"Get three chairs. Get four. Get at least three," Char told me, and started counting the women again.

I handed her the stack of printed-out discussion questions and went back up. Every time I came down with another dining-room chair, I checked on our drop-in. Roux seemed fine, easy in her skin, moving group to group. Everyone I saw her speaking with seemed to smile a little wider, laugh a little louder. They were trying to impress her, and I couldn't blame them. Roux looked so interesting, like a woman with a passport full of stamps, who would know how to make pâté from scratch, who'd probably had sex in a moving vehicle. Maybe on the way here.

I came down with the last chair just in time to see Roux holding out a hand to shake with Tate Bonasco. I paused to watch. I couldn't help it. Tate had never recovered from being pretty in high school, and she brought an eau-de-tenth-grade-lunchroom to neighborhood politics. She called me "the pit bull" behind my back, partly because I had short, sandy hair and an athletic build, but also because I'd thwarted her book-club coup. When we outgrew Char's little house, she'd cited her big den as an excuse to jack the whole thing.

"It'll give Charlotte a break from planning it, too," she'd cooed, acting as if she were doing Char a favor.

I called her on it, saying out loud, in front of everyone, that Tate only wanted it because Char had worked so hard to make it shiny and popular, plus, with Tate at the helm we'd be reading Kardashian biographies every month.

It was bitchy, but losing the club would have broken Char's heart. And it worked. In the end we moved to my large basement rec room with Char still in charge. Given the history, I couldn't help but enjoy watching standard-American-pretty Tate meet exotic Roux. Tate straightened, one hand going to smooth her hair, then excused herself to the restroom. Two minutes later she emerged with fresh lip gloss and her T-shirt knotted to show a strip of flat, tanned midriff.

Charlotte began banging out chimes on Lisa Fenton's wineglass, then motioning with the spoon for everyone to find seats. Unfortunately, Roux happened to be standing in front of the leather wing chair. Roux didn't even look. She sank backward, and the wing chair received her. It was the tallest chair, the natural focal point of the circle, traditionally Charlotte's. Char jerked like she'd received a small electric shock when she looked up from herding ladies and saw Roux already settled there. I took a seat in one of the dining-room chairs that I'd pushed up against the fireplace and motioned Char to join me.

"Honestly," Char whispered as she sat next to me. "I mean, she didn't know, but you'd think someone would have mentioned."

Instead there'd been a minor traffic jam as five different women tried to claim the seats on either side of Roux.

"Next time I'll set the printouts in your chair to hold it," I said, and Charlotte brightened. She liked having a plan.

I was thinking that I wouldn't have to. Braless, rental-house Roux and her bird tats would not be back. She didn't strike me as a joiner, much less a woman who wanted to talk potty training and the lighter side of classic literature. She'd end up at bunco, or maybe nowhere, if her business got done fast enough.

Tate and Panda Grier finally closed the circle, cramming together on my padded piano bench. They'd made a quick dash to the wet bar for a final splash of wine, and no other seats were open.

Charlotte split the stack of printouts and sent pages both ways around the circle, saying, "Take one and pass, please." She culled discussion questions from every book-club guide she could find on the Internet. "So how many of you finished *House of Mirth*?"

Almost every woman present put a hand up. Me, too.

She smiled, bright and approving, though I suspected that more than a few were lying. I sure was. I'd read most of it, but Oliver had been up and down all last night. When I rocked him to sleep this afternoon, he'd felt as toasty as a little jacket potato on my chest, his bald head reeking of delicious baby. I'd drifted off. We'd both slept hard and long. Madison had helped me throw together a dinner, and Davis had cleaned up after so I could skim Wikipedia to see how it ended.

"How many at least got partway through?" Char followed up, and now every hand was raised, including Roux's. "Super, but if you didn't finish, fair warning! Our talk will be chock-full of spoilers."

"Oh, no, Lily Bart dies?" soft-hearted Sheridan Blake said on my other side. She'd been reading ahead in the discussion questions.

"Before we start, we have a new neighbor," Charlotte said. "This is her first time at book club. Let's all welcome . . . um, Roux."

A murmur of hellos went around the circle, and Tate whispered something to Panda. Panda nodded, like always, but maybe less emphatically than usual. Panda Grier was top-heavy and matronly, with both a plain, sweet face and a delicious husband. She'd made Tate her best friend the minute the Bonascos moved in, petting her, bringing over fruit and coffee almost every morning. It was as if Panda thought Tate was a smoking-hot volcano god that must be propitiated, lest she erupt with sex all over Panda's marriage.

Now Roux was in the room, an obvious expansion of a dangerous pantheon, and Tate was bristling at the competition. Panda couldn't serve both gods, and I was small-town enough to wonder how it would play out. I thought she'd likely stick by next-door Tate. The Sprite House was four blocks farther away from the beautiful Mr. Grier.

"Hello," Roux said. "Maybe y'all could introduce yourselves back?"

The contraction sounded wrong in her mouth, even though Pensacola, Florida, sat right between the ocean and Alabama. About half my neighbors had a soft southern slur, but Roux didn't sound like them. "We could go around the circle. I want to know who y'all are." Maybe she'd lived south long enough to pick it up.

I felt Charlotte's elbow jab my arm, hard enough to telegraph outrage.

"Well, but we all know each other. And we only have an hour," Charlotte said, in a voice that was sweeter than I knew she was feeling. One person grinding the whole club to a stop strictly for her own benefit was exactly the kind of thing that Charlotte hated. Char was addicted to fairness. It was one reason I loved her so. The world all around her was patently, consistently unfair, but Charlotte lived like a kid at the beach with a little red bucket, sure she could fix it so every ocean had the same amount of water.

I backed Char, saying, "Plus, we've got such a crowd tonight—how many names will you remember? If you come again, you'll get to know us naturally."

"You're right. I won't remember," Roux said, smiling at Char. Char smiled back and inhaled to speak again, but Roux talked in the gap, looking across the circle, right at Panda. "You're Panda, right? I remember that. Because it's unusual, sure, but also because you struck me as so funny." Tate's smile got brittle as Panda's whole face pinked up with pleasure. "But you aren't a Panda. Not at all. Not with those killer cheekbones and that sense of humor. Sly, sly, sly. You're a fox, aren't you?"

She leaned forward, intense, as if Panda Grier, who barely seemed to own cheekbones, was just so damn interesting. She wasn't. We weren't. We were just regular women living near a college in a midsize seaside town. We were wives and moms, adjuncts and administrators, professors and librarians. *Roux* was interesting, elbows resting on her knees, her legs set wide, and her dress hiked up so the full skirt hung down between. Her thighs were trim and very pale, and she was wearing scuffed cowboy boots. I could feel her charisma like it was a wind she'd set loose in the room, pushing us all forward in our seats.

Panda, still blushing, said, "What do you mean? I should be named Fox?"

"Not at all," Roux said. "It's just you *are* one. Fox is your spirit animal." She said it as if this were a known thing. Like this pack of mommies, clutching our printed sheets and paperbacks, had spirit animals tucked under our chairs instead of designer leather bags we'd bought on the cheap, three seasons late, from TJ Maxx. I would have bet money that the number of women here who had ever spoken to a spirit animal could be counted on one finger. And that one was still talking. "What if we did that? Instead of a regular and—you are so right, Charlotte—useless formal introduction. If you each tell me your spirit animal . . . well, believe me, that's a thing that I'll remember."

Women in the circle were turning to one another, ripples of energy and whispers spreading. With someone like Roux listening, they wanted to talk. They wanted to have spirit animals, and they wanted to say them. I felt a spark of it, too, but this was Charlotte's club, and she was my best friend. Across the circle Tess Roberts was bright-faced and excited, while Liddy Sleigh was uneasy, looking our way for a cue. Tate glowered, sending psychic demands for Char to shut this down. I felt us all wavering, as if we were balanced on a peak and the merest breath could blow us one way or the other.

Roux turned to Sheila Bowen on her right. "Lila? No, Sheila. Yeah? What kind of animal are you?"

"A tiger," Sheila said promptly, and I felt us tip.

"I see that! You've got those yellow eyes, like some kind of huntress," Roux said, and an affirming murmur ran around the circle. Sheila did have tiger eyes, but none of us had noticed that before. Roux said, "Keep going, keep going, I can hear," as she got up and left the circle, heading for the wet bar.

She loaded every leftover wine bottle into her arms, though we usually all stopped pouring when we took our seats, finishing our last half drinks during the discussion. She plopped them clanking down onto the coffee table as Lavonda Gaffney introduced herself and claimed to be a lion fish.

I felt the elbow again. Harder. I gave Char a commiserating glance. Charlotte had had a rough first trimester, and all the vomiting had made her more impatient than she usually was.

Next to Lavonda, Tess was talking in her big, goose-honk voice, claiming to be a sparrow, while Roux twisted off all the screw caps.

Then Lisa Fenton introduced herself and said, "I'm in the red brick, between your house and Charlotte's. Come over if you need sugar or an egg, whatever. As for my animal, that's hard. I need to think."

Roux was now making her way around the circle with two open bottles, nodding to Tess, saying, "Red or white?" soft, like a waitress.

Charlotte whispered to me, "This is a total hijack!"

I gave her an apologetic shrug.

"I think you're a hawk. So there," Sheridan Blake said.

Roux nodded, pouring cups and glasses to the rims, instantly affirming. "I can totally see that."

Lisa blushed, so pleased, and said, "With three kids under five, I guess I have to be. I do see everything."

I put a calming hand on Charlotte's arm while Chloe Fischer declared that her spirit animal was "mama bear." But then she paused and added, "Or maybe I'm an egret?" She looked to Roux for confirmation.

"What's an egret?" Panda asked, which spawned a lot of explanations about seabirds, and everyone kept drinking, drinking, drinking.

Roux decided in the end. "Definitely a mama bear. It's just you're built so delicately, it's hard to see that bear inside you. But it's there."

Char leaned in and whispered, "Bear my butt. Chloe Fischer's just a monkey. We're all monkeys. That woman has us wearing cunning little hats and dancing on cue. How did she do that?"

I wasn't sure. Nothing had ever derailed Charlotte's rigorously scheduled book club. Nothing derailed Char's rigorously scheduled anything, and as much I loved her, I couldn't help but think this might be good for her. I couldn't help but find it interesting.

Shy Allie Whitaker was playing now, peeping up from under her bangs and claiming that she might be a tiger, too. Inside. Very, very deep.

"Yeah, you have some jungle teeth hidden in you. I can see them," Roux said, and Allie shrugged, almost wriggling in her pleasure.

Char kept checking the clock, watching the minutes leak away, as the women picked animals and emptied the glasses that Roux kept sloshing full. I knew Char'd been looking forward to talking about beautiful Lily Bart, drifting to her doom by inches; the whole discussion hour was nearly gone, and we hadn't even started the questions.

Roux kept pouring, egging them on, until they were talking over one another, all claiming to be piranhas or panthers or peacocks. The only true peacock in our bunch was Tate Bonasco, who had bee-stung lips and (Char believed) a boob job. And even she would be a zoo peacock.

Truthfully, we were domesticated animals, all of us, except for Roux. She hadn't said her animal, but I thought it must be wild, or maybe feral.

The wine was nearly gone, and Roux was back at the bar, making up a mixed drink like she lived here, though the last thing any woman in this room needed was more alcohol. The conversation was so loud and rowdy now, women slurring and cackling, that I was glad all the bedrooms were up on the second floor. Oliver slept light, and Davis got so uncomfortable when folks were sloppy drunk.

Roux came back to the circle just as it was my turn. She handed me the mixed drink, and I was surprised at how observant she was. I hated wine. Could not bear even the flat, sour smell of it. I drank gin and tonic, but my first had been a very light pour. After that my drinks had been gin in name only, like always. "One-Drink Whey," Davis called me.

I took a sip, and it was piney and brisk. Cold in my mouth, but so strong that I felt it as a heat by the time it reached my chest. No way I would drink much of this, though it was delicious. She'd rubbed the rim of the glass with fresh lime, a tart finish on my tongue.

Still, loyal to Char, I only said, "I'm feeling like a porcupine. A porcupine who really wants to talk about *The House of Mirth*. Maybe we could—"

"We're almost done," Roux said, wiping my words away with a lazy wave of her hand. I was surprised at how much I minded the dismissal. She'd made a fuss over all the selections, so opinionated, finding an animal that made every woman there feel good. Until me. I wasn't anything like a porcupine, but she accepted it as my animal, when I'd meant it as a dig. She'd already turned her gaze on Charlotte. "Of course I know your name, but your animal is tricky."

"I'm a porcupine, too," Char said, tight, and popped her lips shut.

Roux sized up Charlotte, eyes lingering on the roundness of her belly, just now starting to look like more than a big lunch.

"I think *this* is Kanga," Roux said, and shot a sly smile at me. As if we had a private joke. The warmth of being included, after that dismissal—I felt it. I won't deny I felt it. My mouth smiled without my permission. Charlotte's eyebrows went up so high they disappeared into her bangs, and I hid my face in my strong drink. I took a long, deep swallow. Roux went back to Char's usurped chair.

Finally Jenny Tugby, who was as warm and bland and comforting as oatmeal, claimed to be a Komodo dragon and said she had to get home. Her baby hadn't started cereal yet, and she was flexing her shoulders and pulling at her bra. Her breasts had her on a timer, and she needed to go pump and dump her wine-soaked milk. Oliver and I were down to nursing first thing in the morning and at bedtime, but I remembered that tight, skin-stretch feeling from early days, back when my body made everything that fed him. I couldn't blame her, but at the same time humans were herd animals. As soon as she broke the circle, others would feel it as a pull to take their leave.

Sure enough, as Char finally got to begin her questions, women started leaking away in pairs and singles, quietly, with apologetic waves. First the ones with the newest babies, then the ones with full-time jobs. Most of these light-drinking ladies were rambley and yawning, listing as they disappeared up the stairs. By ten o'clock there were only six of us left.

Tate and Panda had joined Lavonda the Lion Fish on the sofa now that the room had cleared. Tate was very full of pinot noir, with a sweaty forehead and her mouth stained purple at the corners. Roux was back at the bar, slicing up more of my limes on the cutting board.

Charlotte said, "Maybe we should call it." She looked tired, with pink circles under her eyes.

Roux said, "Definitely. That book was a nonstarter. We should do something else." She blinked, and her neck elongated, as if a clever thought had only now occurred to her. "I know. Let's play a game."

Char bristled. "That's not what I meant at all."

"It is getting late," I said, trying for loyal, but I was tempted by the idea of a game.

I'd chosen a husband who liked meat loaf on Monday, tacos on Tuesday, dinner out on Friday with sex after. Charlotte was a lot like Davis; I was naturally attracted to anything orderly. But now I had a baby. I loved Oliver in a whole-body way I'd never known existed, but every day with a baby was the same day.

The closer he came to weaning, the more I missed teaching at Divers Down, both the joy of introducing new divers to the secret world under the waves and the color and noise of the kids in my swim and Seal Team classes. Most of all I missed diving itself. No one dives pregnant, and these first eight months of motherhood had been a sleep-deprived blur. I'd gotten under only half a dozen times since Oliver came, and I was starting to get truly itchy for it.

Now, if Roux had suggested a bank job or even a bungee jump, I would have shown her to the door, and this last gaggle of tipsy mommies alongside her. But staying up past ten on a weeknight to play a game? It was a rebellion that sounded about my speed. I wanted to play.

"Too late to start a game, I think," Charlotte agreed, trying to sound regretful but not quite making it.

"Poor Kanga," Roux said to her. "You should definitely head on home. You're resting for two."

"Yesh, s'fine. You go on home, Kangroo," Tate slurred, cutting her eyes at Roux. She'd been very quiet so far tonight, drinking her resentment.

But Char had meant for everyone to go. It was her club, and she was closing it. She paused, and I knew she didn't want to leave me with some of my least favorite neighbors, all three already drunk, and this usurping stranger. I was torn, wanting to see what happened, but at the same time I didn't want to end up cleaning Tate Bonasco's vomit out of my sofa.

"I do not like this," Charlotte said to me. "Not one little bit."

Roux was carrying limes and rocks glasses and my room-temp gin back to the coffee table. She overheard Char, and a sly smile spread across her face.

"You aren't a porcupine," Roux said, setting out the glasses and expertly pouring shots, not measuring. "You aren't Kanga either. I know you, lady. You're that fish. That orange fish in a bowl from *The Cat in the Hat*. *That's* your spirit animal."

"Oh, my God, you are," Lavonda said, laughing so hard she choked.

"Roux should not be here when your mother is out," Tate said in an uptight Fish voice, reaching across a giggling Panda to pat Lavonda's back.

"Go get some sleep. We're almost done here," I assured Char, turning her toward the stairs before she had a rage stroke.

"Yes," Roux said, "Amy, you play Up-Up-Up with a fish," making herding motions toward the stairs, and that put the sloshed trio on the sofa into hysterics.

Char stomped up ahead of me, the back of her neck crimson.

"Hey, did you really read the book?" Tate asked over the laughing, so loud we heard it at the tip-top of the stairs. "Because I only read the Spark Notes."

I closed the door to the basement.

"Good grief!" Char whispered with a fierceness that I rarely saw in her. "How will you ever get them out of here?"

"I don't know," I said.

Except for pregnant Charlotte, I was the soberest woman in the house. Even so, I could feel the gin in my veins. I took another little sip. I wanted to be back downstairs playing, not up here disapproving. Still, loyalty had me walk Char to the door, nodding agreement as she whisper-railed.

"Who comes into someone's house, someone's club, and takes it over and makes everybody drunk and stupid? If I were you, I would go right up to bed and just leave them there to realize how stinking rude they're being. Except I wouldn't trust that Roux not to steal something."

Upstairs, Davis would be in bed reading with an ear cocked for the baby monitor. Oliver was no doubt enjoying the sleep of the innocent, his arms thrown up over his head. I was naïve enough to assume that my stepdaughter Madison was upstairs in bed, too.

"Yeah, that was pretty . . ." I trailed off, because what word came next?

Interesting.

Which, though I'd never say it out loud, book club often wasn't. Char's selections were heavy on Ladies and Society. She liked white-gloved books that explored long-dead social mores. On my own I read high-stakes fiction: Margaret Atwood, Stephen King. Or memoirs like *The Glass Castle* and *Wild,* the ones by women who'd lived risky and survived.

I understood, maybe better than anyone, that the saying "May you live in interesting times" was the cruelest curse that could be laid. I didn't want my life to be interesting ever, ever again, but I liked interesting on paper, contained between closable covers. I didn't mind this Roux person hijacking our decorous, mild fun. Just this once.

To Char I said, "We can discuss *House of Mirth* ourselves, after our walk tomorrow," and I resolved to get up early and read the last third. I would give Char her book talk, to make up for this disloyalty. For thinking, for just a moment, *Dear God, she really is a little like that orange fish, fussing in his bowl.* "I'll make us lunch, and we'll do every question."

Char's eyes pricked with tears, the pregnancy hormones maxing out every emotion, and then she lurched at me and hugged me. I hugged her back, tight, feeling the arc of her inflating belly pressing against my hip. Char's extended family was very small. An elderly, unwell father and a military brother who'd married a German girl and still lived overseas. I was nearly estranged from my own family as well. It was one reason we were so close, forming a do-it-yourself support system.

"God, you're so nice to me. And I am such a whiner," she said. "Okay, okay. See you tomorrow."

I opened the front door for her, and there was Madison. She stood barefoot on the grass by the lowest porch step. She was wearing an outsize T-shirt that she often slept in, but under it she'd pulled on black leggings. Out on the lawn, just past her, the pale face of a boy floated in the moonlight, his dark clothes and darker hair blending into the night. I drew up short.

Char whispered, "That's Roux's kid."

Madison turned when she heard us coming out, smiling and lifting a casual hand. She didn't act like someone who'd been caught. She wasn't doing anything wrong, after all. Just talking on the lawn, still within the golden halo of porch light, safe. I didn't like it, though.

"Hey, Mads," I said, like I'd known she was out here the whole time. "Who's your friend?"

"This is Luca," she said. "He's new. Luca, this is my stepmonster, Amy."

"'Sup," Luca said, not reacting to my nickname. He jerked his chin by way of greeting. He had his mother's hair but his own face. It was very angular, with long, narrow eyes and a sulky rock-star mouth. His black T-shirt had some kind of band logo on it, and he'd paired it with ripped, dark jeans and shitkicker boots. He looked as if central casting had sent over Boy Trouble.

"Nice to meet you, Luca," Char said, stiff. She didn't like it either. "I'm Charlotte Baxter."

"Nice to meet you," I echoed. "Mads? It's about time you came on in. School night."

"Oh, no, Monster, really? Ten minutes?" she said.

"I think now is good," I said, mild, but I flashed her a wicked-stepmother face, so that she knew I was about to become so embarrassing.

She rolled her eyes at me but said, "See you tomorrow," and turned to the steps.

"Later," Luca said, and he went slouching off into the darkness.

"Mm," Char said to me. "I'll see *you* tomorrow." She

gave me a look that said we now had more than a book to talk about, then started off home.

Maddy pushed past me into the house, saying, "It's barely even ten, *A*-my." She bore down hard, very judgmental, on the first syllable, the way she sometimes called Davis "*Da*-ad" when they were close to getting into it.

She never used to say my name this way before Oliver was born. The baby had changed so many things. These days I sometimes forgot that I'd loved Maddy first, falling for her the very day Char brought the Wheys to Divers Down, close to seven years ago. Char'd told Davis that Seal Team was exactly what his unhappy kid needed—friends, fun, physical activity. Char had been doing a little matchmaking, introducing her single swimming teacher and her handsome, divorced neighbor. But when I first met Davis, an econ prof in button-down shirts and penny loafers, he struck me as an uptight ass. My heart had gone out to nine-year-old Madison, with her puppy-fat belly sticking out from under her crop top and her eyebrows set in a permanent scowl.

That scowl had not changed, and she gave it to me full force over her shoulder as I followed her in. Then she went stomping up the stairs to her room with no idea that the basement still held a gaggle of bombed book-clubbers.

I took a final bracing sip of G&T, then set the glass on the counter. I could feel gin buzzing in my hands, and this right here was about as tipsy as I got. Ever. I opened the door to the basement. I could hear them cackling. I shut the door fast behind me and started down, hurrying so as not to miss anything more.

Tate was saying, "Everybody does that. It's just some people lie about it. It isn't *bad*."

Panda talked over her, saying, "No, no, I know, like, I'm not a prude or anything. It's just that Francis, he barely ever wants to . . . you know. When it happens, it's great and all, but he's . . . he's . . ."

"He's a sex camel," Roux finished for her as I got to the bottom of the stairs, and they all laughed.

They sat on the floor, four women inside a fairy ring of abandoned chairs, clustered around the coffee table. It was littered with sucked-dry lime wedges and paper plates crusted with the dregs of hummus and onion dip. Each woman held a rocks glass with a finger of my good gin in the bottom. Judging by the level in the bottle, they'd already done a shot, maybe two, while I'd been busy shooing Maddy inside.

"A *what* camel?" Lavonda said. "Is that a spirit am-mimal?"

"No, no," Tate said, superior and drunk-wise. "I get it. She means that Francis stores up his humps."

They burst into noisy laughter again. Only Roux saw me. She was sitting like the north point of the compass, facing the stairs. Lavonda had her back to me, and Tate and Panda were the drunken witches of the east and west, in profile. Roux's eyes lit as they met mine. We grinned at each other, neither of us half as drunk as they were.

"Then you took matters into your own hands. So to speak," Lavonda said, giggling. "But that doesn't count as bad."

"Well, but you have to take into consideration that I didn't take things into my own *hands,*" Panda said, sounding sly.

"Panda, you doglet! Do you actually own a . . ." Tate

made a *bzzzzz* noise, as if this were subtler than saying "vibrator." It wasn't.

"I mos' certainly do not," said Panda, smug. "But they make those disposable toothbrushes now. You know the kind? With batteries?"

Roux snorted, laughing now, too. "Okay, but I still think Lavonda's winning. That's gross, not *bad*."

"Except I brush my teeth with a regular old Oral-B," Panda said, and then there was a pause. She made them wait for it, but I got there first and felt a bubble of shocked laughter rising. "Only Francis brushes with the battery-powered kind."

Then they were all laughing like a pack of jackals, covering my own laughter. Poor Francis! I would never be able to look at his lovely white teeth in the same way again.

"Oh, my God," Lavonda said, lifting her plastic cup. A good inch of clear liquid sloshed around in the bottom. "You got me. You have the lead."

"Tate?" Roux said, lofting her own glass. "I don't think you can beat that. Drink."

"Hold on!" Tate said, sitting up very straight. Panda never beat Tate at anything. Tate leaned in. "I frenched a guy last week. Not my husband. Boom, bitches. Why don't y'all drink to *that*."

The hilarity drained instantly. Silence from Panda. Silence from Lavonda. I found myself stepping in closer.

"Who?" Panda said, and there was such outrage in her voice that even sloppy-drunk Tate seemed to hear it. "Who was it? Someone we know? Someone's husband?"

Tate backpedaled. "God, no! No one you know."

I did not believe this.

"Well, that wins," Roux said, wry, and drained her cup.

Panda and Lavonda were still staring at Tate.

"You let him?" Panda said.

Tate said, "No, no, I pushed him right away. I guess I . . . felt sorry. He was saying how his wife was pregnant and she was being the sex camel. I felt bad for him, you know? He misread it, and he tried something. I shut it down. Of course. Not a big deal. Panda wins. Here, I'll drink." She guzzled at her cup.

I was reverberating with a second shock. Pregnant? Did she mean Charlotte's husband? Surely not. The world was full of pregnant women. Just because Char was the only pregnant person in our neighborhood right now, it didn't mean Tate had started something up with Phillip Baxter.

"Who was it, Tate?" I had to know. I couldn't stand here, passive, eavesdropping. Tate turned her head to peer at me with owlish eyes. I don't think she'd realized I was back until that moment. Her eyes widened, and her face flushed a deep, dark red. Panda and Lavonda were her inner circle, but I was Charlotte's. Tate couldn't look away from me, and I could see drunk wheels spinning in her head.

"Just a guy I met . . . um, at the car place. We were stuck in that waiting room, and we got talking," she said, overloud, looking right at me, and she was lying.

"It's just a game, y'all," Roux said, getting up. "Panda won. Come join us for the next round, Amy."

She walked toward me, slow and slinky, like a parody of a fifties housewife, carrying a glass with a shot of gin at the bottom.

I couldn't look away from Tate, who was now aiming her eyes anywhere but at me. She told Lavonda and Panda, "He got the wrong idea. They shunt've named that place Quickie Lube," and Lavonda snorted and laughed, reassured. I didn't. I wasn't. It was Phillip. She had done something with my best friend's husband. I knew it even before Tate peeped at me to see if I'd been taken in by her weak lies and her joke.

I said, "This game? It doesn't seem all that fun to me," to Roux, but I held my gaze level and serious on Tate. She flushed and looked away fast.

Roux sidestepped between us, blocking my view. "It's a blast. You should play. It's like Never Have I Ever, but for grown-ups. We skip the coy denials and go right to confession. You start by telling everyone the worst thing you did today."

That last sentence made me feel as if Roux were running one overly cool, lacquered nail tip down my naked spine. It straightened me into Good Girl posture, shoulders back and down, eyes widened into instant innocence.

"Sure. I'll play," I said quietly, to Roux alone. "The worst thing I did today was let you get this pack of harpies drunk in my house."

Roux laughed and waved away my entry. "We're past that round now."

Over at the coffee table, Tate said, "Let's keep going! Lavonda, what's the very worst thing you did last month?"

I felt Roux watching my reaction. I asked her, sharp, "Last month?"

Roux shrugged.

"No, but wait, were you flirting with the car-place

guy? If it was all him, why is it *your* worst?" Panda asked with dogged, drunken logic.

Tate said, "I must have been putting out a signal, is why it's my worst. But, like, for real, unconsciously."

"Women blame themselves," Lavonda said, trying to smooth it over. "But it's the man. It's the penis. It's the man penis that causes all the troubles."

"Last month?" I repeated, gaze fixed on Roux. "You said it was a game about today."

Roux said, "Round one was today. I won it. This was round two, where we all told the worst thing we did last week."

Last week meant the beer-soaked Back-to-School party Tate had hosted around her pool, I remembered, trying to do infidelity math inside my head. Davis and I had made a brief appearance with Oliver, while Maddy stayed the whole time, basking and splashing with the small pack of neighborhood teens. Char had been there, plopped miserably in a deck chair, sipping ginger ale and eating saltines. Her husband had been pounding down the Rolling Rocks, and Tate's husband had been micro-managing the brats on the Big Green Egg. With Phillip drunk and Tate unsupervised, I hoped for Char's sake it had stopped at just a kiss. But I couldn't worry only about Char right now. Right now I could barely breathe.

"And then round three is . . ." I heard myself saying in an airless voice.

"You say the worst thing you did last month, and if yours is the most awful, then everyone else has to drink," Roux said, eyes on mine, unblinking. "Then we tell the worst things we did last year. And so on."

The three drunken furies at the coffee table were bickering now, locked in their own tension. It rendered them oblivious to ours, but I felt it. Our tension was a long, lithe ribbon winding around us. It squeezed in, cold-blooded and well muscled, binding the two of us together.

"Ish the penis that starts it, but sometimes the vagina *can* send a signal," Lavonda pontificated.

"What kind of signal?" Panda said. No doubt wondering if Tate's vagina was signaling her own very tasty husband. But no, Tate had it aimed at Charlotte's.

But all I could manage right now was asking Roux, "How many rounds? How far does it go?"

"Oh, come on, Amy. A good game has to go all the way," Roux said, and her pink tongue came out for just a moment to touch her pale upper lip. "Think back. What's the worst thing you ever did?"

Somehow that rocks glass was in my hand. She'd put it in there, or I'd taken it. I felt the rim at my mouth. From a distance I observed One-Drink Whey slamming down a shot of room-temp gin. But I needed the heat. My whole body had gone corpse cold.

I couldn't make sense of the angry words the others were saying now. It sounded like cats hissing and growling around my near-empty bottle of Hendrick's. Their sound faded as Roux leaned in, close. Intimate. Like she had a secret to share, and I was leaning as well. As if I wanted to hear it.

"You don't want to play? That makes no sense," she said, and her spirit animal was a more sinister version of the Cat in the Hat. Hers was feral, invading to unpack trouble in a house where no mother would ever come home. In this house I was the only mother, and I had let trouble in. I'd swung the door wide for it, hoped it had the right house, even. "Because, Amy? C'mon. You

would win this. I'm thinking you got these low-stakes
bitches on lockdown."

"Get out," I said, soft, a thousand underwater yards
beneath the drunken, sniping women on my floor around
my coffee table.

Roux heard me, though. She was down here with me,
standing exactly as she had when I first saw her on my
porch, head tilted, hip cocked. She spread her hands
palms up, and I was shot through with a painful feeling
that was akin to pleasure. Her hands were not empty
after all. They were holding my history, invisible but so
very heavy. I could almost see it in her hands.

"Oh, yeah. You would win."

"That's not true," I said, but I was still leaning toward her, as if I wanted more. At the same time, her
sentences ran through my mind in triplets, like the first
movement of the "Moonlight" Sonata, played poorly in
a minor key. *You'd win this. You'd win this. You would
win.* Every sour chord telegraphed itself on my numb
face. *Guilty,* and she saw it.

"Come by my place. Soon. We have a lot to talk
about," Roux said.

"Get out," I repeated, and she brushed past me to the
stairs.

I turned to watch her rise. Behind me I could hear
Tate retching and Lavonda saying, "Oh, shit, grab that
trash can!" and Panda crying out, "Oh, no!"

I wanted to run up the stairs after Roux, chase her to
the front door and drive her out, bolt it, draw the chain.
But it would do no good. She'd cracked open the past.
I could feel it leaking into my bloodstream, spreading
like a toxin through me. She'd brought interesting times.
She'd let them loose inside me.

2

TUESDAY. MAY 28. 1991. *The moon peaked full at 1:36, bare minutes before a rock pinged off my bedroom window. I opened it and stuck my head out to see Tig Simms, hungry and shining with moon madness. He whisper-called, "I need a pork chop," and I went down to meet him. The moon set us in motion, and we zoomed through its light-drenched hours, driving toward a darker morning.*

I used to think about it all the time, this night that started every evil in my life. It led me down a chain of bad, black days and sickened me, left me unable to eat or sleep. I was on medication for high blood pressure before I could vote. It was, quite literally, killing me.

Junior and senior years of high school, it was like living with a tapeworm in my gut, a lithe and sentient foulness gobbling any goodness I might hope to own. I believed that no one could truly know me unless they knew my worst. I thought that in order to forge any new friendship, have any hope of love, I'd be required to lay the live, vile beast of my past upon an altar, belly-creep, and plead my case.

I couldn't do it, so I kept to myself. When I graduated, I ran west to California like a million lost girls had before me. There I tried drinking too much, I tried a variety of drugs, I tried losing myself in the sun-browned bodies of surfer boys and boat rats.

It was diving that saved me. One of the boat rats offered to take me out for a "discover scuba" dive. I agreed, thinking it would fill a couple of hours, or maybe it would be an escape, or maybe danger. It wasn't any of those things.

It was prayer. It was a meditation. It was a stillness and a silence.

Afterward all I could think about was getting certified so I could go back down into that wordless world. I stopped getting high, because no one would let me dive high. I cut my drinking down to a beer every now and again, maybe two. I started exercising, to build my strength and stamina, and I started eating food again. Healthy food, in healthy portions, so I stayed fit for going under.

Sixty, eighty, a hundred twenty feet down in the deep blue, weightless, my breath a thrumming, bubbling rhythm in my ears, I was emptied out, quiet inside. I'd hang suspended in schools of fish who wheeled in perfect tandem, like a living tide. Sea cucumbers and starfish crept blindly on their own slow business. Turtles sailed past, heavy with majesty. Ocean creatures had no eyebrows, no mobile mouths, so each face was set forever in a single shape. Every dolphin smiled, every eel looked faintly angry, every seahorse seemed surprised to see me. They all had such blank, unjudging gazes, and the deeper blues beneath me felt like an infinity. The truth was in the water with us, but it didn't matter; the sea could swallow anything.

In that beauty, so vast and varied, I felt my own smallness in the wide, wild world. It let me forget myself and yet be wholly present. It let me stop trying to die. If I hadn't ever stepped off that first boat, truly, truly, I would not be breathing now.

My life on land got better, too, though it didn't come like a lightning bolt. It was more like the turning of a long, slow tide. I practiced letting any thought about the past sink out of my brain, slide down my spine, and disappear into my own deeps. My history lived below my words, under my thoughts, even lower than my knowing, though it was still as much a part of me as the red-meat organs in my abdomen. I never thought about my liver, but it was always there; it did its silent, dirty work in the dark of me, necessary, unexcisable, but not a thing I thought about. Not ever.

Now when I saw certain news stories, or sometimes on Ash Wednesday, I'd remember it was there, but that was all. I never went down deep enough for words or images. Not even when I found myself inside an echo of my past, like the night that we told Maddy I was pregnant.

Davis was anxious about it. Maddy'd been an only child for thirteen-plus years. Still, she said the right things and smiled. I don't think he saw the worry flash across her face.

Afterward I couldn't sleep. I went down to the kitchen for hot tea, and there was Maddy. She was framed in the open door to the backyard, her feet still on the righteous side, touching the tiles. The rectangle of night I saw around her was teeming with regrets that could last her whole life long, and she was walking right out into it, fearless and young-stupid and so dear.

She looked over her shoulder with the caught face

of a small animal, frozen in the center of the road. But I wasn't headlights. I was only her Monster, who loved her so. I went to her, took her hand off the knob, closed the door. I could feel my worst things, sunk deep, yet still alive inside me. I wanted to dredge it all up, show her, and then ask, *Do you see how high the stakes are, every minute?* But she was just shy of fourteen. She had every wild young animal's faith in its own immortality. The only thing my history had the power to change was the way that she saw me.

"Who are you meeting, girl-child?" I asked instead, quite stern.

"Just Shannon," she said, and I believed her.

I said, "Go text her. Tell her you got busted and she better get her butt in bed or I will call her mother."

"Are you going to tell Duddy?" she asked, nervous.

"Of course. I tell your father everything," I said, and this was almost, almost true. "But I'll also tell him you and I had a good talk and that you won't do it again. Because you won't, right?" She nodded, but she still looked worried, so I gave her a line from *The Princess Bride,* our favorite movie. "'Buttercup doesn't get eaten by the eels at this time.'"

She grinned and kissed me, saying, "You are the best monster," before running, light-footed, for the stairs.

I let the mass inside me sink and settle, unexamined. Just as I had three years ago, when Char came down with the flu while her husband was out of town. She had a fever over 102 even on Motrin, and she was sweaty and so shaky she could hardly stand. I moved into her house, minding teeny-tiny Ruby, keeping Char hydrated with juice and broth. When her fever finally broke, she grabbed my hand and said, "You're my best friend. Isn't that stupid to say out loud? We aren't nine."

I looked at our clasped hands, and I thought, *Char, you have no idea what you are holding.* The urge for confession was so strong—to be wholly seen by my dearest friend—that I felt it move through me like a cold and salty wave made of every unnameable feeling. I saw that moon, fat and full, centered in my mind's eye. But it was not Charlotte's job to forgive me.

All I said was, "We should make each other bracelets," and we laughed.

The closest I ever came to letting it rise was almost five years back, when I went over to Davis's house for dinner and found that Maddy was at a sleepover. We only spent time at his place when she was home, the three of us watching PG-13 movies, ordering pizza. Later he'd walk me out to my car. We'd been dating almost a year, but sex had only recently begun between us, and always in my studio apartment, lights off, blinds drawn. He never stayed the night. When Maddy woke up every morning, her dad was there alone, scrambling her eggs.

That night he made dinner for me. Oven-fried chicken, steamed green beans, salad, mashed potatoes. Davis cooked like a man who'd gone straight to Betty Crocker for advice after his wife had left him with a second-grader. Basic American meat and three, seasoned with salt and pepper. It wasn't bad, but he pushed the food around on his plate like a TV actor pretending to have dinner.

"What's wrong?" I asked.

He shook his head. Swallowed all the nothing in

his mouth. He looked so grave, so sad, that if I hadn't understood him so well, I would have assumed he was breaking up with me.

"I'm going to say yes. To you, to Mads, the whole package," I told him, but he sat there staring down at his uneaten food. I added, quietly, "I'm not the kind who'll ever leave you."

He met my eyes then. Nodded. Still solemn, he pulled the small velvet box out of his pocket and slid it across the table to me. The ring was simple and elegant, a rose-gold band with a modest marquise-cut stone. His ex-wife's was smaller and cut round. I'd seen it in the picture of her that Maddy kept in her room.

"Yes," I said immediately, and then, blushing, "I mean, did you want to ask?"

He laughed. He came around the table and knelt to do it right. After that he relaxed and we had a nice meal. We cleared the dishes, I rinsed while he loaded, and then we went up the stairs to his bedroom for the first time. I drew the curtains, turned out all the lamps.

After, I lay wide awake in the arms of the man who would be my husband. Who would put his only daughter even more deeply in my care. He deserved to know what he was getting, this good man with his upright posture, his patient dedication to my orgasms, his 401(k). I ran my thumb over the ring. It fit. Of course it did. Davis did his homework. I rolled to be the inside spoon, and Davis turned with me, his hand spanning the small, soft rounding of my lower belly. I wondered if he could feel the ripples of old stretch marks, faint souvenirs from back in high school, when I was so heavy.

We whispered in the dark back and forth, talking late into the night in the way of new lovers. I already knew about his hardest time, when Maddy's mom left. Laura was drinking every day by then. When they fought, she said bitter, drunken things that attacked the very roots of him. I knew that he drove her to rehab and that two days in she left the program. She never came back home.

That night he told me more. How he'd wept with Maddy, who was wild with rage and sorrow, but inside all he felt was relief. He confessed that the house without Laura in it had felt bigger, airier, like suddenly there was enough oxygen in all the rooms. He still hated his raw and secret joy in the face of his child's abject misery. It felt so disloyal. The vicious blackout drunk was the remains of Laura, after all, and she had been his love. He'd once stood up with her in a church and made such promises. I held him, feeling a faint, whole-body tremor as he whispered to me about how he'd failed her.

I assured him he had not. He'd never made a vow to grocery-store box wine, and by the end Laura was lost in it. I told him he was good and dear and loyal.

If ever there was a time to let my past rise, show it to him, tell him everything, it was then. He had laid his failure down in front of me, asking if I could know his weakest moment and still love him. I'd promised him I could, and in the wake of it, in his peace, I wanted my own. What a relief it would be, to loose truth in the smallness of this room. To feel it in the air around us. To be fully seen. I could feel words rising. I could see a sky I had not seen in years.

Tuesday. May 28. 1991. The moon peaked full at 1:36. . . .

But the words stayed in my mouth. I lay in his arms in the darkness, and I let that moon sink. I did not even trace its descent. I didn't need for him to love the girl

I'd been, and I wouldn't ask him to forgive her. I hadn't.
Why should he? I only needed him to love me now. I
stayed silent, listening to his breath grow deep and even
until he was asleep.

But now Roux had gone dredging, reaching down so
deep inside me. That old moon rose, and there was no
way not to see by its pale light. No way not to remember.

At fifteen I'd jet-dyed my sandy-colored hair into sub-
mission, so that it hung down my back in lifeless hanks.
I had thick-cut Betty Page bangs, too severe for the soft
moon of my face. They got in my eyes as I leaned out
the window to wave to Tig Simms, drenched in moonlight, asking for a pork chop.

I'd been waiting, my big body filling up my papasan
chair like I was a scoop of ice cream in a wide, round
cone. I was already dressed for school tomorrow in a
plaid skirt and a navy uniform top. Beside me I had a
tote bag with a can of Lysol in it, though I'd half hoped
Tig wouldn't show. It was the first night that the moon
looked full, and tomorrow or the next day would be so
much better—assuming that he showed at all. He didn't
come every month, and more than once he'd woken me
up, unprepared, on random, near-moonless weekdays.

I whisper-called down, "Gimme a minute."

He grinned up at me, pushing his wild hair off his
forehead. In sunlight it had a metallic cast, like he'd
gilded it in bronze, but now it looked almost black.
Brighton's dress code required short-haired boys and
long-skirted girls, but Tig's tight curls saved him from
paying for a lot of haircuts; if I grabbed one and pulled
it straight, it would likely reach past his shoulder.

He motioned for me to come down again, urgent. I
gave him a thumbs-up, flushing at my own staring dork-

itude. I drew the window shut. I'd have to sneak through the house and out the back door. My unwieldy body would not let me shimmy out, creep along the roof, then leap to the oak and climb to the ground, the way my older brother often did from his room next door.

I stuffed my feet into my stretched-out flats, grabbed my tote and my guitar, and snuck downstairs, barely breathing, careful not to bang the instrument against the banister. Creeping put me inside my body, though. All at once I was hyperaware of the way it sloshed around me. That xylophone sound effect that played on cartoons when people tiptoed started plinking in my head, and I knew with bitter knowing that not much was funnier than a fat thing sneaking.

Once down I hurried silently through the living room, more at ease with every step that took me farther from my parents' bedroom, into the kitchen. Usually on these nights, after we'd gotten baked and played for a couple of hours, I'd ask Tig to take me to Waffle House. Chez Waffle we called it. *Your gas, my treat,* I'd tell him, because he rarely had money. We'd walk through Lysol clouds to kill the pot smell and go eat with the truckers, Patsy Cline on the juke, all of us grainy-eyed from being up all night. We'd drink tons of coffee, mine khaki colored with half-and-half. Then we'd go straight to school. Since my dad left for work before dawn and my mother slept in until eight, no one knew except my brother. Connor couldn't rat on me; he snuck out more than I did.

I wished Tig and I could Waffle House tonight. God, bacon sounded good. Hash browns scattered, smothered, and covered with a waxy slice of American cheese. Pancakes, and I could almost feel the thin spread of maple-flavored syrup on my tongue. But I was broke; just this week, after her "big announcement," Mom'd told me she was going to start putting my allowance directly into my savings account. She'd also emptied out my pig, depositing my saved-up babysitting money. *For college,* she'd said, though thanks to Nana's trust my college was covered. More than. We both knew she really did it to stop me buying food.

I grabbed four pears from the ceramic bowl on the counter and threw them into the tote with the Lysol. I checked the pantry. Canned soups, jars of oil and olives, five kinds of cereal that all looked and tasted like the cedar chips in the bottom of my hamster's cage.

I opened the fridge and found packages of skinless chicken breasts stacked up like a wall of bland, waiting to be baked dry. I fished a plastic envelope of ham, 98 percent fat-free, out of the deli drawer. I divided the slices in half and made two sandwiches on the extra-thin-cut diet bread. There was no cheese or mayo in the house. No ketchup either, because of the sugar. I squirted on some mustard and bagged them up.

These were the best things I had to offer Tig, moon crazy and wanting meat. Tomorrow I'd have better. Our neighbors down the street, the Shipleys, had a new baby that wouldn't sleep at night. Pretty Mrs. Shipley had asked me to come by right after school and babysit, so she could get a nap. I could tell Mom I'd been at the library and keep the money.

Plus, three-year-old Lolly and I would have snacks, screwing the tops off Oreos, eating the filling, then dipping the sides in Mrs. Shipley's whole milk. We'd get milk mustaches and color pictures of Ariel or Muppets while baby Paul cooed and drooled in the bouncer.

Mrs. Shipley never noticed that I snuck extra cookies or her Pringles home in my backpack. She wore peasant blouses that slipped off one delicate shoulder and narrow-cut capri pants; no way she ate junk food. I couldn't imagine Mrs. Shipley eating anything but leaves.

But Tig was here now. So it was pears and diet bread stuffed with rubbery, fatless ham. In desperation I checked the lower cabinets. Tupperware and pans and kitchen gadgets, nothing good or even edible. Until I looked under the sink.

In the very back, behind the cleaning products and the extra sponges, I saw a large green bottle lurking. Red wine? It had been left there so long that the top was dusty, and the big bottle meant it was cheap. Too cheap to be seen in the living-room bar. I vaguely remembered Dad bringing it home a few months ago. To make sangria. Mom had told him, "I said *inexpensive wine,* not salad dressing." That was like Dad, though. He did it wrong so Mom remembered not to trouble him with errands.

I paused. Except for tastes of my mom's champagne at New Year's or weddings, I hadn't really ever had a drink. But I might like it, and Tig for sure would be impressed. Plus, Mom owed me some fun. She'd taken all my money and ruined my summer in one fell Monday swoop. And it's not like I'd get caught. Mom was blind to cheap stuff, and Dad only noticed the things that were not right there waiting when he wanted them. If I made off with the Blanton's, he'd bellow, *Janine!* at my mother right at 7:00 P.M. sharp. But this? It was invisible. If my brother had ever looked in this cabinet, he'd have snootched it long ago.

I had to shift half a dozen cleaning products to get the giant jug out, careful to avoid any kind of clanking. Then I put everything back and hurried away, slipping out the back door and into the night.

Tig waited at the edge of the yard, dressed in his uniform as well, though his pants were frayed at the bottom and his hand-me-down shirt had faded from navy to a muddy royal blue. I lumbered toward him, hampered by my guitar, the heavy jug, the tote bag on my shoulder. As I got close, I saw that the bruise on his cheek had faded to an odd army green in the moonlight. Last week he'd gotten into it with Assholio, his mom's new boyfriend, but he didn't have new bruises. Not anyplace that I could see. I lofted the jug as I reached him, and he mouthed, *Damn, Smiff, yeah!*

He always called me by his own slurry, punk-rock version of my surname, Smith. Never Amy. Smiff or Smiffy. I loved how cool it sounded, but I hated that it turned me into some kind of buddy-buddy. Practically a boy.

He took my guitar with careless chivalry, and the two of us hustled in silence for his car. It was a gleaming cherry-red steel tank of a car, a 1967 AMC Ambassador, or most of one. He'd built it himself out of cast-off parts in a garage bay at his ex-stepdad's garage. It looked as danger-sexy as Tig himself, especially at Brighton, where it hulked among Jeeps and hand-me-down BMWs and convertible Miatas. Now he was gathering chunks of 1978 Chevy Novas and putting them together into another car, maybe to sell.

"Want to practice driving?" he whispered, holding out the Ambassador's keys.

He'd offered last time, too, but I'd said no, instantly.

Not because I didn't want to. I had my learner's permit, and I was wild to drive. But I'd worried I wouldn't fit behind the wheel. I'd had an instant horror flash of my gut catching, of me pushing and grunting and trying to wedge my body in with Tig watching. I'd turned him down, but then I "accidentally" left my purloined Shipley snacks in the car. Once he was settled, I went back for them and tested it. I'd slid onto the bench seat behind the wheel just fine. I hadn't taken Tig's long legs into account. I'd been hoping that he'd offer again.

"Hell, yeah," I whispered now, and took the keys. He had his license, so that made my learner's permit legal. Or would have, if he'd been a grown-up.

"I been thinking about the band name," Tig said once we were in the car with the doors shut. In my neighborhood every house was a custom build on its own huge, wooded lot. No one was going to hear us from the road.

"I thought we were the Failicorns?" I said, pulling at the silver hardware on the seat belt, blushing.

The Ambassador had only lap belts, and the one on the driver's side was set for Tig's slim frame.

"Failicorns sounds like an all-girl band," he told me.

"Screw you," I said. I had the lap belt clicked shut now. I turned the key, and the muscle car's big engine growled to life. "What's wrong with an all-girl band?"

He fished in his curls for the joint he'd tucked behind his ear but almost dropped it as I lurched us forward. He laughed, and I tried again, struggling with the clutch pedal. I'd learned to work a manual transmission in driver's ed, but Tig's car didn't handle like Brighton's limp fleet of hand-me-down mom sedans.

I began winding my way out of the neighborhood. Not to the front entrance, where a decorative wrought-

iron gate said WAVERLY PLACE in scrolling letters. Toward the undeveloped land at the back. Tig tucked the
joint between his lips and did that cowboy move with his
Zippo, zinging it against his jeans so the lid flipped up
and the light flared. I hastily rolled my window down;
Lysol could only cover so much. He got himself a good
lungful, then passed it over.

"Nothing's wrong with an all-girl band, except that
by definition I can't be in one." He talked airless and
weird, holding smoke.

I took the joint, sealing and unsealing my lips to let
a lot of air in as I toked. I liked to get high, but not too
high. Mildly stoned made me the best kind of hungry;
I was always hungry, but high I could eat without feeling the shags of fat hanging off my frame, without feeling invisible eyes judging me, without the aftertaste of
shame. I'd even eat in front of Tig—a thing I never did
straight—snarfling down whatever Waffle House would
bring us. If I oversmoked, I felt a weird pressure, like
a band around my chest, squeezing my heart. I also got
paranoid, and way too free. What if I got so high I forgot myself? I might lurch at him with my hungry mouth
open, my greedy hands grasping his body; it would
destroy whatever the hell this weird friendship was between us, and I lived for our rambling lunchtime conversations, our study sessions at the library, and, most
of all, these nights.

"What about Ragweed?" I said. "Because I'm such a
bitch, and you . . . well, you know."

Tig shook his head. He didn't get it.

"Like, I'm always on the rag and you're always on
the weed."

Tig laughed so hard he snorted. "You don't go *on* the weed."

"I know," I said wisely. "You *do* a weed," and I thought he might bust something. I loved making him laugh, and the farther we got from my house, the lighter I felt. The joint helped, too, so I had another puff off it.

"Ragweed. You and me," he said, when he could talk again. "Perfect. Especially since the whole damn school is allergic to us."

I grinned, because it was so true. We were outliers, defaulted into friends because I was fat and he was poor. No one else was either one of those things. Not at Brighton. There were a couple of chunky girls, one podgy boy, but I was the biggest human in the school. Maybe even bigger than the secretary with the huge, mothery boobs and the wig. She was Nana-aged, so no one cared if she was fat. They didn't even care if she was breathing. She sometimes passed me Starlight Mints, sad eyes downtilted as if to say she understood that we were the same, and I hated her so much in those moments. I took the fucking mints, though.

Tig was actually, really poor, the only full-scholarship kid in the whole school. Every other scholarship was partial, doled out to a few kids with middle-class parents and 4.0s. Tig's ex-stepdad owned Vintage Wheels, a garage where a clique of Brighton's major power dads rebuilt classic cars for fun. The ex-step had brought Tig, who was a certified genius, to their attention. Tig took the scholarship, but he didn't really embed. He walked the halls alone. He read smart-kid books—*Brave New World, Cosmos, The Jungle*—but he didn't sit with the smart kids.

Before Tig I'd sat with them, anchored by the desperate friendship of Peg, the second-fattest girl. She'd liked hiding her body in the wider shade of mine, making me fat camouflage, but she'd never once called me up to see a movie on the weekend. Still, I couldn't have done what Tig did before he had me, just plop down alone at a small corner table, reading while he methodically ate every scrap of food on his school lunch tray. I envied his metabolism. It didn't occur to me that the free lunch the school gave him was most of what he got to eat on any given day.

I passed the joint, then braked as we got to the railroad tracks. We were out of my neighborhood now, into undeveloped land. Loblolly pines rose high all around us. I lumped us over the tracks, slow and careful.

Tig said, "Pussy move, Smiff," but with no rancor. He liked to speed up and try to get a jump off, though most of the time he only jarred us so hard it rattled my teeth. Once or twice, though, it had really felt like he'd gotten his muscly steel monster airborne. I was scared to try it. What if I did it wrong? I'd scrape the muffler clean off.

As I turned onto the dirt road, Tig took another huge drag, then carefully tamped out the half joint and left it in the ashtray. He started digging in the bag, hunting meat. He came up with a sandwich.

"Oh, yeah, Smiffy, you are God."

"You're welcome," I intoned, Godlike, and Tig snorted.

He flipped on his radio. It was set for 101.5, which was alt-rock and old-school. He had every button on his car radio set there, because he said it was the only station worth a preset. A solid three weeks back, I'd changed all the button settings to a fluffy pop station he would hate, but he had never punched one to notice. I was tired of waiting, so I did it for him. Morrissey cut off mid-dirge, and there was MC Hammer, making whoa-whoa noises.

He punched button four, button two; it stayed MC.

"Smiff, you total asshole," he said, so fondly that I flushed.

He fished the ham out of his sandwich, dandling it over his face like a pink meat rag. He sang the duh-nuh-nuhs along with the music, but at the end he said, "Ham Time!" and snapped at it with his teeth, cracking us both up.

"Ham time! Ham time!" We sang together. The car wobbled on the trail, branches scraping the side.

"Whoa!" Tig said, still laughing, and I righted us and slowed. I crept the last half mile into the woods, stealing tiny glances at his Roman nose, his sharp-cut jawline, his long-fingered musician's hands.

Tig sang with MC, and ate his sandwich, and never felt my gaze. I was good at it. I'd learned at school, looking at girls. My eyes seemed to point themselves at girl bodies in a way that disturbed me; it felt so hungry. The meanest girls had the prettiest bodies, as if slender legs and perky breasts and clear, fresh skin were day passes to cruelty.

They didn't deserve those breezy bodies that they flexed and swayed inside. What would it feel like to run without feeling my fat jouncing around me, turning every sprint into a humiliating lumber? Would I be a bitch, too, if I could? As it stood, I was careful to stay jolly and kind.

Once, in the girls' locker room, after laps, I forgot myself, staring openly at Shelley Gast and her friends.

They were shifting from one foot to the other, leaning on things, touching their own narrow waists. They were all so bendable inside their cream or pink or olive skins, the only shades on regular display at Brighton. Shelley stood closest to me, near naked by her locker, underpants riding high up on the half-moon curves of her tidy little ass.

"Why don't I have any boobs at all?" she lamented.

She did, though, pencil-test-ready B cups with cotton-candy-colored nipples. I watched her tuck them away inside a polka-dot bra. I had small poinks that jutted from the fatty expanse of my chest. They seemed sexless to me, not breasts so much as smaller dandles of fat above the triple loaves of my hanging gut. Shelley caught me staring.

"Lesbo much?" she said, pulling her uniform shirt over her head, and I giggled nervously.

"Just thought yer bra was cute," I said, jolly, jolly. I didn't want to be the Fat Lesbian. Being the Fat was bad enough. "I need new ones."

"Dillard's, but it won't come in your size," Shelley said.

After that I learned how to look in little sips, to never get caught yearning. When I found myself behind one of those girls in the hall, I'd flick my gaze around, taking in the pieces. A bank of lockers, then slim hips. The window, then bare legs making the plaid uniform skirt flare and bell. The pile of books braced on my belly, then a sleek ponytail ticktocking between narrow shoulders.

These days I used the same technique to look-stalk Tig Simms. He was tall and just as lithe as those girls. His ribs showed when his shirt rode up. His hand-me-down khakis hung off his hip bones, but he had broad shoulders, tanned skin, dark eyes. That crazy hair.

I parked us in the dirt turnaround. We had to hike the last hundred yards down a narrow trail to reach the fire pit. I made Tig go first, to break any spiderwebs. I hated that feeling of a web strand on my skin. Tig carried our acoustics, and I grabbed the picnic, the jug wine, and a waxy paper Mickey D's cup that I dug out of the backseat. Tig kept a flashlight in the glove box, but the night was crazy-bright with moon, and anyway we knew this path by heart.

Three splintery wood benches surrounded the ashy pit, and we each took one, unpacking our instruments. Behind us there was an old shed with a dank mattress inside, so stained and ill-used that sitting down on it could probably get me pregnant. If this was a weekend, someone would for sure be using it. A lot of kids knew about this place. But now, after 1:00 A.M. on a school night, we had it to ourselves.

"Did you bring a corkscrew?" Tig asked, handing me a fresh joint and picking up the jug. I was crestfallen, but he grinned. He unscrewed the cap and held it up to show me, like he'd done a magic trick. "It ain't no nevermind, Smiffy. I got me some redneck ingenuity." It was the voice he used to make fun of Assholio, and I laughed. How on earth had I thought that the jug would have a cork?

He poured the waxy paper cup near full and then gulped at it.

"Ahhh Smiffy," he said, "That's the stuff. Tastes like desperation."

He offered me the cup, and it smelled flat and sour, very much like bad salad dressing. I drank it anyway.

Three long swallows, holding my breath like it was a draft of medicine.

Tig's eyebrows disappeared into the curls flopped on his forehead. He often liberated a couple of canned beers from his mom and Assholio, but I didn't like the taste. I'd never been invited to the hunch-punch parties the Brighton kids threw down at the bluffs either.

Tonight, though? I wanted to fit my lips over the exact spot where his lips had touched the cup. Plus, the pot had given me dry mouth. I drank again, and it went down a little easier.

I would have committed murder for some cheese popcorn right about then. For cheese of any kind.

We played—the Smiths, Violent Femmes, the Cure— passing the cup back and forth between songs, then smoking the joint. Tig sang, soft and growly, and I liked how our voices wound together. I wanted to do some Pixies, and as we sang "Here Comes Your Man," the notes rose up around us, almost visible. At this thought I knew that I was really, really stoned.

I felt so light. I forgot my body, became only my essential self, the piece that could sometimes feel like a filament, bright and hot and burning. I wasn't stumbling on the chord shifts now, even though Tig was the musician; he'd been teaching me on an old guitar my brother, Connor, had abandoned. Mostly I strummed easy chords while he played lead. But tonight it was like I knew what Tig would do, where his hands and voice would go, as if we were a single thing. I met him in harmony, effortless and perfect.

"Ragweed's rocking it, eh, Smiffy?" Tig said when we took a break to eat the pears, split the second sandwich, drink and smoke more.

"Oh, yeah. But, God, I hate pears," I told him, pouring. The jug had gotten lighter, and the world seemed to slosh faintly along with it as I overfilled the cup. Wine splashed out, and I corrected, giggling.

He laughed, too. "I never seen you drunk."

"You don't feel it?"

"Naw. S'just wine," he said, and chugged more.

Well, he was used to it. He talked about slamming forties and playing drinking games with his friends in his neighborhood. He lived in a wasteland of decrepit blocks behind the dilapidated Krispy Kreme that everybody called Downtown, and there he had a whole life I only knew from stories on nights like now. He hung out with Buddy and Carl, who did cars with him. He talked a lot about some girl named Toya. She was not his girlfriend, but it seemed like from his stories she'd had sex with him. Also Crystal, who for sure went all the way, because she had a baby. I wondered what her body looked like; a lot of girls were fatter after babies. I was pretty sure Tig had had sex with her, too, this potentially fatter girl, but the baby wasn't his.

I knew because one time I'd asked, and he'd said, "Nah. I wrap that shit up, you know?"

I had nodded, stoned and owlish, but I hadn't known. Two days later, in civics, it suddenly hit me that he didn't mean he wrapped it up as in "closed down before sex." He meant he used a condom. Tig Simms had for sure had sex. Tig Simms for sure knew how to do it.

After that the way I watched girls changed. I couldn't stop imagining myself getting *in* them. If I could only body-swap, I'd change with Shelley, walk away covered in pretty. I'd go Downtown and show Tig Simms my brand-new teacup breasts, the curvy little belly she

hated that I thought looked so taut and sexy. I'd lie beneath him, slim legs tangling in his. Shelley had sex all
the time with Cliff Mayes, everybody said, so my new
body would know how to do it, too.

"Well, I want to be drunk. So there," I said. Defiant.

Tig looked at me with kind eyes. "Bad week?"

I nodded, and he leaned his shoulder against mine. I
tried to be still and cool. I could feel my fat, and it was
both me and a living wall around me. I sat inside my
body, yearning. If he put his arm around me, he would
feel the lumps and folds of my waist. Some nights I pretended my hands into his hands. I would grab squashy
handfuls of my own ass, suck in my gut, and touch the
ripe flap of it still hanging down in a dandle. My own
hands were repulsed, so I knew I couldn't let him touch
me. Even so, I'd send one of my Tig-hands snaking between my legs, to touch the place where I was just like
any other girl, to rock against the pretend of him.

I was not one of those loose-hipped, saucy girls from
way down in his neighborhood, but when he leaned his
shoulder against mine, my body didn't seem that bad a
place to be. We sat quietly together, and then I said a
true thing.

"Mom's sending me back to camp."

"Ugh," Tig said. "Camp Celery?"

"Yeah," I said. "Camp Sweat."

She'd announced it Monday night, watching me eat
my allotted roll as if she begrudged me every dry, un-
buttered bite.

I'd burst into tears. At fat camp mini Reesey cups
were valid currency, same as Camel Lights in prison.
Last summer I'd huffed and puffed through daily aer-

obics with floppy, uncommitted arm movements, half a beat behind. I'd doodled cats and ballerinas all through the nutrition classes, learning nothing except that I was an exceptional candy smuggler. I came home only six pounds lighter, and I'd quickly gained those back and then some.

"Please, no! It didn't even work," I'd begged my mother, crying.

"You didn't mind it so much last year," Mom said, but last year I hadn't had a Tig to leave behind.

"Camp Fuck That Noise. You'll be gone all summer?" he said, like he might miss me. Like I mattered.

I nodded, and then I said a thing that made me feel more naked than I had ever been with another person. The words came quiet and ashamed. "Camp Get Less Disgusting."

"Hey. Don't say that," Tig said, turning his head. We looked at each other, faces close, still leaning on each other's shoulder. "You don't call you disgusting."

"I know what I am," I whispered. I could smell the wine sour on his breath. I liked it.

"You're my best friend," Tig said. "Don't talk that way about my friend."

I warmed. All of me warmed.

"I know what I am," I told Tig again, and he shook his head, and then he kissed me. He slipped his shoulder sideways and ducked his face in. A real kiss. No sad cheek smacked with pity-lips, but the real thing, like I'd seen in movies. Like I'd seen pretty girls get kissed in the hallways, pressed up against their lockers by their boyfriends. My mouth opened under his, all of me alight and atremble.

He pulled back, and I pulled back. I was conscious of the night around us. The mattress behind us. The moon making him crazy.

He grinned. Ducked his head. Finally he spoke. "Shit, Smiffy, we are real bad drunk. We can't ruin this. We can't do this wrong."

I wasn't sure what he meant. Ruin this thing that he started? Ruin our friendship by starting this thing? I just waited, panting, my mouth going dry again.

He leaned away to get the jug, and I hated the loss of that small pressure, his shoulder on mine. He poured the wax cup full, handed it over. I gulped at the wine, which felt so cool and good now on my sandpaper tongue. Tig relit the half joint, and we traded it and the cup back and forth, not talking. I wasn't sure if we were comfortable or crazy. I wasn't sure what time it was.

"I gotta eat somefin'," I finally said.

The big green jug was close to empty, but I didn't realize how bad it truly was until I stood up. The world lurched and tilted around me. I spread my arms out, braced my feet against the whole huge earth. I could feel it rotating under me.

"We're so stoned," Tig said, jerking his thumb to point behind us. "Let's havver nap?"

When he said it, my chest filled up with a host of tiny, popping bubbles. He meant that mattress. He was asking me to lie down on it with him, and what would happen? He might fall asleep, snoring as I yearned—pathetic. He might roll to me and touch me. Kiss me. I thrilled to this, but what if he meant sex, all-the-way real sex? Would I be naked, my folds and creases open to him in the moonlight? I wanted. I wanted so much, and yet I shook my head, near panicking.

"I gotta eat," I insisted, though I wasn't actually thinking about food. I reached down and grabbed his hand, hauled him up. He let me tug him along the path, but it was my choice. My fear and my self-loathing.

I set us in motion, and we went.

The growly engine roared like a living thing, and Tig started singing that Pixies song again. I heard my own voice from a distance, winding in and out around his. The tires slurred against the dirt, and this was a song, too. We hit the railroad tracks, so fast, so fast. Up and over into a weightless moment, where my body disappeared around me and I was only motion, suspended in the darkness, and Tig Simms had kissed me.

The trees and the dirt road ended together, and ahead was a watery wall of moonlight glowing off the asphalt where the road became real. We went sailing out of the woods, into that white wall of light, and in that moment the road dropped out from under us and the music turned to clanging glass and the shriek of tires. Inside those sounds time itself changed. The stars spun, and they are spinning. The sky turned, and it is turning. I am inside a slide show of noise and flashing color. The lap belt cuts into my stomach as I jerk and flail to the grinding rhythm of metal ripping.

A small black beat of lost time. Am I asleep? Tig said that we should take a nap. Am I still asleep? Did he kiss me at all? My mouth floods with salt.

"Marmee?" Lolly Shipley calls, and her marmee must be sleeping, too. I must be babysitting. I have to go get Lolly. I swallow, gulping brine, and my mouth instantly refills. "Marmee, Marmee?" Lolly calls. She has blond pigtails, a soft belly, fat cheeks like my hamster. Little tiny things, hamsters and babies, they are so cute when they are fat. I touch my mouth, and my fingers come away sticky, my blood shining black in the moonlight.

Now I am standing in the moon-drenched road, Tig's car behind me, and I am lurching forward, trying to follow Tig across the street. I am swayed by currents into a winding stagger toward the other car. I know this car, little and light and sporty, but the front side is now bent and twisted to an unfamiliar shape. It is so far away, shoved half onto a grassy, sloping lawn. Tig reaches it, and he is moaning, falling to his knees.

I see Lolly, and Lolly's face is red. Her blue eyes are bruised pansies, wide and wet. Baby Paul, who never sleeps, wails in his car seat. Driving him to sleep worked, I remember Mrs. Shipley saying. Paul is beside Lolly in the back half, which is whole and like a car. But the front is strange and curved and lacy white and black with jagged metal. The nose is crumpled in profile, and the driver's door is smashed. Pretty Mrs. Shipley stares silent at me through the missing window, and below her collarbones her body is smashed, too.

I go nearer, and Lolly sees me, and she says, "Amy, Paul is cry?"

I say, "Mrs. Shipley?" but I can see now that all the black wetness that is in the folds and crumples of the car is Mrs. Shipley. From the shoulders down, most of her insides are on the outside. Her face is still so pretty, even with the red-black wet splashed across it, even with the glassy open eyes that are so dead.

I feel myself toppling, the asphalt biting my bare, broad knees. I throw up salt and black and purple in the road.

Lolly cries, "Marmee? Marmee?" and it sounds softer

now. Lolly is tired, and I must be tired, too. Paul wails from far, far away. Please let us be sleeping, napping on that filthy mattress, like Tig said. Tig lows like cattle, moaning on all fours.

Mrs. Shipley's pretty body is folded and opened, and this is a thing I chose. I dragged us down the trail to the car. I understand this. This is a choice I can't take back.

My face is stuck in an expression. My face is so surprised. I did not know I could lead us to a thing so big, so mean, something we can never undo or remove, that will echo in my life, in all our lives, forever.

I lie down in the road near my sick, and Lolly calls, *"Marmee,"* and of all the things I sank so deep down inside me, Mrs. Shipley's dead, dead, pretty face, blood in strings like spiderwebs across her white skin, her eyes wide open, their blue washed down to pale gray in the moonlight, was the last. The hardest thing to never, never see.

3

I STIRRED, TUMBLED IN the horrid wave of fear and worry that had pulled me into dreams of drowning and rolled me in and out of sleep all night. Drifting between sleep and waking, I was certain, for an endless, awful second, that Angelica Roux had all my past in her possession. If she owned my past, then she owned me with it. She could center it in her palm like a tiny gift—a fig, a wish, a duckling—and hold it out to Davis, to Maddy, to Charlotte, every neighbor, all my coworkers. Would it change me in my husband's eyes? The very thought knocked me fully awake, left me breathless and askew.

I scrubbed at my face, sat up. It was impossible for Roux to know my past. Truly impossible, unless she was a mind reader. The gray light at the window told me it was dawn, and logic told me that Angelica Roux could have no power over me. But not even taking diver's breaths, slow and even, could set my heart to rest. I kept hearing her throaty voice, seeing her knowing eyes as she told me, *Come by my place. Soon. We have a lot to talk about.*

A thin, unhappy humming began piping through the baby monitor. Oliver's waking-up-hungry sound. I got out of bed and turned the volume down to zero in case he started sounding serious about it before I could reach him. My husband was sleeping. I wanted him to stay asleep.

I changed Oliver's bloated overnight diaper and then brought him back to our bed. He blinked up at me, giving me his gummy, lopsided smile with its lone pair of tiny teeth poking up from the center bottom. He seemed mercifully oblivious to my anxiety.

I smiled back in spite of myself, whispering, "Morning times, good baby."

He rolled to me, making little grunty snuffles and rooting, and I hiked up my T-shirt so he could latch. He settled in to nurse in earnest, his hands fisted in my top. I wondered if the storm of bad memory that had been released in me was dripping into my baby as surely as the gin I'd pumped and dumped last night would have. I breathed, tried to be only in this sweet and quiet now, to only see my boy.

The very shape of him was beautiful and so dear to me in the faint light. I loved his big, round Charlie Brown head, still mostly innocent of hair. *Takes after his dad,* Davis liked to say, wry and smiling, rubbing at his own hairline, which was just beginning to recede. Oliver did favor Davis, but he had my eyes, wide-set and Irish green. He was unequivocally a good thing, and I had made him. I had put him in the world.

I rested my hand on his back to feel the pit-pat of his small, strong heart. Nursing released a cloud of hormones that could blunt life's sharper edges. Most mornings doing this most basic job reduced the wide, black world to the rise and fall of my husband's broad chest, the knowledge of our Mads sleeping right down the hall, and outside my fall pansy bed getting prettied up by dew to meet the sunrise. But not today.

I couldn't shake the feeling that Roux's game had been aimed specifically at me.

That could not be true. It only felt that way. It was a game for gaining social leverage, like something Tate would pull if she were smarter. I should have seen it when Roux took Char's seat, the obvious power chair, as if she happened to be standing there. That had been choreography, designed to up herself in the pecking-order game women played with each other at our very worst. She'd gone fishing for guilt, and her hooks had sunk deep into me and Tate Bonasco. She'd hauled Tate up in one smooth move. But really, Roux only knew what Tate herself had confessed; she could have no idea how high the stakes were for me.

All I had to do was outbrain Tate—not a high bar to clear. Last night I'd overreacted, panicking. It had made Roux home in on me. All I'd revealed, though, was that I felt guilty about something, which was an almost universal human condition.

The thought gave me no peace, even as I ran my fingers in slow whorls on Oliver's warm back, watching new sunlight spill lemon yellow into the room. I'd never had so much to lose. The last near-seven years had given me Char, then Maddy and Davis, now Oliver—one by one they had barnacled onto me until I was at home, for the first time in my life.

I'd grown up in a family where Mom preferred my brother and Dad preferred his job. After the accident it got worse. Dad blamed me for his having to make a lateral career move that landed us in Boston, and as for my mother? It was as if I had been coated in Teflon. Before the accident, she would at least look at me to telegraph her disapproval, her gaze twitching and flicking over my surfaces. But after, her eyes never seemed to light on me at all. I finished high school, barely, and I think it was a relief for all of us when I picked a tier-three college all the way across the country. With my grades I thought it was a miracle I got in, but I had Nana's trust. Kids who can pay can always get in somewhere. I moved to a studio apartment by campus and I registered, but I never once went to class. It didn't seem to matter.

The terms of the trust earmarked it for college; I couldn't touch it if I wasn't going, so I waited tables and then later worked at dive shops to make rent. I dated West Coast boys with tats and slouchy walks, lost souls who reminded me just enough of Tig to prick my heart. Not one of them was ever half as nice to me as he'd been. At nineteen, before I found scuba, when I was still heavily self-medicating, I went to Vegas with a surf rat named James Lee, and we woke up wearing rings. I liked James fine, but I felt alone even when he was sleeping right beside me. We split up a few months later with no drama, using a form we got at the county court clerk's office. The only thing I kept was his last name.

My California time was like childbirth; once it was over, I forgot how awful it had been. Until now. Roux's damned game. It had gotten inside me in a way that felt like an infection, heating and roiling the deeps within me, and things long buried were bubbling toward the surface. I hadn't felt my past as a weighty physicality in years, but now it was a pressure in my abdomen, a humming in my hands.

Maybe I *should* go talk to Roux? Casually. Not about

the game. I could make her some blondies as an excuse. Our set always baked for new families—another Char initiative—and I helped Char maintain a current database of neighborhood phone numbers and trusted local businesses: plumbers, roofers, lawn services, even the ever-changing crop of teenage babysitters. We didn't usually bake for Sprite House people because at most they stayed a month or two, but Roux had come to book club.

I could walk two blocks down to the cul-de-sac, light of step, cheery, very off-the-cuff. I'd talk about raising teenagers and *The House of Mirth*. If she did the same, I'd know that her game had not been aimed at me. Then I could relax.

If she did bring the game up, asking me why I'd gotten upset enough to kick her out of my house last night, I could act affronted. Not even act—it was an affront, her digging in my business. I would tell her plain and simple that her awful game had brought up bad memories from my childhood, which was true enough, and tell her to back off.

Now that I had a plan, I was eager to get up and get it over with. Oliver was deeply asleep again, still latched. He was a good baby, as long as he got all his naps on schedule. If not, he could be a howling terror. I pressed one finger against the corner of his bottom lip, feeling his breath puff out warm as he released. A little milk went in a dribble down his cheek, and he rolled onto his back, chubby legs akimbo.

"Davis," I said quietly, and my voice sounded so normal. "You have Oliver. Please don't mush him."

He cracked an eye and rolled toward us on his side, putting one big hand out to span Oliver's chest.

"No baby mushing," he mumbled.

I slid out of bed and changed into yoga pants and a fresh T-shirt in the near dark, then went to stir Maddy as if this were any morning on a school day.

She was nothing but a grumpy heap of covers that said, "Go away, Monster."

I grinned. "You'll miss the bus."

"Got a ride," the heap whined, so I let it be. When Shannon's mom drove them, she could stay in bed an extra fifteen minutes.

I went downstairs and pushed the button on the coffee machine. I was still off caffeine, though I'd sometimes steal sips from Maddy or Davis. I swung into my morning routine, getting a load of the never-ending laundry going, emptying the dishwasher, sautéing mushrooms and tomatoes for the scrambled eggs.

It felt like a performance, like I was saying, *See Wheys, and Char, and neighborhood, and world? I am the kind of person who makes real food, protein and vegetables, to start her family's day off warm and right. The kind who sets a healthy three hundred calories' worth aside on a plate for herself.*

No one had come down by the time I'd finished cooking, so I folded their eggs into tortillas with avocado slices and salsa and wrapped them up in tinfoil to keep warm.

I went to the foot of the stairs and called, "You guys are running late."

"Poo-splosion!" Davis called back. "Don't come up here, honey. Run. Save yourself."

That made me smile. The kind of small disaster that defined my current life was unfolding normally upstairs. "Hey, Mads? You better not be still in bed."

"Blah!" Maddy yelled back. She sounded vertical at least.

Just as I finished my breakfast, Davis came hurrying down with a nearly naked Oliver in his arms. He shifted his hands under Oliver's armpits, then held him out to me. "Take this wretched, pooping baby!"

"Ahmamamama!" Oliver said, reaching, babbling a sound that wasn't quite a word but I thought still meant me. His dangling legs kicked in excitement, though he saw me every day, all day.

I propped him on my hip, and he got himself an anchoring fistful of my hair. Davis pulled a onesie with cartoon dogs sprinkled all over it out of his pocket and offered it to me, draping it over his arm with a flourish, like a maître d's napkin.

"I had to strip the sheets," he said. "They're in a plastic hamper on the landing, and this boy here? I ran him under some warm water in the shower because otherwise it would have taken enough baby wipes to create a whole new landfill."

I looked at my husband, standing in our sunshiny kitchen, having a regular morning-time conversation while the baby we'd made together pulled my hair and blew raspberries. I had to turn my back and blink away the tears that sprang up unexpected in my eyes. This ordinary life, full of laundry and diapers and kitchen curtains with apples printed on them, was so precious to me. This morning it also felt frail.

"You were very brave," I told Davis, working to make my voice sound normal as I got his to-go breakfast off the counter. "I'll put the sheets in as soon as the washer clears, and then I'll bleach the bathroom."

"Bleach can't save it. Once Maddy leaves for school,

you and Oliver should go outside and burn the house down." He checked his watch. "Sorry to leave it with you, but . . ."

"I got this," I said, trading him the egg burrito for the onesie.

"Southwestern style?" he asked, all hopeful, and when I nodded, he said, "I do not deserve you."

"True," I said, and hoped it didn't sound as ironic as it felt.

He dropped a kiss on the corner of my mouth, and he was gone.

I got Oliver dressed and then popped him in his high chair, sprinkling a handful of Cheerios on the tray to keep him busy while I mixed baby oatmeal with stored breast milk and opened up a jar of pureed apples. I was about to call Maddy again when a car horn sounded and she came hurtling down the stairs. She'd paired her short blue shift dress with green knee socks patterned with demented deer heads. These things didn't go together on any planet, nor with her battered orange-and-aqua tennies. As she dashed past, I caught a glimpse of mascara and a smear of gooey pink lip gloss. My girl lived ninety percent of her life in leggings and ratty T-shirts, so why was she decked out in full Mads regalia?

"Love you, Monny-Monster!" she hollered over her shoulder.

I stood up. "Breakfast!"

"Not hungry!" she shouted from the living room.

"Hold up, Mads!" I called. "Madison!"

The only answer I got was the front door banging shut. Loud. I scattered more Cheerios on the tray to keep Oliver busy, grabbed the burrito off the counter, and ran after her.

I yanked open the front door just in time to see an Infiniti convertible, cherry red and gleaming, peeling away with the top down. Maddy's bobbed curls ruffled in the same wind that was streaming Luca's long black hair.

I wanted to leap off the porch and run after them, shrieking like a harpy, I was that angry. She'd never once been allowed to ride to school with an unsupervised teen driver, much less the male of the species. I'd gotten deliberately misleading words from the grumpy heap of covers, and then she'd lurked upstairs until the last second, no doubt to avoid conversation that might lead her into a direct lie. But they were already too far for me to catch them, music blasting too loud for them to hear me. Plus, I couldn't leave Oliver alone with Cheerios for more than five seconds without worrying about choking.

I went back to the kitchen. I half wanted to hustle Oliver into his car seat and take off after them. It would be an overreaction, though, and it would embarrass Maddy nigh unto death.

I sat down and put breakfast into the baby as he banged around with his "helping" spoon, spattering us both with oatmeal and apples. His world was so small and so safe, but Maddy had ridden off into a much larger one, in a car, with a shady boy. And why would a kid who looked like Luca be offering our Mads a ride to school anyway?

Maddy was beautiful, to us. To most adults. But not the kind of beautiful that played in high school. She had her dad's bold nose and a heavy brow line, and two weeks ago, in a fit of despair over the rash of pimples that kept appearing on her forehead, she'd grabbed the meat shears and cut herself a thick wedge of unflattering bangs that poinked out in all directions. She was the kind of girl who would come into her own in college, when ideas about beauty widened to include girls with striking features and flashing dark eyes, and when the boys themselves got a dollop of emotional maturity.

Luca, meanwhile, was teenage-dream-style beautiful. Cheekbones for days and that sulky James Dean mouth set in skin so clear and flawless that he looked like he'd been carved. Add the hot car and he was cheerleader bait. I couldn't see him fitting in with the spotty herd of magnificent weirdos in Maddy's clique.

Unless he was gay? Please, God, let him be gay, because I doubted that Roux had taught her boy to be gentle with girl hearts. Last night she herself had come to book club with a battle strategy. And what kind of mother would put an adolescent male behind the wheel of a car like that? But of course I knew what kind. I had met her. A shit stirrer. With a great big spoon.

When Oliver finished eating, I called the school office to make sure Maddy hadn't had bigger, badder plans to skip with Luca. She was on the attendance log for homeroom, so the stolen ride had been the end of it. Still, it was more drama linked directly to Angelica Roux, and on a morning when I was already full up with her.

I released Oliver into the babyproofed keeping room. There the TV and a pair of comfortable brown leather sofas shared the space with Davis's armchair and a ton of built-in bookshelves. The lower shelves were full of soft, squeaky toys. I latched the baby gate to keep him from the kitchen while I was baking, watching him pull up on the low coffee table as I mixed ingredients, answering his babbles and blowing raspberries back.

Once the blondies were in, Oliver and I went upstairs to clean the bathroom, get the ruined sheets in the washer, and remake the bed. We'd just come back down so I could check on my baking when I heard my front door opening.

"Amy?" Char called from the foyer.

I checked the microwave clock. Nine-fifteen, damn it.

"I'm in the kitchen," I called back.

I power-walked with Charlotte every weekday morning. The time had gotten away from me. My head was really not on right. Worse, caught up first in my own invented worries and then with Maddy's deception, I hadn't considered what I was going to do about Tate Bonasco and Charlotte's husband. Now, *that* was a real problem, concrete and immediate, and it wasn't like me not to put Char first. She'd been a priority ever since she'd poked her nose nervously into Divers Down almost seven years ago, right after I started working there, asking if we had adult swimming lessons.

I'd been sitting in the empty shop, thinking about all the ways I'd already given up my mission. I'd come to Florida after my thirty-fifth birthday. That was the year Boyce Skelton, a lawyer at the firm who managed my family's money, called me to tell me the clause earmarking Nana's trust for college had expired. The money, well over half a million dollars by then, was wholly mine, to do with as I pleased. As soon as he told me, I thought about Tig Simms. Even before I got off the phone, I was forming a half-assed, nebulous plan to give the money to Tig.

But first I'd had to find him, which meant coming back to Florida. He'd always been close with his ex-stepdad, Toby, the one who'd gotten Tig into Brighton in the first place. I'd gone by Vintage Wheels and asked about a fictitious classic-car-themed Christmas present for my equally fictitious husband. As Toby and I had chatted, I'd mentioned, offhand, that I used to know Tig. I'd made it sound like I knew him from Downtown, not school. Toby'd told me Tig was doing great, living an hour and change away in Mobile. He'd started his own business, another classic-car garage and parts yard. Restoration, it was called.

I got into my car and headed straight for Mobile, but I turned back before I even breached Pensacola city limits. I tried again the next day. And then again, days leaking into weeks, then months. I got the job at Divers Down to cover rent and food, driving toward Mobile a couple of times a week, inching a mile or two closer, then turning back. It was like a failed game of Mother May I?, though I knew damn well what my own mother would say.

That day I was sitting in the empty dive shop considering going back to my empty life in California. There at least I could blame my cowardice and inaction on the distance. But when I saw Charlotte's face peeking in the door, young and round and earnest, cheeks pinked with the embarrassment of admitting her fear of the ocean, I'd thought, *Here. Here is a small, good thing that I can do today.*

I'd signed her up with no presentiment that my life was already shifting. In a few short months, Char would become my closest friend. I owed her so much, and not only because she was Char. She had led me to Maddy,

who led to Davis, and now Oliver. She had gifted me
with my whole sweet second life here.

Now she came bustling into the kitchen, pushing
Ruby in her stroller with the little pooch of her new
pregnancy wagging before her. A toddler, a baby on
the way, and what the hell was Phillip Baxter thinking? Not that I was completely surprised. I had never
been fond of Charlotte's smug little husband. He took
her so for granted. Davis called him "the Vegetables"—
something I had to dutifully eat if I wanted lovely Charlotte on my plate.

I started to apologize, but she waved it away.

"I figured you were a little bit hungover? And oh, my
God, when did she get out of your house!" she said, in
lieu of hello. There was no question who "she" was.

"Wee hours," I said.

"That *bitch*," Char said, no hesitation, though she
only mouthed the second word in deference to the babies. Still, my eyes widened. Char, in a temper, said
things like "rats" and "phooey."

Ruby was already unclicking her stroller belt, saying,
"Eh-mo! Eh-mo!" and opening and closing her hands at
the TV. She usually got to watch *Sesame Street* when
Char hung out in my kitchen.

"Roux wasn't even the last one to leave. The rest of
us had to wait for Tate to finish puking," I said, lifting
Ruby over the baby gate.

"Hi-ho, Obbiber," Ruby said.

"And whose fault was that?" Char said, getting the
remote off my counter and firing up the keeping-room
TV. "Red or white, red or white, like it was her house.
Like she was the hostess. What happened after I left?"

I found myself telling her about Roux's game, because she was Charlotte, and for seven years now I had told Charlotte almost, almost everything.

Char said, "I bet Tate won every round. She's so competitive, and she hasn't got the good sense God gave little fishes. She'd confess anything. Did you play?"

It was a casual question, but the words were tinged in green. Char must have felt how interested I'd been in Roux before it all went bad.

"Hell no," I said staunchly, though I mouthed the first word. Ruby was singing along with the Muppets, waving her stuffed lamb at Oliver, but she was notoriously bat-eared and of an age to repeat every single thing she heard. "I stood by my stairs drinking too much gin and trying to look poisonous enough to make them leave."

She laughed, reassured. "I can guess how well that worked. Honestly, it's the stupidest game I ever heard of. I don't want to know the worst thing every neighbor ever did, or even the worst thing they did last month. How far did they get? Did anyone give up something super juicy?"

"Not far. They were all so drunk," I said. I didn't much want to talk about the actual confessions. That road led right to Tate Bonasco and Phillip at the Back-to-School barbecue. "I missed most of it. I was upstairs with you, evacuating Mads from that front-lawn flirt session."

"Oh, yeah! That kid Luca? Trouble. And I would say that even if I hadn't met his awful mother. He's way too cute," Char said. "But I wouldn't worry. He'll find his own crowd, and it's not going to be the honor-roll kids in marching band."

"That's what I thought, but then he gave Mads a ride to school this morning." Char's mouth popped open, and before she could ask if Davis and I had lost our minds, I explained, "Mads played me. I assumed 'a ride' meant Shannon's mom. But no, she went roaring off in his completely inappropriate red sports car."

"That's not his. That's Roux's. Or anyway it's the only car I've ever seen in their driveway. It's brand-new, like this year's model." Char paused, sniffing the air. "Are you *baking*?"

Char had struggled with food issues as a teen, and I'd said enough for her to understand that I had, too. She knew I didn't keep sweets in the house.

"Blondies. For Roux," I said. I wasn't going to lie to her about minutiae. Her eyes widened. "I printed her out a copy of our neighborhood directory, too. When I drop it off, I'll very casually mention that most of the moms with teenagers go to bunco instead of book club."

Char laughed then. "That's brilliant. Pawn her off on them!"

The doorbell rang. Char looked a question at me, but I wasn't expecting anyone. I shrugged, eyes too wide, because I knew that it was Roux. Had to be. Come back to finish her damn game, and this time with Charlotte as a witness.

"Watch the littlies?" I asked Char.

I turned away so she wouldn't see how plastic my smile had gone. I went through the swinging door to the long hall, with its wide arches to the formal living room and dining room on either side. The walk to the front door at the end took about a thousand years.

It was only Tate Bonasco. She was actually the second-to-last neighbor I wanted to see this morning. Still, my breath puffed out with relief, and only then did I realize I'd been holding it. Tate had a white bakery box from Publix, and she was smiling so wide that all her teeth were showing.

"Hey, Tate," I heard myself saying, as if this were perfectly normal. It wasn't. I could count on my thumbs the times Tate had dropped by to see me all impromptu. Hell, I could count them on my wings—it had never happened.

"Hi," she said, drawing the *H* out long. "Can I come in? Do you have a sec?"

As she spoke, she ran her free hand down her glossy ponytail, smoothing it. It did not need smoothing.

"Oh, I'm—" I said, and faltered, turning and gesturing behind me, supremely conscious of Char, right down the hall, through that flimsy swinging door. Tate took it as permission, ducking past me into the house. Before she could start talking, I called out, very loud, "Charlotte, Tate's here! Can you check the blondies for me?"

At Char's name Tate paused, her gaze flying to meet mine. Her cheeks flushed, deep and red and confessional.

I turned toward the kitchen, washed in a whole-body discomfort, but Tate grabbed my arm.

"Did you say anything?" she whispered, gaze flicking from one of my eyes to the other, searching. She must have found her answer, because she blew her breath out and nodded. "Please don't. It was just a kiss. A little drunken kiss." When I didn't respond, she tightened her grasp and changed tacks. "You could really mess her marriage up."

"Could mess yours up pretty good, too, huh," I said, quiet but not so quiet that she couldn't hear the acid in my tone. She had the grace to drop her gaze.

"Please," she said. "It was nothing."

I looked away. Last night it had sure as hell sounded like more than a sloppy smear of lip on lip. Tate had been implying something truly juicy, but she'd back-pedaled in the wake of Panda's shock and Lavonda's disapproval. If they had leaned in, smiling and dirty-interested, she might have had more to tell.

But "might" was a big word. And damn Tate Bonasco for putting me in this position anyhow. She had me whispering in the hall, behind my best friend's back. I had to do the right thing for Char, with no idea what the right thing was. I didn't want to hurt Char, but if it was more than a kiss, she needed to know.

What if telling wrecks our friendship?

The thought rose unbidden, but it was a valid question. Women in denial shoved at people who told them truths they were not ready to hear. Shoved them hard, all the way out of their lives.

Then I was ashamed. I had to do what was good and right for Charlotte, even if it boomeranged on me.

"I don't want Char to hear it elsewhere," I said.

"Panda and Lavonda won't gossip about me," Tate said. "I'm going to go make nice with Roux, but even if she does talk, she thinks it was some stranger at the car place. They all do. I'll never tell a soul that it was . . ." She paused and then jerked her thumb toward the kitchen, indicating Char.

Maybe nothing *was* the right thing to do. I tried to put myself in my friend's shoes. If it were Davis, would I want Char to tell me?

The answer was a blankness. There wasn't enough beer in the world to make Davis into a man who would fall into a clutch with Tate Bonasco at a barbecue. Davis was . . . the word was "decent." It wasn't an announcing quality, just bedrock goodness, quiet and ever-present. It was his base. When I first met him, he'd seemed so stiff that I could see why Maddy sometimes called him Fuddy or Duddy instead of Daddy. But I came to see that if Davis said something, he meant it. If he made a promise, then he kept it.

"Please," Tate said again, sharp this time.

At the end of the hall, the kitchen door swung open and Char poked her head through. "I think they're ready. I took them out. Hi, Tate."

"Oh, hi, Charlotte," Tate said without enthusiasm.

"There's some coffee left. Want it?" Char asked, smiling as we came down the hall and back into the kitchen. "Amy says you had a tough night."

Tate smoothed her ponytail again. "I don't know what got into us."

"Don't you?" Charlotte said. She went to get Tate a mug, as comfortable in my kitchen as she was in her own. "Because I have a pretty good idea of what got into you."

"A bucket of wine?" I said, sounding lighter-hearted than I was. Most of my good gin had gotten into Tate as well, though, to be fair, she'd given it back directly, right into my unlined brass trash can.

"Excellent guess," Tate said. This would normally be good-natured neighborhood teasing, but for me, today, it had an edge to it.

"Actually, I meant Roux. Roux is what got into all of us," Char said plainly. She must have felt the edge, too. She poured Tate the last of the coffee and left it black. Tate didn't waste calories on cream or sugar.

"Yeah. I'm not crazy about her after last night either," Tate said, shooting a fast glance in my direction.

I turned away slightly, checking on the babies. Oliver

was edging around the coffee table, both hands on it for balance. An Elmo segment was on now, and Ruby was transfixed.

"Amy told me about the game," Char said, and Tate's whole body went stiff. Char didn't notice. "It's not even really Never Have I Ever, except maybe on steroids."

Tate shook her head. "It isn't? I haven't played that game."

"Sure you have," Char said. "Everyone who's ever been to a high-school party has. Roux's game is similar, I suppose, because you do learn the worst things everyone has done. You say, 'Never have I ever cheated on a test' or 'Never have I ever frenched a boy,' and then everyone who *has* frenched a boy has to drink." Tate was nodding now, and Char asked, "So who won?"

"Oh, Amy didn't tell you?" Tate said, shooting me another drowning glance.

"Hadn't gotten to it," I said.

"Most of it's not worth repeating," Tate said, overbright. She laughed, but to my ears it came out sick and sad. There was an awkward pause, and Tate could not meet Charlotte's expectant gaze. Finally Tate said, "Panda won, really."

Surely Tate wasn't going to tell Panda's toothbrush story? Panda was her best friend, and she must be dying of embarrassment this morning. But Tate launched right into it. I busied myself cutting up blondies while Tate explained "sex camel" to Char and dropped her voice to a salacious whisper for the punch line. Char laughed, her cheeks flaming pink, but the easy way Tate sold out her friend made me sick to my stomach.

"Oh, my God," Char said. "Amy! You were holding out on me!"

"I shouldn't have told it either," Tate said.

"No. You shouldn't have," I said, but Tate ignored my tone.

"Panda would kill me, and really, we shouldn't judge. I mean, has anyone in this kitchen been an angel? I could have confessed all kinds of stupid things, meaningless in the big picture, but that I'd find so embarrassing," Tate said, and I could feel her gaze boring holes in my skin. "Maybe we should all agree to pretend it never happened."

"Never have I ever played a naughty game?" Char said, smiling.

Tate didn't seem to get it, so Char reached for Tate's untouched coffee and took the tiniest sip.

Then Tate looked confused. "Wait, but—drinking means you did do the thing. You didn't play. You left before the game last night."

"Well, sure, but I've played naughty games. Truth or Dare and stuff," Char said. "Once? In middle school I even played Spin the Bottle." She took another tiny sip.

"Tramp!" I said, trying to lighten Tate's reaction.

"Mm. I miss coffee almost more than I miss wine," Char said, putting a protective hand low on her belly.

But now Tate wouldn't let it go.

"If Amy and I don't drink, can we all agree that we never played Roux's stupid game?" she asked, staring hard at me, weighting the moment with a ridiculous amount of meaning. Did she really think that if I passed on a sip of coffee, I was entering a pact with her? She was asking me to pretend I'd never heard her damn confession.

It was possible to consign her sin to silence. I knew it better than anyone. Pass the cup, seal my lips, never

mention it again. Let it sink. Let time roll over it, pushing it ever deeper. We stared at each other, so intense
about it that Char's eyebrows went up.

"It's just a joke," I said, firm. I took the coffee mug
and lifted it in a toast at Char. I sipped from it, hearing
Tate's angry little exhale as I did so. I put the mug in the
sink and changed the subject. "What brings you by this
morning, Tate?"

"Oh, right. Can you print me out one of those neighborhood directories?" Tate asked, and I knew what she
was going to say next even before she lofted the bakery box at us and added, "I realized last night we'd
never taken Roux a welcome gift, and I thought if I
went by . . ."

Char laughed out loud. "There's one on the counter.
Amy made these blondies for the same reason. I don't
think she liked that game any better than you did, and
as for me . . . well. That woman flat ruined book club.
Amy was going to try to pawn her off on the bunco
bunch."

Now Tate's eyes on me were speculative. "Was she?
Great minds."

I smiled, but inside I was horrified. Tate showing
up on my doorstep this morning had read to me like
full confession. Now she was belly-crawling to Roux's
house to try to play down last night, and that would be
a confirmation for Roux, as well. Her ploy was so obvious that I was instantly ashamed, because it was my
ploy, too.

If I showed up at Roux's with baked goods, the four-
page neighborhood directory flapping in my hands as
flimsy as my excuse for being there, I'd be telling Roux
that *her* guess was right—that I could have won her

awful game hands down. It stank of nerves and weakness. I might as well show up wearing a T-shirt that said YES, YOU DID SEE SMOKE. YES, YES, THERE IS A WILDFIRE BURNING HERE.

Just then Oliver lost his grip on the table. He sat down, hard, and made a pre-fuss noise, sharp and surprised. Char said, in a loud and cheery voice, "Whoopsy, Obbiber! Who fell down?" Her reaction reassured him, and he decided not to cry, but his eyebrows were still knit up.

I went through the baby gate to get him. I could feel Tate's eyes still burning holes in my back, but I did not turn or meet them. I stayed with the babies, letting Char give Tate the directory and walk her out. I wouldn't make Tate any promises, even unspoken ones.

As for Roux? There was nothing to be done. Nothing was the best thing, really. Talking to her, kowtowing like Tate, it would only make her interested in me. I felt unsettled now, nervous and worried, but this was mostly in my head. If I left her alone, nothing would come of it, because nothing could.

I knew that Roux could not have recognized me. There was nothing of the panhandle in her voice, but even if she was from here, she looked too young to remember me personally. No one my age or older remembered me either. Folks I recognized looked right through me.

My second day back in Florida, on a grocery run, I'd literally banged into my past in the form of my old youth pastor, my cart kissing his when he zoomed around the corner into the cereal aisle. He had looked right at me. Right into my face. All he said was, "'Scuse me, ma'am," and then he went back to his shopping. I'd stared after him, my mouth opening and closing, but no words came out. A few days later, I saw my father's former secretary at the library, and my first week at the dive shop, the boy I'd sat beside in freshman English came in to sign his daughter up for swimming lessons. They didn't know me either. No one did. Not even in that vague, "Have we met before?" way. The girl who killed Mrs. Shipley had lived in this town for less than three years, and she was two decades, a hundred pounds, and three names distant.

I never had made it to Mobile to see Tig Simms. Instead I'd hired a local lawyer to investigate him, and I'd learned that his business was in trouble. Two mortgages, the second at a high interest rate. With Boyce Skelton and the local lawyer's help, I'd created a corporation called Fresh Starts, whose stated purpose was to help small businesses thrive. Its actual purpose was smaller and more singular—to help Tig Simms. Fresh Starts paid off close to three hundred thousand dollars, saving the garage, and I'd let that be the end of it. Since I'd never faced him, no one from my past knew that I was back in town, so no one could have told Roux about me.

Roux could not have run across my story in some law-enforcement file or even in an old newspaper. The court records were sealed because we'd been minors, and my picture and my name had never appeared; I'd barely been a footnote in those stories.

Even if she did somehow know, I told myself, Tig and I had been children. We had believed we'd owned those roads at 3:00 A.M. We had never meant for it to happen. That night Mrs. Shipley lost her life and her family was shattered. It was horrific. What I did altered the future for so many people, and in such painful and irrevocable ways—but it *had* been an accident. Reckless, careless, but not malicious.

And yet these thoughts gave me little peace. The pressure in my chest had the added weight of everything that happened after. It was rising now, called up by Roux's knowing manner and her godforsaken game, even though only two people walking God's green earth—me and my mother—knew that killing Mrs. Shipley was not in and of itself the worst thing I had ever done. It was only the beginning.

4

"YOU USUALLY WENT TO Waffle House," the new detective said. "So did Tighler Simms decide on his own to drive back to your neighborhood that night?"

I sat on the sofa in our living room, wedged between my mother and my main lawyer, feeling both much older and much younger than my fifteen years. I wanted to say, *No one calls Tig "Tighler." Not even his teachers.* I wanted to ask, *Is Tig okay?* I wanted to know, most of all, *Can I please see him?* But at the intake of my breath, my lawyer laid a soft, restraining hand on my shoulder and talked before I could.

"Asked and answered."

"Well . . ." the new detective said. He was a schlumpy older guy, balding, with a broad, pale face. He seemed kind, more like a dad than the one who'd talked to me at the hospital. He seemed more like a dad than my own father, who was leaning in the doorway that led back to his study, radiating impatient anger. The detective sat across from me, leaning forward, so that I felt hemmed in on all sides.

The police hadn't even talked to me right after the accident. I was a stoned, drunk minor, bleeding profusely from the mouth, throwing up more blood and sour wine, moaning and struggling. They sent me straight to emergency, although I had no memory of that journey.

I'd almost bitten through the right side of my tongue in the crash. The doctor numbed it, making it feel like a foreign piece of meat invading my mouth, then cut away a small wedge that was too mangled to save. I'd needed fifteen stitches. They had also shoved a tube up my nose and down into my stomach to siphon out alcohol and the blood I'd swallowed, then sent me for a CT scan and admitted me.

When I woke up, sober and sorry late the next morning, my mother was sitting by my hospital bed. She was brittle and excessively cheerful, tapping and dabbing at me with her hands, trying in her way to be comforting. Really trying. At first. No recriminations, no lecture, only assurances that she was going to fix this. Money was her love language, and she told me she'd already found me an excellent lawyer; he was on the way. When he came, she presented him as "the best defense attorney in the state," with the same look on her face she had when she served beluga to her party guests.

He had a power tie and silver-gray hair that folded away from his face in a majestic swoop, and he questioned me for a solid hour. My tongue was still swollen, pulsing with pain around the stitches. It was not up to telling stories, but I did my best. My answers seemed to satisfy him, and my mother sat nearby, nodding encouragingly.

It went well, right up until the end, when he told me Tig had been arrested at the scene for possession; they'd found half a dime bag in his front pocket. Other charges against Tig were pending, he said. That was when I burst into tears.

My mother's lips thinned, and she leaned toward me. I noticed she had brand-new circles under her eyes, shining faintly purple through her concealer. "Are you crying over that boy? Don't you dare! You need to be worried about you. You could be charged, too, underage drinking or possession, Mitch says. Tell her, Mitch!"

The lawyer shook his head. "Leave all that to me. Even if the worst happens, Amy is looking at a misdemeanor. Community service."

"She'll have an arrest record," my mother said. "That will follow her—follow all of us—forever."

"Follow us where?" I asked, confused, tears streaming unstoppably down my cheeks.

"She doesn't mean it literally," the lawyer said, kind.

My mother shook her head. "Yes, I do. We have to move. My God, the Shipley house is two blocks down. Excuse us a moment?" This to Mitch, who took a purely ceremonial step away and turned to face the window. My mother leaned in, putting her face close to mine. "First tears I've seen, and they're for that boy?"

I shook my head. I was so overwhelmed by guilt and sorrow I could hardly breathe. Why hadn't I gone with Tig back to that mattress? In the hope and terror that had gripped me after the kiss, I had insisted we leave. I had put us on the road that led us to poor Mrs. Shipley. Last night I'd cried myself down to a rag over that choice. I would again, many times, but I had tears for Tig, too. I tried to sputter an explanation with my thick tongue, but my mother's veneer of calm support had cracked.

"Do you realize this is going to change your entire family's lives? Your father is talking to headhunters. Do you understand? Your brother will spend his senior year at some strange school." She blew air out her nostrils, lips compressing, and she was close to tears now, too. "We are all making sacrifices here. For you, Amy. We hired Mitch, and his retainer alone is— Yet here you sit, crying over the awful boy who got us into this mess." Her voice rose. "And you could go to jail!"

"She's a minor," the lawyer said, still facing the window, as if making an observation to the clouds outside. "I doubt she'll be arrested. Even if she is, it will be sealed."

But that did little to propitiate my mother. She straightened, crossing her arms, nostrils flared.

"I'm sorry," I said, hitching and snotting as I tried to stop my tears. I had never been the kid she wanted. Maybe, after perfect Connor, who was born sporty and swaggery and smart, she'd thought children were custom orders. Maybe, if I'd been trim and glossy or if I'd been a boy, she would have been the doting mother I saw parenting my brother. But she got an awkward, compulsive overeater who stole cheap wine and snuck out of the house with a boy from the bad side of town. I'd made our shiny, much-admired family the topic of whispers and thinly veiled op-eds about tragedy and underage drinking, and now I was weeping over Tig instead of being grateful and impressed by how much she had shelled out for a lawyer. "I'm not only crying for Tig. I keep thinking about Lolly and Pau—"

"Well, stop that!" she interrupted, and I realized I had somehow made it worse. "You want to drop by and make sure they know you're sorry? Those kids with no mother, that widowed man, should they pause their grieving to hear your apology? They aren't sitting around their house wondering, 'Is Amy sorry?' We are moving so they do not have to look at us—to give them some peace."

"But I am sorry," I promised, weeping so hard that the lawyer could no longer pretend himself out of the room. He turned back and handed me a crisp white handkerchief. My mother stared at me, her face registering such a tumbled mix of emotions that I could not read a single one.

"Just answer Mitch's questions," she said at last. I had almost stopped crying when she added, "I only hope they don't find a way to sue us because you brought that boy the wine."

By the time the first detective came to take my statement, I was so wrung out that the whole interview rolled over me in a wash of words. I could barely talk around my tongue, but I mostly told the truth, only skipping the kiss, my small, bright secret, now totally eclipsed. What we had done next negated it, ruined it, made it into a mistake, too.

The first detective kept pressing me for details about the accident itself. But after Tig had kissed me, we'd finished off the wine, smoked more, and the night had become a kaleidoscope of tumbling colors and shapes that made no sense now. I told the truth, though the truth was only three words long.

I don't remember.

I said it over and over, and in my swollen mouth the words came out mostly vowels. *I 'onn rem-em-ba.* After we left the clearing to get food, my first solid memory was Mrs. Shipley's face. Lolly's piping voice. *Amy, Paul is cry?*

I did not remember. It was true then, hand to God,

and it was still true six days later, in the second interview, when the new, dad-like detective shrugged and said, "That was last week."

My lawyer smiled, revealing his movie-actor teeth, square and pearly white in the wet pink flesh of his mouth. My parents had those exact same teeth, but neither one of them was smiling. I sat, a silent lump, though my tongue no longer hurt. It was miraculously nearly healed, just as the doctor had assured me—something about all the blood vessels making tongues heal abnormally fast. The rest of my body, however, was sore down to the bone. Under my clothes I looked like a ruined peach, bruised yellow and black and deep purple and brown.

My lawyer said, "Nothing has changed since last week."

"Let's go through it again," the detective said. "That could trigger—"

"She's doing that. With her therapist," my lawyer interrupted. "Should her therapy bear helpful fruit, rest assured we will contact you."

"Her testimony could—"

"Yes," my lawyer cut him off again. "I realize it would be very convenient for you if she did remember. With her testimony you could convict that boy without having to look for any pesky evidence or investigate. But that is not her job. Her job is to get well."

I stared down at my hands. In one of the occasional chairs, off to the side, some sort of junior lawyer was taking notes and looking stern. There was a junior cop, too, sitting opposite him, with an equal and opposing notebook. They didn't really matter in this room. The people who mattered were my lawyer and the detective.

After that my parents. Dad tall and imposing in a be-
spoke suit that cost more than this cop made in a month
and my mother, sitting slim and straight beside me. I
should speak, I thought, but me and the lackeys, we felt
so incidental. I had no power in this room.

"My job is to sit here and ask questions until I get a
thorough statement," the detective said, firm.

"I'm sure that suits Mitch. He bills by the hour," my
father said, and my lawyer chuckled, holding up a calming hand.

"We all know who caused the accident," my mother
snapped, uncalmed.

We did. Tig *had* been driving. My parents and my
lawyer said so. The police said so, and it made sense. It
was his car. He always drove.

Except the once, earlier that same night. But I hadn't
mentioned that.

I'd left that out. But not on purpose. Not like the kiss.
I had just . . . left it out.

My lawyer said, "You arrested the boy for it already."

I'd known it was coming, but still. My gaze flew
to the detective's face for confirmation, and I found it
there. My mother put her free hand on my thigh, a hard,
grounding grasp that dumped me into my body. All at
once I felt my bulk taking up more than my fair share
of the sofa.

When I glanced up, the detective's eyes on me
seemed so kind. He seemed to see my misery, my fear.
He looked at me as if the lawyers and my parents and
his junior cop were more pieces of expensive furniture.
As if I were the one who mattered in this room.

He said, right to me, "Sometimes people don't remember things because they don't want to. Because

it's hard. Now, your friend made a bad decision, and he has to pay for that. But he's a kid, and I want him to get treated like one. You should know the D.A. is willing to deal. Tighler will have to serve a little time, no way around that, but hopefully in a juvenile facility. If it goes to trial, though, the D.A. will push to try him as an adult. He could be looking at fifteen years. Inside a real grown-up prison. Your statement could be the lever he needs to take this plea. You'd be helping him, Amy."

My mother's hand clamped harder, pulling my gaze down to her slender fingers digging into the meat of my thigh. She wanted me to say that I remembered Tig driving. She wanted it maybe more than the cop did. I heard her draw breath, breath to make words, and my lawyer cut her off so smoothly he did not even seem rushed.

"But Amy does not remember the accident. She shouldn't lie and say she does"—he paused, nostrils flaring, and his next words came out dripping with sarcasm—"even to *help* her friend."

"It could help her as well," the detective said, unfazed. "When he heard all the charges, Tighler Simms finally gave us his statement. He says she was driving."

Beside me my mother gasped, and I heard my father's sharp inhale as well. In my lap my hands went cold. My fingers felt like my tongue after the emergency-room doctor had injected it with the local. Dead flesh, not my own. My bruises pulsed in tandem with my heart.

At that same moment, three memories bloomed whole in my brain, perfectly captured in vivid Technicolor.

Me, fishing Tig's car keys out of my skirt pocket.

Me, sliding behind the wheel.

Me, stabbing once, twice, three times at the ignition and finally feeling the click and twist of the key sliding home.

My whole body thickened into a solid. No breath, no flowing blood. My gaze flew to the detective's eyes, and he was looking back, watching my reaction.

"But she wasn't," my lawyer said in a bored tone. "So what's the point?"

"She sees the point," the detective said. He looked at me with deep empathy, as if he were sorry to be saying these hard things. "Whatever loyalty you're feeling, Amy, it's not reciprocated."

"That little shit!" my father exploded. "How dare he! How dare he!"

"Jim," my lawyer said, a warning tone.

"No, Mitch, that delinquent is slandering my family!" my mother said. She bent toward the cop now, her tone demanding. "When did he come up with this fabrication?"

The cop was still looking mostly at me, but he answered her.

"Earlier today. He was arrested for possession at the scene, but we had to wait for his mother before we could question him. She refused to let him give a statement then. Asked for a lawyer." I felt my head shaking, back and forth. Tig's mom had probably been high, because she was almost always high, and she hated the police. "We got him a public defender, but those guys are overworked. Not like this guy you've got," the cop went on, jerking a folksy thumb at my lawyer, like he and I were together on this.

I stared at him, still frozen. He was coming at me, just like those memories had come at me, rushing in and hitting me dead-on, so that I was still shaking with the impact.

I closed my eyes. Nothing in the room mattered. Only that night, that road, that lost time.

I concentrated inward, peering down into the well of memory, but I saw nothing more. It was still true that I did not remember driving, only the brutal kiss of steel rending Mrs. Shipley's sporty little tin can of a car. I did not remember getting out of the Ambassador. I only remembered standing in the road, after. But oh, I had remembered enough—I'd had the keys. I'd slid in behind the wheel. I'd started the car.

My lawyer was talking now, but his calm voice sounded so far away. "Don't make this about loyalty or her feelings for this boy. It's almost as if you want her to lie for him. This is about the truth, and the truth is, my client was traumatized by Mr. Simms's actions. She watched her neighbor die. Let's not forget, this boy gave her drugs and got her so drunk she had to be treated for alcohol poisoning. The crash itself was traumatic. She simply doesn't remember."

I opened my eyes a crack. I could see that the detective was still focused entirely on me. He said, "Time passes. Memories come back."

He was right. Memories did that. They did come back. I closed my eyes again.

I could see my hand stabbing the key at that swaying ignition slot, the homecoming feel of it sliding in at last. I was so numb I only then realized that my mother's grip had become painful, squeezing a chunk of my leg bloodless.

"There is nothing more my client can tell you," my lawyer said, but that was no longer true.

I wanted to speak. I did. I wanted to open my mouth and say, *I think Tig might be right?*

But I wasn't supposed to. I wasn't allowed to, unless my lawyer gave me specific permission. *And what if I'm remembering wrong?* I asked myself, desperate. Desperate and silent. What if the detective had put those memories in my head by telling me about Tig's accusation? It was Tig's car, after all. I didn't even really have a license. He had to have been driving.

Maybe after I turned the key in the ignition, Tig slid in behind me and I scooted down the bench seat to the passenger side. Maybe we changed seats sometime later, in an unremembered pit stop. Surely if I'd been driving, the police would know. They would figure it out. I told myself all this, picturing scenes like I'd seen in movies. Teams of cops and scientists and doctors, seeking truth. I didn't understand that a sleepy, midsize college town in 1991 didn't have those resources.

The relevant truths were few and already written down: It was Tig's car. He was a kid from Downtown, while I lived in Waverly Place, backed by parents who regularly dined with the mayor. I had one of the best criminal attorneys in the state standing between me and every question that might have revealed the truth. The only person who cared enough about Tig's statement to check on it was this cop. But he was no match for Mitch and all my parents' money. I didn't even have to lie. Not out loud. All I had to do was sit quiet and let all the wrong things happen.

After the detective left, and my lawyer left, and my father went back to work, my mother made us lunch. We sat in the dining room, each of us in front of our own untouched salad. I was never comfortable in this formal room with its lacquered table and wall-length china cabinet displaying all her Raynaud dishes. It was painted a weird neutral, taupe and beige mated to make a putty-colored baby. River Stone, my mother called this color, though I'd enraged her once by calling it Hint of Wart.

She was still so tense she was vibrating like a violin string, every bit of her pulled taut.

"I think . . ." I started, and then stopped. I had said nothing to the cop, but I needed to tell someone. "I think I may have been . . ."

I stared at her, and she stared back, searching my face with a depth I was not used to. She never looked at me the way she looked at Connor. She gazed at his face with the only kind of hunger that she ever seemed to feel. Now she was looking into my eyes, but it was different. It was as if she were seeking confirmation or perhaps the truth.

Whatever she was looking for, she found it.

"Jesus," she said. "You were . . ." She couldn't bear to finish the sentence any more than I could.

"I really don't remember," I said instantly. Now I *was* lying, so I amended it. I tried to make it be true. "I don't remember driving."

"You don't remember driving?" my mother repeated, questioning but also nodding.

"I don't," I said. "But Tig said I was, and I do remember that I had the k—"

"You don't remember driving," my mother said, fast and edgy, and this time it was an order. She reached a hand across the table and left it there until I gave her mine. It struck me that this, today, was the most my mother had touched my body in weeks. I could not remember the last time her hand had rested on my leg or squeezed my fingers. "Don't let this boy put things in your head. If you try to remember too hard, your brain can make things up. Like all those kids who said the satanists were at the day care, or whatever that was. None of it happened. And if you had been driving, the police would know. So you weren't."

We sat for a moment, and I said, "What if memories come back, like that detective said?"

My mother shook her head. "Any new thing you think you remember, you can't trust that. That policeman put it in your head. So let it go. You aren't going to talk about it. With anyone. Ever again. This isn't just about you, Amy. If you invent some big confession, you could hurt your dad's career, and I am already feeling so judged. And your brother—he has a very bright future. You have embarrassed us enough."

"But if Tig wasn't dri—" I started, and she jerked her hand away. Her voice went from almost pleading to chilly and dismissive.

"Amy, don't get dramatic and choose martyrdom. Do not orchestrate some grand romantic gesture for this boy. Because that would be pathetic. You are hardly Juliet." And now her gaze did go to my body. "Do you understand me?"

I did. I understood her perfectly.

And God help me, I did what she said. I swallowed it down and let it sit inside me. It filled me, like a lump of clay in my stomach.

Part of me believed that it would fix itself without me. Surely I had behaved suspiciously enough that that old, dad-like detective would tell someone, *We got it wrong. I see now! It was Amy at the wheel.*

Then I could say, *That may be so, but I do not remember,* and let justice happen.

But no one ever talked to me about it again. Not the police, not my lawyer, not my family. Tig took a deal, pleading guilty for a reduced sentence, and no one even told me that. I saw it in the *News Journal.* I had no way to know where he was sent or what happened to him there. I had no contact information, no shared friend, and I was too ashamed to call his mother or his ex-stepdad. My father took a job in Boston, and we moved away.

For the next three years, the length of Tig's sentence, I couldn't eat. Food had long been my comfort, and I did not deserve to be comforted. I wanted the hunger. It was an angry, alive thing that I let loose inside myself as punishment.

I thinned and dwindled, and though I was wan and weak, my skin a little loose on my young frame, I finally looked like a daughter that my mother might have wanted. But what I had done could not be shed, and her gaze still slid toward me and away, glancing off air, never quite landing on me, as if my edges were still two feet farther out than my surfaces. Shame had applied itself onto my bones, swelling around me until I was mired, and, to her, fat and shame were almost the same thing.

We never got much better. These days my relationship with my family was a lukewarm phone call close to Christmas or my birthday, in which we traded empty words about getting together sometime.

Now I had made my own family, and we weren't like that. I let Maddy be her mercurial, brash self, and Oliver was growing up secure and adored. With me Davis had felt safe enough to whisper that he'd wanted his wife gone, not fixed, even though her absence hurt his kid down to her small bones. I had made our home into a place full of love and acceptance, but I had locked myself outside it.

I never did whisper my worst thing in the dark to Davis. I kept the lights out when we made love, so he wouldn't see the stretch marks on my body; I never told him about the night that Mrs. Shipley died, much less that moment, mid-interrogation, when I'd remembered sliding in behind the wheel.

This was why Roux's game had gotten to me. It wasn't the gin, or the force of her personality. In that moment, in my basement, I'd felt that she saw me, fully, all the way down to the bottom. She'd looked into me as if she knew what I was capable of doing and sustaining. It had horrified me, and yet a piece of me had liked it. A piece of me had wanted to drink more gin, lift my shirt to show her the faint white marks on my breasts and belly, let the truth be in the room with us. Isn't that what diving gave me? To float in the same space as the truth, silent and unafraid.

I knew from long experience that I only had to wait the feeling out. People say, *I don't know how she lives with herself,* but every single one of them was living with their own worst thing, just fine. No one walks around holding their ugliest sin in the palm of their hand, staring at it. Our hurts are heavy, and we let them sink. Every day they drift lower, settling in murky places where the light can't reach. All I had to do was wait. My bad would fall down into darkness again, because the bad things always do.

All I had to do was make blondies. Update the neighborhood directory. Call Divers Down and get back on the teaching schedule. Feed the baby. All I had to do was all my jobs, and let time pass.

Today my job was Madison.

I needed to talk serious with her about boys and cars and lying by omission. My jangled nerves demanded that I hand down groundings and extra chores, too, but I wasn't going to do that. Maddy wasn't me, and Luca wasn't Tig Simms. They'd stolen a two-mile ride in a cool car, dead sober, in the sunshiny morning. This was normal teen behavior, and I would react to it as such, not to my own past.

I was in the keeping room playing peekaboo with Oliver when I finally heard the front door open and Maddy's stompy walk ringing out against the hard-woods.

"I'm home!" she hollered.

"Back here," I called. "Come see me."

I stood up, Oliver cocked on my hip, but when she came through the swinging door, she had Luca with her. This I did not expect. Oliver bounced himself joyfully, smiling his silly, two-tooth smile at the sight of her. He was crazy about Maddy.

"You remember Luca?" she said, coming all the way to me to give Oliver a little tickle on his belly. "Hi, stinky baby." Her cheeks were pink with pleasure.

Luca gave me a casual hand wave. He slouched by the breakfast bar, looking like a godlet in his perfectly cut jeans and Doc Martens.

"Hello, Luca. It's great that you're here, actually," I lied. I didn't want any damn thing Roux-related within a mile of me today. But this was my job, and I would do it. I made sure my tone was friendly but also firm. "I wanted to talk to you about our house rules. We don't let Madison ride with teen drivers. Kids need at least a year of experience driving alone before they start toting other kids around. Especially if the kid is ours. Got it?"

"Yes, ma'am," he said, and that surprised me. The "ma'am." It didn't even sound ironic.

Maddy's pink cheeks had gone all the way to crimson. She knew she was busted, and she was begging me with her eyes not to ground her, not to make this boy go home. Oliver was still reaching for her, so she took him, then buried her blushing face in his neck.

"How long have you had your license?" I asked Luca.

"Ummm," he said, thinking, and then he shrugged. "Not a year."

That was reassuring. That meant he was likely still sixteen. A junior.

"We all understand each other?" I said to both of them.

"I'm sorry, Monster," Mad said. She put her face by Oliver's face and smiled. "Am I to be executed with the sunrise? Should I bid my dumpling of a baby brother a final farewell?" She kissed Oliver's cheek with a resounding smack, and he giggled. I couldn't help but smile back at the both of them.

Part of me still wanted to ground Maddy, mostly so I could send Luca away, but that would not be fair. Plus, in an hour Maddy's mother was scheduled to have her weekly phone call. Laura lived in Birmingham, and while the court had granted her supervised visitation, she only managed to show up for it once or twice a year. There was a good chance she wouldn't call at all, which was one kind of awful, and an equally good chance that she would call very late, or drunk, or both. Wednesdays were hard, but today, with this boy in tow, Maddy was being silly and charming and kissing on the baby like it was still Tuesday.

"'Buttercup doesn't get eaten by the eels at this time,'" I told her, and she grinned.

"Go see your mommy," she told the baby. I held out my hands, and Oliver lurched toward me. I perched him on my hip again.

Maddy turned away and plucked at Luca's shirt, pulling him back toward the swinging door.

"Where you going?" I asked.

She froze. "Upstairs? I wanted to show Luca this video."

"Run up and bring the iPad down," I said, and then fixed Luca with a firm gaze. "We also don't let Mads take boys up to her bedroom." Maddy shot me an agonized look for saying "bedroom," but I was not here to play. "Why don't you sit down at the breakfast bar. Have a snack. I've got homemade blondies."

Maddy looked like she was hoping the earth would mercifully open up and swallow her whole at my offer, or maybe she was hoping it would swallow me. But Luca was a teenage boy, and he perked up at the mention of food.

"Great," he said.

"Milk?" I asked him.

"Oh, my God," Maddy said, but Luca said, "Yes, please," at the same time.

I began the process of getting plates and napkins and blondies and pouring milk one-handed, with the baby "helping." Luca wandered past us, into the keeping room, looking around while I got their snack together. Maddy plopped onto a stool at the breakfast bar, staring daggers at me, trying to eye-stab me out of the room.

"These are cool," Luca said. He was over by the sofa that sat against the side wall, looking at the photo grouping I'd hung there, eighteen pictures in various sizes of undersea animals. He pointed at the center shot, a spectacular purple-and-orange Spanish shawl. "What's this guy?"

"A nudibranch," I said, and he chuckled. "Yeah, it's a weird name. They're little shell-less mollusks, and they come in a ton of crazy colors and shapes. Believe it or not, that blue-and-white guy with the wings in the next picture is a nudibranch as well."

"That animal is the same thing as that?" he asked, looking back and forth between them.

"Yeah. Monster took those pics. She's a dive instructor," Maddy said, proud in spite of herself.

"Really?" he said, glancing over his shoulder at me with new respect. He pointed at a tiny blushing octopus. "That's my favorite animal. I had a stuffed octopus when I was little. I dragged him around until his legs fell off."

"Mads took that one," I said, and he turned to look at her with the same respect.

"You dive, too?" he asked her.

"Oh, yeah," she said. She tucked a curl behind her ear, grinning self-consciously. "I've been junior-certified since I was ten, and even before that I was pool diving."

"That's so cool," Luca said, and Maddy's eyes flew to my face, instantly pleading.

"Monster could teach you," she said.

"I'd be into that." Luca came over and sat by Mad,

his elegant slide in contrast to the way she had hurled herself down, and took a huge bite out of his bar. "This is amazing," he said, with his mouth full. He swallowed, then said to Mad, "We never have crap like this at my house."

I believed him. I somehow couldn't imagine Roux in an apron, licking beaters.

"Did your mom give up sweets for Lent and not go back?" Luca blinked at me, confused by my joke. "You know, when you give up sugar or cussing—before Easter?" He shrugged, and I gathered that Roux was not religious. I also felt a small flash of shame, grilling the kid. Luca was an innocent bystander, and with better manners than I would have thought a boy raised by his bitchy mother would possess. But I still wanted to know about her. "I meant your mom is not a baker?"

He shrugged. "She doesn't, like, keep any kind of bread in the house."

"Does your mom—" I began, but Madison interrupted me.

"Let's go to the basement. Watch the video on the computer down there."

The bedroom was a no-brainer, but I didn't know if Davis would want his daughter down in the basement alone with a boy either. We hadn't set boy rules, because up until today there hadn't been a need. It seemed to me a girl could get just as pregnant on the cushy rec-room sectional as she could on a bed, and polite as he seemed, Luca was still a sixteen-year-old boy. But maybe I was letting my feelings about his mother spill over onto him. Would I feel this way about any teenage male who wanted to watch videos in the basement with Mad?

I stalled. "All right, all right, I can take a hint. Run up and get the iPad, Maddy, and you can have the keeping room. I'll get out of your way."

I evacuated to the living-room sofa to finish *The House of Mirth*. Oliver rolled around on a play mat, making sleepy noises. I'd need to rock him if he didn't drift off on his own soon. He was still on three naps, and he needed every one of them to stay his cheery self. The teenagers got louder and less self-conscious once I was out of the room, their conversation drifting down the hall. I couldn't make out individual words, just tone, but it was clear they liked each other. Maybe boy-girl like, maybe the friendship kind, but the talk sounded easy and lively on both sides.

Tig and I had been like that. Both outsiders, we'd defaulted into lab partners, but we'd found each other strangely easy to talk to. There'd been instant, simple chemistry—that odd, almost audible click that happens when you meet your kind of person. It had happened for me with Charlotte, too. She was smart, and funny, and endearingly fussy, and there was never an awkward lag when we were chatting. What was happening in the kitchen sounded like that kind of connection. I shook my head, then went back to reading until Oliver started making grumpy sounds.

As I carried him upstairs for his bumper nap, I could hear Maddy still chattering happily, though 4:00 P.M. had come and gone with no call from Laura. Normally Maddy would be wrecked, waiting and listening and pretending not to do either. I paused, hearing Luca's baritone say something that made her laugh. Not a coy giggle either. Maddy's real, full-throated, head-thrown-back guffaw.

In the nursery I tucked Oliver against my shoulder and sat down in the rocker, a lump in my throat.

So this boy was going to be a thing.

Well, Madison was a normal, healthy teenage girl. At some point some boy or another was bound to be. I wished Luca weren't quite so beautiful. I hoped Maddy wouldn't get her heart crushed. I wished, most of all, that Luca weren't Roux's kid. The very thought of Roux got me agitated, both worried and intrigued.

Oliver stirred, rearing his head up, fighting nap. I patted him and hummed, soothing us both.

Just wait, I told myself. *Pack it away and let it sink.*

Tomorrow I would feel less anxious. Less anxious the day after that. The stirred silt of my past that was choking the air around me would settle. I would shift all my anxiety to Charlotte. She was the one with an unimaginary problem. I would concentrate on helping her, and in a week or two I'd run into Roux at the CVS or Publix. I would be cool and calm. We would talk kids and yards and movies, in the way of neighbors. I would see that my fears had all been mostly in my head, that her game had not been aimed at me.

Over the next week, I stuck to this plan as best I could. It was hard not to think about Roux, given that I could hardly spin around without finding her son. Luca was at our house every afternoon, even on the weekends, from two-thirty until almost five, every day. Maddy was the main draw, but he was also always hungry. I fed him carbs and forced myself to not ask questions about his mysterious mother, treating him like any other neighborhood kid. Davis and I talked, and we decided together that boys in the basement were okay, as long as the door at the top of the stairs stayed open.

The tightness in my chest did ease. I helped Char put together the neighborhood newsletter, and she picked yet another Austen novel for book club. I taught a one-day refresher course for out-of-practice divers. Oliver let go of the coffee table and took one staggery almost-step toward me before tumbling back onto his butt.

Everything is settling. Everything is fine, I told myself.

I even believed it, right up until the moment Roux got bored of waiting for me to break. Right up until she came to see me.

5

THE DOORBELL RANG NOT five minutes after I'd packed Davis and Maddy off to their respective schools. I perched Oliver on my hip and went to get it, wondering who was stopping by so early. It was still half an hour before it was time to meet Char for our walk, and she always let herself in anyway.

I opened the door to find Roux standing on my porch, exactly as she had the very first time I'd seen her. Hip cocked, hands empty, wearing a different long, sheer maxidress. An ombréd aquamarine this time, gauzy and expensive-looking. I found myself tugging down the hem of my rumpled T-shirt, splattered as it was with bits of baby oatmeal, as if it could hide the last eight clinging pounds of Oliver weight.

"Hi there, Amy Whey," she said, and her lips twisted up on one side in a half smile. Instantly the last week fell away. I felt my spine lengthening, a small current of excitement running through it. At the same time, an anxious drumbeat started in my chest.

"Hi, Roux," I said, my voice as casual as I could make it.

"Mind if I come in?"

She was inside almost before she finished asking. I

wasn't entirely sure how she did it. She stepped forward as if there were room for her, and my body melted back and made it true.

"I have a spare minute," I said.

This was what I'd been waiting for anyway, I told myself. I'd wanted our paths to cross, for us to have a normal conversation about kids or recipes. I hadn't pictured her slithering into my house to have it, but here she was.

I closed the door, but moved to block the way out of the foyer, because a conversation could be both normal and very, very short. Oliver would help. He sat quietly on my hip, regarding Roux with serious eyes, but this was a very active playtime for him. He would want down soon. "What can I do for you?"

She tilted her head to the side, that half smile still quirking up her lips. "What are my options?"

"I don't know. Did you need to borrow something?" Her eyebrows rose, but I stuck to my cool, calm guns. I wouldn't let her see the sick, strange eagerness spreading in my middle, at war with the fear that her version of Never Have I Ever had been aimed at me. "Did you want to know what book club's reading next? It's *Persuasion.* I can get you on the e-mail list."

"Austen, huh? It must be Kanga's turn to pick. Or is it always Kanga's pick?" She must have seen the answer on my face, because she laughed. "I'd rather read something with teeth."

"I like Austen," I said, though I had long wished Char would choose books I'd describe in just that way. More teeth. "So. What did you need? Because I know you aren't here for a cup of sugar."

"I like sugar," she said, and now she was the one

lying. She used the exact same intonations I'd just used, claiming to like Austen.

"You don't look like a person with a sweet tooth," I told her. This woman didn't allow bread inside her house. No way she had a bedside drawer full of Mallomars.

"I like sugar," she insisted, stepping in. Close. Too close, so that it felt like a double entendre. "But I don't let myself have everything I like. Do you?"

I stepped back, almost involuntarily, and she breezed past, the elegant skirt billowing around her slim legs. She beelined down the hall between the dining room and living room, passing the stairs down to the basement, going right for the swinging door into the kitchen. I followed, all the way to the keeping room. Oliver blew another raspberry, misting my cheek with a fine spray of baby spit.

Roux finally stopped by the far leather sofa, examining the photo grouping of muck diving pictures, exactly as her son had. By then it felt too late to say something sarcastic, like, *No, please. Make yourself at home.* I'd been thrown off guard. Of all the ways I'd imagined our first postgame meeting, fending off a pass had never crossed my mind.

Oliver was struggling in my arms now, bending toward the floor and saying, "Babababa." I closed the baby gate and let him down. He went speed-crawling toward the bookshelf full of toys.

"I've been thinking about you," Roux said. She was still looking at the pictures, her back firmly to me, but there was something flirty in her tone. "All week."

"Well that's . . . a little weird," I said. I'd been thinking about her, of course, too much. But not in the way she was implying.

"Have you been thinking about me?" she asked, as if she'd plucked the words out of my mind.

"Not really," I lied. I was glad her back was to me. She'd looked at me and known I was lying about liking the book-club picks.

She didn't say anything else. Instead she drifted in small steps down the length of my sofa, studying every shot. I felt more awkward every second, but I made myself wait her out, practicing diver's breathing, readying a calm, cool smile. When she came to the end of the pictures, she peeked over her shoulder at me, coy. The silence stretched, getting thinner, making even the air feel thinner. I kept the smile, though it was starting to feel plastic.

It occurred to me that this was a game, too. A silent game.

That ticked me off, but I was almost glad. Irked wasn't good, but it was better than anxious.

"I don't have time to play 'who'll talk first' this morning, Roux," I said.

Her eyes sparked with amusement. "See, I do. That's why I just won."

"I don't have time to play anything," I said, snappish in spite of myself, and her spark became a full-blown grin. She came sauntering back toward me.

"You don't like games?" she asked.

Acknowledging the silent game had been a mistake. "Games" wasn't a topic I wanted to explore with her. She'd thrown me off balance, though, and now she was coming way too close again. I held my ground this time, even though I could feel how guarded my eyes had gone, could feel my body still wanting to bend away from her.

"Are you trying to—" I didn't know how to even ask. It seemed so presumptuous. And yet she was now so close I could smell her breath, minty and cool. I put my hands up and stepped back. I couldn't help it. "Whatever this is, it's fine for you, but it's not my thing."

She smiled at me. It was a seductive, almost predatory smile. If I had been gay, or male, I was willing to bet it would have gotten my attention. All my skin had gone in prickles.

"You like men?" she asked.

"I like my husband," I said, firm.

"How very Stepford of you," she said. "Relax, I like men, too. For fucking anyway." She seemed oblivious to the unstated mother rules about cursing, dropping the f-bomb as if my baby weren't right there with his language centers all wide open, seeking his first word. "You're perfectly safe alone with me."

"We aren't alone," I said, my voice tight. Oliver was three feet away, investigating a plastic stand stacked with brightly colored concentric rings.

"Alone enough. That doesn't even talk," she said, glancing at him, then back to me. "I'm straight as they come. I go for lawyers, mostly. Not just because they are one kinky-ass batch of humans, though that's a perk. I like them because if you fuck 'em right, they talk. Lawyers gossip easy as a gaggle of drunk women at a book club."

That was another direct reference to the game, and exactly the conversation I wasn't going to have with her.

I said, "Ease up on the language?" very mild. "I don't

want to have to convince my neighbors that Oliver's first word is 'truck.'"

She didn't laugh at my joke, though. Not even politely. Her head tilted again, the other way. She was looking at me like I was a puzzle piece and I wasn't going in my slot.

"Second-favorite fuck? Bankers," Roux pushed on, as if I hadn't spoken. Her tone was insistently breezy. This felt like yet another game—a familiar one. Suburban Mom Chicken. I'd seen Tate and Lavonda playing it, one-upping each other with toe rings and tattoos, seeing who would say or do the edgiest thing. "You should try a banker. They're like practice for lawyers, because they aren't as crafty."

She was trying to provoke me, and since she wanted it, I had a perverse desire to keep my cool. I fixed her with a bored look. Shrugged. "You can have my share. I'm married."

She shrugged back, mimicking the exact set and twitch of my shoulders, as if she'd decided to join my sex-with-lawyers moratorium. "I'm married, too."

"Really?" I said, interested in spite of myself. Except that she didn't eat carbs, this was the first hard, concrete information I had on Roux. "I've never seen him around."

She smiled. "We're separated."

"Small wonder, considering how many lawyers there are in the world," I said. It came out tart, barely south of bitchy, and a startled laugh escaped her.

"You don't rile easy, do you?" she said.

I shrugged, and I liked this feeling, liked surprising her while she tried and failed to shock me. It made me want to be even calmer. I sank into myself, breathing like I did on deep dives, my face blank, my body still. She could do a donkey act on my coffee table, I decided, and I would blandly hand her the Lemon Pledge and ask her to clean up afterward.

She said, "I thought you'd be prudier. Maybe because when I met you, you were Kanga-adjacent. She's wound pretty tight."

I shrugged again, but she was correct. If she came on to Char or did that lawyer-humping monologue in front of Ruby, Char would have a stroke. I had opted out, though, and it had given me the upper hand. I liked the feeling of being one up on her. I breathed, slow and even, and I could stay like this forever now. I wasn't going to break the silence.

She waited, too, her gaze measuring me. At last she said, "Okay, then." She cocked one hand on her hip, almost posing. "Let's try again."

I wanted to say, *Try what? Not being an asshole?*

But that would be playing. This was grown-up time.

I gave her my best hostess smile, blank and friendly. "We have gotten off on the wrong foot. And we are neighbors. Maybe we should stick to what we have in common."

"Okay. I have a pulse, for example. Do you? Because I'm beginning to wonder." She said it wry, not mean, though.

"We both have pulses," I assured her.

She sat down, sinking gracefully onto the leather sofa, and crossed her legs. Sunlight streamed in from the big picture window to land full on her face. Her forehead was as pale and smooth as an egg, and her eyes had a slight fixed brightness. She'd had a little work done, I realized. Fillers for sure, maybe a little Botox, though if I'd had a different mother, I might not have known. It was really good work. Subtle, which meant pricey, and also very effective. She was probably close to my age.

"We have something else in common," Roux said. "We're both one-percenters."

I shook my head. My parents lived in a zip code that was one-percent-adjacent, but I hadn't truly been a member of the Smith clan for years now. Davis and I lived solidly middle class. I did have close to three hundred thousand dollars left from Nana's trust, but it was sitting quietly in a bank in Boston, waiting. It was more than a lot of people had, but it hardly put me on a par with billionaires. As for Roux, the only financial assets I'd seen were the red car and her designer wardrobe. And her expensive face.

I shook my head. "Hardly. We're comfortable. . . ."

"I mean we're both divers," Roux said, gesturing over her shoulder at my pictures, and I got it. She meant the one percent of people who scuba.

Half the tension I'd been hiding ran out of me, and I felt a twinge of something that was akin to disappointment. Suddenly I wanted to laugh at myself. Was that all this was? Every afternoon Luca had asked me about scuba: how to get certified, what it cost, how long it took. He must be driving her crazy at home. She was here to ask about lessons for her kid, and I needed to calm my ass right down. Roux liked to stir up trouble, but it was my own uneasy guilt weighting the conversation.

Oliver was busily throwing his toys off the bottom shelves now, checking to see if gravity still worked. Rattle Bear, teething keys, soft cloth books, he grabbed them one by one and let them fall. I had a lot of toys stored there, enough to hold him for a few minutes.

Long enough to work out scuba lessons. I walked over and sat down on the end of the other sofa, catty-corner to her.

"So Luca is serious about it, huh? Divers Down does an open-water class at least once a month, and I'm back teaching now. I think it's a great idea, especially since you dive already."

Her face didn't change. Her body stayed in the same shape, legs crossed, leaning back, one arm draped comfortably along the sofa. Even so I felt a shift in her. A flex of muscles tightening under her skin.

"When did you talk to Luca about diving?" she asked.

"All week," I said. "Every day he has another question."

Her arm dropped, and she leaned slightly forward. "Luca was here?"

She didn't know her kid was at my house? Not that I minded him anymore. He didn't seem to have romantic or even sexual designs on Maddy, though I worried about how gone she was on him. He was charming, and twice I'd invited him to stay for dinner, though he hadn't taken me up on it.

"Yes. He comes home with Madison after school."

"Luca homeschools," Roux said, tight. That surprised me. Homeschooling didn't seem to fit Roux's demographic, but then what did? Her brand-new shiny car didn't match her peeling rental house, her expensive clothes and her equally expensive face did not belong in our neighborhood. She got up and walked away from me, over to the picture window, picking her way through Oliver's mess. He was still pulling toys off the shelf, examining or mouthing or shaking each before dropping it, babbling quietly to himself.

"Do you work afternoons?" I asked, curious how she hadn't known her kid was at my place in those hours.

She shook her head, impatient. "That's when I'm at the gym."

She's at the gym two-plus hours a day? I thought, but looking at her body silhouetted against the picture window, I believed it.

"Maybe he just didn't mention it. It's all pretty innocent," I said, very offhand and dismissive. I liked it, this reversal, me cool and her a little on edge, but at the same time I hoped I hadn't landed him in hot water. I'd come to like the kid. "I've kept a close eye on them, believe me."

"He's hanging with your stepdaughter," Roux said, almost a question.

That made me laugh. "Of course. He's not here to learn how to keep his colors bright and his whites from getting dingy."

She smiled. "I suppose not. That boy can't even get his socks into the hamper."

Her tone was very light, but I could still see tension in the lines of her body as she looked around the room. I liked it. I resisted the urge to get up, move a little closer. Her gaze settled on a family picture on a shelf too high for Oliver to reach: me, Maddy, and Davis, dressed for Easter service. Oliver was in the picture, too, a huge, round presence belling out the skirt of my lavender maternity dress. She went over and picked it up, studying us, seemingly unaware of the baby playing at her feet.

"This is her? Maggie? The step?"

"Maddy," I said. "Yes."

She cocked an eyebrow at me, looking from the picture to my face. "Hardly Luca's speed."

I felt my whole body flush with instant anger. And

yet—hadn't I thought the same thing? I hadn't phrased it in her blunt, dismissive way, but I'd thought it.

"They're just friends," I said, my voice gone cool.

"Sure," she said. She set the photo down a little too hard and turned back. "I'm not really happy with this visit, Amy. I told you to come see me, and you didn't, so I had to come to you. Now I'm here for fifteen minutes before it occurs to you to say, 'Oh, by the way, your kid is sneaking over here.'"

Much as I liked pushing her buttons, this was about her child. I'd had the same reaction when Maddy scammed me and rode to school with Luca. I had to treat this seriously.

"I would have said something if I'd thought Luca was sneaking. Mother code," I told her, and I meant it.

"Sure," Roux said, exactly the way she'd said it when I'd asked if she'd read *The House of Mirth*. Agreeing, even though both people in the conversation knew that it was bull.

"I would have," I insisted. "But he's what, sixteen? It's fine. He and Maddy eat popcorn and talk about taste-makers, which is apparently a real job now, and listen to music. Nobody's drinking, nobody's high, nobody's getting pregnant. Not on my watch."

Roux's arms were crossed, but she gave me a grudging nod. "I told him not to get embedded. I'm here on business, and I don't want weeks of moping when it's time to go."

Now we actually were on common ground; I understood moody teenagers. But more important, it sounded as if Roux would not be around long. "Oh, is your work short-term?"

"I hope so," she said, which could mean anything.

I asked, "What do you do anyway?"

No one in the neighborhood seemed to know. According to Char, who had of course followed up, Roux'd been vague at book club. She'd said something about web design to Lisa and hinted to Sheridan that she got big-time alimony. Tess had come away with a vague impression that Roux was some kind of artist, maybe a dancer.

"I don't want to talk about my job," Roux said dismissively. "It's not going very well, to be honest."

"Bah!" Oliver said, disgusted. All the toys were off the shelf now. I got up and came over, since Roux apparently wasn't going to help him. She got out of the way as I approached, walking back toward the sofa.

"Okay. Well. If it's not about scuba lessons, why did you come by?" I got onto my knees to put all the toys back in handfuls. She was silent, staring at me in an assessing way I didn't like. She drew herself up tall, literally looking down on me, and I felt a subtle power shift. She was calm again, and I had relaxed my defenses, talking kids and diving. Now I was on my knees. I thrust another handful of toys onto the shelf and scrambled to my feet.

"You know why," she said, and with those words she changed. Her whole body changed. Her shoulders set. Her neck elongated. Her hands fisted and then flexed. "I came so we could finish."

"Finish what?" I said. My heart rate quickened, because I did know.

"The game," Roux said, the very words that I was thinking. She tilted her head again, such a quick and birdlike movement, inquisitive and foreign. "Don't be coy, Amy Smith."

"I have no inter—" I was halfway through the sentence before it registered that she had used my maiden name. I hadn't been Amy Smith since I was nineteen and married James Lee for fifteen minutes. It wasn't a name I'd ever used again. "What did you say?" The question came out involuntarily. I realized my hands were twisting together. I made them be still.

"Amy. Elizabeth. Smith," Roux said, very slow. "Yes, I know your name. I know you. Do you know me?"

I didn't.

I bent and began picking up toys again for Oliver, though he'd only thrown a few, staying on my feet, though. I needed to give my eyes a place to look that wasn't her. The teething keys rattled in my shaking hands. Oliver giggled, oblivious, thinking it a game, grabbing the keys the second I set them on the shelf. I picked up another handful of toys, thrust them onto the shelf, bent to gather more.

"What do you want?" I said to Rattle Bear. Because she had to want something.

"Justice," she said. The one word. Quiet. Strong.

I froze, my gaze pulled to her face. It was set in avid lines as she watched the word sink into me. Rattle Bear tumbled out of my hands onto the floor. I found myself straightening.

"Justice," I repeated, and the word felt strange and heavy in my mouth. As if it were French or Spanish. Not a word I knew or owned.

"There it is," Roux said.

"There what is?" I asked, and she spread her hands, almost apologetic.

"Your real face," she said. "I've been looking for it since I got here. God, you're hard to read. But you do know me, Amy Smith."

I didn't. "What do you want?"

Time stretched as she stepped toward me, once, twice, and I realized I'd stopped breathing.

She said, "The wrong kid went to prison. You were driving."

"I don't remember who was driving," I said. My old lie. It came out automatically, so fast it was said before I realized that this denial was wrapped around admission. I shouldn't have reacted at all, shouldn't have telegraphed that I knew exactly what she was referring to. I wasn't sure why this mattered, but I felt its truth on instinct. I tried to backtrack, but my hands had twined together again, twisting hard, and inside I could feel that fat moon rising. "I don't know what—"

"Yes you do," she said, so flat and sure that my denials died inside my mouth.

She knew. This was happening.

No, it had already happened. The world had already shifted.

My body flooded with an enormous, shaking feeling. It was something like relief, if relief could be so cold it burned. For the first time in years—decades, even—I was in a room with a person who saw clear through to the bad in me. I could feel that gaze, crashing through me, into me, all the way down.

"You know me," I said.

"I do," she answered. Coming close again, but now there was no flirting in it. It was a terrible proximity.

She was so close that all I could see was her pale face. I hadn't realized how much work it was, to hold truth in and under, to stay silent, every day, every day. My buried past was so much larger than the space I'd sunk it in. She'd started days ago, at book club, dredging at me. Now it was rising, pouring up and out of me. It filled the room, enormous, roaring all around us.

"You were driving. You killed Dana Shipley," she said. "I know. I saw you. I was there."

I shook my head, a violent, physical no. Because she could not know this. The police had canvassed for witnesses, but all the people in the nearby houses had been asleep. The crash had woken some of them, but by the time they got up, grabbed robes, came to their windows or their porches, Tig and I had already left the Ambassador. We'd been all the way across the road, beside Mrs. Shipley's car.

"I was," she insisted. She stepped even closer, moving slow, eyes on mine. I could not look away, my unsaid words still locked tight in between us. But she knew, as certain as if I had already released them. "I saw you climbing out from behind the wheel. You let that boy go to prison."

I could feel my head shaking, back and forth, back and forth. At my feet Oliver said nonsense to his bear. I heard him, but from very far; in this moment it was only her and me.

"No one saw," I said, but had she? The police canvassed for witnesses, but had they talked to children? Exactly how old was she? The roads had been deserted, but there'd been windows all around us, dark and silent, each its own glass eye.

"I was there," she insisted. "When the cars met, the sound of metal ripping was like screaming. Remember?" Roux asked, and I could hear it. "That smell, from the tires, burning against the road," she said, and I could smell it.

She leaned in even closer, her blue eyes widening and

glistening. Now I was right back in it, back inside that night. My house, my tidy room, even my baby, babbling softly to his toy, faded further into darkness. There was only the taste of my own salt, choking me. Only the bite of asphalt on my knees. I saw myself reflected in her eyes, pale blue like Mrs. Shipley's. Like Lolly's, wet and bright as damaged forget-me-nots. I could hear Lolly's piping voice. *Amy, Paul is cry?*

She said, "It's all right, you can say it. I already know."

I was driving.

God, those three words. I could feel them roiling through my body. I'd been waiting for permission to loose those words since I was fifteen years old. I'd wanted to say them, to save Tig with them, undrown the truth, let it be alive.

Roux said, "You killed her, and you sent that boy to prison for you."

I could feel the breath that made her words touching my face, and she was the voice in my head, saying everything I'd repeated on a loop when I was out in California. When there weren't enough drinks or drugs or sun-browned boys in all the world to stop the truth revolving in my mind. When there was never, never peace or silence. All that she'd set loose roared through me and around me, and words came with it, fast and soft.

"I never meant for it to happen. I never meant to lie. I didn't remember that I was driving. Not at first. I never meant. I never meant. I swear to God."

"But you killed her," her voice said, and it was more than her voice. It was my own. It was the voice of God.

"Yes, I did," I said, and all the weight escaped my body.

I thought I might fall. I thought my heart might simply stop, or I might rise up in the air and fly, and this, this feeling, this was why there was such a thing as confession. This was why Roux's game had worked at book club, why we all played, why we all said too much. To speak, to release, to let go, to let this truth be shared between our human bodies, breath and blood, in sunlight. I hated her, and I was almost in love with her, for making this moment. For knowing. For letting me say these words out loud, at last, at last, at last.

"Good," Roux said. "Good. Now. How are you going to make it up to me?"

I blinked, disoriented still. "Make it up to *you*?"

"To me. Surely by now, you've guessed who I am?" Roux asked.

I shook my head, still puzzled.

"That night? It's my first memory. I was in the back, strapped into my booster. I saw my mom die. I remember. I saw my babysitter staggering out of the car that killed her. Driver's side. And it was you."

I landed back in my body, hard, only to find that my bones had all gone rubbery and soft.

"You aren't Lolly Shipley," I told her. My hands came up to touch my head. When I thought of Lolly and baby Paul—and I tried not to ever, ever think of them—all I saw was clear blue water. No way to see past it.

"Tell me that you're sorry." Her eyes were so intense, boring into me, but I did not know them. They were the eyes of any blue-eyed stranger. "Tell me that you're sorry that you killed my mom."

I stepped back, gulping, sick and dizzy, my legs so weak I nearly lost my balance. She wasn't Lolly. It was impossible. "You aren't her."

"How can you say that?" she asked. Her lower lip trembled. Unshed tears welled up, sparkling on her lashes. "How can you look right at me and deny me?"

My vision pinholed, the world tilted and spun, and Roux tipped sideways. No, I did. I was falling. I was under. Blue waves billowed around me, around Roux's terrible, beautiful face, so close to mine, and I found Lolly after all. I saw her the way I used to see her when I lost control, early days, when the real worsts at my core would come unfolded, showing me everything I owed.

I saw Lolly in the water, holding Paul, struggling, kicking, trying to pull them both up. All the air leaving her, bubbles tumbling toward the surface and the sunlight, up to where she could not go.

But what had I done? What had I said?

Lolly sank into a blue so deep and velvet it was almost black. I saw bubbles rising, but Lolly, she went down. She went down fast, and I went with her, into a silent darkness.

6

I WAS LYING ON the floor. It was dry. No waves, no water. The blue I saw billowing around me was only the skirt of Roux's long dress. My head was cradled in her lap. Had I fallen? Somewhere a baby was making noises. Not unhappy, but getting there. Readying to fuss.

Not Paul. Not Lolly. They were not here. They could not be. It was my baby. It was Oliver.

Roux peered down at me, saying, "Welcome back. You fainted," but that could not be right. I wasn't the kind to faint.

From a thousand miles away, I heard my front door bang open. Someone was calling for me. "Amy?"

"Shit!" Roux jerked, looking up. "Is that Kanga? Does she not knock?"

"Amy?" It was Charlotte, calling from the foyer, coming for our walk.

Roux pushed at me, rolling me away so she could stand. I flopped back and lay flat, sick and dizzy. She bent at the waist, leaning over so her eyes met mine, talking in an urgent near whisper. "Tell her— No, too complicated. Get rid of her, fast, and come see me.

Today, or I swear to God . . . You owe me. You owe me, and you are going to pay."

I knew what she was then. Too late, I understood her game.

Char's footsteps were coming closer, down the hall, pausing by the stairs to call up, "Amy? Are you up there?" and Roux was running lightly to the back door. She slipped through it and was gone.

"Ahmamamama," Oliver said to me, reaching for me, close to crying.

I sat up, groggy and sick, and I reached back. Of course I did.

But, God, what had I done?

Charlotte took one look at me, half lying on the floor, my back propped against the sofa, and drew up short, still safely in the kitchen.

"Oh, Lordy, is it flu?"

Ruby caught any stomach flu that came within a hundred yards of her.

"Just an awful headache," I assured her, and Char, that saint, offered to watch Oliver so I could go to bed. She wouldn't take no for an answer either.

"Do you know how many babysitting hours I owe you? I'm at least a million in the hole. And we like Obbiber, don't we, Ruby? Get a nap, but you have to pick him up by two, okay? Ruby has her checkup."

I let her take him, closing my eyes while she gathered diapers and baby food and frozen breast milk. I was trying not to scream and scream and scream.

They finally went banging their awkward way out the front door, Char managing two strollers. Even before it closed behind them, I was scrambling to my feet. I went directly to the pantry, Roux's voice an echo in my head.

You owe me. You owe me, and you are going to pay.

There, in a Tupperware container on the second shelf, were the stale remains of last week's batch of blondies. Only four, thanks to Maddy and Luca. I pulled the lid off, let it drop, and ate them methodically, one after another, hardly tasting them. When they were gone, I tipped the Tupperware back and poured the crumbs into my mouth, then let it fall to the floor, too.

This was about money. She'd come at me, truth in her hands, wielded like a weapon. But she wasn't Lolly, and she did not want justice. She wanted a check.

She'd seen the accident; she knew I was a Smith. *We're both one-percenters,* she'd said, pretending she only meant scuba, when we were both from a neighborhood where the houses sold for multiple millions. As a child she'd seen Mrs. Shipley die, watching from a window. Too young for the police to question her hard, old enough to never lose the memory. Her expensive clothes and car and face, so at odds with the Sprite House, meant that something had gone bad wrong in what had begun as a very privileged life.

Now she needed money. She knew my family had it, so she'd come to find me, pretending to be someone I owed a debt that I could never pay. It was smart, and cold, and utterly amoral. What wouldn't I give if Lolly Shipley asked?

I shook my head, sick and so dizzy. My past was loose, alive inside me, roiling in my head and in my guts like a thick, tangible howling.

I took down Maddy's Saturday-only cereal, shoveled a handful into my mouth. It was like eating sugar-crusted Styrofoam, sterile and chemical. There was no pleasure in it, but I kept putting it away inside myself. It stopped me thinking. I ate it until my tongue burned from the sweetness, until my belly was a hard ball pressing at the band of my yoga pants. I thought that I might vomit. I leaned my head against the shelf, shaking.

I was not this girl. This was Amy Smith, and Roux had conjured her. Roux had pulled her out to play.

This was a game to her. When she first told me the rules, I'd been thinking small and personal. I worried about neighborhood politics, as if she were Tate trying to take over Charlotte's book club. I'd worried what would happen if she gossiped. Then she'd come to me saying "justice" and caught me up in that moment. It had all felt so huge. The confession she'd peeled from me, incomplete as it was, had felt so freeing.

But this game was larger than a petty power play and smaller than real karma. *You owe me,* she had said. Twice. *You are going to pay.*

Sick from all the sugar, I looked at the almost empty box of cereal. I surely did not owe her this. I dropped the box on the floor, the last Froot Loops scattering out.

Thirty seconds later I was upstairs pulling on an old lime-green tankini, throwing a loose cotton dress on over it. I hurried to the guest-room closet, where I stowed all our dive equipment, and started packing up, gear-checking as I went. I had two full tanks on hand. I knew they were nitrox, 32 percent, but I calibrated my analyzer and tested the gas content anyway.

This was good. This claimed my whole attention. Everything had to be right, because I was about to bet my life on these machines, these tubes, these frail connections. On the way to the car, I checked the weather and the tides on my phone app and then drove straight to the abandoned fishing pier. Here in September, midmorning on a school day, I was alone on this sunny stretch of beach. I hadn't even called Davis or the shop to tell someone where I was. Smart divers did not solo, I told my students. Not even at familiar walk-in spots like this one. But I dropped my bag and peeled my dress over my head and kicked my sandals off anyway. I geared up and did my final checks, then walked into the green-blue waves.

The water rose around me, slowing my unwieldy steps, until the low waves were slapping at my upper thighs. It was enough. I fell forward, arms out, and the water caught me. It took me in. It let me under.

The ocean was thick with bits of green seaweed. Low visibility, but I was almost glad. I didn't want to see too far ahead. I had no desire to look behind me. I wanted only to be in this now, the water a living world of green surging around me. The ocean had its own breath, and, suspended in the huge, relentless inhale-exhale of the tide, I matched mine to it as I slipped my fins on.

For the first time since Roux had said that word to me, "justice," I felt as if the air I drew got all the way inside me. I exhaled in regulated, even ways, using my own breath and the ocean's to keep my body angling ever downward, following the sloping sand into this sacred, silent space. It was huge enough to hold the things inside me.

I came to the wreckage of the pier, where the baitfish churned in schools, flashing silver in the green gloom. They swam, like with like, hundreds banded into a single organism. Each was its own self, but they all stayed in formation, each hoping it would not be singled out. Two long, thin shadows took shape in front of me. Barracuda, drawn by the baitfish, and this was the way the world worked. Predators came, drawn to easy meat. They watched me go by, impassive.

Near the end of the old pier's remains, a nurse shark lay basking under a rock ledge. He was a good-size fellow, almost as long as I was. He regarded me in profile with his calm, taupe-colored eye. A remora, slim and busy, worked around his gills.

I was more than thirty feet down now, and I kept on going, gliding past him, to the remains of the last pylon. If I wished it, I could simply keep on swimming, out to where there was only ocean and more ocean. I could follow the sloping sand down so deep I'd get narc'd. Giddy-high on oxygen, I could press on until my gauge told me my tank was in the red. I'd drink my last scant air while I stripped down mother-naked. I'd hold my weights, to keep me in the cool, dark deeps. Then I would learn what the real Lolly Shipley had learned, the day she walked into her neighborhood pool. I could watch my last bubble rise, follow it with my eyes as high as I could see but not rise with it. My past would sink with me.

I could see how it would be. I was not afraid of it. If Roux had come seven years ago, I might even have done it. Just kept going, south and down and out. But the life I had now was so sweet, so very dear. Above me, somewhere in airy sunlight, Oliver played with Ruby, safe under Char's watchful eye. Davis worked in his office, maybe grading papers. Maddy was sneak-texting or doodling her way through math. I had to return to them.

But not yet. And truthfully, if Roux had come seven years ago, I wouldn't feel this way. Seven years back I *had* been easy meat. I might simply have given her whatever she wanted. But now? The stakes were higher than she knew. I could feel my heart rate rising. Too much thinking. I was breathing hard now, sucking gas like a newbie. I had to shut it down.

I breathed myself up a foot and flutter-kicked toward the largest heap of rubble, and as I passed, the nurse shark stirred himself and followed, curious. He sailed easily past me, then circled back, clearly used to divers. He angled in close, pushy as a cat, and I scratched his head gently with my fingertips. His skin was smooth and cool, a pleasure to my bare fingers. He slid past, then circled again, coming back in for another scratch.

For this small and stolen moment, I let there be no shore, no small son needing me, no family, no friends, no job. No Roux, invading, knowing things she could not know.

There was only breath and now. The ocean surged around me, teeming and seething with urgent life, each animal, each plant, each cell bent to its own singular business. Time passed, though I was not truly aware of it as time. It was only numbers winding down on my computer, reminding me my stay was finite as I moved in easy loops around the site, the nurse shark shadowing me.

Near the end I found a blue crab peering at me from under a slab of rock. He spread his claws out wide, trying to make himself look bigger, just in case I was a thing that dragged crabs out from under rocks and ate them. I found myself smiling around my regulator, charmed by his bravado. I was all right again. I looked at the crab, fronting large, and I knew what Roux was. I knew I owed her nothing. I was ready to face her.

I made my way back, angling up the sloping sand toward shore, making a safety stop and then surfacing. By

the time I'd stowed my gear and traded my wet suit for
my damp and sandy dress, it was past noon. I repacked
the car, my mind a calm blank, and got in behind the
wheel. I didn't start the engine. Instead I dug my phone
out of the glove box and went to Google Docs.

Char had added Roux's contact info to our shared
files. We kept the phone list alphabetical by first name,
which put Angelica Roux in second place. The pettiest
little piece of me didn't like seeing her name just under
mine, almost touching. She didn't go by Angelica, so
why not shove her down among the R's where she belonged? I resisted the urge. She had my secrets, and they
were not safe with her. I knew what she was. I had to
seem compliant, keep her calm. I pushed my salt-thick
hair back from my face, breathing steady, staying centered.

When I was ready, I dialed. It barely had time to ring
twice before she picked up.

"Hello?" She sounded tense.

"Hey. It's Amy," I said. "I think—"

"You take your own sweet time, don't you?" she said,
and I realized she was not just tense. She was downright
angry. I couldn't afford to like this, but I liked it. "Are
you coming?"

"In a little bit," I said, and she snorted.

"Oh, in a little bit? God, who are you?"

"Who are you?" I asked her back. "When you said I
owed—"

"Never on the phone. Come over. Now." And that
was all.

"Oh, you bitch," I said, soft, into the dead connection.
Half of me wanted to regear, take my second tank, go

straight under again. But I was as ready to face her as I was going to be.

By the time I got back to my neighborhood, it was past one, and I had to pick up Oliver. I didn't want to take the baby to Roux's, but Char had that appointment. I left my car at the house and walked two blocks farther down to the cul-de-sac to collect him, not even stopping to clean up the mess I'd left in the pantry or change. I was mostly dry by then anyway.

I thanked Char profusely, promising to pay her back the time with interest. Oliver'd gone down for his big nap, passed out in his bucket seat. I snapped it into the top of the stroller without waking him and wheeled him two doors down.

The red car was gone, but I could hear faint music playing inside. Somebody was home.

I rang the bell, and almost instantly I heard footsteps coming. Roux jerked open the door. Some kind of jazz was on in the room behind her, janky and discordant. She was barefoot, wearing low-rise yoga pants and a workout top that barely covered more flesh than a bra. She was not as calm as I was, her mouth set in an angry line, her forehead furrowed as much as her Botox would allow.

"Come in. I sent Luca to run errands, so we have the place to ourselves." She stepped back to let me push the stroller in.

I found myself in a dingy living room, crammed with the kind of ugly, durable furniture that ends its life in rental houses. I got an instant case of déjà vu, and yet I'd never once set foot inside the Sprite House. It was dim, mostly because a thick gray blanket had been tacked up over the picture window, but as my eyes adjusted, I could see Roux staring at me with big, wet eyes, both furious and wounded.

She was still in character.

"I can't believe how long you kept me waiting. Considering."

"Stop it," I said, the way I might tell Mad to stop clicking her spoon against her teeth in that enraging habit she had while eating cereal. "You are not Lolly Shipley."

Roux's wounded eyes went high-beam. "How can you say that? I saw the whole thing—"

"Not from inside the car. Plastic surgery isn't a time machine, Roux," I said, bald and mean. "You're pushing forty, I would guess."

A fraught pause, and then she straightened. All her accusing sorrow, it slithered off her like a cape she'd been wearing. I could almost see it puddling at her feet. Her anger stayed.

"I'm not forty," she snapped. "I could easily—"

I cut her off. "Lolly Shipley died." Simple. Bare. I kept my eyes on hers, steady. I did not allow my voice to shake.

That took her down a notch.

"Well, shit," she said. "When?"

"She was five. She drowned," I said, as calm as I could be, considering.

"Are you fucking kidding me?" Roux said, a different kind of pissed now. It was as if this information had inconvenienced her. She stood looking at me expectantly.

I didn't want to say another word. The last thing I wanted was to hand her the keys to more of my guilt.

After Mrs. Shipley's death, Mr. Shipley hadn't done well. Drinking. He'd lost his house, his business. They'd moved to Milton, Florida, to a crappy neighborhood with one amenity: a shared pool.

I skipped the history and simply said, "Paul, the baby, walked into a pool when he was two. Lolly jumped in after. To try to save her little brother."

I said it as flatly as I could. I didn't tell her that Mr. Shipley had been right there, four feet away, asleep in a deck chair. I didn't tell her that he'd been drinking. I stopped talking, and I stopped thinking, too. It was a discipline, long practiced, never to think of Lolly—of any of the Shipleys—past this moment. The blue. The bubbles. I let her go down into them.

It was not a bad place, under. It was the place I felt most at home in all the world. I paused, breathed in, breathed out. Strange to tell this story with my own sleeping baby in the room, so wholly innocent.

Roux turned from me, muttering, "Shit! I should have followed up on that."

She paced away, toward the switchback stairs on the other side of the room. I took the moment when her back was to me to scrub fast at my eyes. When I looked up again, my sense of déjà vu got stronger, and yet I'd never been here before. Not in this house, and certainly not in this position. Maybe it felt familiar because on some level I'd been waiting for it, for truth to come at me in some shape or another, suspended between fear and hope for all my quiet years.

"I don't remember any Rouxs from the neighborhood. Is that your married name?" I asked when she turned to face me. Her gambit had failed, but she had seen me get out of the Ambassador on the driver's side. She had a good hold on my past, which meant she had a hold on me.

She took a long time before she answered, and I recognized the expression on her face. I had just felt it cross my own. She was trying to decide how much she needed to tell me.

"Not important. You know I was there. You know what I saw." She walked toward me, around Oliver's stroller, until we were face-to-face. "You know enough to give me what I want."

"Which is?" I said, although I was pretty sure I knew that, too.

She smiled. "Take your clothes off."

She said it as if this were our obvious next step. My arms crossed, instantly, protectively.

"I'm not doing that," I said, confused but vehement. Money we could talk about, but this?

Roux chuckled. "I'm not after your virtue, dewy maiden. Please. I told you, I'm straight."

I swallowed. She was close to naked herself, in her yoga togs. I took in the bare flesh of her willowy waist, her elegant breasts in the sheer top. I felt my eight pounds of leftover baby weight swelling around me. They felt like eighty as my eyes traced the faint, sleek muscles in her arms and legs, visible even in the soft curve of her abdomen. In this soft light, she looked no more than thirty again. The sight of her shoved me back in time. Toward young Amy with her hungers and her cowardice, both mossy green with age but still alive. I made myself focus only on her face. I would not see the past.

"Then why?" I demanded.

She rolled her eyes, now sounding both bored and impatient. "I need to be sure you aren't wearing a wire."

"A wire? So I can record *this*?" I said. The last thing I wanted was any kind of record of our conversations.

"People do," she said.

She stepped to a battered glass-top end table and picked up an iPhone. She fiddled with it, shutting off the jazz. I heard a voice coming out of it, tinny and far.

"—*never meant to lie. I didn't remember that I was driving. Not at first. I never meant. I never meant. I swear to God.*" The voice shook and quavered, both foreign and undeniably mine.

"*But you killed her.*" Roux's recorded voice unspooled a foot away from her closed mouth.

"*Yes,*" my voice said. Just one word, but it was enough.

She stopped the playback. For a single, shocked second, I felt a coiling in my body. I would leap at her, wrest the phone from her fingers, smash it, ruin it, make it gone.

Roux saw it in my eyes, or else she expected it, because she was already talking. "This app backs up into the cloud."

"Oh, my God," I said softly, shaken in spite of my resolve.

"Taping conversations is a good idea, Amy," she said, setting the phone back down. "I need to make sure it isn't one you had. Because we're about to have a real-ass conversation."

"Is that legal? Taping me like that?" I asked. As if this mattered to her. She was smack in the middle of blackmailing me, after all.

"It's called single-party consent, and it's legal in

thirty-eight states." She smiled. "I told you, I sleep with a lot of lawyers."

That landed, in spite of my shock. She'd been talking about lawyers, at my house, before her bullshit claim that she was Lolly Shipley. She'd gone on and on about it, sex with lawyers, but then she'd changed directions. I could almost see it, why this mattered. My gaze skipped around the ugly room, then back to Roux herself, shiny and expensive-looking.

"Hurry up and strip," she said.

I lost my train of thought, my arms still crossed defensively over my body, my mind still reeling from hearing my own confession. There was no way in hell I'd let Roux's doctored, lineless eyes peruse the little roll at my waist, the old silver stretch marks on my thighs and belly. I had some newer ones now, too, redder and more visible, that Oliver had gifted me.

"You can play that tape on *Good Morning America* before I'll take my pants off," I told her, fierce, and to my surprise she threw her head back and she laughed.

"I think you actually mean that. Damn. I have to say, you aren't what I expected." Well, neither was she. We stood there at an impasse until she blew out an exasperated breath. "Fine. A compromise. We'll do this the old-fashioned way."

She came back around the stroller as if it were another table, not even glancing at my sleeping baby. She paused just shy of touching me, eyebrows raised. I made myself breathe and dropped my hands at my sides. She took it as permission. She started in my hair, the pads of her fingers running across my scalp, sure and thorough. She checked my ears and my neck, pressing the seams of the dress's collar.

I did not want her hands to move lower, to outline every imperfection in my body. It was work to hold myself still.

I focused my eyes over her shoulder, staring at the fireplace. It was ugly brown brick, flanked by built-in bookshelves. It reminded me of Char's before I'd helped her paint it white, and then I understood the déjà vu. This house *was* Char's. The exact same floor plan, only backward. To my right was the hallway to the master suite, and opposite that an arch led to the kitchen beside switchback stairs.

But this was a shabby negative of Char's crisp white walls, Colonial blue-and-yellow prints, and breezy sheers. Roux's furniture was covered in a dull, durable weave, and her bookshelves were mostly empty. A stack of old board games had been crammed onto the lowest shelf, and the top shelf held a vertical pile of tattered mass-market paperbacks; I suspected that these, like the ugly furniture, came with the house. The only thing that might be hers was a small framed picture propped on the mantel. It was a simple line drawing of a naked woman flopping on her back, legs akimbo. She had both her eyes on one side of her face like a flounder, her wonky breasts pointing in odd directions. It was signed. Picasso.

"Is that real?" I asked.

Roux paused to glance behind her, her hands on my shoulders like we were slow dancing, middle-school style. "Of course."

"So you moonlight as an art thief?" I meant it as a dig, but she shook her head, as if it had been a real question.

"Without the provenance, art's just paper and lines. That was more like a gift."

"Sure," I said, the way she used that word. Sarcastic.

She smiled, recognizing the inflection. "People like to give me things. I'm nice if you give me things. You'll see."

I understood then; she'd done this before, traded secrets for things she wanted or needed. Maybe this was all she did. Her mystery job.

Meanwhile her hands found the tied strings of my suit, the tankini top still damp under my dress. "You went to the beach? You smell like beach." I didn't answer. "What the hell are you? I have your whole life in my hands. I told you to dump Kanga and get over here, and you . . . what, you geared up and went diving?" She sounded almost admiring, her fingers running along the suit's underwire. She brushed her thumbs across the cups, and I jerked.

"Are you searching for my nipples?" I asked, acid. "Because you found those."

"Just a mike," Roux said. "Or a gun. Little knives. Ninja stars."

It sounded like a point of pride. It sounded true.

"Oh, do people often try to kill you?" I asked, deadpan. "Fancy that."

"Well, I did mention I was married," she said, and then added, "Rimshot!"

I didn't think she was joking all the way, though. There was a serious edge to it, and I took it as another drop in my meager pool of knowledge about Roux. She was married. She'd once lived in my old neighborhood. She didn't eat carbs. And now this: She'd known violence.

Her hands were lower now, feeling my waist. I sucked my stomach in. I couldn't help it. It was easier to stand her hands on me when we were talking, so I talked.

"You don't seem married. Hearing how you talk about men, I don't think you like them very much."

She shrugged. "Men are useful. I like useful things."

She knelt then, running her hands down my right hip, then my leg.

"See, right there, that's animosity," I told her, and I wanted to make her uncomfortable. Wanted to invade her space, the same way she was muscling into mine. "Has it occurred to you that you're raising a man?"

I felt a stillness come into her body, but it happened in her core. Her hands stayed in motion. "Luca is a boy. Boys are sweet."

"What do you think boys grow up to be?" I pushed.

"Men. Mostly. But at that point don't they also get the hell out of your house?" She grinned, tossing the remark off, but my dig had landed. She did have a soft spot. Her kid. Now she was checking my sandals. "You're pretty fit, especially considering how big you used to be. You should dedicate a day to abs, though."

I'd hit her and she'd hit back, immediately, landing a low blow. I closed my eyes, breathed in, as her hands swept up my other leg. Imagined I was underwater. Imagined her movements were waves and current pushing at me. It worked, too, right up until she put one hand directly between my legs. I cried out and stepped back, my eyes flying open.

She cocked an eyebrow. "Relax, Amy. People always think no one will look there. It's the first place I think of and the last place I check."

"Satisfied?" I asked, my voice tight, as she stood and stepped away from me.

"Not yet. But I mean to be." She gave me a brilliant smile. She looked down at Oliver, snug in the stroller,

sleeping in the abandoned way of secure and happy babies, both arms hurled up over his head. He'd kicked the
blanket off, as he always did, exposing one perfect, pink
foot. "See, now, boys *are* sweet."

It was the first time she'd ever acknowledged him as a
person existing around her, and she said it in an offhand
manner. She reached down, and I thought she was going
to fix the blanket. Instead she searched my boy as if he
were a handbag, impersonal, her movements brisk and
thorough.

I felt my own hands fist at my sides, and this was
more an invasion than her groping me had been.

"If you wake him up . . ." I said, a warning whisper,
but he was already stirring.

She didn't know it, but this meet was over. Oliver
was a monster baby if anyone pulled him out of a nap.
He was beginning his high whine that would become a
squall and then a howl. His gummy eyes fought to open.

Roux put her face close to his, then placed one hand
on his chest, one lower. She bounced him in little pushes,
like a gentle version of baby CPR, making a noise that
sounded like a quiet train.

"Chicka-chicka-chicka."

His eyes focused briefly on her face, then he slow-
blinked once, twice. To my surprise he settled, going
limp again.

"I'm a baby whisperer," she said, peeping up at me
with a sly smile. "They fucking love me."

This from a woman who had acted like he was a
houseplant every time she'd shared a room with him.
She bent lower to check the diaper bag I'd stowed under
his stroller. My cell was in it, and she pressed the button
and swiped, powering it all the way down. When she

was finished, she walked, brisk and businesslike, over to the sofa and sat. "All right, you asked what I want. I want the money from your college trust fund. After you liquidate and pay taxes and fees, you should clear around two hundred and forty thousand. You give it to me, all of it, and I will go away."

It took a moment for that to sink in. I'd guessed that she was after money, but this was so specific.

"How can you know how much . . . ?" I started. But it sputtered out. That wasn't even the question. How did she know about the trust itself? For the first time since coming up from the dive, I was truly off balance. She seemed to like it, a creamy smile spreading across her face.

"I looked you up on Boyce Skelton's laptop."

I straightened up. I knew the name, but it was so far out of context, it took me a moment to place. "My lawyer?"

He was an attorney at the investment firm that managed my family's money. Not one of the important ones. He handled people like me, who had small trusts and relatives that mattered. He'd come to my parents' house for cocktails a few times, trailing his bosses, just after we moved to Boston. I was turned entirely inward that year, focused on the live, wild hunger that I'd let loose inside me as a punishment. It was new, but minute by minute I could feel my big body dwindling in its grip. Boyce blipped on my radar only because Mom had told me he was handling my college trust. He'd been a podgy young man with a receding hairline. We'd spoken on the phone a few times over the years. He'd done his damnedest to talk me out of liquidating half to pay Tig's mortgage.

"Boyce Skelton lives in Boston," I said.

"Yeah, well, I took a little trip up there," Roux said.

I shook my head. "Why would he show you my file?" I asked. He wouldn't. It could get him disbarred.

"I helped myself while he was in the shower. His place, because Luca was back at my hotel. It was not a PG-13 kind of night," Roux said, and showed me all her teeth.

"You went to Boston to have sex with my lawyer. So you could sneak a look at my investment portfolio," I repeated, stupidly.

Boyce must be in his fifties now; I could not imagine that puffy little yes-man, grayer and podgier, having sex with Roux. But I could, I realized, imagine Roux cold-bloodedly seducing him to see a file. I was still taking this as personal, as if it were about me. It wasn't. She was a professional.

She flirted one shoulder up, dipping her chin in an acknowledgment that was half nod, half bow. Her pink tongue came out to touch her teeth, and she smiled a conspirator's smile.

"Do you know he keeps his password on a Post-it note? Right in the laptop's carry case. I looked you up, and I did the math. I'm good at math," she said. "He's a missionary kind of guy. A traditionalist. A lot of those Boston banking types are into truly freaky stuff, Amy, but not your Boyce, you'll be relieved to know. I always think people feel better knowing their money is in the hands of a man who doesn't need to lick boots."

I glanced at Oliver. He was still deeply out. Even so, I wanted to grab the stroller, run him from the room. I didn't want this conversation touching air he breathed.

She was making me feel this way on purpose, I realized, and something akin to admiration pinged small at my center. She didn't mean these things. She only thought saying them would knock me off balance. Just like at book club, just like at my house, earlier.

"Why do you keep trying to shock me? You're black-mailing me. I'm shocked enough," I said. I made my-self sound calm and cool. If she wanted me shocked, she would get the opposite. It wasn't even hard. I'd lived wild in California, unhappy enough to do almost any-thing to stop myself from feeling. I mimicked her little shoulder flirt, her offhand tone. "I'm not some medie-val nun who's scared of lesbians and never saw a show on HBO."

She let out a startled bark of laughter, and that ping of admiration at my center found an echo inside her. I could see it. She leaned back, as if reassessing me, and I didn't like the way we were positioned in the room. She was lounging, at ease, while I stood there like some naughty child waiting to hear my punishment. I should sit, too. I felt it on instinct. But I didn't. I was in the room with a predator, and I could not bring myself to move away from Oliver.

She said, "No, you're right. That shit doesn't work on you."

"I can't imagine it works on anyone," I said, like a criticism.

"It would on Kanga. And Lisa Fenton," Roux said, unaware that what I had just done, mimicking, had worked on her. She sounded ever so slightly defensive. "I've seen your husband, and he looks wound up, with the little spectacles and those knife-sharp creases in his khakis. It would work on him."

She was right, but I didn't acknowledge it. I had her

off balance. I could feel it, and now I knew one more thing about Roux: She took pride in her work. She'd gone to Boston to screw exact amounts out of my lawyer, cased my neighborhood, interviewed my friends; it was no accident that Char had met her first. She'd manufactured a game to use on me like a tenderizer, softening me up so she could tear me open, cause words that I should never say to come spilling out. She was good at this, and proud of it, so I didn't acknowledge it.

"You don't really know them," I said instead, dismissively.

Her smile got tight. "Fine. I'll stop talking about rolling Boyce. I won't even show you the pictures. Instead let's discuss the statute of limitations for felonies connected to a death here in the lovely state of Florida. Oh, wait. There isn't one."

When I tapped, she hit back hard. The muscles in my abdomen tightened. I swallowed, swamped with sudden fear, as she'd intended. I pushed it down, away.

"Okay," I said. "I know what you want. I know the stakes. I'm going home now. I need to think about it."

She blinked, surprised enough for it to show. "Oh, you do? You need to think about it?"

I nodded, and she stood up, abruptly, as if she physically could not stay seated. She came two steps toward me, as if drawn. I'd seen her have a lot of feelings, but most of them had been manufactured to work me over. This, though, this rising interest, this was real.

"What are you?" she asked. "I get people, Amy. I *know* people. I know women like you in neighborhoods like this. You don't have anything interesting to say, so mostly you talk shit about each other. You puff and squawk, and you get nervous when anyone steps outside the safety of your little, line-filled lives." She was so intense, eyes narrowed above bared teeth. It was as if the rhythm of the conversation had gotten away from her. I stayed cool, though I had one hand on the stroller bar, gripped so tight I was surprised the metal didn't dent. She couldn't see that hand. I kept the rest of my body loose and easy, turned inward, focused on my breathing, as if I were a hundred twenty feet under and every molecule of oxygen was precious. She came closer, still talking. "Why aren't you like that? Like your friends. You have your shit on lockdown, all big eyes and tight lips. I tell you to come see me and you go diving. I have your ass in a vise six ways from Sunday and you tell me, cool as a pudding, that you need to think. There is nothing to think about. Either you liquidate your trust and transfer the money or I go to the cops and fuck your life, forever. That's it. A or B. Your call. So make it. I'm fine either way."

The things that she was saying weren't all true. I looked at her, and the contrast hit me again. She glowed, so expensive and soft, in this rough and ugly house. This was not her natural habitat. She wouldn't be here, wouldn't have her kid in a place like this, if she had other choices. She needed my money, and she wouldn't capriciously blow a chance to wring it out of me. If it were twenty thousand, maybe. But not almost a quarter of a million.

"What's it worth, that Picasso sketch?" I asked.

That took her aback. "Why? You want to buy it?" When I didn't answer, she relented. "More than your car."

I shrugged. "It's not that nice a car."

She laughed again, nonplussed, while I breathed, in and out, twice, thinking.

She'd started down one path, to blackmail me. Something about sex with lawyers. She'd meant to shock me, knock me off my guard with what she'd done to get to see my file. She had a path charted that I could not imagine, but I knew it started with Boyce and led to me incriminating myself. She'd needed that tape. A child witness, twenty-five years later, was not enough for policemen or lawyers, and therefore it was not enough to scare me.

I'd stayed calm, unshocked, and then our talk about Luca had derailed her off that path. She hadn't been able to get to me, so she had upped the stakes, pretending to be Lolly. That had been a risk. A gamble. She hadn't done the research.

Maybe she was bad at her job, but I didn't think so. If she were, I would have seen her before now. She'd saved me in her pocket for a rainy day, which meant that up until now she'd had a lot of success, a lot of sunshine. Now here she was, in this house that smelled musty and foul, and I knew it must be raining hard indeed.

"I don't think you are fine either way," I told her. "Otherwise you would have done the research. About Lolly. You were in a hurry, so you skipped steps and came at me before you were completely ready. Look at this place. Not your usual digs, I'd guess. You need me. You need my money as much as I need you to keep your mouth shut."

Her face had gone to stone. It told me nothing. I gave her the same face back. The quiet game again, but this time I decided I would age out and die, right here on her floor, before I lost. I would not lose, and this knowledge was a wild, red pleasure. The silence stretched, and there was a clock somewhere in the room, I realized. It had been ticking this whole time, but now I was aware of the sound, each second being marked as it slipped past us. In the end she broke it.

"What the fuck are you?" she asked. She tilted her head to the side with birdlike curiosity, maybe even reptilian. My heart sped up, just a little, as if it had decided to race the ticktock sound. "I came armed for small-town-wifey-with-a-past. I know the species. Not a hard target. But you? You're like me. You're all folded up and secret down inside, like you're made of fucking origami."

The door banged open. I jumped, but she didn't. Luca came in, toting five or six plastic bags from Publix, one-handed.

"They didn't have cashew milk, so I got almond?" Luca said, and then he saw me. "Oh, hey."

"Almond is fine," Roux said, and now her smile was genuine. She loved her kid.

"Hey, Luca," I said. My voice was shaking. Just a little, but I could hear it. I hoped she couldn't. I bent over the stroller, fixing Oliver's blanket, though he'd only push that exact same foot out again within a minute.

"Whatcha doing here, Ms. Whey?" he asked.

I had no answer, but Roux stepped in, smooth, her voice bright and cheery. "Working out your scuba lessons."

That was interesting. Did Luca not know what his mom did for a living?

Luca brightened, and he looked back and forth between us. "For real?" Then a faint shadow of worry crossed his face. He turned to me. "Is it expensive?"

So he knew about the money trouble. He was a bright kid, and I doubted this house looked like their real home, wherever that was. I wondered if he knew how his mother planned to recoup their losses. I didn't think so. He'd have to be a better player than his mother, to eat my blondies and chat about my pictures, all the while knowing I was one of her hapless victims.

"You let me worry about that," Roux told him. "Go put the groceries away and let us work out a schedule for your lessons."

"Cool," he said. "That's so freakin' awesome." He disappeared into the kitchen. We could both hear him in there, banging around in her carb-free fridge.

I went to the stroller. "I need to think," I told her, soft, insistent.

"No you don't," she said.

"I do," I said. Exactly how broke were they? She had the Picasso sketch, and she could sell the car. That would get her, what? Maybe fifty, sixty thousand? That was a lot of cash, but maybe not to her. And not next to a quarter mil. I thought I had some wiggle room. A little. So I pushed it. "I'm not impulsive, Roux. You give me time or you go to the cops and you get nothing."

It wasn't true. I'd bend if she pushed me now. I'd have to. But I shoved that truth way down, into my most secret spaces, deeper than the worst parts of my past. Down to where the worsts that I was doing every day lived, the things inside me that I could never, never look at. My real worsts, that this woman, who owned my past, must never know. I met her gaze head-on, and I saw my bluff land. I saw the very moment she believed me.

"I'll give you until tomorrow," she said, and I felt

a small but fierce exulting. She raised her voice, loud enough for Luca to hear. "Thanks, Amy. I'll come by tomorrow about nine A.M. and do the paperwork so he can get started."

Luca appeared in the doorway, grinning at his mother under a nut-milk mustache. "Like you'll be up at nine."

"I walk right then anyway," I said, staring her down, pushing it even further. "Let's make it ten. I can't miss my workout."

"Sure," she said, but with an edge. Luca wiped at his mouth and then rolled off the doorjamb. He went galloping up the stairs. A moment later we heard a door slam, and then music turned on, loud and bass-heavy.

"I have to go. Maddy will be home any minute," I said.

She didn't answer. She stayed silent, and I took it as permission.

I put my other hand on the stroller bar, began turning Oliver around. He was still out, dreaming. Something good, by the look of it. His mouth worked faintly, as if he were nursing. I pushed him to the door.

Roux's voice stopped me. She was right behind me. She'd come to me, silent, barefoot, and so fast.

"Are you playing, Amy? Are you in my game?" I could feel her breath on my neck. I made myself be still. I didn't answer. "Don't. It's just money, and you aren't even using it. Fifteen years is a long time. That baby will be as tall as Luca by the time you're out." She was almost whispering, but every word she said landed like gospel. "Be here, tomorrow, ten A.M. If you bounce off to the goddamn beach again, I will pack it in. I'll move down to the next bitch on my list. Yeah, I need the money, but there is always a next bitch. So do not test me. If you play me, if you make all the setup I did on this into wasted time, I will fuck your life so hard on my way out. Believe it."

I said nothing. I didn't even look at her, but I believed. I pushed forward, out the door, fleeing with my boy into the sunshine.

7

ALL AFTERNOON, AS I took care of Oliver and scrubbed my kitchen and bathrooms to keep my hands busy, the choice was churning in my head. Roux was pushing me down toward memories and guilts that were sunk too far for anyone to see them. Not even me. I'd thought they were deep and distant, but Roux had said I was like origami; maybe she was right. What if they were only folded away? She'd brought my worst things close and made the barriers that kept me from them feel as thin and frail as pleated paper.

Scrubbing the grout as if it had personally offended me, I knew that if prison was my only fear, even my main fear, then I did have a choice. When I was fifteen, I'd learned that justice bent to money. I could afford to hire a lawyer. Assuming I did not pay Roux, I could afford the best damn lawyer in the state. Well-spoken white people from prominent families came out on top in our broken court system. It wasn't fair, but it was true. If I went to an attorney right now, the two of us could go straight to the D.A., get in ahead of Roux. Make a deal.

The max was fifteen years. I couldn't bear to think of Oliver navigating all those rocky years to adolescence with no mother. Perhaps I deserved it, but he didn't. In fifteen years he would likely be taller than me yet still vulnerable and innocent, like Maddy. But Roux had told me fifteen years to scare me. Given my youth at the time and my current life, I would not get the max.

I was a tax-paying wife and mother, valued in my community. Tig, a kid from the wrong side of town with a bag of pot in his pocket, had gotten only three years. It was likely, though by no means guaranteed, I would fare better than he had. I might even get probation and community service.

But "might" was a big word, especially when I held it up beside my child's future.

What if they gave me Tig's exact sentence? Oliver would be older than Ruby was right now. Ruby already had friends, ideas, opinions, passions. I could not miss three years. Or two. Or even one. Oliver was changing every day, and the near-walking bold explorer I had now was nothing like the tiny, soft potato I'd been handed in the hospital. In a year he would have a fifty-word vocabulary. He would be running in that stumpy toddler gait, flat-footed and charming. I couldn't miss that time.

And that was only the legal side. If Roux told my secrets, it would wreck my world in ways I could not bear to think about. It would put cracks and dents in every relationship that mattered to me. Everyone would know. I'd have to move. Davis might not forgive me, much less move away with me. This could smash my family in half. The night he proposed, I'd promised him, *I'm not the kind who'll ever leave you.* And I had meant it. I still meant it. But what if my secrets broke us? I didn't want Maddy, who was my Mads now in so many ways, to be unmothered twice in her short life. I did not want Oliver growing up between two houses, much less two entirely separate states.

That was as far as I could think.

That was as far as I would allow myself to think.

I could not look directly at all the other consequences looming. It was like staring into a sun so bright it hurt. But that didn't make them any less real.

Either I had to pay Roux off or I had to tell everyone who mattered most myself, then go to a lawyer.

The master bath was gleaming. I repacked my cleaning basket and headed to the laundry room. The dryer was finished. I pulled the warm clothes out, heaping them onto the counter to fold. I'd thrown in some of Davis's plaid boxer briefs to make a full load out of Oliver's small onesies. Intimate clothing, warm as skin, smelling springtime fresh.

I bent and put my face into the pile, breathing in everything that was clean and sweet.

If I told, I'd start with Davis. The very thought made my heart hurt inside my chest. I straightened, wiping at my eyes with a soft onesie. Of course, Davis first. Then Char. The two of them before a lawyer, even though I could not bear to imagine the look in Charlotte's eyes when I told her all the truths I'd hidden. I owed her so much. Not least she had gifted me with Davis in the first place.

"You're too cute to be single," she'd told me early in our friendship. We were eating frozen yogurt from a little stand out by the beach. They had picnic tables near the water, and we sat side by side on a rough wooden bench, watching the waves roll in. "There's a guy who works with Phillip, very attractive, about your age. He's not all the way divorced yet, but he says he's ready. Or there's my dentist. He's a widower. It's been almost four years, so he has to be ready."

I shook my head. "You talk like these guys are grocery-store avocados. I'm not up for doing any pinching right now."

Char grinned and stole a bite of my yogurt. "Sorry. I can't help matchmaking. I love being married. I want everyone to be this happy." Since I had not yet met Phillip, I thought this was charming. "Oh, I have the perfect one! My neighbor down the street. Davis Whey. He's so nice. One daughter, Madison. She's a headstrong little thing, but very darling. He's been divorced a couple years now, and he's super, super cute."

I demurred, changing the subject, but not three days later Char brought Davis to Divers Down, giving me significant, waggling eyebrows as she introduced us. I was polite but cool, shooting Charlotte a quelling look as I asked Davis how I could help him.

Just then Maddy came slouching up behind them both. Her dark curls were limp and greasy, and her heavy brows were pulled down into a scowl that seemed permanent. I knew she must be nine, ten at most, but she was dressed like the kind of teenager who is busy going bad.

Too-tight jeans, too-short crop top, and she'd drawn spiderweb tattoos all over her arms in Sharpie. Not the kind of creature who inspires love at first sight, but Char presented this sulking kid and her exasperated father to me as if they were Christmas presents.

"This wants swimming lessons," the man who would one day be my husband said, jerking a thumb at his scowling child.

I didn't like him calling his kid a this, but she responded, "No, this does not."

"This is having swim lessons," he said. "Charlotte says you have a team? A swim team here?"

"Swim team is for nerds," Maddy said, not to me. Appealing to some higher court.

"Good," her father said. "Nerds almost never go to rehab or have accidental babies. Be a nerd."

"Davis!" Char said, shocked.

I didn't recognize it as wry humor, but Maddy snorted with laughter.

"Gross," she said. "And anyway, I know how to swim. Miss Charlotte said diving."

"Wait, do you mean scuba diving?" Davis said, looking around as if he only just now understood what sort of dangerous fun house he had staggered into. "I thought you meant, like . . ." He crossed his hands, leaned a little, mimicking a person diving off a board into a pool.

"Dad, I know how to dive. I want to scuba," Maddy said.

"That's insane," Davis said mildly. "They don't let nine-year-olds go scuba."

"Sure we do," I said, and he turned his skeptical face toward me. It was a good face, I had to give Charlotte that, hiding behind the fusty, 1950s dad glasses. And what looked like a good body, too, buried under the tweed.

"This needs scuba lessons," Maddy said, pointing at herself, her eyes shining. She broke away from us, heading to the side wall where the wet suits hung in sleek, black rows, dappled with pops and edgings of bright color.

"I'm going to kill you," Davis said, still mild and calm, to Charlotte.

"If you don't want Maddy running wild, you need to let her do something she wants to do," Charlotte said. "Busy kids are happy kids."

"Don't they have a needlepoint club?" Davis asked, and again I didn't recognize his humor. He was so dead-pan. But Char laughed.

"I'm sure they do, and you can sign up right after you swap out Maddy for an entirely different child," Char said, and turned to me, adding in a confiding tone, "He caught Maddy smoking. Cigarettes! She nicked them from her friend Shannon's disgusting, smoky uncle."

"Do we need to go into all of this?" Davis said.

This struck me as the kind of Waspy, hide-the-dirty-laundry crap that I'd been raised on, and I decided that I didn't like Davis Whey very much, cute or no.

I looked past him to his daughter, already pulling a Lotus that was way too big for her off a hanger, trying to strap it on, hollering, "What's this vest? Does this hose go to the air-tank thingy?" over her shoulder, flushed with pleasure.

She was hooked before she'd ever gone under, and I think I fell for the kid right then and there. I'd had a cold, stiff, distant father. I'd come from a family that buried anything ugly or painful, even if they had to bury their own child right along with it.

I saw myself in Maddy, so I called back, "That's a buoyancy-control device—call it a BCD and you'll sound like a pro," as I pulled out paperwork and set it on the counter, giving Davis a cool, professional smile. "She can start with the Seal Team kids doing pool dives and learning the equipment and safety procedures right away. After she turns ten, we can get her in the ocean."

"There, you see?" Char said. "Tell him how safe it is. Better yet, come with us for ice cream and tell him. Aren't you about to get off work?" She knew darn well I was. Plus, she was dangling ice cream as extra bait. We were pretty tight by then; she'd told me how she'd flirted with an eating disorder as a teen. I'd downplayed my own war with my body, but I'd admitted that I'd flirted, too. She knew that I only ate sweets when I was out with friends, their presence controlling my portions. "Maddy? Want to go to Scoops?"

"In a minute," Maddy called. She was reading a colorful poster about gear packages, pointing to the list of beginners' must-haves. "It says here I get a knife! And a strap to put it on my thigh, which is so freakin' cool. I want to strap a knife to my leg! Why do I need a knife?"

Before I could answer, Davis said, "To stab the shark while he's eating you. So he will at least regret it."

"It's in case you get entangled," I explained, irked.

I thought he was trying to scare her off, but Maddy laughed again—she had a huge, honking, rowdy laugh—and then mimed stabbing the air, saying, "Back off, shark!"

"Are there sharks?" Davis asked me, serious.

"Well, it is the ocean," I said. "That's where we keep 'em." His forehead creased, so I added, "But it's not like the movies. Maybe we should go get that ice cream."

I wanted to talk about my sport with him, set his mind at ease so he'd let Maddy dive. And not for nothing, I wanted a chocolate-mint chip.

Char, thinking I had other motives, gave me a series of embarrassing winks and thumbs-ups behind Davis's back.

At Scoops I began to realize he wasn't half as cold and stiff as he seemed on first impression. Davis unbent enough to flick Maddy with a few sprinkles from his spoon when she sassed him, and I saw that the snarky talk was really banter, part and parcel of a deep connection. He wasn't like my father at all. He was battened down, sure, but he loved his kid like nuts just under. It was buried so shallow that a single afternoon revealed it. Plus, he had really nice biceps and a clear sense of right and wrong. Within a month Maddy was my secret favorite Seal Team kid, and I'd been on seven dates with Davis. I knew by then that I could love him. Really love him. I was even getting a sense of the kind of life the two of us might build together. I could see its outline, forming. It looked very, very good.

In part it appealed to me because Davis loved rules, and tidiness, and order. He fell for the Amy I was now: disciplined and mature, quiet and strong. Even after we were lovers, even after he had whispered his own worst thing to me in the darkness, I had not told him mine. I'd talked about my background, my chilly, moneyed parents, my much-preferred brother, but he didn't know about my wars with food and my own body. I'd downplayed how wild I was when I lived out west. I kept my secrets, telling myself that they were the past. I ignored the ones that were still alive. The ones that touched my every current breath, the ones I couldn't even tell myself.

If I did not pay Roux off, he'd see all of it. See all of me.

I did think that he would forgive me. I was his wife. I loved and looked after his girl, and I had borne his son. He'd be the easiest person to tell, so I tried to picture it, how it would go.

Davis, at book club we played an awful game. It was a lot like Never Have I Ever.

I could line up shots on the kitchen counter, though Davis, a one-beer-on-a-hot-day guy, hated to see people getting sloppy drunk. Still. I would need to kill both my inhibitions and my instincts for self-preservation.

Davis, never have I ever lied to you. Drink.

Never have I ever kept a secret. Drink.

Never have I ever taken a human life, or stayed silent and let my best friend bear the blame, or watched him go to prison for three years while I said nothing. Drink. Drink. Drink.

And after that—

No. It was unendurable. Roux was unendurable.

I was so preoccupied as I made dinner that the salmon came out rubbery and the broccoli was practically mush. When we sat down to eat, I was snappy and distracted, daring them with my eyes to say a word about the food.

Davis and Maddy filled up on rolls and salad, and I saw them exchanging a purely Whey look, coming to a silent agreement that they would tiptoe around Monster tonight. It made me furious and guilty all at once, and after that I did my best to be quiet and spoon peas into Oliver and not bite anyone's head off.

At bedtime, when Oliver was down for the night and Maddy was in her room reading or, more likely, sneak-texting Luca on her phone, Davis called me out.

"You want to talk about it?" he asked as I emerged

from the bathroom, teeth brushed, in one of his big T-shirts that I salvaged from the hamper. I liked to sleep in them after he wore them, when the smell of his aftershave and his own warm scent was caught inside the fabric.

He was already in bed, propped up against his pillows, a book about Civil War spies open facedown on his lap. I was putting lotion on my arms, getting ready to climb in on my side, but I froze at the question, feeling how serious his gaze was.

I'd redone this bedroom right after we married, wanting to make it ours instead of his. Or rather his and Laura's. I'd replaced her stark modern furniture with a sleigh bed, queen instead of king, making room for a pair of cherrywood nightstands. I'd painted the walls a warm, rich gold, bought chocolate-brown and cream bedding, added a few pops of cranberry and rose with throw pillows and in the print of the love seat I put by the window. This room was a haven. No TV and a lock on the door. It was a place where we were two, a couple instead of a foursome. I didn't want to barefaced lie out loud to him in this room.

"I'm sorry," I told him. I sat down on the edge of the bed, an excuse to turn my back on him, and began putting lotion on my legs. "I'm having a bad day."

"You've been having a bad week," my husband told me gently, and a week ago—that was the day we had book club. I hadn't realized how much the strain I'd been under was showing.

I shrugged, and a waiting silence fell. We were both quiet people, neither of us big on chitchat. We talked at dinner about family things, but at night we liked to sit side by side, reading in bed, exchanging a few words about our books or plans for the week or events of the past day. His physical presence, his heartbeat, his breath usually combined to make me feel content and safe, but now the silence felt brittle.

What would happen if I simply let all the silent truths I kept deep buried spill into the room? Davis loved me, I knew this. It would hurt him, but it might not be a fatal wound. He might forgive me, and I knew how relieved and free and lightened I would feel. Roux, damn her eyes, had taught me that. There was such solace hidden in confession.

Her power over me would be instantly cut in half, and I would have an ally. Davis had such a strong, sure moral compass. He would know the right thing to do. Or the rightest anyway, because there was no purely good move I could make.

I teetered on this cusp, a thousand words piling up in my mouth. I looked over my shoulder at him, the tube of lotion forgotten in my hands.

"Honey, what?" he said, genuinely concerned now, his spine elongating, his brow furrowed. "What is it? Just say it."

I opened my mouth, and what came out was, "The Vegetables might be cheating on Charlotte."

I wasn't sure if I said it as an alternate truth or as a way into a larger conversation. I only knew that these were the words my mouth made when I let it open.

Davis was quiet for a moment, but I could feel his concern change direction, moving out of our inner circle to the larger world that Char inhabited.

"That idiot," he finally said.

"You don't seem surprised." I put the lotion back in my nightstand and got under the covers by him.

"Well, the Vegetables," he said, like this was explanation enough. It almost was. I had never trusted Phillip with Char's heart. "Still, how can he sit through dinner every night, face her across the table?" I didn't answer, even though I certainly could have. I understood the mechanics bone deep. Amazing, the human capacity to compartmentalize, and, dear God, Roux was right; I was made out of origami, and so was Phillip, though I hated having anything in common with him. Davis, still thinking it through, asked me, "Did Charlotte tell you? Is she sure?"

"Char doesn't know," I said, and his eyebrows went up.

"Then how do you?" he asked.

I broke it down for him, but I left out the game. It was too complicated, and it opened a conversational door to questions I wasn't yet sure I would answer. I didn't want him wondering if I'd won any of the rounds. So I told him only what I'd overheard Tate saying to her friends at book club, how I'd guessed it was Phillip, how Tate had shown up the next day in a move that was tantamount to a confession. I also told him that Tate had written it off as sloppy-drunk kissing, a meaningless, unrepeated mistake.

Davis sat silent for a moment, digesting. Then he asked, "Do you believe Tate?"

"I don't know. That's part of the problem." Davis's dark eyes were serious, empathetic, but they held no answers. I asked him, "Would you want me to tell you?"

"If you were cheating on me? Yes, please," he said, very dry. "Preferably before you give me syphilis."

That made me smile in spite of myself, but at the

same time I felt another question rising. And it wasn't only about Charlotte.

"Let's say Tate's telling the truth. Put yourself in Charlotte's shoes. Would you want to know?"

He cocked an eyebrow. "If you made out with Tate Bonasco at a barbecue? Hell yeah, I'd want to know. I'd probably want pictures."

I smacked him lightly on the chest, laughing in spite of myself. "You're not funny."

"I'm a little funny," he said, smiling back.

"I'm serious, though," I said, because I was, and this wasn't only about Phillip now. The stakes were higher than that, and I thought I could let him decide, right now, my larger course. "Really think about it. What if I had done something. Something bad, but it was in the past, and I was never going to do it again. Knowing it would hurt you, though. There would be consequences. It might wreck us. Would you want someone to tell you?"

He did think about it then, and I could see he was taking it seriously. He asked. "Does everyone know your secret thing? Are they all feeling sorry for me?"

I shook my head in an emphatic no. "Only me, and I'm not talking."

"Then I think I wouldn't want to know." His answer clearly surprised him as much as it surprised me. But it had the ring of truth.

"Why?" I said.

He smiled then, his beautiful smile. "Because I'm happy, Amy. I'm really happy. I want to stay that way."

I thought about our son, asleep in the little nursery room next door, snug and warm inside the house I'd made into a loving home. I thought of Maddy, with all her bounce and vigor, the way she spilled out her exuberant love all over us and crept to me for solace when she was caught inside her stormy sorrows. And Davis, this good man who smelled like sandalwood over his own essential warm, male smell and who quietly made any room we were both in feel complete.

"I'm happy, too," I told him.

But he wasn't finished. "If Tate's lying, though, if it was more than one mistake, if it's still ongoing . . ." He trailed off, then swallowed. At last he said, "I didn't know last time. I should have. If betrayal of any kind is ongoing, then yes, I'd want to know."

In his words I felt the ghost of Laura, the woman I had banished from this room with cherrywood furniture, new paint, and my own scent. He sounded so hurt, remembering, that I scooted close, pressed myself against his side, resting my head on his broad, bare chest.

"I'm sorry," I said, and I was. I was sorry for a thousand things. Not least of which were all the things my silence allowed him to assume. No, all the things my words led him to assume. This was what Roux did, wasn't it? Davis was having one conversation, honest and truthful, and I was having at least three. I didn't want to be that kind of person, but it was in me. It was a part of me, and it was oh, so very useful at this moment.

He put his arm around me, still talking, pulling me in closer. "By the end she was drinking all day every day. Driving Maddy to kindergarten blasted. Toting Maddy's little friends around in the car, too. Every minute of her life, she was lying. She never said a word, but it was lying, all the same. God, yes, I wish I'd known.

I'd have gotten out much sooner." He shook his head. "It sounds like I'm off topic here, but it applies. You need to be sure what happened before you act. If Tate's telling the truth, then stay out of it. But if it's an ongoing lie, an affair, you have to tell Charlotte. So she can get out and not waste any more time."

I had my answers then. For every question. Even the one I'd actually asked, the one about my friend. Char was in real trouble, separate and distinct from mine. I'd let my worries about her husband slip off my radar, and that wasn't like me. I had her back, always.

But I had to know if Phillip was seeing Tate before I acted. If he was cheating, he wouldn't be too hard to catch. Smug, entitled Phillip would leave a trail. As soon as this ugly business between Roux and me was settled, I would devote myself to finding out. When he told Char he was golfing, I could call the course and ask for him, to see if he at least was where he said he was. I could keep up with Tate on social media, see if her absences matched his "boys' weekends."

The answer to my unstated question was even more clear.

Davis preferred the past in the past, so I would leave it there. Even though my lies were a living thing, they were not about him, or us. Not really. I was not actively betraying him, so that was that. Of course, he might not see it that way. His old hurts from Laura, they ran deep. I wouldn't risk it. Silence was my best, my only, choice.

Yet I couldn't simply hand the money to Roux. Not if I could help it. I'd done good with the first half of Nana's trust. I had put a little justice, that word that Roux had tried to use against me, back into the world. I needed to do good with the second half as well. It would be wrong to use it to save my own ass, to let Roux bask in unearned luxury.

That meant I had to find a third way out.

Roux had begun this as a game. She'd told me not to play. But I already was. I had to. More than that. I had to win.

It was an easy thing to say. *I have to beat her at her own game.* But I had never played before. I didn't even know all the rules, and she was a pro. It was as crazy as my challenging LeBron James to a driveway round of Horse, and yet I couldn't see another choice.

Also? I was pretty fucking good at it.

My past and my quiet, watchful nature combined to make me a natural. I'd seen through Roux, after all. She'd gambled, claiming to be Lolly Shipley without all the facts. God, if it had worked? I'd have given her anything. It was emotionally smart. But it had tipped her hand. Coming at me unprepared like that, plus the dingy house—I'd understood gut deep that she was under some external pressure. Money or time, she was short on one or both. I'd used that understanding to buy myself this night to decide. How much more rope would she give me if I pushed her?

Quite a bit, I thought. She only had the one great big red button. She wouldn't push it. Not as long as she believed she'd get my money in the end. The moment she understood that I was never going to pay, I had no doubt she'd wreck me, but in this gap I had some room to work.

I was up half the night, staring into the darkness, thinking while Davis slept deep and easy. I could hear Oliver through the baby monitor, sighing and shifting every now and again, but mostly sleeping sweetly, innocent.

I needed a plan that did not involve the police or an appeal to Roux's better nature. The first option ensured that all my secrets would come out, and as for the second—a better nature—Roux didn't seem to have one. At some point I shifted from waking to dreaming, falling into a fantasy world where Roux had simply disappeared. Mysteriously. Never to be seen again. I understood that this was on me. If she disappeared, it would be because I made it so.

I jerked awake, startled and sweating. Beside me Davis stirred briefly. I froze, waiting for sleep to reclaim him, my body stiff, my eyes staring wide into the darkness.

Disappearing Roux was a road I would not let myself go down. Not even in dreams.

I had once, long ago, taken a human life. I understood the kind of gap that created in the world. It was greater than the sum of its parts. I wouldn't purposefully create another absence, no matter what, I told myself. I didn't have the stomach for it. Roux was awful, and she deserved to be in prison, but she also had a child who clearly loved her, needed her.

Perhaps that was the key? Her human connections. For the first time, I caught a glimpse of a narrow path, a crevice I could maybe squeeze through between paying her and the truth. Every person has a soft spot.

Hers was Luca. Each time I brought him up, I felt a stillness in her. Motherhood was too powerful for even Roux to be immune to it. Oliver had caused a shift in me, waking me to depths of love I'd never suspected lived inside me. I'd loved Maddy and Davis before he came, but his arrival had deepened those loves. He'd been so small and sleepy, so fully in my care. His vulnerability in the face of the cold world made me understand how vulnerable Davis and Maddy were, too, and how very mine.

Mother love must be alive inside Roux, or her kid wouldn't be so . . . nice. As much as I hated Roux, I couldn't deny that Luca came across as a kid who'd been loved from birth on up. Not that she deserved some kind of medal for it. Every mammal protected its own babies, including rats and weasels. It was hardwired into the biology. Even my own mother, cold as she was, had once upon a time hired me a lawyer.

What if I could dig up some equal and opposing dirt on Roux? Something truly ugly, that could buy her silence sure as money could. I was willing to bet that Roux had dirty laundry—plenty—and every mother had a secret grown-up life apart from her kid. If I owned that, could I own her the same way she owned me? We could stare each other down, crouched over our big red buttons. Mutually assured destruction.

I felt a sparking of real hope. She was better at this than I was, more experienced, but I didn't have to win, after all. I only had to play down to a draw, get enough to make her walk away.

I needed two things: a secret and to know who she was hiding it from. I didn't know how to get the first thing, not yet, but I did have a line on the second. If I was willing.

They were here on business, Roux had said. She'd warned Luca not to get embedded. That meant that somewhere Luca had real friends. A father. Roux herself had claimed a husband more than once. I needed to find their home base. No sense threatening her with exposure if I had no one to expose her to. She could take Luca and vanish, then destroy my life from afar.

At least I knew where to start looking. In 1991 she'd lived in my neighborhood. She'd seen the wreck, or at least seen me stagger out on the driver's side. That meant she'd lived in one of the few houses that faced the woods at the T intersection where Rainway Street met the woods and the old dirt road.

I had to go back there. It was the last patch of earth I ever wanted to revisit, but I had to see which houses had windows that overlooked the sight of the wreck. The lots were large, so it couldn't be more than three or four. I'd find out who owned those houses back in 1991. I was pretty sure the county would keep records on that down at the courthouse. If not, there were other ways. People remembered things like that, so I would ask. I would find Roux's family.

It wasn't much, but it was something. An idea. A direction I could walk in. It was better than feeling helpless, and I thought I could get some sleep, even though right now my plan truly amounted to just three words:

Blackmail her back.

8

I GOT TO ROUX'S house half an hour before her deadline, feeling as if my stomach had been filled with bees. I was here to promise her the money and buy myself some room to maneuver. This morning, in the scant time between Maddy and Davis leaving and my meeting Char for our power walk, I'd called Boyce Skelton and instructed him to convert my investments into cash, just in case. I was going to play, but I could lose. I needed to be liquid, with all my options open.

Boyce had started in with all the same arguments he'd given me when I'd asked him to liquidate the first half, but I'd cut him off. I wasn't interested in taking life advice from Boyce Skelton. He hadn't exactly put me in this situation, but he hadn't helped. He'd sloppily given a criminal access to a computer containing my files, and the files of God-knew-how-many other clients.

He had paid, though, a little. On a hunch I asked him what kind of car he was driving these days. He fell silent, then mumbled something about its having been stolen. I pressed, asking what kind of car it had been. He described Roux's red convertible. Stolen my ass. Boyce was married. I was willing to bet that Roux, with her penchant for recording, had gotten more out of her time with Boyce than a peek at his files. I could hardly stand to talk to him long enough to get the wheels in motion. If I ended this with any of Nana's money left, I was damn well moving it to another firm.

While we talked, I put Roux's name in Google to see what the Internet might know. There were a few people on social-media sites with that name, but none of them were her. Only one was American, and she looked about thirteen. It was disappointing, but I supposed "black-mailers" were like the least likely professionals to join LinkedIn.

The door opened even as I was reaching for the bell. Had she been watching for me from behind the ugly blanket over the big picture window, as anxious as I was? I hoped so, even though I could not imagine Roux antsy. She seemed cool as a cat as she stepped outside, pulling the door closed loosely behind her. She wore another set of black Lycra gym clothes that showed every line of her honed body. My own clothes gave her pause, though.

"Is that a pool cover-up?" she asked, looking me up and down.

"It's a jacket," I said.

It was cousin to a jacket anyway, a lightweight, baggy thing that came down to midthigh. I peeled it off so she could see that underneath I had put on her game's re-quired uniform. Yoga pants, sheer and fitted, with a half tank that I wore as a jog bra and she'd wear as a shirt. I didn't want her hands all over me again. She twirled her finger in the air, and I spun slowly, feeling like her fun-house mirror image, shorter, squatter, thicker in the hips.

"Good. Good job. Now pass me that abomination," she said, holding her hand out for the jacket.

"Can we go in?" I asked.

I didn't like standing in the scant shade of her azaleas in what, truthfully, was underwear. Char was two doors down, and what would she think if she came outside and saw me playing strip-'n'-spin on the porch with this woman she so disliked?

"Hand it over," Roux insisted, so I did. She began feeling along the lining and then checking the pockets.

I waited, fidgeting, looking all around for passing neighbors.

Roux ignored me, pulling my phone out and making sure it was powered down.

"Now can we go in?" I asked again, glancing around, my arms crossed over my bra top.

Roux handed my things back. "You don't want Kanga to see us together. Is that it?"

Well, yes. That, too.

I downplayed it, shrugging my way into my jacket and repocketing my dead phone. "You went out of your way to make her feel jealous at book club. So."

Her voice shifted into a singsong chant. "Amy and Roux, sittin' in a tree, cheatin' on Char, and Phillip makes three. . . ." My eyes narrowed. Phillip makes three what? Cheaters? Had she connected Phillip and Tate? I'd promised myself that I would find out if Phillip was embroiled in a full-blown affair, and here was Roux, a professional at digging up secrets. She might already know, definitively. That was a topic worth exploring. But she was still talking, saying, "She's very small-town, your little friend. They're like that. Territorial," as if she and I were one thing and Charlotte was another. "Luca's in the den right now. We could slip off behind her back to a cheap motel? By which I mean a coffee shop."

I ignored that. "Does Luca not know? What you do for a living, I mean." I kept my voice as casual as I could.

She paused, her eyes sizing me up before she spoke. "Amy, did you come to play?" I saw it then. She *had* been antsy, waiting for me. She still was, and I thrilled to it, though I worked hard to keep it off my face. She honestly didn't know which way I was going to swing.

I decided not to answer directly. "This isn't a game, Roux. This is my life."

She steepled her fingers, and her smile went wolfish. "Everything is a game. Asking if you can use my job against me is a play. You think you can threaten to tell Luca. Make me back down."

I could feel a blush heating my cheeks, but I kept my chin up, met her eyes. "Maybe I'm trying to see if you have any shame."

That made her tilt her head, her eyes gone sharp and bright, like a bird catching a glimpse of something shiny.

"I really don't. And I shouldn't," she said. She stepped in just a little closer, but she wasn't trying to intimidate me, and it wasn't sexual. It was almost confiding, and I had the sense that whatever she said next, it would be true. "People do awful things, Amy. They have to pay for them. They want to pay, even. It's the only thing that will give them any peace. I make them pay me specifically, but it gets the job done. I'm practically a fuckin' priest. Why wouldn't Luca know? I'm not ashamed." She gave me that quirky, one-sided smile. "He has no idea that you're a client, though. I would think, since he's friendsies with that stepchild of yours, you'd prefer that."

I felt my lips tighten. "Of course I would."

I didn't want Luca to think of me as anything but Maddy's nice Monster. I found myself peering at Char's porch through the azaleas again. I couldn't help it.

Roux sighed and relented. "Let's go to the back patio. The privacy fence will live up to its name."

I followed her inside. Once again my eyes took a moment to adjust. It was a summery Florida fall day, but the gray blanket and low ceilings made this room instantly gloomy. The windows on the other side were bare of blinds or curtains, but between the screened-in porch, the trees, and the tall privacy fence, they didn't let in much natural light.

Luca was on the sofa wearing what looked like pajama pants with a T-shirt and a pair of bulky headphones. His long dark hair was still sleep-snarled. He was hunched forward toward the coffee table, tapping frantically at the keys of a shiny black laptop. On the screen a little soldier ran across a weird landscape, shooting monstrous bug things. Typical teenager. His mother had stepped onto the porch for three minutes and already he'd abandoned math or history for pixel murder. He looked up when we came back in, and his soldier got fragged.

"Crap!" he said, I thought because he was busted gaming during school hours, but he grinned and added. "You got me killed!"

"My bad," Roux said.

Luca pushed the headset down around his neck, looking eagerly back and forth between us. "Hey, Ms. Whey. So is it worked out?"

I blinked, confused. Roux stepped in smoothly.

"There's not a beginner scuba class scheduled until next month," Roux said, and that was true. She must have checked the website. His face fell, but she wasn't done. "Amy's going to teach you herself. One-on-one. No waiting."

"Really?" Luca said, which was exactly what I was thinking. Was she serious? It was so presumptuous, as if my time and expertise were in a bundle with my nana's money, and it all belonged to her. But Luca was looking at me, hopeful as a Labrador. I couldn't help but like Luca, especially when his cool reserve broke and he acted like the kid he was. "When do we start?"

I smiled, plastic. "We're talking about it."

"We're going to go sit on the patio," Roux said, giving his hair a fond tug as she passed.

"So you can get back to your schoolwork," I said, fixing him with universal mom eye. I couldn't help it. He laughed and pulled the headset on again, restarting his game.

Roux said, "He will. Don't worry." She paused then and said, as if it had only just occurred to her, "Where's your baby?"

"Lisa Fenton's watching him," I said.

I hadn't asked Char. I felt bad enough about the "headache." But Oliver made me soft, and I also didn't want him getting baby-whispered again. Not to mention the field trip I had planned as soon as Roux and I were done. I was going back to Waverly Place. My old house. That intersection. I couldn't take Oliver to that neighborhood, that road. It was too soaked in bad history.

"I'll grab us some water," Roux said.

She went past the stairs into the kitchen, leaving me

alone with Luca. He was deep into his game. I stayed where I was, searching the room with my eyes, trying to figure out what was Roux and what was rented.

I could pick out bits of her, her tastes so expensive that anything hers practically glowed in this room. A spectacular raw-silk dressing gown draped over the sofa. The computer Luca was using. It was big for a laptop, gleaming new, with a red dragon logo on the back of it. Did Roux use it as well as Luca? If I had ten minutes alone with it—

"Come on," Roux said, startling me.

I hadn't heard her bare feet padding in. She held up two curvy glass bottles of sparkling water with a French name. Nothing I'd ever heard of. Nothing I could pronounce. She was treating this meet as if it were a social call. I didn't want to sip a refreshing beverage, cozied up with Roux to discuss how she could best rob me like we were besties organizing a bake sale. I took the water anyway, made myself smile.

Only moments ago she'd spoken to me about being like a priest. I'd had the sense that for the first time I was face-to-face with Roux. Not some character she was playing to keep me off balance. The real thing. I wanted to see more of her. Needed to, if I was going to beat her. I followed her out onto the small screened porch.

Roux sat down on the love seat. It was part of a cheap set of outdoor furniture, made of plastic formed to mimic woodgrain, topped by mildewed cushions in a faded tropical print. I stayed standing, my unopened water in my hand.

She said, "This is the last real conversation we'll have until it's time for you to transfer the money."

"You're still worried I'm going to try to record you?"

NEVER HAVE I EVER   175

It occurred to me that she could be recording, and I should have thought of that already. Trying to think like her—like a criminal—was new. I needed to learn faster. I couldn't stay the fox in this hunt, let her have all the dogs and guns and horses. I gave her a tight smile. "What if I am? There could be a carful of FBI men a mile away with a directional mike pointed right at you."

She dismissed that with a wave. "Please. No way feds stepped in on this small-time BS that fast. It would be the local yokels. I know what they use here, and you're not wearing it. Not in those pants. I think you came to seal our deal, and I'm glad. It's the best choice. For you as well as me."

"For me?" I asked, and a little outrage leaked into my voice. I couldn't help it.

She nodded, serious, and this was her again. Roux. Not playing. Talking to me as if I were an equal. "I've seen your financial records, Amy. You blew half your wad setting up a foundation to pay off that poor schmo who went to prison for you. But it didn't fix you, did it?" She looked me right in the eye, speaking with conviction. "People think they can buy absolution at their leisure, or on someone else's dime. It doesn't work like that. You have to pay the universe."

My eyes narrowed. "You aren't the universe."

"I'm what the universe sent," she said, almost off-hand, but I had the feeling it was the most honest thing she'd ever said to me. She twisted the cap off her water.

Was this how she justified herself? But she had no idea how I'd felt or what I'd done, trying to pay for my mistakes. This was crap, and I told her so. "I paid off Tig's mortgage because I owed him. I don't owe you."

"No. You gave him exactly what you felt comfortable

giving, anonymously, in the way that suited you best," she said, and there was an edge of sorrow to it. It was as if she felt bad for me, but it didn't change what she had to do. She took a sip of water and then set the bottle down. "You enjoyed paying off his mortgage. It made you feel good. But this? This hurts. This feels unfair and random. That's the kind of paying the universe demands."

I had to ask. "And what's the universe going to do to you?"

She chuckled, and her walls came up. "Let's stay on topic."

"I'm not that obedient," I said. It felt good, to dig at her, trying to keep her real face in the room. "Seriously, I want to know. What do you think the universe will do to you for all the bad you're doing to me right now?"

She stopped smiling then, taking it seriously. Her eyes on me were very cool. "I've prepaid, bitch," she said, and then she brushed her hands together briskly, done with honesty and metaphysics both. I could tell that she believed it, though, that she had prepaid. Good. It hinted at a darkness in her own past. That darkness, her own worst thing, was what I had to find. "Sit. Let's get down to it."

A puff of mildewed air escaped as I took the sagging chair catty-corner to her. I set my unopened water down on the low table so I could cross my arms. I needed to curl my body into a smaller shape, to feel my own warmth.

"How do I know you won't come back? What's to stop you from bleeding me forever?"

Roux scoffed, and now she was insouciant book-club Roux again. "What would I come back for? Your signature necklaces from Chico's? Your copper-bottom pans? Pay me and what you'll have left is plain old middle-class equity. That shit won't call me or attract anyone else like me. Once you pay me, something magic happens. You become a regular lady, with no secret money, no secret plans. You'll even have bought the right to keep pretending you have no secrets." Her tone was light, condescending, even. Like she was explaining to a toddler how to use a spoon. Even so, her words felt as invasive as her hands had felt last time, when they'd gone rummaging around my body and my baby. She was watching my face, closely, and now she gave a sly little smile. "Speaking of secrets? Mine aren't on that computer."

"What computer?" I said, to cover my blush.

"Luca's. You were ogling it inside," Roux said. I hadn't even realized how hard I'd been staring at the computer, and, sweet God, she didn't miss a trick. "It's strictly his. We homeschool, I told you. If you don't believe me, stick your head in the door, ask if you can borrow it. You can read his civics paper. Maybe do some algebra."

"Or play shooters during school time?" I said, tilting my chin up, but I could feel heat flood my cheeks. I had to be better at this. I had to get better, fast. But how? Most of my lies, my whole life long, had been lies of omission, keeping silent when I should have spoken. I needed to learn to lie like Roux did, with my words and my body language, maybe even my thoughts. Yesterday had gone better, when I'd been running on instinct and adrenaline. Now I was overthinking it. I made myself look her right in the eye, and I said a thing I hoped I didn't mean. "I don't care about the computer. I thought everything through, and I don't see an alternative. I can't go to jail. I can't leave my baby. I'll give you the money."

It came out so plain, so resigned, that even I believed me. I wanted to keep Roux focused on her legal threat, as if that were the thing that scared me most. I had to keep her believing she had read me right, that she truly owned the worst I'd ever done. So I gave her this partial truth, and something in my demeanor must have telegraphed as honesty, because she leaned back, smiling.

"When can we do the transfer?"

"It's a trust. It'll take a couple of weeks to dissolve it," I said, lying on instinct again. I was surprised she'd asked. It seemed like something she would know. But I needed time, and she'd just handed me an opening to buy some.

Her eyes kindled, and she leaned forward, bracing her forearms on her knees. "Goddamn it, Amy! You're playing."

"I'm not," I said, letting my anger cover my dismay. "There's all these stipulations—"

She was laughing outright now, and I felt my voice fade to nothing.

"Jesus, you are all the way in. And you're pretty good. You snapped right to that. But you are not in your league, kid. I know my way around an investment account. There are no restrictions anymore. Not since you turned thirty-five. You can get it liquid in three days."

My face had gone so hot I was likely cherry-colored. She'd laid a trap to see if I was as resigned as I seemed, and I'd gamboled right into it, dumb as a fawn.

She threw her head back and ran her hands through her hair, shaking it out. "You're going to make me work for it, aren't you." Not a question. "We'll do the transfer Friday."

I made myself meet her eyes. "You're off by a little. Liquidating takes three full business days. I won't have it until Monday."

She leaned forward, agitated, studying my face again. Now her cheeks flushed, too, but with temper.

"Bullshit," she said.

I pulled my phone out of my pocket. "You want to see the e-mail confirmation?"

She regarded me with hooded eyes. "Yes. Yes, I do."

We sat in uncomfortable silence while it booted, Roux leaning forward, tension in her body. I navigated to my e-mail. Boyce had sent one, exactly as I'd requested. Roux scanned it. It was only a few lines long, Boyce confirming he was liquidating my account and estimating that it should yield just over two hundred forty thousand, after fees and taxes. Lastly the e-mail said the funds would be available on Monday, by noon. What the e-mail didn't say was that I'd instructed him to hold off on starting the process until after noon today, to buy myself the weekend. Roux took it at face value, though. She lost her temper.

"You should have fucking done this yesterday."

I felt my pulse quicken. I'd gotten something past her.

I hit back. "You should have told me you were on a deadline."

Instantly she dialed it down. Her body relaxed, softening, but too quickly. I could see it was an act of will.

"My rental on this place is up on Sunday," she said.

That might be true, but it hardly explained her overreaction. Roux had stumbled. Just a little, while I'd been crashing and flailing around like a bull moose. But still. Now I knew that she was on a timeline, and I'd learned it by reading her, same as she'd been reading me. All my years of lying by omission, lying so deep that I even believed me, had schooled me in dishonesty. I knew it when I saw it. Perhaps I wasn't as far out of my league as she believed.

"Gee, sorry," I said, using sarcasm to cover my excitement. Now I knew she had a deadline, some threat she had to counter or avoid. Could I find it? Could I speed it up? "I guess you'll have to shell out. Buy yourself a few more days in paradise."

She shook her head, so very casual, almost perfect, but I could see a hint of effort at the edges on her smile. "Oh, don't worry about it. I'm not the kind of woman who pays her own rent." That was interesting as well. Did she have a lover, or a friend, or an accomplice who paid for the house? Maybe the mysterious absent husband. He or she could be a soft place in her armor, just like Luca. Or it could be another of her "clients," someone caught in her net, like me. A possible ally against her.

She stood up, paced away a few steps, staring through the screen out at the yard. It was unkempt, a balding patch of grass with a lot of hard, dark earth showing. No flower beds, just more overgrown azaleas near the windows and a stand of tall loblolly pines near the far end. When she finally turned back, her anger had been packed away. But it was still there, inside her. I could see it in the lines of her, even as she made her voice sound casual and calm. "Monday, then. On the bright side, you can take Luca for his open-water dives over the weekend. I thought you'd only have time for the coursework and the pool dives."

I crossed my arms even tighter.

"So you want a quarter mil and free scuba lessons for your kid?" It seemed so petty, as if she were robbing me and then putting out a tip jar. "Would you like anything else of mine? A stick of gum? A kidney?"

That made her laugh. "I wish I didn't like you," she said. "To be honest, Amy, I just want you busy. You get ideas. Idle hands and all that. Getting Luca certified will eat your time. Plus, he really wants to do it."

"We can do the classroom work. I have the DVD, and I can get him a book and administer the tests." I was negotiating. If we did the full course, I wouldn't just be busy. I'd be watched. "I can't do his contained-water dives. The pool schedule at the shop fills up weeks in advance."

This was true, but it didn't faze her. "Borrow Tate's pool."

That made me almost laugh. "Have you met Tate? She's not going to do me any favors."

"I'll ask. She likes me," Roux said, smiling blandly.

That was patently untrue. Tate was a natural queen bee; she didn't like beautiful women. I bit my lip. Unless Roux had dirt on Tate? Was my possible ally Tate Bonasco, of all people? If so, then my gut was right; Tate was having an actual affair with Phillip. Because what else could Roux's leverage be? I didn't want to get distracted, but I had promised myself I would find out, for Char's sake.

"What do you have on Tate?" I asked.

The question caught her off guard. I saw surprise

flash across her face. I didn't think she'd expected me to be so blatant.

"Tate doesn't owe me anything," Roux said, but that was not an answer.

"Neither do I. I owe 'the universe.' Isn't that what you said? Why is Tate going to loan the universe her pool?"

"Touché!" Roux said, almost admiringly, and that weird head tilt was back. Birdlike, or maybe reptilian. She smiled, and it was genuine. She actually did like me, I thought, in her odd, carnivorous way. If we'd met in California, I would have liked her back. Now she leaned in, confiding. "I'll say this—it's not karma with Tate. It's just psychology. Tate thinks she has a nicer house than me, what with the pool and that brand-new IKEA dining set." Her voice dripped disdain, but it was wholly aimed at Tate—and possibly most of the other women in our neighborhood. I had the sense that I was outside it. She was speaking to me almost as a peer. "She's competitive, especially with other women, so she'll like it that I have to ask for a favor. I'll make it sound as if I'm coming, too. She wants me to see her house, her things, and compare them with this shit here. She wants a win with me, and so far she's zero for try-hard."

That sounded like the Tate I knew. It didn't let Phillip off the hook, though. Roux might be covering for Tate exactly because Tate was a client, which left me still on the fence about what, if anything, I should say to Charlotte. It also sounded as if Roux would not come with Luca for lessons. I didn't ask, though. It might be bait, like when she'd asked me how long it would take to liquidate the money. I wasn't going to snap fast at any opening she dangled. I was learning.

"Fine," I said, flip as I could. Maybe I could make

it work for me—get Luca talking about his mother. He might let something useful slip. "He can start the book work today. Can you line up Tate's pool for tomorrow and Friday? Then Saturday and Sunday, we'll drive over to the jetties for his open-water dives." Maddy was going to be ecstatic about scuba all weekend with Luca, so that was a teeny upside.

Roux was shaking her head, though. "No jetties. Book us on a boat. You have some prime wrecks around here. I love a wreck dive."

She grinned at the face I made. Not what I wanted, to spend the last of my precious days out on the ocean with her, but I had no better option at this moment.

"Fine," I said again.

"After this, when our paths cross, we won't discuss our arrangement. Even when we're alone. We'll chat about casserole recipes that use those yummy cans of soup, or whatever passes for banter around here. Then Monday meet me here at noon. You'll transfer the funds to an account I give you, and I'll be gone. Really gone. Won't that be nice?" Roux asked, stretching, lithe and pleased in her body at the thought of all my money. She straightened, leaned in again, and captured my gaze. "Or you screw with me. And I blow your life and this town, easy as I blew your lawyer."

"Fine," I said. It was starting to feel like the only word I knew.

"I'll go tell Luca to get ready. You can take him with you."

I shook my head. I had plans.

"I need to go to Divers Down. I have to borrow some equipment," I told her. It was even true. Like most scuba junkies, I had a walk-in closet's worth of backup dive gear, but I needed to pick up full tanks and a new open-water book with blank quizzes. Plus, every wet suit and BCD I had at home was cut for women.

She sized me up, and then she came to a decision. "Okay. I'll send him your way in an hour or so."

I stood, keeping my shoulders tense so I didn't tele-graph relief. I couldn't let her see how much I wanted this stolen hour. She was taking me seriously now; twice today she'd even come close to confiding in me. She'd dropped her provocateur's mask, as if I were her peer. I threw a final glance over my shoulder, trying to look nervous and resigned. I needed her to underestimate me. I hoped she was. If she was estimating me exactly right, then I was screwed.

I went home, got my Subaru, and headed out of the neighborhood. If I was really going to do this thing she called playing and I called fighting for my life, I had to go to Waverly Place. I pointed my car north, away from Divers Down, away from the ocean, driving myself di-rectly toward my own long-buried past.

9

TIME FELT AUDIBLE, TANGIBLE, counted in the pound and pulse of my own heart. Five days to learn how to play Roux's game. Five days to find a way to win.

It felt surreal to see this neighborhood again. I'd been back in town for close to seven years now without once going near it. It was a carefully curated blank spot on the map, present but unexamined. Only twenty minutes from my current neighborhood, yet I felt I was driving toward some dark and distant made-up place, dystopian and bleak.

The sign was the same, scrolling metal words hung on a wrought-iron gate, purely decorative, permanently open. When I was a teenager, Waverly Place was the "it" neighborhood, but it had aged. The houses were large and probably still overpriced, but the wealthiest people in town now were building on prime lots overlooking the bluffs.

I crossed into the neighborhood itself, and though years had passed, it all felt so familiar. I recognized houses where other Brighton kids had lived or I had babysat, and the carpool pickup spot on Maple Drive.

Maple intersected with my own old street, Clearwater. I kept my gaze deliberately forward as I crossed over. My parents' former house was on this block, and two blocks farther on would be the Shipley home. I had no desire to see what trees were still standing or if the paint colors had changed. I didn't want to be here at all.

I drove directly back to Rainway Street, though I almost went right past it. I was looking for the back of the neighborhood, but the woods were gone. Rainway had houses on both sides now. The newer ones were smaller and more homogeneous, brick-fronted with an array of coordinating pastel colors on the HardiePlank sides.

I turned onto Rainway, and there was my old classmate Shelley Gast's house. That put me two blocks down from where the dirt road had once run. I could feel myself getting close. It was like driving into a vortex, being pulled toward a dark center. The air became sharper, more electrical, as if the place itself had sentience and judgment. All the little blond hairs on my forearms rose, and my hands prickled on the wheel, as if they had gone to sleep. I stopped exactly on the spot, in front of what had been Mr. Pratt's house, a white Colonial perched up high on a hill.

When Tig and I came roaring out of the woods in the Ambassador, Mrs. Shipley's little car had skidded all the way across the street and partway up the slope, tearing gashes in Mr. Pratt's manicured grass. The crash had awakened both the Pratts. Mr. Pratt was the one who'd called the police.

I got out of my Subaru, my legs shaking so hard I wasn't sure they'd hold me. I realized I was hungry. So hungry. I hadn't eaten yet today, and I had mostly pushed last night's dinner around my plate. Once I noticed the feeling, it became huge, almost omnipresent. To be this savagely hungry felt almost righteous, a dark sensation close to pleasure. It made me remember I deserved to be this empty.

I closed my eyes, made myself breathe slowly. I was not that girl, and I was here on business.

I looked around. On the old side of Rainway, the lots were much larger. To the right of the Pratt house, the hill subsided. I could see the windows of just three more houses, which meant only these four had a clear view of this spot.

The Pratts had already been quite elderly at the time. Even their grandkids had been grown then, so Roux was not a Pratt. The house next door to them had been for sale, I remembered. Empty.

Could Roux have been a squatter? Not a child of privilege at all but a runaway, ten or twelve years old, camped out in the empty house?

It didn't ring true. It wasn't that kind of neighborhood. Waverly Place houses had alarm systems, plus a private security company drove around checking for interlopers.

The next house was Jesse Cannon's old place; he'd been a Brighton kid, the youngest of three boys. No sisters. That left one house, sand-colored brick with a roofline that rose into three peaks.

I had no idea who had lived there back in 1991. I stared at the windows, and they stared back like empty eyes. It was the last house on the block. After it, Rainway curved.

I walked close enough to read the numbers on the stone mailbox: 226. I'd have to call my local lawyer, the one who'd long ago worked with Boyce to set up the bogus foundation that had paid off Tig Simms. He could dig through the records at the courthouse and find out who'd owned the place in 1991. I had to get to Divers Down and then pick up my baby. I didn't want to keep Luca waiting so long that it became suspicious.

Still, I lingered by the mailbox. Why not simply ask? My stomach growled audibly inside me, like an animal. There was no harm in asking.

I climbed the steps to the porch and rang the bell. It pealed out Westminster Quarters, fronting like Big Ben. My mother had installed a bell like that, grand and clear, in the Boston house.

A woman came to the door. She was older than I was, tricked out in the kind of all-white resort gear that costs more than a night at a really good resort. She was as expensive-looking as her clothes, ash-blond highlights concealing any hint of gray, her face lightly and expertly made up. Like Roux, she'd had some work done, but she was older and hers was showing. The plump skin of her cheeks and forehead didn't match her neck.

"Yes," she said, eyebrows arched, pre-impatient, as if I were holding out a booklet about hell or vacuum cleaners. Waverly wasn't the kind of neighborhood that tolerated door-to-door anything.

"Sorry to bother you, and when I'm such a mess," I said. I touched my hair, apologetically. "I just came from yoga. But I was passing by and . . . well, I grew up here. I was trying to find my house. It's so confusing, with all the new builds."

"You grew up on this street," she said with a healthy amount of skepticism.

My old Subaru, visible behind me on the road, was surely not helping, and neither was my baggy jacket. It did look like a pool cover-up, damn Roux for being right.

"Yes. Near Shelley Gast's place. Shelley and I went to Brighton together. If I could find her house, I'm sure I could get to mine. I walked that route a million times when I was a kid."

Her face cleared. "Oh, we knew the Gasts. Lovely family. They moved to be closer to the grandkids. You aren't far off. Go that way, maybe ten houses down?" She pointed back the way I'd come.

"Thank you!" I said. "How long have you lived here? Did you know my parents? The Dennings?"

"I don't know that name, no," she said. "But we've only been here fifteen years."

"Yes, they'd moved away by then," I said, perky. "It's strange, but I don't remember this house at all. Who did you buy it from?"

"No one," she said, and chuckled at my blank expression. "We built it. This was an empty lot. No wonder you're confused, between our place and Shantytown across the street."

I did my best to give her a sympathetic look. Poor her, beset by climbers who could only afford homes in the high six figures.

"I can't believe the woods are gone," I said. It was the only sympathetic thing I could say that was true. "Thanks for the directions."

I walked back toward my Subaru. This house hadn't even existed, and I'd ruled out the others. So where had Roux been standing?

She'd seen the crash. She'd described it, on the day she'd come to wring a confession out of me. She'd asked me if I remembered the sounds, the smells. . . . I stopped dead in the middle of the road.

Those things were the same in all car crashes.

She'd claimed she witnessed the wreck when she was pretending to be Lolly Shipley.

She'd never said she saw it from a window. That was my assumption. She'd gone along with it. But what had she known, really, that I had not prompted?

She knew my maiden name. Knew my history. Knew about the accident. That I had money. That I had so much guilt I'd already given tons of it away.

She'd sought Boyce out, in fact, *because* she knew my story. If she wasn't a witness, then how had she known all that? Most especially, how had she known that I was driving?

When I asked that question, it got simple. Because the list of people who knew that I'd been behind the wheel was very short.

Me, but silence had long been my specialty.

My mother, but she had the knowledge buried so deep that she did not admit it even to herself. I knew exactly how that worked.

"Shit," I said out loud, because there was only one more person.

Only one person alive who could have sold me out to Roux.

Tig. Fucking. Simms.

10

I DROVE TO DIVERS Down to pick up wet suits and air tanks. Then I had to go straight home, and yet every molecule in me yearned west, bending toward Tig Simms. Anxiety came in waves, and at the crest of each I was sure that Tig was in on it. More than in. The orchestrator. He was Roux's mystery husband, Luca's father, and the whole plan had been his from the start.

But if this was true, then he had to know that I'd paid off his mortgage. Why send Roux? He could have come to me himself, said, *Do you really think that was all that three years of my life were worth? Write another check.*

Maybe because this hurt more. If hurting me mattered, then they'd done a gonzo job. This hurt like hell. But when I put his three incarcerated years in terms of Oliver, in terms of losing that time myself, I deserved it.

Then the wave would pass, and hope would swell behind it. I would be suddenly, equally sure that Roux was using him. Tig was her unwitting pawn. He would know things about her—her maiden name, her home base, more of her "clients"—that could help me. Assuming he had any desire to help me.

But why would he? I would ask, and anxiety would rise again.

It was an unceasing, churning cycle, but I couldn't go to Tig and end it. I had to retrieve Oliver, meet Luca, keep Roux happy and complacent. She'd been smart to book my time up, keep me watched and busy.

As I pulled in to my driveway, I saw Luca already sitting on my front porch steps like an orphan, staring deep into the mysteries of his cell phone, wearing his expensive wireless headphones.

I made myself smile and call to him, "Hey, Luca," in a normal voice. To him I was only Maddy's nice Monster, doing him a favor, not one of his mother's "clients," paying the universe for all the bad I'd put into the world.

He must have heard me over his music, because he looked up and turned the beam of his white smile on me. It was so spectacular that my breath caught. When I was fifteen, what would I have done to get a boy this beautiful to make that smile for me? Anything. That was the answer, and my heart quailed for Maddy. Luca hurried toward me with unabashed excitement, pushing the headphones down around his neck.

"Hey, Ms. Whey. This is *so* cool. Thank you!" he said, sounding genuinely grateful.

I planted him on my keeping-room sofa with some OJ and the open-water textbook. He got to it, studying, and the right way, too. Each chapter had learning objectives in the form of questions at the front, and he was underlining the answers as he came to them. He didn't even put headphones on, giving the book his whole attention.

I kept catching myself staring at the kid, seeking Tig in the straight lines of his nose, his wide, full mouth, his chiseled jawline. I couldn't see it.

Which meant exactly nothing. Genes were funny things, and anyway, Tig could be Roux's husband whether Luca was his child or not. He could just as easily be her business partner. Or her patsy. Watching Luca, I wished I had a textbook, too. *The DIYer's Guide to Blackmailers. Machiavelli for Dummies.* Something that would help me figure out Tig's motives. The only way to know for sure was to go to him. Ask him myself.

The hours ate themselves. Roux did not check up on me, perhaps too busy with some wretched business of her own. Luca read the first two sections and passed the quizzes before Maddy got home. The two of them went bounding downstairs to "hang," whatever that meant. Hopefully nothing horizontal.

I made sure that the basement door was open, and after half an hour I toted down Cokes and some disingenuous sliced apples. I was reassured to find them sitting innocently side by side at the computer, watching something goofy on YouTube. Luca was wholly absorbed by the screen, but Maddy was watching him watching. My girl was headed for a heartbreak, but hopefully a small one. So far it looked like an unrequited crush, and its object would be gone too fast to leave a large mark. I hoped. Meanwhile its object had me stuck inside my house.

I had to steal some time tomorrow. Roux hadn't left me much room, but I thought I might find some at the starting edge of day.

While the kids were downstairs, I practiced lying in the master-bathroom mirror. To beat Roux I had to do more than lie with silence, more even than lying with my mouth. I needed whole-body dishonesty, deception folded into my smiles and the way I manually kept my shoulders loose and my hands still.

Over dinner I tried the lines I'd practiced, telling
Davis and Maddy that I'd been asked to sub in on an
early-morning dive class for a sick coworker. Not a boat
trip, I told them, just a walk-in at the beach reef. I'd
be home by nine, plenty of time for Davis to make his
nine-thirty class and to meet Char for our walk. I even
ate like a liar, as if I enjoyed the way my good meat loaf
clumped, thick as clay, in my dry mouth.

They believed me. So easily it scared me.

I was good at this. Too good. At bedtime Davis had
no questions about what was bothering me or the dive
I'd purely invented. I lay awake for a long time after he
fell asleep. I felt sick with guilt, and I was glad of it.
Roux, in my position, would sleep as sweetly as Oliver.
She was making me a better liar, but she couldn't make
me like it.

By four I was up, layering a light cotton dress over
a flowery tankini, dressed as if I really were heading
to a dive. Even my clothes were lies, and worse, I was
sneaking out to meet Tig Simms. Again. The last time
I'd done this, it had ended so, so poorly. That thought
nearly shut me down.

Before the sun rose, I was close enough to Mobile Bay
to smell the salt. I wished I could keep driving, straight
in and under. Down where it was quiet and blue and no
one knew my name. Seven years ago I'd started down
this highway so many times. At first I couldn't even
make it out of Florida. As the weeks passed, I'd pushed
closer, but I'd never once gotten past the Baldwin Beach
exit. There had been a quarter century's worth of shame
blocking my way.

This time? I gunned it, racing toward Restoration

Garage with my foot heavy on the gas, though I had no idea what I would find. I couldn't let the complicated swamp of feelings that were choking me slow me down.

Restoration was on a quiet county road, a long, low building covered in green corrugated metal siding. There was a chain-link fence running all the way around it, with a roll of barbed wire at the top. It had a gate with a keypad, but I didn't know the code, and it was dark inside.

Tig's house was on the property, too. I remembered that from when I'd paid off his mortgage. It was a small, red brick ranch outside the fence. I followed a fork in the gravel drive down to it. An old Mustang was parked in front, a low-slung beast of a car, deep blue and gleaming. I parked behind it.

The house had no porch and no awning, just a concrete pad, and no lights were on. I crossed the lawn, wet with morning dew, and though the air was warm and humid, I was shivering. The back of my throat felt sour with remembered wine. I'd imagined coming to this very place so many times, but not under these circumstances. Never in this mood. The shame and sorrow I expected—deserved—were present, but laid over with a thousand other feelings.

I lifted a shaking hand to press the doorbell, and it chimed obligingly. I waited, but the house stayed dark and silent. The Tig I'd known was a night person, but how much of that Tig was left? As a kid he'd stayed up late, sometimes all night, especially if the moon was full. Those were the nights he'd come to ping rocks off my window, whisper-calling up, *I need a pork chop.* Right now the moon was a fat disk hung low in the lightening sky, barely on the wane. A sliver was missing from its edge. Did a moon this full still make him hungry, steal his rest? He could be out now, roaming.

I pressed it again. Twice. After thirty seconds I banged on the door itself, and a light came on. My hands dropped and began twisting together in front of me. I had to press them together to make them stop.

I thought, perhaps foolishly, that all I needed was to see him and I would know. A quarter of a century had passed, but there was no love like first love. I'd lost a thousand hours studying his face, tracing its planes and angles. I knew what every muted feeling looked like as it crossed his features. If he'd sent her, then his deep green eyes would narrow, the lids pulling up from the bottom. He would press his lips together. His thumbs would worry at his knuckles.

And if he hadn't, what face would he make? What would he feel when he saw me on his porch?

This I could not imagine.

I could hear footsteps padding toward me. Closer and closer. I think I stopped breathing. The door swung open, creaking loud on its hinges.

He was still in the process of pulling on a shirt, and I caught a glimpse of a tattoo as the cloth dropped over his abdomen. It was a plain white tee, the kind of thing Davis would only wear under a button-down. Tig was still wire thin, so his ancient pajama bottoms rode low, hanging off his hip bones. They were banana-colored, covered in tiny cartoon monkeys, too silly for the occasion. His familiar face was creased with sleep. His hair was the same, a halo of crazy corkscrews shooting out in all directions. The light behind him caught the bronze, and I saw there was some silver in it now, too.

He scrubbed at his eyes, then met my gaze.

There was nothing there. Not even irritation at being jerked from sleep. Just a pleasant, mild politeness.

"Gate stuck again, or did you forget the code?" he asked, then blinked at me, as if trying to remember my name. "Do you— I'm sorry. It's really early. Do you have a bay here?"

He didn't know me. Not at all.

"Tig," I said, and stopped. I just looked at him, helpless.

He blinked at the sound of my voice. It was like watching him wake up again.

"Smiff?" he said at last. "Smiffy, is that you?"

I tilted my chin up. "Hey."

He shook his head, a little disbelieving, or maybe shaking the last sleep away. Then he stepped to me, so fast it caught me off guard. My hands came up, defensive, but he bowled into me, wrapping his arms around me, squeezing me so tight. My own arms were trapped between us, and I thought he might be laughing. I snaked them out, wound them tight around his body. He lifted me up off the ground for a second, my feet dangling, then bent, still holding me, until I touched down. My face was pressed into his chest, and he smelled the same, exactly like Tig, a little pot smoke and a little copper in his tang.

"Shit, Smiffy. Look at you. What, you need a waffle?" he said into my hair. Just as if it were a thousand years ago and we'd been up all night rocking it as Ragweed. As if dawn were nigh and we were played out and hungry and had school in half an hour.

In his arms I understood how desperately I wanted to believe that he was not in league with her. Surely if I were his mark, he would have recognized me? He couldn't be working with her. I wanted it to be true so badly I didn't trust myself.

"No, I'm good," I said. My voice came out as creaky as his door.

Finally he pushed me back, arm's length, his eyes searching my face like he was hungry for the sight of me. "Jesus. You still look just like you."

I shook my head, old shames at war inside me. "I do not. I'm a couple of decades older. And there's a hundred pounds or so less of me."

"Yeah, but you still—" He stopped, seeking the words. "I don't know how to say it. You look like you. You're you." He grinned, as if this were a good thing, hands still so warm on my shoulders, staring at me so long and with such pleasure that it almost got weird. He felt it, too. He must have, because he dropped his hands, laughing, and said, "Shit, come in. I shoulda— I'm sorry. I was asleep. You want some coffee? I need coffee."

He swung the door open wide, but I stayed where I was, eyes welled up, shaking so hard I was shocked my teeth weren't chattering.

"Why are you happy to see me?" I asked.

He blinked, shook his head. "Aw, Smiff. I've wanted to see you for a long, long time. So bad. I should have come to you. I know that. It was on me. Please, come in."

He led me into a little living room, and it was a very Tig space. The Tig of old. Messy but not dirty, with books everywhere, double-stuffed into built-in shelves and in tall stacks near the fireplace and the couch. A Leatherman sat on a short stack of *National Geographic*s, sharing the coffee table with a water pipe and two more books, both open facedown to keep their place. A single lamp gave off a mellow, golden glow. The sofa and a couple of chairs were crammed into half the room to accommodate a drum kit, two big amps and a baby one, and five guitar stands. The one on the end held Tig's ancient Fender. I would have known it anywhere.

The kitchen was a small, dark square on the other side, separated from the den by a breakfast bar. Tig went around it, not bothering to turn more lights on, and I slid onto a stool. A Bunn coffeemaker waited on the counter with a plastic pitcher full of water, premeasured, right beside it. He poured the water, and within a couple of seconds coffee started streaming through.

"You're serious about it, huh?" I'd only seen that kind of coffee machine in diners, never in someone's house.

"Cut me. I bleed black," he said.

Looking around, I didn't think any woman lived here, least of all Roux, with her silk dressing gowns and Picasso sketches. She might go slumming here, like she was at the Sprite House, but nothing I could see was hers.

I checked his hands. No wedding ring. His knuckles were smudged with ink or grease. He saw me looking and grinned, then came close and fisted them for me, holding them up so I could see the remains of old, old tattoos. The jailhouse kind, and I felt my throat get thick. Simple block letters, one per finger, showed faintly on his fists. L O V E, his right hand said. I had to squint to read the left one.

"'Love . . . Cake'?" I said, smiling in spite of all the history in the room.

"Yeah. It's a joke. You know, like how bad-ass men get 'Love/Hate' tats on their hands."

"But you got 'Love/Cake'?"

"I was seventeen. It seemed funny at the time," he said, sheepish, but then he added, "And I didn't want my body to say hate."

I liked that. Too much to say so. I dropped my gaze.

He turned back and opened up a cupboard. It was piled with dishes, all mismatched shapes and colors. The Bunn was already finished, so he pulled out two random mugs and filled them.

"You still take cream and sugar?" he asked. "I have milk. I think."

"Black's good," I said. I hadn't had a whole cup of coffee in a year and a half, thanks to Oliver. Caffeine made him so hyper. But right now that life seemed far away.

He came around the bar with our mugs. His had a map of the world curved around it. Mine said WORLD'S BEST DAD.

"You have kids?" I asked, taking it.

"Not that I know of." It was a very Tig Simms answer. "You?"

"Two," I said. "My stepdaughter, Madison, is fifteen, and about eight months ago I had a baby. Boy. Oliver."

"Eight months? Shit, you do look good," he said, and that was all.

"Thanks."

I liked that my weight loss didn't seem to be that big a deal for him. Anyone else, we'd be talking about it still. It had happened over and over as my body changed in Boston. People would express amazement, delight, and ask how I was doing it. I never told the truth. Never said, *I eat less than five hundred calories a day, I throw most of that up, and then I take a laxative.* I'd murmur something about walking more, and they would overpraise me, acting as if I were beating cancer. Tig didn't do any of that. He was simply glad to see me.

He said, "Gimme a sec, okay? I just woke up."

He set our coffees on the bar and disappeared into the back of the house. I could hear water running.

I took a sip of mine. Now that I was here, time felt different. As if I'd driven backward through it, back to find myself fifteen again, landing in a place where Tig and I were friends. Early days, before it all went south. As if we had yet to break anything that could not be mended.

I ought to get up while he was gone and search his house for signs of Roux. But now that I'd seen him, it was very hard to treat him like a criminal. I didn't want to ask about Roux, or blackmail, or even if he'd hated me for a time, in spite of what his hands said. Not just yet.

In the wake of his surprising joy to see me, what I wanted to know most was why he'd kissed me, all those years ago. Pity and chemicals, I'd thought then, because my mother had taught me that fat girls don't get kissed or touched or loved. I did not believe that anymore. I'd used food to hurt my body in a lot of ways over the years; when I was ninety-eight pounds, I'd felt as unworthy of love as I had when I was over two hundred.

Now I'd been at relative peace inside my body for long enough to wonder, had he loved me?

I should have gone back to that old mattress when he asked. We might have kissed more, or talked eye to eye about drunken, silly things, or slept off our high, side by side.

If only we had.

I could see it, like another world. One where Mrs.

Shipley drove in circles until her fussy baby fell asleep and then they all went safely home. I would be an entirely different Amy. My family wouldn't have moved to Boston. Tig and I would have finished high school together, gone off to different colleges, lost touch. Or maybe not. We might have stayed friends. We'd both have been home summers. We might have kept kissing, on and off, over the years. Maybe now I would be raising curly-headed babies in a house like this, near a garage. Or maybe he would be designing car engines for Lexus and I would be studying literature in France. I had no way to see how our lives might have unfolded. I could only see the things that would not be.

In that world I never met Charlotte. She never brought me Davis. He and Maddy picked someone else. And Oliver? He never came to be.

I wouldn't wish Oliver away for anything. Not on the earth or off it. And yet I still wanted to know. Had Tig loved me then, a little?

He came back, now in jeans and a Restoration logo shirt. He sat down on the second stool, angling to face me. The space was so small our knees touched, and I could smell the new mint on his breath.

"I want to say things to you," Tig said. He had always been the chatty one in our old friendship. The idea guy, waving his hands around for emphasis and punctuation.

"Me, too," I said. "I want to say a lot of things."

This close, even in the dim, warm glow of the single lamp, I could see all the ways he'd gotten older. There were deep scores on both his cheeks, like parentheses around his mouth, and creases at the corners of his eyes. I hoped they meant that he'd smiled a lot since I'd seen him. His teeth were the same, with that little overlap on both sides where his canines tilted in.

"Why'd you pay my mortgage off?" he asked.

The question didn't surprise me. Roux knew I had paid it off, and if she'd learned about my past through him, of course he knew, too. They had to be connected. Somehow.

"I owed you," I said simply. "When did you know it was me?"

He shook his head. "Not at first. I was too damn happy to question it, you know? I was gonna lose the place, and then pow. Magic happened. Who looks a gift grant in the mouth? A few weeks later, these guys I jam with were over, and we got all Auld Lang Syne-y. Playing Pixies. 'Monkey Gone to Heaven.' God, you loved that song."

"I remember," I said.

"So I'm singing it, right, and you were in my head. You always are when we play Pixies. I thought, *Oh. It was Smiffy*. Had to be. You were my only rich friend, ever, and there's no such thing as a bunch of free money that comes looking for you. You have to hunt that shit down. I wanted to see you then. I wanted to thank you. Ask you why you did it."

Now he really had surprised me. Of course he knew why I'd helped him. Was he lying? I still had no doubt that his path had crossed with Roux's at some point. He'd told her all about me. About us, and what we'd done. Nothing else made sense. But why would he sell me out to Roux if he wasn't angry or vengeful? If he was grateful? It made no sense.

"Tig," I said. I looked at my coffee, because I couldn't

look at him right then. "You know why. I owed you. I think I probably still do."

"You don't owe me shit," he said.

I couldn't let that stand. "You wanted to sleep it off. I'm the one who said we had to go. I'm the one who—"

He cut me off, repeating, "You don't owe me shit. I owe you."

He took a sip of his coffee. Then we sat in silence for half a minute, because clearly he didn't want it said out loud, what we had done. He didn't want me to call up the ghost of Mrs. Shipley.

I had to break the quiet, though. I was on the clock. Timeless as the room felt, it was ticking on, relentlessly, outside this place.

I said, "Can you tell me about Angelica Roux, then?"

I was looking into his eyes, but he had no serious reaction. A little puzzled, maybe.

"I don't know her," he said.

If he was lying, he was better than me. Better than Roux, even.

"You must. You told her about me, the accident. You told her—" He was still looking at me, open-faced, but what I was saying did not seem to be connecting. "She's beautiful, tall and pale. Long dark hair. Crazy yoga body. She has a teenage son, same hair as her—"

His face cleared. "You mean Ange Renault."

The name was similar enough to pause me. I shrugged, but he was pulling his phone out of his pocket. He scrolled to a picture and showed me. "I've never seen a woman that beautiful who was camera-shy, but I only got this by accident."

It was a picture of a car, a Firebird in terrible shape.

The house was in the background, though. There, out on the lawn, a woman very like Roux stood in profile, talking to someone who wasn't in the shot. I zoomed in, her perfect face growing fuzzier as I got closer, but I had no doubt. It was her.

I closed my eyes in a long blink. Angelica Roux was not her real name. How naïve I had been, with my assumptions and my Googling! It had never occurred to me that she would lie on this most basic level. But of course she would, and now that I thought about it, her name didn't even sound real. It sounded like the pirate queen from the pages of a bodice ripper. No wonder there was nothing—literally nothing—about her online. Ange Renault didn't sound much realer, though I'd Google that name later, just to be sure. Both names were dramatic, and French, and had the same initials. Maybe she chose noms de plume that sounded close to her real name.

If I had her real name, what kind of power would that give me? She was using fake ones for a reason. There might be a warrant for her arrest. That seemed likely, given her profession. Her real name might be all I needed to own her.

"Rumpelstiltskin. Rumpelstiltskin."

I didn't realize I'd whispered it aloud until Tig said, "What?"

"Sorry, I— Ange Renault. This is her. This is who I meant. When did you meet her?"

"A couple of weeks ago," Tig said.

"Two weeks?" I said, shocked.

"Maybe three," he said.

God, but she moved fast. She'd moved in fast on me

anyway. She must have left here and gone straight to sex with Boyce Skelton, then landed in my neighborhood twelve days ago.

"Tell me about her. Tell me everything."

And Tig, unlike any other person on the planet, didn't ask me one damn question. He simply told me.

He'd met Roux at a junkyard he frequented. He was skimming for parts. She was there to sell a beater Honda so ancient that Tig wouldn't have let a dog drive it. Luca was with her, sitting in the office playing with his phone, but at first all Tig saw was Roux, sexy as hell and clearly in a mess. She didn't have the paperwork for the car, only her word that she owned it. The junkyard owner, a shady guy named Pete, was negotiating price with her.

Pete took a phone call, and Tig and "Ange" had started talking.

"The car was stolen?" I asked.

"Technically, not that that would bother Pete much," he said. "But it was hers-ish."

"'Hers-ish' is not really a legal term," I told him, and he smiled.

According to Roux, her husband had the pink slip, but it was her car. She and Luca, whom she introduced as "Randy," had left the husband; he wasn't good to her. He wasn't good to her boy either, she'd said, in a way that was pregnant with subtext. The husband was looking for them, she told Tig, eyes wide, clearly frightened. Tig asked her if it was a custody issue. He didn't want any part of a kidnapping charge.

She swore it wasn't. The husband was Randy's stepdad. His real dad wasn't in the picture, and that made sense to Tig; she'd obviously had the kid quite young.

I had to work hard not to snort there. Sure she had.

Tig believed her. She talked about taking a beating like a woman who knew how. Plus, she'd had old bruises on her back and hips.

"You saw her hips?" I said, though this was not germane. And not at all my business.

He shrugged, giving me another sheepish grin. He was good at them. "Eventually."

But that was getting ahead of the story. He talked Pete into giving her a break, and he offered Roux a place to crash for a night or two. No strings, though he admitted he would not have made the offer to some beardy hipster guy in equal trouble.

I couldn't blame him. Roux had gone full damsel on him, and I knew how charismatic she could be when she chose to shine it on.

"Ange and Randy Renault" stayed with Tig for a few days, until she got in touch with a friend who wired her more money. I translated this in my head: She played her game and found a local client, or she retapped an old one. Either way, she got flush, and Tig drove her and Randy to the airport. She didn't tell him where they were going. She said it was safer if he didn't know.

But I knew. They had gone to Boston. She was hunting me by then. Tig had somehow put me on her radar. The story she'd told Tig sounded like lies to me, but maybe not all lies. She was on the run from something.

I still thought a warrant was the most likely scenario, considering her profession and her use of fake names. Roux, who loved Botox and raw silk and sparkling water from France—she wouldn't be in a beater Honda unless things were desperate. And the timeline was so short. She'd been in enough of a hurry to come at me unprepared, claiming to be Lolly Shipley.

"You told her about . . . what happened with us, when we were fifteen. About me," I said, not a question but asking for an explanation all the same. I wondered who I was in Tig's version of our shared story. The spoiled rich girl who sold him out? But then why had he greeted me like the dearest of old friends?

"Yeah. Like, her third night here," he said. He still didn't ask the questions I expected, but I could see them rising in his eyes. "I told her a lot of stuff. That woman, she's a good listener. She asked me a thousand things, about everyone I ever met, felt like."

That sounded familiar. It was what she'd done at book club, getting everyone talking, playing games that made them overshare. She'd had her ears cocked for any useful story, anything that might lead to a payday. Someone in my neighborhood was covering her rent, I was pretty sure. I hoped not Tate and Phillip.

"Why did you bring me up?" I said.

"She asked about these." He ran his hand over the faint letters on his knuckles. "A guy with tats like this has been inside, nine times outta nine. Women see tats like this, they ask. Smart women anyway."

He *had* been inside, and that was on me. "What about the tenth time?"

"The tenth time he lies and says he wasn't," Tig said, wry. "I mean, you meet a woman, it goes good, and she asks about the tats. You don't want to lead with, 'Yeah, so me and this friend, we kinda caused this lady's death, but it was a long time back, and hey, you want to come on back to my place?'"

"So you had an edited version. To get women to sleep with you?" I asked.

"Well, yeah. But to be fair, I told it to women who

were probably already gonna sleep with me," he said, and shrugged. "Look, Smiff, I was nineteen when I got out, and these tats were so fresh that girls could see 'em from space. They would ask about them. It was short-hand. A way to ask if I was safe. My story of how I ended up in juvie—it was a way of telling them I was not the kind who would hurt a woman. My story of how I got sent up is not a hundred percent true, but the girls who asked weren't looking for a husband. They wanted whatever they wanted from me and to feel like they wouldn't get killed or beat while having it. I got asked a lot, back in my twenties. I was kind of a dog. I told that version of the story so many times I stopped thinking of it as a lie. I wanted it to be true. So bad. When I was telling it to some girl, it would almost feel true. Does that make sense?"

Yes. God, yes. I nodded.

"I grew up, though. I stopped tomcatting around like a fool and started having actual relationships. I was with this one lady six years. And then, about seven months back, she bailed. It's okay. She wanted something dif-ferent. I haven't been seeing anyone, not since she left. So here's this Ange, right? Beautiful. Staying here. And her third night, Randy bagged out early. She gave him half an Ambien. Said the kid hadn't been sleeping good on the sofa."

I swallowed a scoffing noise. I'd have bet a million dollars that "Randy" had been sleeping just fine. Roux gave him the Ambien so she could work on Tig. She was protective, I'd give her that. But drugging your teen so you could weaponize sex hardly made her mother of the year.

"And then she asked about the tats?" I said.

"We were talking back in my room, so we wouldn't wake him up. We smoked a little weed, and she was playing with my hand, like, tracing the letters, asking me a million questions. One of them was about the tats. I knew she was heading out soon. She was a ship. She was passing. And I found myself telling that old story."

"The story I'm in," I said.

"Yeah," he said. "I was high, and it was this déjà vu situation. I told her about Ragweed. Sneaking out. The accident. I told her you were driving, but I didn't talk mean about you. I never did, not to Ange or anyone. In the story you're the classic poor little rich girl, all the money in the world but no one who gave a shit about you. From what I remember, that part's accurate. I make myself out to be this up-and-comer, talk up my scholarship, a bad kid about to make good, except this awful accident happens." To me that sounded accurate as well, but he was still talking. "In the story version, I don't sell you out. I never tell the cops a damn thing. I eat the blame, so I come off real noble, right? It's shitty, but I always wished so hard it had gone down that way. It's the story that I always wanted to be true."

His eyes were so sorry and so sweet, and in this light, except for those deep-cut parentheses scored around his mouth, he could have been the boy I'd known. I could see it, too, how the boy in him wished he hadn't talked to the cops. The story turned his hard pain into heroism, and I could see why he still liked it. There was a lot of boy alive inside him still. Not married, no kids, a life of cars, guitars, and weed. Still so charming. I wondered if this was on me, too, that Tig had not grown up. If he'd graduated from Brighton, colleges all over the country would have fought to give him a full ride on his math scores alone. He might have a family now, be someone who designed cars instead of fixing them.

"Why are you sorry?" I said. "It's fair. I was the bad guy, Tig."

His head shook in an instant no.

"Oh, Smiff, naw," he said. "In my story there's no bad guy. There's just stupid kids who do a lot of damage. One pays for it, because, you know, he kinda loves the other."

"Did you?" I said. Because I had to know. The love-starved girl I used to be, so hungry, she demanded that I get her this answer.

He smiled. "Of course. When I came to Brighton, Jesus. I was lonely as fuck-all. Even before. I mean, back in the neighborhood I had friends, girlfriends, my mom. But no one like you. Of course I loved you. I still sold you out. I been waiting years to say I'm sorry."

It was sweet, but it wasn't fair. All he'd done was tell the truth.

I leaned in, urgent. "No, I am. You have nothing to be sorry for. It was me."

We stared at each other, our gazes both so gentle, and this, this forgiveness, it was what I'd tried to buy seven years back. Now I'd come here and found that I'd already owned it. It had been here, waiting, mine all along.

He leaned in, too. Not much. Only an inch, but I recognized it as an invitation. It was for the fifteen-year-old girl who was still alive inside me. That girl had had the best first kiss. The best. But what came after had sucked the sweetness out, ruined it, made it shameful. Shame on top of shame, but no matter what that girl did later, she had deserved that kiss. She hadn't done one damn bad thing wrong then. Not yet.

I wanted, in that moment, to reclaim it. If I leaned in, too, Tig would meet me in the middle. It was in his eyes, in the set of his shoulders. I understood that this was not about true love. This wasn't about breaking my family in half and claiming some old, other life. This was only about right now. This morning. This moment.

There was another mattress somewhere in the house behind us. Clean, probably with at least three books tumbled in the bedding. I looked at his face, so dear and so familiar. I looked at his ink-smudged hands, clutching his map-of-the-world mug in a house where no woman lived. I could have this. Have him. Just for a single half hour, outside time. I could have it if I wanted it. And God help me, I did. I did want it.

I stood up abruptly, almost knocking over the stool. I passed him, hurrying around the counter to the coffeemaker, even though my mug was still nearly full. I almost ran, like a woman who was desperate for a warm-up. It was too dangerous to stay close to him.

Right now Davis was home, playing with the baby we had made together. Oliver was a morning person. He would be paddling his feet, gurgling, and chatting nonsense with his father. Maddy, not at all a morning person, would be stomping down for coffee with her hair in crazy tufts. The night he had proposed, I'd told Davis, *I'm not the kind who'll ever leave you.* Those words had held more than their legal meaning. I'd been saying I was his, that I would not betray him. I wouldn't make those words a lie. I was getting too good at lying already.

I was sorry for that girl who had loved Tig, but she was gone. I'd tried to bury her in her own meat, I'd tried to starve her out, tried drugging her to death in California. Before I'd found a way to kill her, she had gone into the water. She'd gone into the water, and I'd come up, new.

"I'm married," I told Tig. I was blushing hard.

"Okay," he said, smiling.

"Happily. With a baby."

"Okay," Tig said, holding his hands up again, palms forward. An easy surrender. "It was just a thought. Nostalgia. Look, I'm letting it go."

He held the thought up in a pinch between two fingers and then blew on it. I could practically see it fly away.

Still, I stayed where I was, the counter between us. I didn't want to smell him, so familiar. I was already bargaining with that dead girl in my head. *No sex,* she told me. *Just a kiss.* But that was a hard no. I would not play chicken with betrayal, trying to get right up to the line. If I kissed him, I would be no better than Tate Bonasco at a barbecue.

"So why are you asking about Ange? You clearly know her," he said, changing the subject. He was making it easy for me to be decent, and that was damned attractive, too.

"It's complicated," I told him. I set down the coffee I didn't want by the sink. "I need to leave in less than half an hour, and I'm sorry, but I don't have time to explain it all, even though I owe you that. I've done this morning all wrong. I even sat here and let you apologize to me, which is crazy. You can't know how much it's meant to me, to come here and see that you'd already forgiven me. But now I need to apologize."

He looked almost alarmed. "That's crazy. For what?"

A thousand things, and he should know them. My eyebrows came together.

"Because I never said anything. I let the cops blame you. I sat there, silent, and you lost three years."

Tig waved one of my three great shames away with a lazy hand, like it was nothing. "What would you have said? Name one thing you could have said to help me."

Was he being disingenuous? It didn't seem like him. But maybe he just wanted to hear it. Out loud. I had given it to Roux, those words, and she was using them as weapons, hard against me. They were already in her hands. I could do no more damage to myself here, and I owed him this. Him more than anyone. I stilled my body, cleared my mind. I looked him in the eye.

"I should have told them I was driving," I said.

He actually laughed. A disbelieving little sound. He shrugged his shoulders, spread his hands out.

"But you weren't," he said, and then he saw my face. "You know that, Amy, right? You weren't driving. It was me."

11

THE THING THAT STAYED with him, the one thing he knew for sure, was that moment on the railroad tracks. On the way to the clearing, I'd eased us over them so carefully that he'd teased me. *Pussy move, Smiff.* On the way back, rocketing down the inexorable path that would intersect with Mrs. Shipley, we had taken the tracks at such high speed that we'd soared.

Jumping the tracks was his move. He always jumped them. So he thought he'd been driving.

He'd never questioned it, though he did not remember his hands on the wheel, his foot on the gas. His last clear memory was kissing me. We'd pounded down more wine and smoked more, after, and we'd already been wrecked. For both of us, the walk to the car was little more than a slide show. The drive itself was a black patch with that single airborne moment in the middle. The next thing he remembered was weeping on his knees beside the wreckage.

"I had the keys," I argued. We'd been over this already. "I got in behind the wheel."

"But you don't remember driving." He said it like a challenge.

"Neither do you," I shot back, and he laughed, a raw, sad bark of sound.

"You never would have taken the railroad tracks like that," he repeated, but then he jammed his hands into his hair. "If you'd been driving, I would know. Wouldn't I?"

"No," I said. "A lot of times people don't remember car accidents. The mind blanks out trauma, plus we were hammered. We have to look at what we do remember. I had the keys. I got in behind the wheel. I kind of do remember jumping us, now that we're talking about it."

He spun on the stool, his fingers steepled, thinking. When he came back around, he gave me a wistful, wry smile.

"I believe that you believe it. I still think it was me. I knew it was me even when I told the cops that you were driving. I said it because my lawyer kept telling me I was going to get tried as an adult. My mom was freaking out, saying your rich-ass parents could get you out of anything, but I'd be screwed. So I caved. I did what they wanted, and my lawyer leveraged it to get me a better offer. God, I felt almost as bad about that as—"

"Tig!" I interrupted. "We were both kids. We were scared, and we felt so guilty."

"We both lied to the cops. We both thought we did it, and we both blamed the other." He didn't sound angry, though. If anything, he sounded relieved. "It's like the asshole version of that O. Henry story. Where she sells her hair to buy him a watch chain and he sells his watch to buy her some combs."

That made me smile. I came over and leaned on the breakfast bar across from him. Closer, but not too close. I wanted to offer comfort, but I kept the solid cabinets and countertop between us.

"I was driving." I said it like it was urgent, and maybe it was, even though I wanted it to be him. I wanted it to be anyone but me, though my heart knew better. There was one thing more I could say to convince him. It was hard to say with him just across the breakfast bar, smelling of mint and copper and history. But he deserved to hear it. "Tig, you kissed me. It was the nicest thing. I was wild with joy, and wine, and wondering. If there was ever a night in my whole life when I would have gunned it at those tracks . . . well, that was it."

It was true. I could see it in my mind's eye, how I jumped us, hungry for another weightless, flying moment.

He closed his eyes, as if he were using them to look inward. After a moment he opened them again and met my gaze.

"Okay, Smiffy. Maybe. But we got no got'dam way to know for sure." He shook his head. "You know what's weird? It's easier to forgive you than myself."

I felt the same. I turned away, pacing in the small, dim kitchen. Back and forth.

It didn't change what had happened. My guilt remained, and I did not regret paying off his mortgage. I was inarguably the one who'd put us on that road. He'd wanted to sleep it off, but I'd insisted, and everything that had happened after happened. The past was set into its shape, permanent and unyielding.

The present, however, could still undergo a sea change.

I made myself stop pacing and turned to him. I didn't believe that Tig had been behind the wheel, but Roux might. Here, finally, was something that could help me. If Tig were willing.

"She's blackmailing me. Your Ange Renault," I said,

no hedging, bald and simple as I could. That took him aback. He sat up very straight, disbelief writ plain across his face. "She wants every bit of money I have left, or she'll send me to prison. She has me on tape confessing that I was the one behind the wheel, not you. That I let you take the blame."

He must have heard the urgency and stress locked in my voice.

"Motherfuck!" He slapped his hands down on the breakfast bar. "Are you serious?"

"Yeah," I said.

"Because I told a story to get laid?"

I shook my head. "No. It's not you. It's her. She collects stories from every human that she meets, looking for one she can use. You told that story probably more times than I want to know about. No one ever took it and used it like this. She's the bad person here."

"How did she get you on tape?" he asked, and I could see he had a million other questions rising behind that one.

I checked my watch. Time was zooming, and I had to get home. I could not be late. Davis and Char would ask questions, and I was still trying to keep my lies to people I loved at a minimum. I also couldn't risk tipping off Roux. Not when I finally had a little leverage. A lot, actually, if I could use it smart. If Tig would back me. If I could keep Roux believing that jail was the thing I feared most.

So I nutshelled it for him, telling him everything as quick and dirty as I could. I only left out the part where Roux pretended to be Lolly Shipley. I didn't want him to know what had happened with Lolly, after. That was mine to carry. But I told him everything else.

It felt good, not to be alone inside this mess.

Maybe a little too good. Was it disloyal? I wished I were telling Davis instead. This story felt too intimate to share with a man I'd come within six inches of kissing.

At the same time, I was glad that Davis was fifty safe miles distant from it. He felt clean and good, like a faraway home that I wanted only to go back to. If I could get there, I wanted to find him whole and just the same. I wanted the life I'd built exactly as it was, and I could have it. But only if I beat Roux.

When I finished explaining to Tig, I crossed my arms protectively over my body and asked, "Would you tell her that it was you? Driving? It wasn't, Tig, I swear, but I want to bluff her." His eyebrows knit together as he thought, and I hurried to add, "It won't cost you anything. You already did the time. I know if I confessed, it could clear your name. But does that matter? Your records are sealed, because you were a kid. So it's not like you have to put it on job applications or . . ." I petered out. It was baldly self-serving, even cold, asking for this, but I was desperate.

He thought about it for less than three seconds.

"I don't ever have to fill out job applications. Because you saved this place. I got'dam love Restoration, Smiff. What you're asking for, it's nothing. Give me your phone," he said. I fished it out of my back pocket, brushing my thumb on the print pad to unlock it, and passed it over. "Turn on that light?"

I saw the switch by the coffeemaker and hit it. The overheads flicked on, harsh and fluorescent, making me blink. Tig turned my camera on, pointing it toward himself.

"This is Tig Simms. Tighler Simms. Amy was too

drunk to remember, but I was driving. I'll say so in court." He glanced at me to see if it was enough, and I nodded, giving him a grateful smile. He looked back into the camera anyway. "So you can fuck right off, Ange," he added, and then stopped it recording.

He didn't hand it back, though. Not immediately. He bent his head over it, navigating to the keypad.

"This is my cell number," he said, tapping away at it. "I'm going to text myself on your phone right now, so I have yours. If you need anything else, hit me up. You got it already. Understand me? Whatever you need."

I felt a lump rise in my throat as he slid it back to me. There was a lot I wanted to say to that, but I was out of time. It was a good thing, to be out of time. I didn't want to stay in this small room with him, feeling this grateful for his profanity-laden knight-in-shining-armor act. It charged the very air between us, warming me. I needed some distance. I hoped fifty-something miles was far enough.

"I have to go," I told Tig. "I don't know how to begin to thank you."

He shook his head, looking away. "No. I should thank you. I—"

"Stop!" I said, and it made me laugh, how neither of us could stand to be thanked by the other. "It's not even, but let's call it even. For the sake of both our sanities."

"Okay. It's not. But we can call it that," he said. He pretended to spit on his palm, puffing air at it, and then reached across the counter. I laughed and took it, his hand warm and firm in mine. He did not shake, and he did not let go. "We'll stop apologizing. We won't argue about who did what a thousand years ago. We'll just be friends. Okay?"

"Okay," I said. It was the first lie I had told him.

I took my hand back. I had to go. I loved my husband, and there was too much history here. Because I loved my husband, I left it behind me. I could not be friends with Tig Simms. I hurried to my car. I would not be texting him. Not if I could help it.

I raced back toward Pensacola, going nine miles over the speed limit, hoping any speed traps would give me a pass. I wasn't out of the woods yet. Not by miles, but I had a move. I could use this. I could lay these cards down and pretend it was my whole hand. Roux believed that her main hold over me was jail. With Tig's video I could take jail off the table. I could force her to negotiate, as long as she did not see through me. As long as she did not see under.

The sun was up, and the roads were getting crowded. The return trip took longer. Davis was texting me, asking if he should take Oliver in with him to school. The university had drop-in day care, but it cost the earth. We only used it in emergencies. I voice-texted him back through the car, telling him there was no need. I was ten minutes away. He didn't answer, probably ticked off, but I hoped he would wait. When I went to meet Char for our walk, I wanted everything to be normal.

It was already ten past nine as I turned in to my neighborhood. I met my eyes in the rearview mirror and practiced an apologetic shrug. Just sorry enough, a little flustered, putting the lie into my whole body, where it felt quite at home. "Sorry. The traffic back from the beach . . ."

I turned onto our street. Tess Roberts was out in her yard gardening, her toddler helping. I made my regular smile for her, gave her a completely regular wave, like

I was normal Amy Whey heading home from an early dive, a woman whose biggest problems were finding a math tutor for Maddy or a more exciting recipe for chicken breasts. Not a woman practicing to slide yet another lie past her husband.

I parked my car in the drive and trotted quickly up the walk. The front door was unlocked.

I let myself in, calling, "Davis? I'm home! I'm sorry!"

I'd hoped to find him pacing in the foyer, ready to thrust Oliver at me and dash away. Had he taken Oliver into school with him after all?

"Davis?" I called, heading for the kitchen.

"Guess again," a woman called back.

It wasn't Char, though. I knew the voice. I knew it. It was *her*. I froze, inadvertently. My feet stuttered to a stop. Everything in me seemed to pause, my breath, even my heartbeat. The kitchen door swung open, and there was Roux, looking daisy fresh in a short yellow swing dress and some low-top sneakers.

She was holding Oliver, and instantly the hair on the back of my neck rose. I didn't like seeing my child perched on her hip. She really was a baby whisperer, because he wasn't having any kind of stranger anxiety. He bounced his legs, happy, a hunk of her long hair fisted in his hand. When he saw me, he held his arms out, babbling, "Amamama," and that unstuck my feet. I hurried forward, reaching back.

She passed him over as if he were a sack of groceries, then leaned in the doorway, smiling a practiced smile that did not reach her eyes.

"What are you doing here?" I asked. I wasn't ready yet. I had one move, and it was a bluff. I'd planned to come home, practice it in the full-length mirror. "Where is Davis?"

"He had to go to work," Roux said. "Better question. Where the fuckin' fuck have you been?"

Her tone was pleasant, well modulated, but she was angry, all right. Seething with it, just under her skin. Her smile was close kin to a sneer.

"I had to lead a dive."

"Sure," she said. She came toward me, one hand reaching out. I flinched, I couldn't help it. But she only grabbed the shoulder of my cotton dress and jerked it sideways, exposing the strap of my tankini top.

Her eyebrows went up. "That's a bathing suit."

"I know," I said, as if I had the moral high ground. "It's what you wear when you go into the water."

She ran her thumb along the strap. "It's dry."

"Of course, it is," I said, super cool. "It was a long drive back."

"Bah," Oliver said, as if he did not believe me either.

She was shaking her head, her temper receding, pushed out by a grudging admiration.

"Your husband wouldn't have checked for a swimsuit. He wouldn't have thought to. It doesn't even show under your dress," she said. "I'd have on a swimsuit, too, you know that? It's rule one. Only lie if you can back it up. I never—" Then she stopped, and her lips compressed. She leveled a serious gaze on me, and I knew we were both remembering the time she hadn't. "Almost never," she amended.

Well, she'd been in a hurry. What a godsend Tig's story must have been to her. She needed a big fish, and he'd dropped one right into her lap. I thought of all the women he must have told that story to over the years. But only in her hand had it become a weapon.

Oliver wanted down. He bounced on my hip, bending at the waist and reaching for the floor. I reshuffled his weight and told him, "No, baby," and then said to Roux, "What are you doing here?"

She smiled with what looked like genuine pleasure, genuine amusement. "Funny thing. I was busy yesterday. Very. We'll get to that later. But I woke up this morning, early for me, feeling like I'd missed something. I was sure that you were doing something naughty. I could smell it on the wind. So I came down here, and guess what—Amy's on a dive. I told your husband that you and Char had invited me to join your little walking club, and I was supposed to meet you here. He must have eaten up whatever bullshit you slathered on his toast like it was jam, because all he was worried about was getting to work on time. I offered to watch the kid so he could go. He took a little convincing, but you were texting by then, saying you were ten minutes away, so he left. Where were you, Amy, really?"

I was instantly furious with Davis for leaving Oliver with, essentially, a crocodile. Even for ten minutes. But how would he know? All the book-club moms traded babysitting, and Roux had presented herself as an invited member of my sacred morning walk, which would have made her seem like inner circle. God, I had to find a way to warn him off her.

I gave her the shrug I'd practiced for my husband. "I was at work, like Davis told you. I'm home now."

I meant to indicate that she should go, but she turned away, walking back into my keeping room.

"I have to change," I told her, following. "I need to

meet Char in five minutes or she'll come down here looking."

Roux sank back onto the leather sofa, like she was about to grow roots into it and live there. "So change," she said, as if it made no never mind. "I'll wait. But I'm walking with you."

That was unacceptable. Oliver was really struggling now, so I closed the baby gate and let him down. He went speed-crawling off toward the coffee table.

"You're angry with me, and it's tense. It could tip her off. You're not going," I told her.

"I'm not mad," she said, and it seemed true, actually. She was perfectly relaxed on my sofa, legs crossed, leaning back. "You don't get mad at a cat for shitting in a box. It's what cats do."

My eyes narrowed. I was so tired of being told that I was like her. I was so tired of her breathing air, using it to make words at me.

"If Char catches on that something's up with us, I will never pay you. Understand me?"

She smiled. "I more than understand. I believe you. It's very interesting, actually. A topic worth exploring, but I'm not done with this one yet. Where did you go?"

I shot a glance at Oliver, happy on the area rug, banging Rattle Bear's head against the floor. It looked satisfying. I wanted to be down there with him.

I wasn't ready. I hadn't practiced, and right now this one shot was all I had. But she was forcing my hand.

"I went to see Tig Simms," I said.

She leaned forward, and it was clear that I'd surprised her. "Of course you fucking did."

"Stop talking like that in front of my baby," I said.

She ignored that, her face avid and interested but still

not angry. "Tell me one good reason why I shouldn't fuck your life from here to Tuesday. Right this second."

"Because you want the money," I said, my eyes as hard as hers now. "No, let me correct that. Because you need the money. Fast." This part was all true, no need to practice. I was correct on this and knew it. I let it show on my face, in my righteous stance, feet planted, shoulders back. "When Tig met you, you were in a crappy stolen car in Eastern Jesus, Alabama. The second you had a line on me, you blew a ton of cash to fly to Boston and honey-trap Boyce. Boyce, I'm guessing, lives above his means, because all you got off of him was his car." I was into it now. These words hardly felt like my words. It was if I were speaking in tongues, a flame alive inside my head, showing me her language. "You're running from something, and my guess is it's close behind you. My guess is you're close to broke. You need money, and you won't say a thing about me, to anyone, because I'm going to give you some. Not a quarter mil. Nothing like. But I'll give you enough to let you move on down the road, find another fat-pocket sucker. You need it too bad to mess with me."

She was looking at me as if I were some kind of fascinating bug, one she'd never seen before. Aghast, and yet almost admiring. "You have been busy."

I gave her a tight smile. "You have no idea." I held my phone up where she could see it. I pushed PLAY.

Tig's tinny recorded voice filled up the room. I let the whole message play, even the "fuck off" at the end. Oliver was still busy banging Rattle Bear's head, and he did not yet speak English, and, God, I wanted her to hear it. I wanted to say it myself, but it was better from Tig anyway. Tig, after all, had been her lover. He and I had only kissed once, and then I'd betrayed him. In spite of all these things, he'd come in on my side. That meant Roux, the amazing sex goddess, had lost a man. To me. I liked how that felt, honestly. I liked grinding it in.

She watched me with bright eyes, her face perfectly composed. It had to be a mask. I'd taken her most potent threat away, and yet she wasn't railing.

"Are you finished?" she asked.

"No," I told her. My phone buzzed in my hands. Probably Char, texting to see if I was heading down to meet her. Any minute she would come looking for me, if she wasn't doing just that already. But I had begun, and there was no way out but through. "I'll be honest with you. I don't want my family to know about my past. I'll pay for that. A little. Say twenty-five thousand. That's enough to get you set up somewhere else. Take it or leave it."

"What if I pick leave it? What if I out you?" she asked, and it wasn't rhetorical. She was interested in my answer.

I shrugged, practiced and small. "Well, that will embarrass me. But only twenty-five thousand worth. You can't send me to jail. I don't think you can break my marriage. I weigh my old lie against a new baby, and Oliver wins. It isn't even close. So. Go ahead. Tell Davis. And get nothing."

It was a straight-up lie, wrapped around a misdirection. Telling Davis was not the worst thing she could do to me. Not by a long shot.

She stayed silent, sizing me up for a few seconds. "You know, usually when people say, 'I'll be honest,' it means they're lying."

I didn't react, though every passing second was an

agony, ticking like Char's busy feet, coming down the road toward my house. "I'm not lying."

"I can't believe you went to Mobile at four in the morning," she said. "Amy Whey, girl detective. Jesus. And you've staked your husband out for me like a yummy little goat, told me to go ahead, eat him up, try to wreck your marriage. That's bold, Amy. Bold and smart."

"I'm not asking you for a report card. Do we have a deal?" I said, impatient, so overloud that Oliver paused and looked up at me.

"Almost," Roux said.

I didn't understand that. "We almost have a deal? What, you want thirty?"

She laughed and shook out her hair, then crossed her legs and spread her arms out across the back of the sofa, the poster girl for relaxed.

"I mean, you almost had me. It was a ballsy try. God, maybe it's narcissism, but I like you so much right now. I don't know if I could have played that any better."

I heard my front door opening. We both did.

"Amy?" Char called.

I turned away from Roux, washed in confusion. I went to collect Oliver, who was sitting flat on his butt, still watching me. I picked him up, and Rattle Bear with him.

"I'm in the keeping room," I called back, and I sounded shaky even to my own ears. "Sorry! I'm running late. Just wait there."

I jerked my head toward the sliding glass door, expecting Roux to slip out, the way she had before. But she wasn't moving. She sat on the sofa like she'd been planted there.

"We'll finish this later," I said, not much more than a whisper.

"Oh, no," she said, in her normal voice, propping her feet up on my coffee table. "I'm not leaving you alone again. Not until I get paid. You are a person who gets ideas. You do things."

"What?" Char called.

I had no answer, and then Char came through the swinging door, pushing Ruby in the stroller, saying something about buying me a watch. The words died in her mouth when she saw Roux. She looked more than surprised. Almost betrayed.

"Roux dropped by." I really did feel as if I'd been caught cheating on Charlotte, a four-edged irony that was not lost on me.

"Hi-ho," Ruby said, oblivious to the tension in the room.

"How are things, Roux?" Char said, her voice guarded, looking back and forth between us.

"Roux dropped by, very unexpected," I repeated, my voice weak.

Char was the last human being I wanted in the room right now. The very last. Better Davis. Or Maddy. Better God himself.

"Hullo, Kanga!" Roux said, grinning a sly little grin. She was still so relaxed, or she looked it anyway. Sprawled, almost.

"I don't really care for that nickname," Char said in a quelling tone.

But to my surprise, instead of goading her, Roux cocked her head and said, "Really? I'm sorry. I think it's cute, how it goes with mine. Kanga. Roux. But if you don't like it, of course I won't call you that."

"Oh. Well. Thank you," Char said, taken aback.

Roux leaned forward, still unleashing a charm offensive. "I was actually heading to your house next, after I finished here."

"You were?" Char said, shooting me a bewildered look. I couldn't hold her gaze. I felt powerless. I had no idea what Roux would say, no way to stop her or control her. I bounced Oliver to keep him happy.

Roux got up and walked over closer to her.

"I was here apologizing. I've been thinking about book club, the way I came in and took over. I can be like that, especially when I'm in a new place. I show out when I'm nervous. I assumed it was Amy's club because it was at her house, but she told me it's really yours. She just lets you use her space and helps with newsletters or whatever else you need. She gave me an earful about ruining the *House of Mirth* discussion, believe me. She's a good friend."

Ruby pulled at the straps that bound her in the stroller. "Out, peas!"

"The best," Char said, tilting her chin up. Roux had fixed Char's hurt at finding us together, but I felt no relief. It was not kindness, because she wasn't kind. Char, oblivious, so generous at heart, smiled at Roux and added, "I'm shy, too. I show it in a different way, though. I get bossy when I'm nervous."

"Amy had an early-morning dive today," Roux said. "She's still in her swimsuit, and she needs to run and change. We can have a get-to-know-you chat while we wait, just you and I." Roux gave me an oblique look, and it was only then, at the very base of me, lower than words, that I began to truly understand. How much she saw. How much she knew.

"I don't need to change," I said.

"We've all had such busy mornings. Amy's been up to all kinds of things. But so have I," Roux said, and I believed her. I'd snuck off to Mobile, feeling so clever, while Roux had been equally busy here.

Char shot me a confused look. "Okay," she said.

"Out, peas," Ruby insisted. "I wanna pay wiss Obbiber."

"Let them play," Roux said. "Amy, you'll be more comfy if you get out of that damp suit."

I set him down by the coffee table. I had to anyway. My arms had gone so weak. Char unclicked Ruby, handed her over the gate.

"Hi-ho, Obbiber!" she said.

"Obbiber!" Roux laughed. "That's adorable." I'd been right when I'd guessed at her spirit animal. She was a cat, and she was playing with me. She'd been playing with me for this entire conversation, like I was small, gray, frightened food. "I did that, too, when I was little."

"Did what?" Char asked, and the whole scene became surreal. The colors grew brighter and sharper. Time slowed and stretched, but it still went forward, and I couldn't stop it.

"Talked like that. Messed up words," Roux said, releasing a practiced trill of laughter. "When I was little? I couldn't say Angelica. I called myself 'Leaky,' like I was a faulty diaper, and everyone in the family picked it up. I swear to God, I was named Leaky until second grade."

Roux gave me another long, sloe-eyed glance, sideways, and my past was just a stone in her pocket. This was not about the worst thing I'd ever done. Not anymore. Tig and I had wrecked that for her, but she'd been

as busy as I had. She hadn't taken what I'd told her at
face value. She'd gone back. Done the research that she
should have done the first time. Checked. This was now
about the worst thing I was doing. The thing I'd been
doing for almost seven years now, to Charlotte. To my
dearest, sweetest Charlotte.

"That's so funny," Char said. She'd been expertly
cued, manipulated, and her next words were unstoppa-
ble. "I was called Lottie when I was little, but I couldn't
say that either. I said it like 'Lolly.' My whole family
and everyone, even my preschool teachers, called me
Lolly. My brother, Paul, he still calls me Lolly-Pop
sometimes."

She chuckled into the ghastly silence that had filled
the room. We all five stood looking at one another. Me,
two babies, my blackmailer, and the woman who had
once been Lolly Shipley, who was now my best friend
in the world.

12

I HAD TO LET her go, down into the blue. It was where I was most wholly myself; I didn't think of it as a bad place to leave her. I took away her struggling, her fear, and let her drift down quiet, her arms around her sleeping baby brother. She never got any older. She never rose. She spiraled down into the deeps, out of sight and thought, waiting for me, under. It was the only way that I could be her friend, once I'd realized she was Lolly Shipley.

I didn't know at first. I swear I didn't know.

Not for months, though in hindsight I do wonder if I didn't recognize her on some level. Maybe I befriended her because I saw my debt limned in Lolly Shipley's round cheeks and soft jawline, both still in evidence on Charlotte's grown-up face. If so, it was deep in my subconscious, because when I returned to track down Tig, I never thought I'd run into any of the Shipleys. I believed they'd left Florida years ago.

I'd overheard my mother complaining to my father about having to relocate, not a year after we'd landed in Boston. It was galling, my mother told him, to think of Dad's lateral career move, poor Connor in a new school for his senior year, her lost home and friends. All this to give the Shipleys space and peace, only to have them vacate. Then she saw me, frozen big-eyed and miserable in the doorway, and changed the subject.

She never talked about the Shipleys, or Tig, or anything relating to the accident in my presence. If I approached the topic, even crept toward it sideways in a delicate verbal crab walk, she tasked me with a chore that took me from the room. I was smarter than any of Pavlov's dogs, so I only had to wash her car and reorganize her gift-wrap station before I stopped trying.

Once we'd moved, I didn't even go back into therapy. My mother didn't want me talking to anyone who might encourage me to examine, or discuss, or remember. She liked my lie, and she threw all her faith and will behind it.

It was, in some ways, a relief to have the topic so forbidden. I had no right to ask anything of the Shipleys, least of all forgiveness. In the face of their huge and permanent loss, my need to apologize was a dust mote, a speck. The best thing I could do, I believed, was leave them to mourn in peace. So I didn't know until after my life and Char's had intertwined that my parents had only been discussing their move out of our neighborhood.

Mr. Shipley could no longer afford to live there; his small import-export business had fallen apart with him. Char had grown up in Pensacola after all, her childhood marked by scarcity. She grew up missing a parent and also short on both money and simple time to be young, because she had to step into the gap I'd made, mothering her little brother.

When Paul was two, he walked into the neighborhood pool, sinking like a stone, and Charlotte, only five, leaped in right after him. She'd been a novice swimmer, barnacled to a baby, thrashing down in the blue. She could see the surface, but she couldn't get them there. She kicked and churned, Paul's panicked little hands yanking her hair. Her father, dozy from beer, was unaware that both his kids were underwater.

Someone—a lifeguard or a nearby mother, Char could not remember—had fished them out. I'd left them there, though. I'd told Roux the same lie that I told myself: There was no Lolly Shipley anymore. As for Char, nearly drowning had left her with both a fear of the water and the understanding that if she did not look out for Paul, no one would. Their father was very busy drinking.

That's how Char came to know Davis so well, at a support group for children and spouses and parents of alcoholics.

It was so intricate, so precise, all the little turning wheels and moving pieces that brought Char to me. I marveled at it later, as I gleaned her history piecemeal from the thousand conversations we had after I'd realized who she was. It astonished me, how everything had unfolded in this perfect chain.

If one thing had been different . . . If she'd spent her summers on the beach getting over her nerves about the water instead of riding herd on her little brother. If she'd gone to the support group at the Baptist church instead of the one the Methodists hosted. If Davis hadn't told her about the foreclosure down the street, so that newlyweds Phillip and Char became his neighbors in a house they otherwise could not have afforded.

But all these things had happened, one after another, until the afternoon grown-up Lolly Shipley poked her head in the door at Divers Down, asking if I taught adult swim lessons. I did not recognize her. She was only Charlotte Baxter, a new bride, confessing that she had both a fear of water and a cute, athletic husband who snorkeled and boated and surfed.

Earlier that morning I'd started driving to Mobile to face Tig Simms. Again. I'd turned back before I hit the state line. Again. In the wake of that shame, I looked at Char and I thought, *Here. Here is a small, good thing that I can do today.*

"Of course," I said, and led her to the water.

We sat dangling our feet in the indoor, heated pool, and she told me about drowning. If she'd said Paul's name then, I might have put it together. But she didn't. She kept it short, tearing up as she spoke, only calling him "my little brother."

We worked together twice a week. I admired her tenacity and her humor as I coaxed her to stand in the shallow end, then bend to touch the water with her lips, then to look under the surface through a scuba mask with a snorkel. It was weeks before she would lie on her back with me supporting her, both arms over her head so she could keep a two-hand death grip on the concrete edge, her wide eyes fixed on the ceiling.

I liked her orderly, checklist approach to terror, as lesson by lesson she gave up one hand's clutch and then the other's, until she was floating with only one of my hands on the small of her back. Once she was actually swimming in the pool, we went out together to the ocean. She was scared that something alive might squirm under her feet, so I put her in scuba booties. She was scared of jellyfish, so I put her in a skin suit. That's how she first waded in—covered neck to toes. But she did it.

Over the weeks we worked together, I came to like her. She was chatty and funny and a distraction from my inability to face Tig; I found comfort in her victory over fear, because I was losing my battle with my own.

Maybe that was why I accepted her invitation to celebrate at Coffee Nation after her first successful ocean swim. I wanted a sugary iced latte and to bask in that small triumph, because I had finally accepted that I wasn't going to make it all the way to Mobile. Not then. Maybe not ever. In the wake of that admission, I'd begun working on my secret way to repay Tig, but I still felt coated in cowardice and failure. Helping Char was my only real win in months.

On the surface we didn't seem well suited to be friends. I was more than a decade her senior, single where she was married, introverted when she was a dedicated extrovert. But we ended up chatting happily for hours. We talked about books, our jobs, her husband, my grumpy landlord. Neither of us talked about our extended families much, though she said enough for me to gather that her mother had passed and she had minimal contact with her father. My quasi estrangement from my own parents doubled our common ground; we shared both a wound and a desire not to talk about it.

It was the nicest time I'd had since I'd arrived, so I said yes to sushi lunch the next week, and then to a girls'-night movie, and so on. Then I found myself saying yes to ice cream when she brought Davis to Divers Down to hook me up.

It was two months later, when Maddy was already the boldest of my Seal Team kids and my secret favorite, when I'd been on nine dates with Davis, that Char invited us, as a couple, to a dinner party. It was an escalation of our odd friendship; we'd never yet gone to each other's home. By then the lawyers were setting up my bogus foundation to pay Tig's mortgage anonymously. All the wheels were in motion, and I could have left Florida.

I didn't. I wanted to keep seeing Davis and Madison Whey.

At dinner I met Phillip for the first time. He was a salesman, compact and attractive in a frat-boy way, with a pug nose and a ruddy complexion under a flop of blown-out hair. Char clearly adored him, catering to him like a 1950s housewife, but I thought the only thing they had in common was a firm and unfounded belief that Phillip was amazing.

Davis was there, and two other neighborhood couples, the Fentons and the Blakes. It was a lovely night, in spite of how little I liked Char's husband. Maybe even because of it, in a weird, small way. Davis didn't care for Phillip either, and we knew this without speaking. It was telegraphed in a single, shared glance that made me realize how well we understood each other. If Char's intention was to show me the sweet possibilities of a life with Davis Whey, then it worked.

At the end of the evening, we were saying our good-byes in the foyer when Phillip asked Davis about his putter. Phillip was in the market for a new one, and it sparked a heated debate. Char grinned at me, giving a little eye roll at how excited they'd gotten over mallets versus blades. I grinned back, but less condescendingly. I was just as bad if anyone asked me to compare different kinds of regulators. Waiting them out, I glanced around the foyer, and my gaze landed on a photo grouping from their wedding.

There was a large picture of the two of them facing each other at the end of the aisle, hands clasped, exchanging vows. Char seemed a little lost inside her enormous dress, but her smile was radiant. Beside it, two smaller frames were hung in a vertical stack, one a photo of Char's and Phillip's newly ringed hands and, under that, a matted, framed copy of their wedding invitation. Thick cream paper with dark brown ink, rich as chocolate, in such a squirrely font that I had to squint to read the words. As I did, I felt a fist closing around my heart.

Mr. Lawrence B. Shipley
requests the pleasure of your presence
at the marriage of his daughter
Charlotte Marie Shipley . . .

I stopped there, unable to make sense of the time and date and address on the lines below.

My hands went icy, and my feet, and my face, as every bit of blood I had rushed to my center.

"Are you all right?" Davis asked, solicitous.

I shook my head, blinked. "I'm fine."

"Goodness, you're white as a ghost," Char said, concerned, taking a step toward me.

Her voice was the only thing that could have pulled my gaze off her printed name; I turned to her. The whole room seemed to telescope, retracting, until her face was all I could see. It was surreal, like a live-action version of that celebrity baby-photo game in gossip magazines, where they show some round-faced, anonymous toddler who grew up to be famous. I wasn't good at it, never guessing it was George Clooney or Julia Roberts until I flipped the page to look, but then it was always instantly so obvious.

Now that I knew, I could see Lolly Shipley. I could see her so, so clearly. The foyer faded, and I was standing by that smashed-in car, swaying on the dark road, hearing Tig Simms moan. These round eyes, still the same shade of blue, fringed with soft brown lashes, had looked right at me. This mouth, still a rosebud framed by full cheeks, this exact mouth had opened, had said, *Amy, Paul is cry?*

So many unconnected details I had culled about her life over the past few months shifted, clicked into focus. The little brother, who had grown up and joined the service and "fallen for a fräulein" while stationed in Germany, that was Paul. Baby Paul, who'd had colic, and who'd needed to be driven round and round the neighborhood by his exhausted mother in the wee hours of the morning. Char's difficult father, who struggled with depression and imperfect sobriety, that was Mr. Shipley, the man I'd made a widower with a business and two little kids to manage alone. Her dead mother . . . oh, I knew who that was.

My vision swam, and I might have fallen if Davis hadn't hooked an arm around me. "Hey, now! Amy! Are you okay?"

I shook my head, tried to laugh, though my hands clutched at his arm. "I probably shouldn't have had that second G&T."

"Let me get you home," Davis said, and then, thank God, he got me out of there.

I barely remembered him dropping me off. I went straight to my bathroom, where I threw up Char's chicken divan, her garlic green beans, and her strawberry shortcake until I was dead empty. Then I knelt on the cool tiles, gagging on my own bile. When my stomach finally stopped spasming, I crept to my bed, and for hours I lay awake, thinking I would quit my job, hurl my belongings pell-mell into my car, and flee back to California. It meant leaving Maddy and Davis—that thought hurt me like a knife drawn slow across my skin—but I had to give Florida back to Lolly Shipley. How could I do otherwise? I didn't fall asleep until almost dawn.

I woke up late, still determined to start packing. While I stared blearily into my first untouched cup of coffee, the phone rang. I picked it up on autopilot, not thinking, without even glancing at the caller ID.

It was Charlotte, calling to check up on me.

"Are you okay? You got the wibbles last night, right at the end."

I assured her I was fine, but she didn't get off the phone. She was rosy with a natural-born hostess's pleasure in last night's success. I could hear her pouring her own coffee, then settling in for a dinner-party postmortem, asking if the chicken had been dry and what I thought of her flowers. I answered as best I could, horrified. I didn't have the right to be taking calls from Lolly Shipley.

But as she went on, rehashing everything Davis had said to me, gauging his interest and mine, making teasing kissy noises, I realized I had even less right to refuse to take her calls.

I was already so connected to her life. I wondered what she would think when she called tomorrow and found that my phone was disconnected. Would it hurt her? The last thing I wanted was to hurt Lolly Shipley. I couldn't simply disappear.

I needed to set it up, talk about a job offer, ease out of her life. This, I realized, meant time. Time with Maddy and Davis, time with her. I wanted it. I wanted every extra minute with a longing so fierce it shook me. It made me understand exactly how deep I had embedded here.

While all this was swirling in my head, Char turned serious. Just for a moment.

"Don't take this wrong, okay? You're barely twelve years older than me, and you're super pretty, so really, really, do not take this wrong," she said. "But Lisa Fenton, last night, she called you my mom-friend. Isn't that funny?"

I knew the term because I taught so many kids and teenagers. In Maddy's class the title had gone to a boy named Simon. He was the one who had to check everybody's trim, who tried to track the whole group's no-stop dive times, who kept saying at Summer Social, *Y'all, don't gulp those milk shakes, you'll get brain freeze!*

"I'm not insulted," I said.

I wasn't. I was overwhelmed. She was joking, but there had been vulnerability in her inflection when she'd asked if I thought it was funny. And this word: mom. Even tethered to a piece of teen slang, it was a weighted word when it came at me out of Lolly Shipley's mouth.

She must have heard that I was choked up, because she turned serious.

"Well, I liked it. Maybe because I don't really remember my own mom. Or maybe because you started as my teacher. But I'm . . . I liked it, is all. When she said that."

I took a long, shaky breath, because in that moment I could see it. A way to stay. I'd returned to Florida to make things right with Tig, and I'd been rewarded with Char's friendship, even though I'd chickened out and only helped him secretly. What if I could help Char secretly, too? And if her brother, Paul, had troubles, she'd tell me, and I could step in. If bad times stayed away, I'd work with my lawyers to set up anonymous scholarships for any kids they had. I would care for all three of them, Tig, Char, and Paul, behind the scenes, if only I could stay.

"Me, too," I said, and I more than meant it. "I like being your mom-friend." I said those words like a promise, like a vow. If I took this silent path, it might lead me toward redemption. If the universe let me have Maddy and Davis, I would know that I was close enough for it to count. I'd know I had done enough right by Tig Simms to count, too.

Char made a pleased sound and lightened the conversation, complaining that Phillip had not helped her with cleanup. Getting her house back in order was taking up the morning, but she'd promised an elderly neighbor she would drive her to the doctor.

I wasn't working until four, and I thought, *Here. Here is a small, good thing that I can do, right now. For Lolly Shipley.*

I had to talk her into letting me, but I won out, seeing it as a start on all the ways I could be present for her.

It wasn't simple. At first I couldn't look at her face without seeing Lolly. I'd come home from every outing, every visit with her, headachy and exhausted. I started misbehaving with food, not eating for ten hours, or twenty, or forty. When I finally broke, I would gorge myself, then purge.

I thought about confessing to her, but what truth could

I have said? Char, when gently pressed, told me simply that her mother had been killed by a drunk driver. A teenage boy, she said. Not "a couple of teenagers" or even "a carful of teenagers." Just a boy. Even if I said, *My maiden name was Smith. I'm Amy Smith,* it would mean nothing without hours of awful explanations. And to what end? Any confession would be for me, not her, to wring her out for drops of absolution.

I couldn't tell her. I couldn't leave her. I couldn't look at her.

I had to separate them out, Lolly and Charlotte. For the sake of my own sanity.

I had the idea while I was diving, hovering over the deck of a wrecked schooner, playing my light over a pair of angelfish to make their sunshine-yellow sides flash. Lolly had gone into the water once, and she'd been trapped in that inhospitable blue. It had left her with a lingering terror. But I had given water back to Char, hadn't I? Now it was a good place for her.

I thought, *Maybe I can leave her there.* Not Char herself, of course. Not even Lolly, but my pain-soaked memory of her, the avatar of all my guilt. I could feel her with me every minute, palpable and so, so heavy.

Down in the vast and breathing blue, she was like all my other sins. She was rendered tiny in the vastness, just like me. Under, she was small enough to carry, weighty enough to sink. All I had to do was let her go.

It was hard to open my hands, though. I imagined her little face, tilted up to mine, peaceful and unafraid. I imagined she was smiling, giving me permission. My fists unclenched, and she went down, faster than I would have thought. I came up from that dive lighter.

Lighter every time, because it became a mental exercise, a meditation. I took my heavy sorrow under with me, every dive, and I let her go into that place of otherworldly beauty, the place where I was most myself. After a few months, I didn't even need to dive to do it. It was a movie I ran in my head every time I filled my mouth with food but couldn't seem to swallow, every time I felt I didn't deserve a bite of bread, or even my next breath. I folded my memories and guilt up in her baby arms and let her sink into the unending blue inside me. I learned to never, never, never go that deep.

After a while when I looked at her real face, I only saw my friend, Char Baxter. When I thought of Lolly, I only saw blue bubbles rising. Diving had taught me how to be present only in each moment. Under the waves there was never anything but breath and now. I could be present in that way with Char, too, I learned. Just breathe, and love the person she'd grown into. It felt so meant-to-be.

I kept my silent promises so faithfully that people in the neighborhood noticed. Davis, as we got serious, told me he loved my loyalty. Lisa and Sheridan called Char and me "the Sister-Wives." Tate, less fondly, had christened me "the pit bull" after I thwarted her book-club coup. She'd meant I was Char's pit bull, and I was. I had to be.

Now Roux had me leashed. She invited herself along on our walk, insinuating herself between us, in the extra space our strollers made. I was almost grateful. I needed her there, filling my sick silence by telling Char all about our plans to get Luca certified this weekend. On Roux's other side, I kept a tight grip on the stroller's bar, kept my feet moving forward. It was all I could manage. I'd been flayed open, all the buried ugly in me rising like gorge, roiling out of me in waves.

I was seeing myself as Char would see me, if she knew. My motives didn't matter. Neither did the genuine love that had grown up in between us, because it was blanketed inside so much deceit. I had killed her mother, derailed her father, changed her childhood. Then I'd stepped in for the mother I'd killed, moving into her most sacred spaces dishonestly and with no consent. I'd made her dependent on me under cover of a thousand silent lies. She leaned on me more than her own husband. How would she feel, to know that the person she relied on most was offering feeble payback under cover of kindness and love?

And everyone would know. Davis and Maddy, my friends and neighbors, my coworkers and acquaintances. In their eyes I would be at best crazy, at worst a monster. That story would enter every room with me, forever, a tide of whispers surging all around me. *She killed her mother, then crept back, years later, insinuated herself into her life, and Charlotte never knew. . . .*

This was the real threat, more tangible than jail. This was the thing I could not endure. Some, those who loved me, might listen to my side of the story. But even then— perhaps in their eyes I would be no better than Roux. I had, after all, done what pleased me and fed me and made me feel whole, all the while telling myself a version of the story that turned me into the hero. I couldn't bear for Char, my family, the world to see me in this light; I could hardly stand to see myself.

"Right, Amy?" Char said.

I had no idea what they were discussing, but I instantly said, "Right," backing her the way I always did.

"Well, I can't blame her. He's a beautiful boy," Roux said, her tone dismissive. I realized they'd been talking about Luca. Luca and Maddy. I assumed Char was asking out of concern, not matchmaking again. "Luca doesn't think of her like that. Not at all."

Char peered around Roux, trying to catch my eye. "What do you think, Amy? You're so quiet."

"Sorry, I'm tired," I said. Her gaze lingered, concerned, and I could feel Roux's eyes boring into me as well. "I think they're just friends."

I smiled, bland and reassuring, even though I could hardly bear to keep my eyes on her. Lolly was back, alive in her face, in her voice, in her nervous little mouse hands tucking her hair behind her ears. I was taking a walk with my guilt made flesh, with nothing but a tiger in between us.

"She's probably ticked that I invited myself along," Roux said smoothly, covering for me. She tucked her own hair back, quick and twitchy, just like Char. "I know it's your special thing, but I wanted to get to know you better, Charlotte. I want us to be friends."

"I can't think of any reason why we shouldn't be," Char said, her eyes flashing to mine, trying to see if it was what I wanted.

"And I can think of about two hundred forty thousand reasons why we should be," Roux said, and Char chuckled. Roux shot me a look, dead serious and full of bad intent. "Yeah, Amy?"

It was a real question, and I understood her perfectly. She meant the money. She wanted me to affirm I'd be paying her in full, come Monday. I'd tried to renegotiate with Tig's confession held like a gun in my hands, but then she'd pushed a button, dropped this bomb.

She'd been as busy as I had, digging at my secrets even while I was digging at hers, seeing for herself what had become of the Shipley kids. I hadn't tipped her off, though. I was sure of it. There'd been nothing dishonest in my voice or my body language when I'd told her about Lolly in the pool. It hadn't even felt like lying—it had been so soaked in truth. Roux was just this damn good at her job. Now, with Char beside her like another big red button, live-wired and close at hand, she was closing negotiations.

"Two hundred forty thousand at least," I said, trying to keep my voice light, for Charlotte's sake. It sounded weak, almost sick, to my ears. I made myself meet Roux's eyes, promising her the money, promising her anything, for her silence now. She dipped her head, acknowledging my meaning.

"I should make you list them all," Char said, thinking we were being silly. "I need the self-esteem boost."

"'You is smart. You is kind. You is important,'" Roux said.

"Is that *The Help*? We read that for book club!" Char said, but she was blushing, flattered and pleased.

"I only saw the movie. Should I read it?" Roux asked.

Roux took my arm now, too, linking me to Charlotte, the flesh of her so cool and smooth. The feel of her made my blood run redder, faster, hotter. My grip tightened on the stroller bar, and she kept up the conversation, laughing and chatting between us. Her voice had taken on Charlotte-like inflections, her head tilting to match Char's angle as she laughed. She could have been a female Mister Rogers, she was so neighborly and friendly. Char was getting thoroughly snowed. Meanwhile I could feel rage leaking into me at our point of contact. It spread up my arm and into my core, like an allergic reaction to her touch.

That was when I knew I wasn't beaten. Not yet. I still had four days left, and as we walked, arm in arm in arm, the two of them chattering, the babies babbling happily back and forth, I knew what I had to do.

13

MY PLAN WAS SIMPLE. Today, while Luca was studying, I would steal his house keys. I'd manufacture an errand, and Oliver and I would run down to Ace and make a copy. I'd do his pool dives before Maddy got home, and then, while she watched Oliver and kept Luca distracted, I'd slip away and search Roux's house. Roux spent every afternoon at the gym; I'd learned from Luca that she went to a yoga class, then did cardio and targeted weights. Every day. She was addicted, so I'd have the place to myself for a couple of hours. She must have her real ID or other pieces of her past stashed somewhere. She was on the run, but she'd had time to grab things on her way out: the Picasso, the laptop, her exquisite clothes.

Her past had to be somewhere, tucked in her freezer or under her mattress. Maybe in a safe-deposit box, which meant I was screwed. But Roux didn't seem like the type to trust institutions. There was only one way to find out: I needed some quality time alone in the Sprite House. Once I had her real name and her point of origin, I could go to Google or even a private investigator and find whatever she was running from.

Then I'd feed her to it.

It wasn't a bad plan, considering, but I hadn't been home from the walk more than fifteen minutes when she came to wreck it. I opened the door expecting her son, and there she was, a shiny bad penny in her yellow dress, turned up on my porch again.

"Where is Luca?" I said, so snappy that Oliver, draped near sleep across my shoulder, reared up his head to look at me with wide, solemn eyes. I patted his back, bouncing him, and he tucked his face back into my shoulder.

"He doesn't get up until after ten unless I set a bomb off, and I couldn't leave you here alone. Not after your little dawn raid on Mobile," she said, unperturbed by my tone. She stepped forward, muscling her way in past me. "You've janked me around so hard already I'm surprised I haven't pulled the plug on this, and I get the feeling you're not done. So here I am. I want this to work out for you, Amy."

I shut the door behind her with more force than necessary, making Oliver stir. I shushed and patted, kept my voice close to a whisper, even though I couldn't help how fierce it came out.

"You want this to work out for *me*?"

"Yeah," she said, like this was only common sense.

She walked down the hall to my kitchen, as easy in my home as Char. I trailed behind her, then stood swaying my almost-asleep baby, my mind churning. Did she mean to stick by me all day, every day, until the money came? I shook my head in a tired, angry no.

"I can't have you living up my nose. It will look weird to my friends. My husband."

"So we look weird for a few days. It's better than looking like a sociopath who stalks her victim's children, isn't it?" She asked this with an odd sincerity, not like a barb.

I felt a dull heat rising in my face.

"What do you think I'm going to do?" I asked. "Go see Tig again? Get him to tell me what he knows one more time?"

She ignored my theatrics and answered the question, calm and almost kind. "I don't know. I wish I did. As it stands, I'm going to sit on you and hatch you like an egg."

"A money egg," I said, bitter, and she smiled, wry and almost apologetic.

"I have to stop you playing," she said. "If you piss me off enough, I'll hit back and blow this for both of us. I want my money, sure. That's the main thing. But I like you, Amy. I don't want to have to hurt you."

It was an insane claim, since she was the one who'd be doing the hurting, but she said it in a way that sounded simple and sincere. I thought this was the real Roux again. All her Char-ish mannerisms from the walk had fallen away, and there was no sign of the exotic new-comer who had fascinated my whole book club. With me she'd alternated between predator and provocateur, keeping me scared and off balance, but even that was gone. This was the woman I had glimpsed before, when she'd dropped the games and talked to me about what I owed the universe. She was being downright human, a woman I would have liked, a lot, if we'd met in California.

In this quiet, before Luca came, I decided to try a different plan. A kinder one. For a moment I would try to be human back.

"That money isn't mine." Opening my cabinet, I got

out a cup and poured her the last of the coffee I'd made for Maddy and Davis, one-handed. "You're not really taking it from me. It's Charlotte's. You understand?" I passed her the cup, and she took it, but she didn't answer the question. "It was always meant for Paul and Char. That money is a wall between them and any bad thing that life throws. If one of them gets sick or loses a job, I have to be able to help." Every word landed like gospel, because every word was true. This was why I'd never touched the remaining funds, or even siphoned more to Tig. It was for Char and everybody she held dear. I could see that my words had an effect on Roux. She was listening, both hands wrapped around the mug, as if for warmth. "You say you're acting for the universe, restoring balance, but you're robbing some kids who lost their mother."

After a moment she shook her head. "That's too easy."

"Nothing about this is easy!" I said, and I had to work to keep my voice down. Oliver was truly out now, a heavy weight on my chest and shoulder. Lord help us if I woke him.

She shook her head again, calm and certain. "That money is. It came from your family. You didn't earn it. If Char got cancer, what would it cost you, personally, to step in and throw cash at the problem? Nothing. After you pay me off, shit gets real. Her chemo or your family vacation? Her meds or your new car? If you cover her ass when it costs you, it will actually mean something."

This was her, the real Roux. The one who had her kid believing she was helping people make amends, balance-checking karma, acting as a twisted version of a confessional. I hadn't realized how deeply she believed it until now. She hadn't been BS'ing me. She really saw herself as some kind of antihero, which meant that deep down she must want to be a good person. It also meant that she was right: We were more alike than I wanted to admit.

I tried again to reach her. "Don't kid yourself. You're not doing something noble, Roux. You stumbled across my life and immediately stuck your hand out."

She looked at me with genuine surprise and then straightened, setting the mug down.

"Stumbled? You think I'm here by accident?" She leaned in, fierce and serious. "Nothing is by accident. I was looking for you, Amy. I sought you like a grail, and that was before I ever heard your name. I knew that your name would come to me. A name always does. I worked to find you, striking up conversations in bars and parks, book clubs and gyms and churches. I know how to get strangers talking. It's not even hard. People are so hungry to be listened to, and most of 'em walking this shithole planet have a story about injustice, the taker or the ruiner who wrecked them on the way through. At the same time, every person alive is starved to confess their own dark moments, because what they really want, deep down, is to pay." She stepped closer, fixing me with the bright eyes of a true believer. "I'm the weapon, not the wielder. I follow the stories, and the road they take me down is the road that was always meant to be. That *has* to be. I was following a different story, heading for Baton Rouge, until I stopped by that garage in Mobile Bay. When Tig Simms started talking, I knew that the road was turning me. I go where I'm sent."

"Sure. Because karma," I said, my voice loaded with irony. It was so easy for me to dismiss her story, see her as the villain. Would it be this easy for Char to dismiss mine? But I couldn't think of that. I had to win, so Char would never have to face that choice. "Not because I had more money than the Baton Rouge guy."

My words landed, but not hard. She laughed and stood down, giving me an acknowledging bow.

"Well. A girl's gotta eat," she said, so glib I knew that her human moment was over. "Go about your business. I'll be here."

And so she was. She stayed all day, watching me like I was television. Must-see TV, even, trailing me from room to room as I put Oliver down, then cleaned up the kitchen. It set me on edge, especially since I felt something disdainful in her steady gaze.

Halfway through loading the dishes, I went and got *Hearts in Atlantis* off my shelf and thrust it at her.

"Stop watching me," I said. "Just sit over there and read this."

To my surprise, she did as she was told, heading to the keeping-room sofa. Even so, the book seemed like a prop. I could feel her gaze following me over the top of its open pages.

"What?" I said at last.

"Nothing. Just . . . this is really what you do? Dishes?"

I fixed her with a baleful eye. "Everyone does dishes, Roux. Even the queen of England has at some point in her life rinsed out a teacup."

"I know. It's just . . ." She shook her head and then waved her own words away, looking down at the book. She didn't say anything more. Not then.

By eleven, Luca arrived, ready to take another quiz, excited about pool dives. Roux made us wait for Maddy, though.

"You don't want to leave your little friend out, eh?" she said, as if Maddy's pleasure were her great concern. Maddy did want to be there for Luca's dives, but I'd told her it might not be possible. Now Roux was taking her side, for no reason I could see. She had yet to get Maddy's name right.

Roux stuck all day, even escorting me to Lisa Fenton's house to drop off Oliver before the dives. She only tapped out when the kids and I loaded the car with equipment and headed down to Tate Bonasco's house.

Tate was blackly disappointed to hear that Roux had gone off to the gym. She was dressed to the nines, her house sparkling clean, wanting to show off for a woman who hadn't bothered to come.

"Is she coming tomorrow?" Tate asked, plaintive.

"Dunno," I said, and herded my excited teenage ducklings to the backyard.

There was a moment, that first moment when Luca swapped his snorkel for his regulator and let himself sink, that not even my current circumstance could ruin. We went down in tandem, face-to-face. Maddy was already under, revolving around us in slow circles like a happy moon. He held his breath for the first three seconds, a reflex, and then he remembered that that was the first rule, to never hold his breath.

He inhaled, and I watched his eyes go wide behind the mask, shining with the magic of it. It was so counterintuitive, to be under, to breathe in. I knew he was hooked. I loved this part of my job, but even as I took him through the skill sets, I could feel time leaking away. He showed me he could clear his mask and recover his regulator, and then I had him give Maddy the signal for "out of air." A secondary air source was standard for safe diving, and Maddy's was built into her BCD. She handed Luca her own regulator and put the alternate in her mouth. Linked by her equipment, they swam the length of the pool together, side by side, sharing air. Halfway to the end, Luca tucked Maddy's arm through his. It was necessity, not romance. The short hose linking them was pulling at his mouth. Even so, when we came up, Maddy's eyes were shining.

Meanwhile Roux was off doing sun salutations, her house empty, her secrets unguarded, and I was held hostage by her own son's safety. She'd bet, quite rightly, that I wouldn't leave a novice teenage diver on his own. Not even in the contained water of the pool, not even with Maddy there.

By the time we finished up, Davis was home. It was a strange night. I felt divorced from myself, almost outside my body, watching Amy Whey make us all spaghetti and meatballs and caprese salad. I was so committed to the role I even ate the food.

I made Amy-style jokes, asked Amy-style questions, and Davis and Maddy both saw Amy. It almost hurt my feelings. Inside I was a wasteland, and they couldn't see. At bedtime Davis read, and I sat right by him, staring at a book I wasn't reading. It was all I could do to turn the pages at reasonable intervals and manually remove the tension from my body. It was like bailing out a sinking boat. I'd find my leg muscles contracting, and I would make them release, concentrating, only to find that same stiffness churning my abdomen or clenching my hands. By the time Oliver began fussing for his nighttime nursing session, I was as physically exhausted as if I'd spent the last three hours at the gym with Roux.

Oliver nursed himself to sleep, and Davis, none the wiser, took him to his crib. He got into bed again and kissed me as if I were the same old Amy I had been for almost seven years now. I kissed him back, just like her, and he clicked his lamp off and rolled away. He was asleep in bare minutes, wholly at peace. It left me feeling so damn lonely.

I lay awake staring up at the dark ceiling, wanting to talk to him. I wanted to talk to anyone, really, but the only one who understood what was happening in my life was Roux, and she was doing it to me.

That was a lie, though. I could fool Maddy, and even my husband, but Roux had shattered my ability to lie to me. She'd unfolded all the hidden spots inside me, then dredged me from the bottom up. I knew there was another person.

At midnight I reached over to my bedside table and got my phone. To my left, Davis was a sloped hill under the duvet, anonymous as landscape. I kept my eyes on the brightness of the screen and navigated to Tig Simms's number. It took me a moment to find it; he'd added himself to my contacts as "Restoration Garage."

That gave me a pang. Tig had guessed that I would want to camouflage him. And he'd been right. If I had any business texting him, there would be no reason for a misleading name. So I shouldn't. I knew it.

I texted anyway. Just to see if he would answer.

Shave and a haircut?

Tig was still a night owl; less than ten seconds later, he answered with an emoji that looked like a quarter: two bits. I smiled in the dark.

Then he sent, Did you get her?

Not yet, I texted.

You will, he sent back, and it heartened me. Two simple words, but I needed someone to give them to me. Another text dropped. Can I help?

No. I got this. Thanks.

The lie came instantly. I sent it before I could consider, before I could process the relief and hope that flooded me at the very thought of not being alone in this. My fingers hovered on the screen, though. Where did my simple human weakness stop, landing me on the far side of betrayal? I was looking for the line. I wasn't sure exactly where it was, but it felt close. Too close for comfort. I closed the window before I could change my answer.

I felt another text land, but I didn't look. I navigated to Settings and turned off vibrations, then put the phone facedown on my bedside table. I had no business asking Tig to do Davis's rightful job. Especially since I hadn't given Davis the chance. He might, if only I asked him. It wasn't my husband's fault that I was a coward. A coward and a liar.

I tried to tell myself that this tiny call and response with Tig meant nothing. But I knew better. It had mattered, because not ten minutes later I fell deeply asleep, wrapped warmly in Tig's faith in me. I woke up with a new plan, fully formed.

Roux arrived two minutes after Davis left, letting

herself in, Charlotte style. She must have been watching the house, waiting for his car to leave. I wondered how long she'd been out there. She was wearing jeans and a linen shirt, casual and easy-fitting. Maybe she'd dressed for squatting in my neighbor's bushes with binoculars, making sure I didn't go creeping out at 4:00 A.M. again.

The day went much like the one before, with Roux watching me go through the motions of my regular life. Luca arrived just before eleven, though unlike his mother he still used the doorbell.

"I finished the next section," he said, waving the textbook at me, and then went galloping to the keeping room to put the DVD in.

Scuba knocked him out of his cool kid's saunter, turning him into the kind of boy I could see hanging out with Maddy. I had no idea what Roux had told him about her sudden need to supervise his class up close and personal, but his attitude toward me hadn't changed at all. Either he still didn't know I was Roux's "client" or he was a better actor than even his mother.

I made grilled cheese and tomato soup for lunch. I skipped it, and the hunger at my center was both punishment and power. Only a few days in, but my jeans felt looser. I was using up the last of my baby weight to feed the baby. I hoped to God I could finish this, get myself back into a routine with food before I lost my milk. Roux declined a sandwich, and after poking around in my fridge she decided to run home and get a green juice.

The second my front door closed behind her, I stopped spooning baby-food peas into Oliver, scattering some Cheerios on his tray to keep him busy. Luca was eating at the breakfast bar, studying at the same time. I leaned on the counter, trying to look casual, but

Roux would be back in five minutes. I hadn't been alone with him yet today. This moment might not be repeated, and I wanted to get him talking. Roux had said multiple times that she was, or had been, married. Luca would certainly know about that.

"I'm excited to get you in the actual ocean tomorrow. You're going to love it."

I sounded like a perky idiot. Thanks to my job and to raising Maddy, I knew a lot of teenagers, but I interacted with them either as an instructor or a parental unit. I had no idea how to get a criminal's child to yammer about his mom, much less about what she was running from.

"Yeah," he said, glancing up, but then he went right back to studying.

"I tried to get Davis into it, but it isn't his thing," I persevered until he looked up at me again. "He's claustrophobic, he says. How anyone can feel claustrophobic in the middle of an enormous, wide-open ocean, I have no idea, but it's a real thing, apparently."

"That is weird," Luca said, but his eyes strayed to the book. He was too well mannered to keep blatantly reading with me standing right there talking to him, but his intentions, his desire were both plain to see. I worried about this kid; I couldn't help it, given his mother. I wondered if he was as deceitful and practiced as she was, but whenever I was around him, I could not believe it. This man-child was so transparent, his gaze flicking to the book again, his hand moving restless on the open pages.

Roux was languorous and unhurried, every move as orchestrated as a yoga pose. Stillness and deliberate motion masked her reactions. I was the same, and getting better at it. Last night had proved that. But Luca? He was a kid, trying to be cool but prone to visible spasms of emotion.

"You're lucky your mom already dives. You'll have a lot of opportunities to get out there, huh?" He nodded. "Does your dad dive, too?"

I was watching him intently, so I caught the way his body froze. Just for a second, but it was a telling second.

"No," he said. And that was all.

"That's a shame," I pressed. "Maybe you could get him into it."

His face flushed, soft red coming into his cheeks, and then he jerked one shoulder up in a shrug. "I don't see my dad."

He looked so unhappy, and I felt a crushing shame. But at the same time, my spine tingled. I was onto something.

"I'm sorry," I said, and I wasn't sure what I was apologizing for. "Are your parents divorced?"

Luca swallowed. His gaze was direct and sincere. "Ms. Whey? My dad—he's not a good person. I don't talk about him. Like, ever."

"Sure, sure. I'm sorry," I said, backing off. Given Roux's occupation, I'd thought the odds were she was running from a warrant. But now I wondered if Luca's father was a more likely reason for her to have hit the road. "Not a good person" could mean a lot of things. I had more questions, but I let him go back to his studying and his sandwich. I genuinely didn't want to hurt the kid. Also, the piece of me that was playing didn't want to tip my hand. Roux would return any minute, and she'd notice if Luca was distressed. Both these reasons existed, but I hoped my gentler, kinder motivation was stronger than the manipulative stir I felt down in my deeps.

I was innocently feeding Oliver again when Roux let herself back in. Luca was engrossed in his book, his thick, perfectly shaped eyebrows furrowed.

At two-thirty Maddy slammed the front door wide and came stomping down the hall. She threw open the swinging door.

"Monster! Luca! Pool o'clock!"

"Hush! Two more pages," Luca said.

She blew him a raspberry, which made Oliver start blowing raspberries back. I was on the floor with him, helping him bang around the wooden pieces of his My First Puzzle.

"Hurry up, already!" Maddy slid onto the stool beside Luca, her shoulder touching his, peering down at the book, even though she knew it backward and forward.

Roux, silent on my sofa, watched Maddy almost as intently as I watched Luca. Both of us mothers were clocking how he reacted to her touch. The answer was not at all. Maddy might as well have been a piece of furniture, but Roux's eyebrows knit together, uncontrolled, as if she had forgotten she owned eyebrows for a moment. I'd thought it might be different with boys, this worry over their crushes. Apparently it wasn't. Luca had a heart, unlike his mother. She was out to guard it.

Maddy, not getting any of his attention, climbed off the stool and dropped to her knees on the carpet by me. She hurled her arms around my neck and gave my cheek a resounding smack. The sound made Oliver laugh so hard she did it three more times, then zerberted his own cheek while he grabbed big handfuls of her curls and yanked joyfully, crowing.

Mad smiled up at me. "How much longer? God, I've missed diving. We haven't gone much since Oliver. I mean, I love him and all." She touched the tip of his nose and told him, "I love you, fat potato," before turning her eyes back to mine. "But I miss us. Doing our thing. You know?"

From the corner I could feel Roux's eyes on us, still.

"I do know," I said. Davis and Maddy were blood, and Davis and I were married. Maddy and I, we were divers, and I hadn't realized that as bad as we'd been missing getting under, we had also both been missing the thing that made the two of us a pair. I ruffled her curls. "I'm sorry, kiddo. I've been lost in baby clouds. But I promise, once we get through this, you and I will start diving on the regular again."

"Get through what?" Maddy asked, and I shook my head a little, laughing.

"Just . . . you know, the class," I said.

"You're a good Monster," Maddy said, and I felt my eyes prick with tears.

"Done!" Luca said, smacking the book shut.

"Good. You can take the DVD home and watch the last section tonight. We'll do the test in the morning, right before your first open-water dive, okay?" I told him, so conscious of being watched. "Mads? Go get on your swimsuit. Luca, you too."

"Want me to jog fat potato baby down to Mrs. Fenton?" she asked, poking Oliver's belly to make him laugh.

"We'll drop him on the way. Run get changed."

Luca's swimsuit was hanging up with his wet suit in

the downstairs guest bath. He went in as Maddy went bounding upstairs. The rest of the equipment was already loaded in the Subaru, ready to be driven down to Tate's.

I flipped through Luca's book, making sure he'd done the practice quizzes. I did not look at Roux. I kept still, so my body wouldn't telegraph anything. It was time to put the plan I'd woken up with into action. If today was like yesterday. If she went to the gym. But she stayed on the sofa.

"She really loves you," Roux said.

"Of course she does," I said, surprised out of my pretend.

Roux's eyes narrowed. "It doesn't always work that way. Not with steps."

"Not always," I said, wondering if a bad step was the reason she was running. While she was in a talking mood, I asked, "Is your husband Luca's step?"

She ignored that. "She isn't jealous of you? Adolescent girls don't like women macking on their fathers."

"There's a little bit of that, but Davis and I make sure not to exclude her." I didn't want to talk with Roux about Maddy, but if I did, maybe she'd talk back. Several times now I'd seen the woman who lived inside her constructs and characters. I'd seen enough to believe her when she said she liked me, in her way. I hadn't yet given up on using that. "I work on it. Davis and I both do. We even planned our honeymoon around Mads."

"Huh," Roux said, a skeptical breath of sound, but it was true.

I said, "We did a destination wedding, just the three of us in Key West. She stood up with both of us. We called her the Best Mad and the Mad of Honor."

"No church?" Roux asked, surprised. "You smell like church to me. No big white dress?"

I shook my head. "It was the second time for both of us. I wore a sundress. We stayed a week, and Mads and I went diving every morning while Davis slept in and then read or golfed. Then we'd all three go hang out at the beach or Mallory Square. One afternoon I said I needed a nap, and I sent Mads and Davis to the Hemingway Home. Mads wanted to see all those cats with extra toes. I did, too, but more than that I wanted her to know that even on our honeymoon she and her father would have their own space." Roux was leaning in, interested. It made me want to say more. I could feel her doing it, and this was part of her job. She got people talking, listened for the cracks and damaged pieces that hinted at their secrets. I talked anyway, hoping she might talk back, tell me something real in exchange, even if it was only to bait me. "What about you? How did Luca manage when you got married?"

"I got married long before I had Luca," she said, which still didn't mean the mystery husband was Luca's father. Not definitively. There had been any number of lawyers post-vows. After a moment she added in a grudging voice, "She's a nice enough kid, your step. But I wonder what you're doing here."

I didn't understand the question. "In Pensacola?" I'd come here looking for Tig. She knew that.

"No. Here." She waved her hand around at my keeping room. "In this brick-front shithole with Mr. Elbow Patches, raising his tweedy baby and a girl who's nice enough but not even yours. Baking whole chickens. Having quiet, don't-wake-the-baby sex every Thursday at nine P.M. I bet you're in the PT-fuckin-A, and how can you stand it? You're like me, Amy. I see you. I see you all the way down. We're the same, except you had advantages I didn't. You were born with a silver spoon jammed up your ass. How the hell did you land here? You could be anyone."

I was affronted, but I worked hard not to let her see it, because this was interesting. She was off-kilter, her words flowing so fast she couldn't be thinking them through. I fixed her with a challenging stare. I was remembering Tate's careful outfit, her scrubbed-clean home, all prepared for Roux, and Roux's disdain for Tate's need to show her up. Did Roux feel that I was actual competition? There was a measure of respect in her words, but maybe this was just another way to work me.

I tested it. "You're so right! Why am I here, when I could be on the run from the law, stealing cars, squatting in the Sprite House smelling mildew with my poor kid jerked out of school and away from everything he knows? What was I thinking?"

It was a solid hit. I saw the flinch, though it was nothing more than a reset of her shoulders.

"You've never seen my real life," she said. "This is a hiccup. Come Monday I'll have the means to start my real life over. Trust me. My real life isn't this . . . small," she said, waving a hand at the walls around us.

I looked at her with something that was almost pity, then down at Oliver. He was lying on his back, tired out, his little fists wrapping my index fingers. I bobbled his hands back and forth.

"It isn't small, here," I told her. "Your eyes are no good. If my life was shit, why would I fight for it this hard? You can't send me to jail, Roux. Tig fixed that. All you can do is mess up this tiny, tiny life you think is nothing. But I'm willing to pay almost a quarter mil to keep it. What I have is valuable and fine. But you can't see that. You're too damn broken."

It was probably the most honest thing I'd ever said to her. I wasn't looking at her, but I thought it landed. I could feel it in the air between us. When I finally did look, she had shaped her face into something insouciant, pitying, but under that I believed I had shivered her. I saw a haunting buried in the back of her eyes.

Maddy came bounding down the stairs then, lithe and young and lovely in her bathing suit, a voluminous sheer cover-up billowing around her.

Roux got up just as Luca came back from the bathroom. Maddy was a dawdler, but I'd wondered what had taken him so long, and now I saw he had already struggled into his borrowed Aqualung wet suit, still damp from yesterday. It was a little short, a slice of bare ankle showing at the bottom, but this time of year the water was still warm enough for it not to matter.

"Gym time," Roux said, though she was still in her street clothes.

I didn't breathe a sigh of relief. I didn't react at all. She paused to drop a cool kiss on her boy's cheek on the way.

"Have fun. Be good," she told him.

"Always," he said.

She saw herself out.

"You could have waited until we got to the pool. That can't be comfortable," I said to Luca.

"I know," he said, sheepish, pulling at the wrist. He did look good in it.

Behind Luca I could see his jeans and T-shirt in a

crumpled heap on the bathroom rug. Typical teen boy, thank God. Here was my chance.

I said to Maddy, "Let me run to the restroom and we can go. Watch the baby?"

I stepped into the guest bath. Once the door was closed, I leaned down and picked up Luca's wadded clothes. I folded the T-shirt neatly and set it on the counter. Then I picked up the jeans and ran my hands around the pockets.

He had a wallet in the back one. I took it out and flipped it open. A crisp twenty in the money pocket. No credit card, no insurance card, but a Maryland driver's license. I didn't know enough about that state to know how real it looked. It couldn't be real, though, because the name on it was Luca Roux. I put it back and checked the front pockets.

I found Luca's key ring. It was a lightweight metal bull's face, goofy and cartoonish. Probably something from a meme I was too old to get or care about. A single key dangled from the ring in the bull's nose. No car key. So Roux hadn't given him free access to the purring red monster she'd jacked from Boyce, which either represented a little bit of responsible parenting or she had control issues.

I slipped the bull in my pocket, then stacked all of Luca's clothes except his T-shirt neatly by the sink. I flushed the toilet for cover and took the T-shirt out with me.

"Hey, kids? I have bad news. I just realized we're short a couple of air tanks."

"Oh, man!" Maddy said. "I can't go? I mean, I know it's just the pool, but . . ."

"We don't even have enough for me. I was counting on the nitrox upstairs, but I burned that on the morning dive I did the other day. It's no big deal, I'll run pick up some more. Can you keep Oliver? You and Luca can watch the last video." I handed Luca his T-shirt. "Take the wet suit off so you don't swelter. I'll be gone half an hour, forty-five minutes tops."

"Sure," Mad said. She reached one easy hand out to the back of Luca's suit, pulling the drawstring to undo his zipper. Her eyes lingered on the bare skin of his back.

"And, Mads, let Luca pay attention to the video, okay? You watch the baby," I said.

"I will," she said, too offhand for my liking.

"He needs to know this stuff so he can dive safely," I told her, stern. I didn't like leaving them alone. Not with the way she looked at him and all the ways he did not look at her. I didn't want her doing things that would mean the world to her and be nothing more than opportunity and hormones for him. He was a nice kid, but he was still a teenager.

Mad was grinning. "You're so mommitty sometimes."

"I'll take that as a compliment," I said. Oliver was yawning, but I hoped his nap would hold off until I returned. He'd make a pretty good chaperone. Since Oliver's arrival Davis and I had learned firsthand how excellent babies were at preventing or at least interrupting sex.

Luca had struggled the rest of the way out of the wet suit, and Mad's eyes slid sideways at his bare chest, lean and pale and smoothly muscled. He was oblivious, pulling his T-shirt on over his swimming trunks, but it didn't set my mind wholly at ease. I'd stolen glances at Tig just like that a thousand times without him ever noticing. Until the night he did.

I went out through the garage, even though I wasn't going to take my car. They were already chattering, wrapped up in the idea of the dive and each other. I checked my watch. Roux had left a good twenty minutes ago. By now she would have had time to change and leave. She was usually at the gym until after five. Or at least that was when Luca headed home.

I slipped out the garage's side door, quick and quiet. I had less than an hour to break in and seek out Roux's real and secret name. There was power in it, or she wouldn't keep it hidden; I was going to find it.

I would find it even if I had to level the Sprite House to the ground.

14

ON MY WAY TO Roux's, I passed Tate's good friend Lavonda out walking her big collie mix. We exchanged cool hellos. Inside, my stomach felt sour and hot, almost boiling, but long before I saw her, I was walking easy, hands swinging as if I hadn't a care in the world. I didn't even have to manufacture a smile for her; I had one ready-made, waiting for whoever needed it. She went right on by, though Lavonda could smell drama or distress from fifty paces. She lived for it, in fact, but she hadn't smelled it coming off me.

I was getting better and better at this. I had always been good at it. My body had lied for me for years now, making itself regular and relaxed with Char. I'd even taught it to lie *to* me. The only difference was now I understood what I was doing.

I wasn't sure that was a good thing.

I didn't see anyone outside when I got to the cul-de-sac, and the red car was gone. I let myself in with Luca's key. Here was the same ugly den with its sad rental furniture, the Picasso still leaned on the mantel. The laptop sat open on the coffee table, but the screen was dark. Roux had claimed that it held only Luca's games and schoolwork, but Roux lied. It might be chock-full of her secrets. I didn't have the password, though, so I ignored it. There was already too much house and too little time. I had to think like Roux, then search smart instead of thorough.

I had seen criminals on television hide things inside toilet tanks, under area rugs, between mattresses and box springs. I'd seen multiple movies where bad guys in cheap hotels unscrewed the vents and hid fat wads of money or drugs or guns behind them. I'd seen that trick so much that my guess was Roux would never use it.

"Think, Amy," I said aloud.

The house was Char's, only backward, which meant I knew it intimately. I knew that the door in the foyer that looked like it would open on a coat closet was actually hiding the ill-placed furnace. I knew there was a small hatch up to the attic in the hallway outside the master. But these were places I might choose to hide things. I needed to think like Roux, not me.

I made myself stop and breathe. I had to pick a place and start. If it were me, I would want my secrets near me while I slept. It felt safer. Roux wasn't all that interested in being safe, but she dripped sex and talked about it as if it were a craft. The bedroom was her power center. I went to it.

It was carpeted in a fuzzy shag so old that the color had become unnameable. Something between sludge and old oatmeal. There was a matchy-matchy pecan bedroom set straight out of the eighties, with large round bulbs on the legs of the dresser and the posts on the queen-size bed. The bed itself was a mess, five or six pillows tossed about, and the sheets frothed up like a heap of meringue. Either Roux was a restless sleeper or she'd had company. I touched the pile of bedding. It had not come with the house. The sheets and the duvet looked and felt like something from a five-star hotel.

I searched the dresser first. I doubted Roux would hide things in her panty drawer like a thirteen-year-old girl with a hot-pink diary, but she might tape something to the undersides of the drawers, or behind them. I checked every hidden surface, especially behind the mirror—a very Roux-like spot. I could imagine her here, preening and primping, knowing that as she looked at herself, she was also looking at her secrets.

Nothing.

The master had two long, shallow closets, side by side, taking up an entire wall. All four louvered folding doors were cocked askew. The one closer to me held dive gear, all of it high-end. In the other a row of her beautiful dresses hung beside a shelving unit filled with folded items, the fabrics all expensive and the tailoring exquisite.

Rummaging through her clothes felt weirdly intimate. She had searched me, and now it was as if I were searching her back, running my hands over the shape of her body. She had a lot of shoes. Heels, sandals, flats, booties in buttery-soft leather. They stood in a tidy triple row, filling the floor entirely, but they yielded nothing when I knelt and jammed my hands into them.

There was a bedside table on the far side, under the window. It had a single, shallow drawer. I opened it, releasing the scent of patchouli and almond oil, and saw a box of condoms, a pale blue vibrator shaped like a large-caliber bullet, and a row of lubrication and massage oils. *To use on lawyers,* I thought bitterly. Behind all this was a vape kit and some boxed cartridges, each containing a different kind of pot. If I were looking for her power center, here it was, and yet I found nothing taped to the bottom or behind this drawer either.

I closed it a little too hard, frustrated, and at the exact same time, I heard the unmistakable sound of another door opening. The front door. The sound of footsteps, light and rapid, were already coming down the hall toward me. I hadn't heard the purring of that sleek red car. I had almost no warning.

I dropped flat onto the filthy carpet behind the bed and rolled under. I ended on my back, staring wide-eyed up at Roux's box springs. My breath sounded so loud. I forced myself to slow down, pulling air silently through my nose.

I was sharing the space with still more shoes. Another row was lined up just under the side of the bed that was closer to the door. Three pairs of athletic shoes and a couple pairs of ballet-style house slippers. Between the sneakers I saw Roux's feet in elegant sandals, framed by the hem of her jeans, walk into the room.

I kept my breath even, hoping my pounding heart was audible only in my ears. What was she doing here? These were her gym hours. The feet came directly toward me, to the far edge of the bed. She kicked off the sandals, and I heard the soft thump of what must be her purse landing on the bed. Then I heard a zipper. The jeans dropped around her ankles. She stepped out, and her hand came down and picked them up.

Dear God, was "the gym" a euphemism? Maybe she'd sent Luca to my house so she could open up her sex drawer and work over some hapless, too-chatty lawyer.

Something damp was under my left shoulder. Moisture was now seeping through the fabric of my lightweight summer sweater, a slimy, coin-shaped wetness.

My skin wanted to crawl off my body and put itself directly into bleach. If she were meeting a man here, there was no way I could stay in whatever this little wet spot was, the box springs scraping my nose as Roux banged secrets out of some puffy old banker's freckled hide.

When her cell phone started to ring, I almost screamed over the cheery electronic jangling, so startling was the ringtone in the quiet room.

"Hello?" Roux said. A brief pause, and then, in a bored voice, she said, "Never on the phone."

Silence. She must have hung up, just as she had when she'd said those words to me.

At least the call wasn't some man checking to see if Luca was gone yet so he could come over. It was a poor soul who was caught in her web, like me. Maybe someone I knew. I hoped not Tate. If Tate was paying her, I would have my answer about Phillip. I almost wished Roux had taken the call, so I would finally know.

As if my wish had power, the phone began jangling again.

Roux ignored it. She got up, bed creaking, and walked away. The phone kept on ringing away above me, on the bed. Her feet disappeared from my sight. I could hear her rustling around near the dresser. I'd checked those drawers. They were full of her gym clothes.

Finally the ringing stopped.

I found myself staring at the pair of athletic shoes closest to my face. They were bright blue, and the soles had an odd stacked look to them. Some kind of fancy support system? They were Balenciaga. I could see the designer's name running sideways above the edge of the sole. Her running shoes probably cost more than our mortgage payment, yet right now she was walking her bare feet across this filthy carpet. We could both be getting all kinds of diseases from it. I could feel the disk of wetness like a crawling on my shoulder, as if it were made entirely out of live bacteria. The rental dust bunnies tickled my nose.

The ringing started again. It had to be Tate. Who else could be so pushy and persistent?

The third ring cut off in the middle.

"Oh, for Christ sake, Panda, just pay the rent," Roux said, but with little rancor. Her voice was coming from the foot of the bed.

Panda? It had to be Panda Grier. Roux couldn't possibly know another. She said something to Roux, so agitated that I could faintly hear her. I couldn't make out the words, though. It sounded like a distraught duck, quacking.

"Okay, okay, okay," Roux said, sounding bored more than anything, repeating it until the quacking stopped. "I can't meet you. You've made me late for the gym already."

This upset the duck even more, but it was a relief to me. No lawyer was currently inbound. Roux would pull on yoga pants and leave. I could finish my search, get the hell out.

"Fine. I'm putting you on speaker, though, so I can dress." I heard a soft thump as the tossed phone landed back on the bed.

"Are you alone?" Panda Grier asked.

"Yep," Roux called back. The shirt she'd been wearing landed on the floor.

"I'm not recording this," Panda said.

"I believe you," Roux said. She wasn't as careful with Panda as she was with me. Maybe because Panda didn't sound like she was playing. She sounded weepy and earnest.

"I'm not going to say anything I shouldn't say, okay? So please do not hang up. I just have to make something clear," Panda said.

Roux came back to the bed again, picking up the phone, I thought.

"Can you make it clear while I pee? I'm late, and your 'special lady' has already filled my quota for bullshit this week. I practically had to blow her just to borrow her low-rent pool."

"Tate is not . . . Don't be gross. . . . Don't . . ." Panda sputtered, sounding near tears. The furious kind. I got that. Roux could be so enraging.

At the same time, I couldn't help but notice that Roux didn't talk to Panda like she talked to me. For Panda there was no avidity, no interest. She could have been talking to the pest-control guy. I felt a sour curl of something, almost pleasure. I had more money than Panda, but I didn't think that was the only reason. The respect that Roux showed me felt too grudging to be faked.

I was also relieved to hear that Tate had been her usual pain-in-the-ass self about the pool. Roux must not have any serious leverage; she'd had to ask Tate for a straight-up favor. Either Phillip was faithful or Roux had been too busy blackmailing Panda and me to dig into the story Tate had told about the kiss.

The bathroom door shut, leaving me alone with whatever kind of lice this carpet had.

I found myself staring once again at the blue sneakers. I felt drawn to them for some reason. I could hardly look away. Then it clicked together in my head with a snap so audible I was surprised Roux didn't hear it. I hadn't seen anything like sneakers in the closet. And Roux was going to the gym. When she got out of the bathroom, she would bend down to pick out a pair, and there we would be. Eye to eye.

The toilet flushed.

I rolled out from under as fast as I could and went scrambling on all fours across the room, into the closet with the dive gear. I slipped past her BCD and some hanging wet suits of varied thicknesses, stepping over a mesh gear bag to wedge myself into the corner. I could see through the slats as Roux came padding back out of the bathroom, naked except for a tiny pair of silky panties, carrying the phone. Panda was still talking, and Roux put her back on speaker in midsentence so she could set the phone down on the dresser.

"—my husband is not gay," Panda said. Her voice was a vehement whisper.

"Sure," Roux said, in that enraging way she had.

I stood quiet in the closet, blinking. A thousand things about Panda and her marriage made a thousand kinds of instant sense.

"He finished the program," Panda said, shrill and insistent. "We both did."

"Sure. And those programs super, super work," Roux said, earnest to the point of parody.

Too many things were happening. My shoulder still felt wet. I brushed at it, and when I did, my fingers touched something that made me jump. A used condom that had been stuck to my back plopped softly to the floor.

I almost screamed. I felt my gorge rising. I swallowed hard, easing away from it, disgusted inside and out. I was sharing space with a used condom, and I now knew things about Panda that I did not want to know, things that made me sad and so very sorry for her. I needed everything to stop so I could bathe in bleach and have a quiet nervous breakdown, but Panda was still talking.

"I'm not gay! We have children!"

"Mm-hmm. I forgot that God strikes gay people barren. Or maybe it's that they spontaneously combust in hellfire if they try to breed. Whatever your church says."

It was true that Francis and Panda went to a very conservative church; they had both been raised in it. Now, in a minute's worth of eavesdropping, Panda and her way-too-lovely husband made an awful kind of sense. I felt so sad for both of them, and even angrier with Roux. Just one pair of shoes in the other closet was worth more than the rent on this place, but she was tearing Panda up over it. If the stakes in my own game had not been so very, very high, I don't know what I might have done in that moment.

"My only sin right now is how deep and wide I hate you," Panda said. "You do not understand anything about me or my marriage."

"Okay, well, then go pay my rent for no reason," Roux said. She'd set the phone down on the dresser, and she was stepping, topless, into yoga pants. "I'm going to check the website in two minutes, and if I see I'm paid up, you can go in peace to enjoy thinking about Tate while you make sweet, sweet love to your not-gay husband's toothbrush. If not . . ."

I could feel my entire body shaking, I was so angry with Roux. I saw Panda's whole life as a picture, captured in this single moment. She hadn't befriended Tate to propitiate her like a sex-volcano god. Panda was in love with her.

What an awful thing, to be so love-starved and to settle for so little. She and Francis were caught up together in a lifelong lie, and Roux had threatened to tell her very straitlaced family, maybe her church. Or maybe Roux had only threatened to tell Tate. That would do it, because now that I knew, it was obvious that Panda had hung her heart on the meager peg of Tate Bonasco's shallow friendship.

"I'm paying it now," Panda said. "Although how I'm going to buy groceries this month, I have no idea."

I wondered then if Panda didn't like me because she saw herself in me. I was excessively close with Char for my own reasons, but maybe, to Panda, my fierce protection of Charlotte acted as a mirror, and Panda didn't want to look too deeply at herself. That I understood.

"Here, I'll make it up to you," Roux said. She was holding a sports bra, but she traded it for the phone. She pointed it at herself, but too low for a selfie, throwing her shoulders back and tightening the muscles in her toned abdomen. I heard the whir of the phone's camera, and then she tapped at the screen. "Check your texts." She waited a few seconds, until we both heard Panda's shocked gasp. Then she said, "Hey, straight girl, are mine as nice as Tate's?"

More silence. Panda had closed the connection. Roux chuckled, shaking her head, then tucked her phone into her purse. I watched, seething, as she put on the bra top. She did bend down and dig out a pair of the shoes that had been right by my face not five minutes ago. She carried them away, moving out of the room and down the hall at a fast clip.

The breath all came out of me, and I felt like half my bones had turned to air and leaked out with it. I was shaking with exhaustion, but I couldn't relax. Not yet. She'd said that she was going to check the website. I eased down the hallway, quiet as I could, my back plastered against the wall. She was in the den. I could hear her clacking at the keys.

I checked my watch. I had half an hour, tops, before the DVD was over and the kids started wondering where I was. So far the only secrets I had learned were Panda's.

Panda must have done as she was told, though, because Roux didn't call her back. She made a soft, satisfied sound and stood up. A minute later she walked right past me, unseeing, and went out the door.

I ran to the computer even as she was locking up on the porch. I had to, before it could go dark again. I hoped to God that Roux hadn't forgotten her gym pass or a bottled water. If she came back now, I would have no time to hide.

On the monitor I saw mostly games, but there was also MS Paint, a calculator, Office. I navigated through the doc files and found that there was literally one saved docx on the whole computer, labeled "Civics Paper." Either the computer was as brand-spanking-new as it looked or Roux was letting Luca slack on homeschooling.

I opened it and scanned a few paragraphs. It was about the judicial branch, and it read like it had been stolen directly off Wikipedia. The mom in me reacted, wondering if Roux knew how to check with those anti-plagiarism sites, and then I blinked and shook my head, almost laughing at myself. This was Roux, amoral as a feral cat; she'd just as likely be teaching her kid how to cheat better so he could beat those programs when he went to college. This really did seem to be Luca's computer, though I knew from my eavesdropping that Roux at least used it to surf the Internet.

Time was leaking away, but I took another precious minute to check the browser history. Like every parent with a teenager, I knew how. I found Airbnb, of course; she'd just checked the Sprite House listing. Before that, Roux had been Googling tropical places, reading up on countries with good coastlines, low cost of living, and no extradition treaties. She'd bookmarked seven sites with information about the Maldives.

My heart jumped. I was right. She was running from the law—she must be. Some client or another had been braver than I was and pressed charges. There was a warrant somewhere, probably with serious time attached. I needed her real name, and I would have her.

But where would she keep such a thing? I scrubbed at my eyes. They felt sandy with exhaustion. She must have a safe-deposit box, or she had simply outthought me. She'd said I was like her, but I couldn't guess her hiding place. Well, I was new at this, and she'd been playing her games for years. Her whole life was nothing but games. Other people were nothing more than playing pieces.

As soon as I thought it, I knew.

I knew exactly where I would find what I needed. I knew it as sure as if Roux herself had leaned in close and whispered it into my ear.

I got up and went to the shelves by the fireplace. A few books rested there, grocery-store bodice rippers and thrillers, the covers tattered from many hands. Perfect vacation reading, they were standard fare for rental houses. Two shelves under that, on the very bottom, another rental-house staple: a stack of board games.

I knelt down beside them.

The fat, square Yahtzee box sat on top of longer, narrow boxes that held Scrabble and Clue and Monopoly. And there, between them, the one I wanted. The game that had to be Roux's favorite. Risk.

I lifted Yahtzee with one hand to slide Risk out, but it felt way too heavy. I set Risk aside and pulled the Yahtzee box into my lap. A weighty object slid and thunked as I shifted it.

I opened it, and my heart stuttered. No dice cups, no score pads. The only thing in the box was a snub-nosed revolver, thick, black, oiled to a dull sheen. The name Ruger ran vertically down its short barrel. A box of bullets snuggled in beside it; it wasn't just for show.

I reached for it, wanting to see if it was loaded, then pulled my hand back. I shouldn't touch it. I had no idea how or even if Roux had ever used it, but I didn't want any trace of me—a fingerprint, a cell, a hair—clinging to it.

And anyway, I already knew that the chambers would be full. I felt it as an instinct. She would keep it locked and loaded, oiled and ready. Roux played for keeps.

It was a simple machine, and it had no safety that I could see. I vaguely remembered knowing that most revolvers didn't have them. That was like her, too, though it seemed insane to put nothing but a flimsy cardboard box between a sixteen-year-old boy and a gun.

Jesus, but I wanted out of here. I wanted to go home, scrub and scrub my hands, peel my sweater off and burn it, and stand under a boiling shower. Then I would abdicate. I was in over my head. Roux had a gun.

She must have a reason. That reason might be stashed

in another of these boxes. I didn't want to know, and yet I had to know. I had to know to win Roux's game, and I wanted to win now for more than me. For Panda, who was still caught in it, and for every other person she was twisting and wringing. I wanted to win all the way. To keep my secrets, keep my money, make her crawl away. I couldn't leave with that Risk box right there in front of me.

I opened the lid.

The first thing I saw was the money. Two neat, thick bundles of twenty-dollar bills in bands. More bands littered the box, broken. If this was all her cash reserve, she was running close to empty.

The other half of the box's contents was both more jumbled and more eclectic. I saw a stack of passports and grabbed the first one, flipped it open. Roux smiled out at me from the picture. The name was Ange Renault, just as she'd told Tig. Was that her real name? I checked the birth date, did quick math. If this was her actual ID, then Roux was thirty-seven. I flipped the next one open, and there was a red-haired, unsmiling Roux with the name Angela Lawry. This was the least romantic of all her names, but I knew it wasn't real because the birth date made her twenty-eight. I heard myself whispering out loud, "Bitch, please."

There were still two more, and these both looked brand-spanking-new. I flipped them open and found a blond Roux with the name Angelica Roux, thirty-four, and a matching one for Luca. In this shot he was blond, too. The dye job or the wig washed him out and made him look somehow younger, like a sad, pale rabbit.

I got my phone out and quickly took pictures of the

box itself, the money and multiple passports, and then one of each passport open to the first page. I would Google the names and birth dates and addresses later.

I turned my attention to a dark green box, the hinged kind with a velvet outside. Inside, a fat diamond tennis bracelet jingled against engagement rings, at least four of them, and a pair of sapphire earrings. I took a picture of these things, too.

Finally there was a big manila envelope, stuffed full of papers and photos.

I dumped it out and sifted through it, taking pictures with my phone as I went. There were two birth certificates on top, both issued from Terre Haute, Indiana, that matched the Roux passports. I shuffled past them and found more birth certificates, matched to her other passports. There was a stack of driver's licenses, too, all from different states. Indiana, Maryland, Texas.

There was a handwritten letter. It was nearly illegible, but I pieced the first few sentences together. They were so racy that they made me blush. Sentimental value? The mystery husband? Perhaps she loved him. Or did she keep it because it was devoted to talking about how beautiful her body was? Perhaps the author was married and this was simple leverage. I flipped it over, but it wasn't signed.

Next I emptied out a smaller envelope and found a little stack of Polaroids. I flinched, involuntarily. The top one showed me Roux, but not a Roux I'd ever seen. Both her eyes were blackened, swollen, the left one near shut. More bruises ran down her perfect cheekbone to her jaw on that side, and violet handprints ringed her neck. Her lips were split at one corner, crusted in blood. Looking at these pictures changed the context of the gun somehow.

She stared at the camera with her slits for eyes, her face expressionless. The other five were much the same, showing that whoever had gotten to her hadn't stopped with the face. There was a profile shot and then body shots. Her abdomen and ribs bloomed with navy and purple bruises, dark as pansies.

I flipped the top Polaroid over and found writing on the back. Just two letters: *NE*

I flipped them all. Each had two or three letters on the back, and when I dealt them out in order, they spelled words in all capitals.

NEVER FORGET.

I wasn't sure if these pictures or the letter said more about her mysterious marriage. Maybe both. Maybe neither. She'd been surprised by how much I loved Maddy. Had she and Luca had a bad experience with steps? Or this might be the work of Luca's father.

He's not a good person, Luca had said. *I don't talk about him. Like, ever.*

It was hard to tell Roux's age in these pictures, she was so badly beaten. How long ago had this happened? Was this the thing she was running from? If so, I would have to move forward very carefully. Because of Luca. What would a man who could do this to a woman, even one as duplicitous as Roux, do to a teenage boy? What had he done already?

I still hoped an open warrant, not a man, had sent her hurtling down highways until she landed with Tig Simms. But now a man seemed much more likely. Worse, it could be both. If I sent her to jail, would Luca be returned to the man who'd done this?

Luca didn't seem like a boy who'd been beaten, but wasn't that how domestic abuse worked? Everyone hid it. I only knew the face that Luca showed me. Maddy might know more, though.

I checked my watch. I was nearly out of time. I started putting everything back, but on impulse I pocketed one of the Polaroids. The first one, with *NE* written on the back. It was Roux facing the camera, recognizable even through the bruising. A record of her face could come in handy, and I wasn't likely to get another. She was camera-shy, Tig had said. His own picture of her was distant and blurry. I didn't take it only to be practical, though. Part of me wanted a record of this, proof that she was vulnerable. Proof that she didn't always win her games. I put everything else back exactly as I'd found it.

I was at the front door, ready to go home, when I realized what I'd almost done. We were going diving tomorrow. Roux would bring her gear. I ran back to the master, stopping by the bathroom for a wad of toilet paper. I went to the closet and fished out the condom. It was right beside her gear bag.

Gagging, I hurried back to the bed and flung it under. Then I flushed the toilet paper and got out of there.

As soon as I was home, I slipped my shoes off, not wanting the kids to hear me coming through the front door. They weren't in the keeping room though. They must have decided to watch the video downstairs, taking Oliver with them. He would be asleep by now. I went to the guest bathroom and slipped Luca's keys back into his jeans, then dropped by the laundry room to change my top. I wanted a shower, but there was no time. I headed for the basement.

The door was closed, a minor no-no, but I eased it open and listened. The cheery sounds of the instructional video drifted up the stairs. The kids had the vol-

ume up to eleven; they wouldn't have noticed if I had
tap-danced in. I'd seen the DVD approximately seven
thousand times, so I knew that it was nearly over. I'd
come home just in time.

I headed down to check on the baby.

I was still in my bare feet, quiet against the wooden
stairs. I could see the kids on the sofa. Oliver flopped
in his bounce chair, sleeping. Luca sat on the end of the
couch closer to the stairs, his back to me, facing the TV
screen where a pretty girl in a wet suit was giving the
wrap-up speech.

Maddy wasn't watching. Something was not right
with her. She was lying down, one bare foot hanging
off the sofa, braced hard and tense against the floor. Her
other bare foot rested in Luca's lap in what looked like
a girlfriend pose to me. Her hands were thrown over
her head, as abandoned as Oliver in his deepest sleeps,
and her head was propped on a throw pillow against the
sofa's other arm. Her face was tipped back, and her eyes
were closed, but too tight for her to be sleeping. Her
eyebrows were knit up, and her cheeks were very pink.
A strange little smile played over her face. It was not an
expression I had ever seen before.

It took me a moment to understand what I was seeing. I even opened my mouth to call her name, to ask
if she was all right, but then I realized Luca's arm was
stretched out, running parallel to the tensed leg in his
lap. His right hand disappeared up under the skirt of her
pool cover-up.

I froze for the endless half second it took for me to
make sense of what was happening. Luca himself was
completely dressed, his other hand innocently resting
along the top of the sofa. Maddy gasped, her head tip-

ping back farther and her little smile widening. It broke
my paralysis. I found myself retreating up the stairs,
rapidly, silently, unsure what to do but very sure I did
not want Maddy to know that I'd seen this.

If they had been making out, I would have slipped
upstairs and then started banging noisily around, giving
them a minute so Luca could wipe away Mad's strawberry lip gloss and she could straighten her hair. But
this? I did not know what the hell to do with this.

Luca watching TV, and yet his hand had been busy,
moving between her legs. What the hell was that? It felt
clinical and weird and not appropriate. They were definitely rounding third base, but they hadn't been kissing.
Her cover-up was still on, all the way, and I'd seen the
strap of her tankini top, so that was on, too. What teenagers go straight to third base?

None I had ever heard of. Especially not with the girl
on the receiving end. I had read all the warning articles
about Maddy's generation, how the boys were hooked
on porn, expecting girls to service them. I'd read that
girls Maddy's age were under constant pressure to send
naked selfies and to give out hand jobs like they were no
more serious than good-night kisses. I didn't want that
for my Mads. Neither did Davis. We had both talked
with her frankly about sex and self-respect, telling her
she didn't owe any boy alive that kind of favor.

But I had never thought to warn her about this.

I wasn't even sure what the hell this was, but I was
sure that Davis wouldn't like it. I was even more sure it
could not be healthy.

"Hey, kids! I'm home!" I yelled down the stairs, trying to sound cheery and not as if my eyes had just been
burned out of my head.

There was a pause, a very short one.

"Okay," Mad called up.

I was still loath to step down far enough to see. For her dignity—and my own. "Mads? Can you come up here?"

I wanted her out of that room. Away from Luca.

"Now?" she called back.

"Right now," I called back.

I found myself hoping, near praying, that Roux was running from a warrant. Warrants didn't beat women the way Roux had been beaten. Warrants didn't produce sons or stepsons with disturbing ideas about sex and boundaries. Luca seemed like such a nice kid, but what if he was on the run from a seriously messed-up father figure? They could be fleeing unimaginable abuse. If I told this man where to find them, I'd be no better than Roux. Considering there was a child involved, I might be worse. Dear God, let Roux be running from a warrant.

I also had no idea how much I should tell Davis. How much would Davis want to know? She was his kid, but dads and daughters—too much detail might do more harm than good. At the same time, how many secrets could I wedge between me and my husband before they stretched us too far from each other?

"We're almost finished," she hollered, and I immediately thought, *Finished with what?* I hoped to God she meant the video. Surely they had leaped to opposite ends of the sofa the second my voice broke into their world.

"You've seen that video a hundred times. Can you please come up here?" I hollered back, my voice cracking with embarrassment and strain.

Thank God, thank God, not ten seconds later I heard Maddy stomping her way up.

"What?" she said. I blinked. I had nothing. "Monster?"

"Is Oliver still sleeping?" I asked at last. "Can you run him down to Lisa's so we can hit the pool?"

"Sure," she said. She didn't look any different to me, except her cheeks were still pink. If I hadn't seen what I'd seen, I wouldn't have known that anything more than earnest scuba learning had been going on. There was a secret world, whole and intricate, inside my stepdaughter, and I was privileged to see only its edges. I didn't realize how intently I was staring at her until she added, "You okay, Monster?"

"Of course," I told her. And then I looked her in the eye, very serious. "Are you okay?"

"Super fab," she said, and bounced back down to get the baby.

The mother in me knew I'd have to talk to her about her decisions and her body, try to guide her out of too-deep water into safety. But I had other pieces, awful pieces that Roux had woken up inside me, whispering.

No wonder Roux had reacted so strongly when I told her Luca had been sneaking over to see Maddy. Luca owned Roux's real name, her point of origin, everything I needed, and kids talked. She knew it, I knew it. All teenagers were a whole and secret world unto themselves, and they revolved around each other, whispering. If Maddy and Luca were as close as they had just looked, then everything I needed to take Roux down was already locked tight inside this girl I loved.

Maddy wouldn't tell me if I simply asked, though. She was loyal to a fault, and her feelings for this boy, though new, ran deep. She wouldn't tell unless I made her. My dilemma was, I could. I could make her talk. I could make her tell me. If she didn't know, I could make her ask him. I could push her, turn her, force her.

She wouldn't want her father to know what I'd seen. I could use that. Maddy was a good person, but she was young, her character not fully formed, and kids, under pressure, turned on each other. I had learned this from that sad O. Henry story that had unfolded between Tig and me.

If I were willing to use her secrets against her, against this girl I loved, I could get ahead on points. Beat Roux. I could win. The thought was so attractive. I felt it as electricity, zinging through my body. I could see myself standing over Roux, her past in my hands, making fear rise in her just as she'd done to me. It was heady stuff.

But it would be wrong.

It scared me how far I was down the road to black-mailing Maddy before that thought came. I was already thinking tactics, exactly how to approach her, press her open, dig the information out. She loved me, and I knew her so very well. I could see exactly how to do it.

But what would be broken in the process? Maddy's faith in me, her trust, maybe her love. I could turn her against me at a time when my lies were creating a gap between me and my husband. I might wring out a way to save my family from Roux only to find I'd wrecked it thoroughly myself in the process.

15

OLIVER HAD FINISHED HIS bedtime nurse session. He was asleep on his back in between Davis and me, limp as a sweet little rag. Davis had his big hand on Oliver's full belly, spanning it. I needed to take the baby to his crib and get some sleep. Spending tomorrow on a tiny boat with Roux was bound to be stressful, and I'd have a brand-new diver in my care. I didn't move him, though. Not yet.

I needed to talk to Davis about what I'd seen, and with Oliver here he would stay calmer. I had to do this. One way or another, Luca would be out of Maddy's life come Monday, but a lot could happen in a weekend. I'd left the kids unsupervised for less than an hour. Davis needed to know how important it was that we keep eyes on them.

I touched Davis's arm, and he looked up from his son. My steady gaze let him know this was serious.

"We have to talk about Mads and Luca. There's been a shift. They're more than friends now."

Something male and primal woke up right behind his eyes, immediate and inadvertent. "They're going together?"

"I'm not sure kids call it that these days." I was, in

fact, absolutely certain that they didn't. He was already tense, though. I was gentle with him. "They got a little bit physical with each other down in the basement."

"How physical?" he asked, eyes narrowing. "Do you mean he kissed her and I need to pretend I think that's sweet or he got handsy and I'm probably going to have to go to prison?"

I smiled, mostly to reassure him. "How much detail do you want?"

I hoped not a lot. Every minute I spent with my husband, relaxed and regular, was already a silent lie. I didn't want to say bald-faced untruths about his daughter out loud in our own bed. But I would if he pushed me. Roux had taught me that. There was no way I was going to tell him the details of what I'd seen. It would raise too many questions about Roux and Luca. He wouldn't want them around Maddy or me, and I didn't have a choice in that matter.

He shook his head, emphatic. "No details. Just on a scale of one to pregnant, how worried am I?"

I leaned over Oliver to kiss him.

"Everyone had their clothes on. But not everyone's hands were in the G-rated zone." That was close enough to truth to count.

"Okay." Some of the tension went out of his body, and I knew that what he was imagining bore almost no relation to what I'd seen.

"They've started down a road, though, and we know where it ends," I told him. "Don't let them sneak downstairs, or anyplace, alone. Things can escalate fast at their age."

"I remember," Davis said ruefully.

I did, too. I'd survived my own sophomore year by

stealing desperate, drinking looks at Tig. His narrow hips in low-slung jeans. The light turning the edges of his curls to burnished brass. Then he'd kissed me. His mouth on mine had cut through clouds of pot, a thousand gulps of wine, waking my body to its own possibilities.

I shouldn't be thinking of that. Not at all, but especially not here, in bed beside my husband. The baby we'd made in this same bed was splayed out, so relaxed he was practically a liquid. But a text from "Restoration Garage" had landed in my phone while we'd been pool diving. Nothing serious. Just six words.

You still listen to the Pixies?

A silly question, and yet I felt flushed and a little trembly when I read it, as if I were fifteen again. As if it were a note scribbled on lined paper, folded three times, and passed up a row of desks to me.

I'd known better than to answer Tig, but I'd answered anyway. We'd texted back and forth the whole time I was making dinner. Nothing deep. Music and nostalgia. I told myself it didn't mean a thing.

Now, this close to my husband, I recognized that for the hollow lie it was. It had meant something. If I were back at Tig's right now, just the two of us, I'd be no more safe than Maddy was with Luca. The difference was, I knew better, and I had no loving father, no hovering Monster, to stop me. I had to stop myself.

Davis said, "That's the worst part. I've *been* a sixteen-year-old male, so I know exactly what that kid is thinking. It makes me want to break his arms. A little bit."

"Poor old Duddy," I said, invoking one of Maddy's pet names for him. He smiled. "She's a good kid. Let's not overthink this. We keep an eye on them and make sure they stay busy. They'll be diving all day tomorrow, and no one ever got knocked up in a wet suit."

He nodded, but his forehead was still creased.

I wished I could tell him that in three days it wouldn't matter. Davis and I might have bigger problems then, as he tried to process all the lies I'd told him recently, not to mention all the lies I'd lived in his presence, every day, for years. Either that or I'd break and give Lolly Shipley's rightful money to Roux. I wasn't sure how I would live with myself if I chose that route, but at least then Luca's wandering hands would be in the Maldives. He'd be drinking virgin daiquiris and not being extradited right beside his mother. I wasn't sure what my face did when I thought these things, but it didn't matter. Davis was looking down at Oliver again, talking softly to his son.

"Thank you for being a baby. You have a single teaspoon of testosterone right now, and we appreciate it." I put my hand on Oliver's chest, grateful, too. Davis looked back up at me. "Do you think he's pressuring her? I read about those bracelets. The ones that tell boys what a girl will do, and the boys act like they're entitled to it. Does Maddy have those?"

"Snap bracelets?" I said, and in spite of everything I laughed. "Davis, that was 2003, and anyway, Mads is not that kid. She's lead clarinet in marching band. She's in the D&D club. That is not the snap-bracelet demographic."

"Okay. Standing down. Trying, anyway," Davis said. His thick, dark eyebrows, so like his daughter's, came together, worried. "Should I talk to her?"

"God no," I said instantly.

Maddy would curl up in a little wad and die if he did.
Not to mention I would lose my leverage.

His face became very serious, and he looked me in
the eyes, putting his hand lightly over mine. Oliver's
breath gently moved our hands together. Up and down.
"This isn't your job. It's Laura's. And mine, but this part
is really Laura's, and she's not doing it. Here you are.
Like always. I can't talk to Madison about what it's like
to be a teenage girl. I have no idea. I'm so damn grateful
she has you."

I couldn't bear his sweetness, his sincerity. I was the
one planning to pressure her into betraying her friend to
save myself. I could tell myself that pushing her into sell-
ing out Luca wouldn't matter in the long run. They were
just kids. She would recover and forgive me. I could not
make myself believe it, though. I'd sold out Tig, and it
still echoed in my life. I knew better. I dropped my eyes.

"I better take this little boy to bed."

"I'll do it," Davis told me, but I shook my head.

"He's had a fussy day. If he stirs, I'll rock him a little
and let him get a bumper nurse."

I took Oliver to his crib, and I did rock him for a little,
sitting in our glider with his weight a heavy comfort on
my chest. When he was deeply, deeply out, I put him
to bed.

By then the house was quiet all around me. I went
down the hall to Maddy's big room over the garage. I
eased her door open, and there she was, sprawled out
dead asleep on her stomach. She had kicked one foot
outside the blankets, just like Oliver always did. Her
phone was by her pillow, though she wasn't allowed to
take it to bed. She'd put it on the charger in her bathroom
half an hour before lights-out, but sometime after that

she'd crept out and gotten it back, no doubt to sneak-text Luca. Probably Shannon, too, getting real-time advice on what to say to Luca next.

I wished I knew her security code. Reading their text history would be less damaging than what I planned to do. Her soft mouth was slack, her curls a riot on her pillow. She was so innocent, and she loved me. I was going to damage that innocence, that love. I hoped we could recover.

I went back down the hall, and Davis had fallen asleep, too. I couldn't bring myself to slide back into bed beside him and curl around him as if everything were normal. Tomorrow, after the dive, I was going to peel his daughter open like a little grape.

All at once I realized I was starving. I couldn't remember the last time I had eaten. I'd avoided swallowing at dinner, moving food around, then dumping it down the disposal. Now I felt so empty I was howling.

I went downstairs on autopilot, divorced from my body. I felt as if I were perched on my own shoulder, watching my hands open the fridge and unpack the leftovers. I picked up half a meat loaf and bit into it like it was an apple. I swiped two fingers through the potatoes, then shoved the whole huge scoop into my mouth. I swallowed without chewing, without even tasting, and went back for more. I knew from long experience that once I plowed through all this, I would want sweetness. I didn't keep desserts in the house, but there were frozen waffles, a whole box, and I had some real maple syrup in the fridge. I got the waffles out, still eating meat loaf from my hand, setting the toaster oven to pre-heat.

I knew what came next. I would eat until I was sick

and sluggish with it, then empty myself in ways that would feel glorious and freeing. Once I was done, I would be swamped in immediate shame, so bleak and dreadful that I might go again, two or three times, eating and emptying myself until I was a husk, raw-throated, my eyes bloodshot and watering. I swallowed the meat in my mouth and bit into the loaf again.

I wanted to stop. I couldn't stop.

I wanted someone to talk to, but I had no one. What I wanted was to not be alone, but my lies left me alone even when Davis was six inches away.

I swallowed another gob of food so huge it stretched my throat. I felt like a snake as the mass moved down. I had the crazy urge to call Roux. She'd been so oddly sympathetic. *I want this to work out for you.* At least with her, I could be honest. Her mocking and her needling had stopped. She'd recognized herself in me, and she was such a narcissist it made her warm toward me. That warmth wasn't going to stop her from wrecking me and tearing my family apart, though. Maybe it even made the prospect more appealing to her, like Munchausen's masochism by proxy.

I couldn't call her. I was not such a beaten dog that I would belly-creep for petting from the hand that held the whip. I bit and swallowed, tearing at the meat. What did it say about me that Roux was the only person I could be honest with? Only she saw me down to my core, dark and deep, bitter as wormwood. All the things that made me hate myself, she actively admired, and she was the only one who saw me whole.

I brought the rind of the meat loaf to my mouth again and stopped.

It wasn't true. There was someone else.

Tig didn't know everything, but he knew my past. And Tig, better than anyone, would understand why I had befriended Charlotte. After all, I'd done it to him, too. I'd stalked him and helped him, all the while staying anonymous. He would believe that my motives at least had been good. I set the last of the meat loaf down on the counter by the Tupperware full of cold potatoes and the waffle box. I turned the toaster off.

I was full, but not sick with it. Not yet. I left all the food where it was and rinsed the sauce and potatoes off my hands in the sink. I grabbed my phone off the charging station and went down into the basement, closing the door behind me. I opened up my contacts.

There Tig waited for me, hidden under the innocuous name of his business. I scrolled down to his entry and opened it as I walked all the way across to the wet bar. I wiped at my mouth, crusted in sauce, and then I touched the number.

It only rang twice.

"Smiffy," Tig said. He sounded awake, though it was now midnight. Same old night owl.

"What are you doing?" I asked.

"Nothing. Reading. You okay?"

"No," I said, and this was a relief to let a simple one-word truth pass through my mouth.

"Aw, Smiff," he said, and I wondered why I'd ever thought this nickname was distancing and sexless. He said it so sweet.

"I'm losing. I can't get a toehold. She's so slippery," I said. I sank down until I was sitting on the floor, legs crossed, bent over my phone. "I was wondering if you remembered anything else? About Roux. Ange. Whatever. Anything that could help me."

Tig paused, thinking, but only for a moment. "I'm pretty sure I told you everything."

"Maybe something small. Like the name of a city, or if she ever called her kid anything but Randy. I'll wait. Just take a few minutes and think back through it. It's important. I mean, obviously. Here I am calling you after midnight."

A longer pause this time. In the end he said, "I got nothin'. Is that why you called?"

The question sounded rhetorical. We both knew it wasn't the only reason, but pretending dressed the call up in respectability. My life would be so much easier if I would only learn to buy my own BS. I shook my head. I'd called, in part, because I was so damn tired of lying. So I didn't.

"No." The truth felt so good I didn't want to stop. "My stepdaughter has gotten awfully close with Roux's kid. So close I bet she knows things. Things that would help me fight his mother. I could ask, but she won't tell me. She'll lie. You know how kids are. You know how we were. But I know things about her, too. I could make her tell me. But, God, I would have to pretty much tear it out of her guts. She trusts me. I love her. I don't want to be an awful person." I was crying.

"You're not an awful person," he said, immediate and sure.

"I don't want to be," I said. "I don't want to lose my family."

We sat there with that for a moment.

"Then why are you calling me?" Tig said, and it was an acknowledgment.

I nodded in the dark, although he couldn't see me. "I know. I know. I called because I'm lonely and I'm tired and I'm fighting, and right now it feels like you're the only one who's on my side."

Another pause. "I am on your side."

On the other end of the line, I could hear him moving, maybe sitting down, or if he was in bed shifting the covers. A rustling, intimate sound.

"I shouldn't call you."

"You're not a bad person," he said.

"Okay," I said.

But Tig was sketchy, a little. He knew a fellow who would crush a car without recording the VIN or reporting it. He kept a water pipe right on his living-room table. He had a good heart. He'd always had a lovely heart. He was loyal and kind. But he could be a little bendy on the ethics. A little situational in a way that Davis never was. But so could I, and I'd gotten even bendier since Roux showed up. Maybe I had more in common with Tig than I did with Davis. Still, I called him on it. Called us both out.

"If I'm not a bad person, what am I doing creeping down to the basement to talk to you in the middle of the night. My husband is asleep upstairs. If this wasn't wrong, I wouldn't hide it."

He gave a low chuckle. "I don't know. All I know is, I'm glad you called. I keep thinking about you. Nine times an hour."

"I'm married," I said. I wanted to hear the words out loud.

"But I'm single, so mostly it's you being terrible," he said, and I let out a startled burst of laughter.

"Did you just throw me under the bus again?" I said.

"Oh, yeah. Too soon?" he said.

But too soon wasn't the problem.

"More like too late," I said. "I love my husband, Tig. I love my baby, and Mads. I love my life here."

I didn't say that life might be blown apart in a matter of days. But we both knew it. There was a good chance this family I'd made would fall to pieces. And if it did . . .

"We haven't done anything we can't walk back, Smiff," he said. "And I haven't been pining. We were close, yeah, but we were also fifteen. I don't know if this, right here, you and me, is anything. All I know is, I want to text you every other minute. I want to call you. I know you're married. But I want you to come back over."

My whole body went still. My hand was wrapped around the phone so tight I was surprised the screen didn't crack and shatter.

"I keep thinking about you, too," I admitted.

"If that's wrong . . . well, hey. I'm not a perfect guy. I never had a friend like you. Everything between us was always so easy. Back when we were kids, I didn't think of you like that, you know? Not like a girlfriend. You were just Smiff. My Smiff, who had my back. I was happy when you were around. That night, before it all went bad, when we kissed, something changed. I thought it did."

He paused, and I didn't think he would say more unless I answered. I wanted him to say more.

"I thought so, too," I said, an invitation to go on. He took it.

"I'd been with girls before. More than a couple, to be honest. I was with a lot more after. But it's never been easy like that. Like we were. Never in my life. I haven't been pining, but maybe, in the back of my head, I compared, you know? Then you showed up, and I can't stop wondering, what if we'd never gotten on the road? What if we'd gone back to that mattress together? Slept it off. Where would we be now?"

I'd wondered that myself, but I couldn't talk. My throat was clogged with tears.

He had no idea what he was saying to me, how much it meant. Back then I'd hated myself. I'd loathed my body so damn much, I'd thought no one could ever love me. But he had. Not *in spite of.* Not *even though.* He'd grown feelings for me simply because of who I was. Who we were together.

"I'm married," I said again. But lots of people were married, and they wrecked it. I could see now how easy it was. It was little baby steps down a road. A text here, a phone call there. The person I was married to was busy, and I was under pressure, and we had this baby, which meant less sleep and less sex than we were used to. Plus, I was lying to him every minute. If my lies came out, I might not have the choice to keep my marriage. "I love him," I said, and that was also true.

"Then don't let me get between that," Tig said. "Because we're heading that way. I mean, you know that, right?"

"I know that," I said.

We sat quiet, listening to each other breathe.

"I better go," I said. And I had to. I had to hang up. Talking to Tig felt too good. It was a safety net. A haven, if I refused to pay and Roux destroyed me. I remembered that night, the night he kissed me, before it all went wrong. I could run toward him now if I chose. It would feel like it had on that dark road, when I stamped the pedal down. I knew then, for certain, that I'd been driving, not that it mattered now. But I remembered exactly how it felt to power us up and over the railroad tracks, dangerous and free, unsure of a safe landing. I could do it again. Tell Roux to fuck herself and let whatever happened happen. Be airborne. Let gravity decide how I came down. It was so tempting.

"You still play the guitar?" he asked, breaking the silence.

I was shaking my head, as if he could see me. As if he were close enough to touch.

"Not for years," I answered.

"You could pick it right back up," he said. "I bet it'd be so easy."

I let that sit, too. It was difficult to talk at all, but in the end I said, "I gotta go."

"I know," Tig said. "I'm here, though."

"I know," I said, and I closed the connection.

16

I WOKE UP WITH a headache hovering at the base of my brain, a low-slung throbbing of anxiety. It was as if I'd slept all night on the edge of a cliff, feeling myself teeter in my sleep. I popped a couple of Excedrin and ignored it as best I could. Maddy and I had to head out for the docks early, leaving Davis to sleep in as long as Oliver would allow.

Roux and Luca were going to meet us there. Roux'd figured, rightly, that I couldn't work against her while prepping for a dive. I didn't have a spare minute, helping Captain Jay and his middle son, Winslow, get the *Miss Behavin'* loaded up and ready.

Miss Behavin' was Jay's smaller boat, a thirty-foot Munson that could comfortably accommodate ten divers. It was late in the season; we were running with seven today. The other group arrived first, a couple who introduced themselves as Tim and Leslie Babbage, plus Tim's older brother, Mark. They were all experienced divers in their late thirties, down from Atlanta on a weekend trip to keep their certifications fresh.

Maddy was talking to Winslow and me on the dock, agitating for the English Freighter, a favorite dive spot of hers, but she stopped in midsentence, staring past me, her breath catching in her throat. I turned and saw Luca hurrying toward us. He was carrying two gear bags, the lean muscles in his arms flexing, and the wind off the ocean made his hair stream back like a baby Fabio's. Winslow, who was forty-something and had two girls of his own, shot me an amused glance. I smiled back, but it was hollow. Luca's eyes were on the boat. He was looking past Maddy to the day ahead, and all she saw was him.

Roux sauntered toward us in his wake, and the very sight of her jacked my heart rate, made me work to keep my smile in place. Not that anyone was looking at me. Both brothers, the married one and the spare, paused to watch Roux. Her pale pink bikini and her skin shone the same through a gauzy white cover-up, the colors and the sheerness conspiring to make her look more naked than naked. Even Captain Jay, who was pushing seventy, stopped to look.

Leslie Babbage smacked her husband's shoulder, and that broke his hypnosis. He laughed and threw an easy arm around her, turning away with her to stow their gear.

The single brother, Mark, kept right on looking.

Roux was aware of his gaze. I could see it in the extra swing she added to her hips, the sly glance she sent me as I walked out to meet her with the liability paperwork.

"Men are too easy. All I have to do is show up and have tits," she said, skipping the greeting to go straight to gross generalizations.

"How clever of you to have tits, then," I said, deadpan.

That made her chuckle, but I could feel the prickle of something electric in the air between us. She was no more at ease than I was, and I was glad of it. If she was on edge, then there must still be a way for me to win her game. God, how I wanted to win.

There was an old picnic table on the walkway just before the dock, and she sat down to fill out the forms with made-up information. It rendered them useless, but there was nothing I could do about that. It was an added pressure pulsing at the base of my neck. The whole day felt like disaster coming, though it was warm and breezy-beautiful, a summer throwback with a high of eighty-seven. In Florida this passed for fall.

My feelings of dread, I knew, had little to do with to-day's dive, and yet they colored everything. The week-end was being eaten up with boat trips and Roux and family obligations. I had almost no room to maneuver, and my time was running out.

Roux was flipping through the pages to find the sig-nature lines. She paused to look up at me. "Take good care of my boy today."

"Of course," I said.

If she'd been any other mother, I would have asked her to do the same for Maddy. I'd tell her what I'd seen down in my basement. But this woman weaponized sex, and she was proud of it. She might be concerned, but she also might laugh and give Luca a gold-star sticker. I didn't know if she was protecting the sweet kid that Luca seemed to be or actively raising a predator to fol-low in her footsteps.

Now she was filling out his forms, putting in his fake name. He was complicit in this much at least. He an-swered to "Luca" like a pro. But if he was trying to keep his mother out of jail, I couldn't blame him. Most kids would do the same. That went double if the two of them were on the run from the man who had pounded her pretty face and her whole body black and purple, until it was as ugly as raw meat.

Every instinct, every minute I had spent with him, said Luca was troubled but not rotten. He was also likely new to this. After all, Roux had three full sets of fake ID. He had only one, and the "Luca" passport had been shiny-new and free of stamps. I believed he'd been protected, kept separate from her career until now. Then something—an arrest warrant, an attack, or a marriage gone so sour that it turned deadly—put them on the road with whatever possessions they could pack up in a hurry.

And Roux loved him. That was obvious. Maybe she wanted better for him than for herself. Most mothers did. As she finished the forms and rose, I decided I had to say something.

"Can I talk to you, mom to mom? About Luca?" All movement in her body stopped, as if I'd hit a button. I had her complete attention. Roux's stillness, the pre-planned absence of any tells, was her tell in and of itself.

"Okay," she said. Light, but I heard wariness be-hind it.

"Don't let the kids wander off together, even if you're just in another room." There was pleasure, only the smallest twinge, in saying it. Earned, I thought, consid-ering how she'd dumped on my girl. Maddy tomboyed around in no makeup and outsize, floppy clothes, and Roux had acted as if Luca were too beautiful and shin-ing to even notice she was female. I wasn't sure what was going on between the kids, but he definitely knew she was a girl. Even so, Roux was staring at me blankly, as if I'd spoken in Latin. I clarified, "Things have heated up between Luca and Madison."

She shook her head, instantly dismissing me. "No. You misunderstood her. He's not into her that way. He told me." That made me laugh, in spite of everything. The real deal, from my belly. Roux's eyebrows rose. "What?"

I said, "You, the cagiest, most suspicious bitch on planet earth, you believe a teenage male who says he's 'not interested in a girl that way.'" Her gaze turned speculative, even concerned. "I'm not basing this on anything Mads told me. Things have gotten physical. I saw them."

"How physical?" Her voice was sharp.

I gave her the same version I'd told Davis, loath to be more honest with this woman than with my own husband. "Everyone had their clothes on, but there were some wandering hands."

I could practically see the wheels turning behind her eyes. Her gaze went to Maddy and Luca. They'd loaded the bags, and now they were standing on the deck together, yammering back and forth, pointing at an enormous pelican who had lighted on a nearby pylon.

Luca did genuinely seem to like her, the way Tig had liked me once upon a time. Maybe, in Luca's head, they were only friends, but something else might well be growing in the depths of him. It had happened that way for Tig. He'd told me so last night, and in spite of everything I felt a little flush of pleasure. Tig would be sleeping now, paying for his late night, but I thought he'd text me as soon as he was up. It scared me, how much I was looking forward to that. Waiting for it, even. A bright spot in a brutal day.

Roux folded her arms, and her eyes on Maddy and Luca went as cool as a shark's. Her face remained as serene as ever, but inside I could almost feel her balance shifting. She slid me a sideways, questioning glance. She knew as well as I did that teenagers talked. They told each other things they'd never tell adults.

She must be wondering what Luca might've spilled. Wondering if I had a way to get that information out of my girl. My dread of the day intensified. All at once I didn't want her in the same ocean as Maddy. I kept my face as serene as hers, though, as if such a thing had never occurred to me. As if we were just two moms, neither of whom was ready to pick out our granny names.

In the end she shrugged and handed me the paperwork, saying, "Okay. Consider me on alert. God. What a puppy." She rolled her eyes. "I told him not to get attached."

I left to help Jay and Winslow with the final checks and to decide a destination. Maddy and the Babbages sat in on that conversation. She was still set on the English Freighter, named for the enormous cargo ship that had been sunk there to form an artificial reef. I suggested an easier site. The English Freighter's stern was in a trench eighty feet down. Maddy kept pushing, though. The bow rested at fifty-five feet, on a plateau with plenty of life, perfect for Luca. I knew why she was pressing. Last time we were there, we'd seen a bull shark. Luca was wild to see one. The Babbages chimed in on Maddy's side, reminding me I had only one student to watch out for. Everyone else was an advanced diver with multiple certifications, and dive conditions were near perfect. Calm seas and sunshine. I gave in.

"The English Freighter it is."

We were ready to go, but Roux and Luca weren't on board. She'd called him out to the picnic table, and they were locked in an intense conversation. She was dressing him down pretty good by the looks of it. She put a firm hand on his shoulder, but he shrugged her off, shaking his head in an emphatic no.

I wondered exactly what he was denying. She wouldn't mind a crush; all kids got them. But she'd care passionately if Luca had been spilling secrets. He turned his back on her and stomped toward the boat, still shaking his head in adamant denial. Maybe he really hadn't told Maddy anything. If they were being chased by the man who had beaten his mother so brutally, he might well have kept his mouth shut. When I confronted Maddy this afternoon, treating her exactly the way Roux was treating me, demolishing her trust in me, would it be for nothing?

Luca came aboard, sitting down by Maddy at the back of the boat, squarely in the sunshine. Roux followed, her face deliberately blank, manually leaking the tension out of her body like it was so much air. The Babbages had all chosen seats under the canopy. Instead of joining Luca, Roux went into the shade and took the open seat by Mark, giving him a brilliant smile.

We set out, and I chose a spot between the two groups, trying to eavesdrop in both directions. The kids leaned over the side on a dolphin watch, hoping some would come and give us an escort. They liked to play in the wake. Maddy was in high spirits. Luca seemed to be as well, but he kept stealing little sideways glances at his mother. The fight had looked like a whopper. I'd need to make sure his head was fully in the game before I took him under.

Roux, for her part, seemed oblivious that she had ever borne a child named Luca. She gazed up at Mark Babbage, asking him how he got into scuba. He was a good-looking fellow, tall and broad and athletic. He and his brother had grown up on the coast of Texas, he was saying, and they'd both been diving since they were kids. They'd met Leslie on a scuba trip to Roatán, and she was as rabid about it as they were.

"What about your wife?" Roux asked him.

"She never got into it," Mark said, and then his smile turned wry. "That's one reason she's not my wife any-more."

"I'm sorry," Roux said, not sounding it. "I'm sepa-rated myself. I know how hard that is. So what do you do when you aren't diving?"

"I'm a lawyer," he said, and almost instantly her body angled itself toward him. He was already turned so far her way that his back was to his brother. I knew then that we'd lost Roux for the duration. She was patholog-ical, unable to stop seeking marks and stories and law-yers. This must have been how she'd looked at Tig, how she'd gotten him talking. I didn't like to think about her hands on him, her claws working into him.

"Want to buddy up? I don't want to watch kids doing skill checks," she said, smiling up at him. "I want to go all the way down to the stern."

"Heck yeah," he said.

I was glad of it. I didn't want her anywhere near Maddy. Plus, I'd have more focus without her eyes on me, and since she and Luca were in a fight, I didn't want her presence distracting him. Luca was still shooting unhappy glances in her direction, so I went to the sunny part of the boat and got my fish ID cards out of my dive bag. I gave them to Maddy, and she started showing him the animals we would most likely encounter. By the time we neared the site, he was deep into it, more relaxed.

We all began putting on our wet suits and doing our final gear checks. I supervised Luca as he set his dive computer. He did a good job, eyes on the screen and not his mother, but when we were done, he said, "Is she not coming with us?"

I shook my head. "She wants to go deep, is all. You have to stay above sixty feet until you do your advanced class, mister."

His nostrils flared. "Sure," he said, sounding just like her.

I understood his disappointment. This was supposed to be a family outing, and his mom had made it into a singles mingle. She was turning now to have Mark zip up her wet suit, giving him a coy smile over her shoulder.

We anchored near the bow of the freighter, and one by one all three Babbages giant-stepped expertly off into the water. Roux paused at the brink, her regulator in her hand.

"Hey, Madison," she called. It was the first time she'd ever said Maddy's name. "You want to come on the deep dive with us? Or stay in the kiddie pool?"

I could feel the little hairs on my arms trying to rise, even compressed by my wet suit. I would not send my girl out of sight, into the sea, with Roux. Not with Luca's secrets likely locked up tight inside her.

"No, thanks," Maddy said, hardly looking up. All her focus was on Luca.

Roux didn't press. She put her regulator in, and then,

with a step and a splash, she was gone. I felt instantly calmer.

"You ready?" I asked.

Luca nodded. He seemed more focused now, too, shuffling in his fins toward the back of the boat. I held my mask and regulator to steady them and giant-stepped in. The ocean caught me. It was in a beautiful mood, sloshing me gently as I followed the trail line out of the way. I turned back to watch Luca make a good entry. He'd remembered to inflate his BCD, and he bobbed to the surface, grinning around his regulator. He signaled Winslow that he was okay, then got out of the way for Maddy.

We stayed on the surface for a few minutes, doing Luca's buoyancy and weight checks. He was light, and I had Winslow pass me another two pounds. It was part of his certification, but it also gave Roux and the Babbages time to follow the side of the wrecked ship down and away from where we would be diving.

We descended slowly, staying vertical, letting Luca get his bearings and equalize. Visibility was okay, about thirty feet, and I saw Luca's eyes widen with excitement when he looked down between his fins and realized we were descending into a huge, weaving cloud of silvery, small baitfish. They parted for us like a curtain, and the bow of the English Freighter came into view. Luca's bubbles stopped.

I touched his arm to get his attention, then waved my hand gently back and forth, the signal to breathe. I heard his Darth Vader inhale, and then his bubbles were streaming up again. Maddy came up on his other side and grabbed his hand, tugging at him, wanting to show him a pair of butterfly fish. They were shadowing each other, mated for life.

He checked his air gauge and then turned with her. Maddy played her light over a flashy little school of blue-and-yellow damselfish, making their colors brighten and shine. I followed, glad to see them sticking so close. This was my favorite place to be on earth, and yet I could not shake my unease. We were all in the water with a predator, much more dangerous than any bull shark.

Luca was doing a good job with his form and his buoyancy, though to stay in position he made little flaily kicks and hand waves, very common for new divers. He only blundered into the bottom once, churning up the silt. The salt in the water made him more buoyant than he had been in the pool, and he'd overcorrected. He inflated and got up without overcompensating, then got into a good horizontal position, Maddy's hand steadying him.

Just to starboard there was a low, cavelike opening in the hull, the edges mossy and jagged. I let myself sink down to peer inside with them. We hovered, and I added my large, bright light to Maddy's smaller one, pointing into the interior. We weren't going to penetrate. Neither Luca nor Maddy had the training, and I did not have the equipment. Our light captured the head of a green moray eel poking out of some rubble. A little sea turtle soared over the eel, hurrying out of the opening past us. She angled up, going for a breath. Luca turned to hurry after her. She sped up, frightened, giving him a disgruntled look over her shoulder. He stopped and simply hung vertically in the water, watching her flippers spinning her away.

I was touched by his instant and intuitive empathy. Whatever had happened between him and my step-daughter, I couldn't believe it was pure, manipulative evil. I hovered, my hands clasped, watching as Maddy took his arm and rolled him, showing him how to lie back and watch the turtle rise out of our range of visibility. Then she tugged him onward, down the side of the ship.

I stayed a few feet behind, letting them play their way down the slope, trusting Maddy. She stopped them right at fifty-five feet. They were still holding hands, though I wasn't sure if this was underwater romance or security. He tried to move down, and she signaled no, showing him her depth gauge. He checked his, then gave an okay sign. He also checked his air again, forming a good habit, and reported it to Maddy without being asked. She reported her air level back. She'd used less, which was no surprise. New divers were air pigs, plus he was male and weighed more than she did.

Watching the kids spin and frolic like seal puppies, I felt my headache abating. The underwater magic was doing its good work in me. The ocean seemed large enough to hold the truth, and me, and even Roux, with room enough to be at peace. We didn't see the other group at all, and Roux's literal vanishing into the depths helped, too. When Luca's air gauge read 1800 psi, I signaled to turn the dive, and we worked our leisurely way back to the anchor line.

Once we reached it, Luca did a perfect pre-ascent check, signaling, noting his time, and then looking up, his hands raised over his head to protect it. We flutter-kicked gently up, deflating as we went, though once I had to take Luca's hose and vent air; he was rising too fast. At fifteen feet we made our safety stop, hovering and letting our bodies decompress while a trio of barracuda hung in the water watching us.

When we surfaced, Luca's eyes were positively glowing. He swapped his regulator for his snorkel, pausing in between to say to Maddy, "Oh, my God!"

"I know, right?" she said, swapping out her own regulator.

She headed for the ladder first, handing her fins up to Winslow. He took them, looking past her to me. I felt a shiver in my spine when I saw his face, concerned and questioning. I gave him the okay sign, but he did not signal back.

I heard him call to Captain Jay, "Dad? Come here a sec?"

Luca headed up the ladder next. Winslow helped him aboard, but he was still darting glances at me, his broad, brown forehead wrinkled. As soon as Luca was out of the way, I passed my fins up to him.

"Where's Roux?" he asked me, quiet, as I came up.

I dropped my regulator out of my mouth.

"She's with the Babbages," I told him, but as I climbed aboard, I saw that all three Babbages were already sitting in the shade of the canopy, eating oranges.

"They came up fifteen minutes ago," Winslow said. I hadn't seen them pass us. All my focus had been on the kids, plus they could have come up the other side. Winslow was still talking. "Mark got low on air, but she had more than half her tank. He said she joined your group?" Mark had a good seventy pounds on her; he would have used his air up much faster.

"We didn't see her at all," I told Winslow.

Captain Jay was scanning the water. I turned, still in

my gear to help Jay look, and so did Winslow. My mind was racing. The sea was relatively calm. If there were bubbles, they would not be hard to find. But there was nothing.

"Hey, where's Roux?" Mark called behind us.

"What?" Maddy said. She'd just finished helping Luca out of his BCD.

I ignored them, looking over the site, still bubble hunting. My heart was pounding. A thousand different things were happening in my head, too fast to catalog or even comprehend. I could see only one thing true and clear: No bubbles meant no breath. No breath meant—

"She was with you," Luca said. His voice had gone high, edged in hysteria.

Mark was talking, fast and defensive. "No, she went to join your group. You guys were right there. We saw you."

"You left her?" Luca said, the pitch of his voice going higher.

"You were twenty feet away." Mark almost sounded pleading, but I kept my eyes on the water, seeking.

No bubbles. No breath.

No Roux. I felt sweat break out all over my body, inside my wet suit. I'd dreamed of this, a world with no Roux. In my dream it had made everything so easy, but now her son was standing right behind me.

Mark was still babbling. "I swear, she was heading right to you when I went up." His brother put a steadying hand on his shoulder.

"Stop," Captain Jay said, firm and calm. "Everyone, put your head over the sides, all the way around the boat. Look for her bubbles."

They hurried to obey, but the pros all knew that it

was busywork. I checked my air gauge. Half empty, but changing tanks would cost me precious minutes.

"Since they came up, I've only seen one patch of bubbles," Winslow told me on the quiet. I let that sink in, my emotions too mixed and loud to read. "We assumed it was all four of you. I'm going to gear up." He headed for the cabin, moving fast.

I called, "Mads, get me a full tank from that rack," then opened the storage chest to dig out one of Winslow's wreck reels.

"I don't see any bubbles?" Luca said, almost a howl.

"Monster, oh, my God," Maddy said, hurrying to me with the tank, tears standing in her eyes.

"What does it mean?" Luca said, following her to me. Maddy turned to put her hand on his shoulder, and he shook her off, like an angry horse touched by flies. "What does it mean? We don't see bubbles."

Mark looked sick and stricken. We all knew what it meant. I was already sliding my fins on again. Winslow was back on deck, attaching his BCD to a fresh nitrox tank.

"If there's not bubbles, how's she breathing? Is she down there? Not breathing?" Luca said. His eyes, wide and terrified, streamed tears.

Either every minute counted, or I had all the time in the world. I took thirty seconds.

"There's a chance she's in the wreck," I told Luca. "If she is, her bubbles are trapped inside the hull, okay?" He nodded, a little calmer. Calm enough to let us all do what we had to do. "Anyone here trained on penetrating wrecks?"

"None of us," Leslie said, speaking for her group.

I said, "Then keep your asses on the boat."

If Roux was alive, she had to be in the wreck. The last thing I needed was a herd of Babbages going in and getting stuck and lost and churning up the silt.

"You said not to go in there," Luca said, as I shuffle-walked to the back.

Winslow was still gearing up.

I called to him, "I'll take the east side, you go west," and then put my regulator in.

"Got it," Winslow said.

I could hear Maddy saying all the right things now to Luca, like a pro. "Because you're not even open-water-certified yet. Monster's penetrated wrecks a hundred times. Winslow, too. They know how to—"

Then I was splashing in, the extra air tank dragging me down. I gave myself more buoyancy and started a controlled descent, horror and a strange, giddy hysteria at war inside me. I breathed, tried to let the chaos and fear clogging the boat stay on it, high above me. I equalized, calmer and sharper with every foot I dropped. I left the spare tank clipped to the anchor line, then kicked away, heading down the east side of the English Freighter.

If Roux was dead, my heart did ache for Luca. That was a real, true feeling, and I clung to it. Luca's father, the man he didn't speak of, could well be the same man Roux was running from, violent and dangerous. If Roux was dead, that man would come for Luca. It would be awful for Jay and Winslow, too. They could lose their business, though they had done nothing wrong. I could lose my job as well, all because Roux had been reckless. I could not let any of this happen, if I could help it. I would not. But another thought slipped through, bubbling up unstoppably.

If Roux was dead, so many things got easy.

I pushed that away. I had to do everything by the book right now. I had to make the same choices I would make if it were Leslie Babbage or my own Mads gone missing. But if Roux was dead . . .

I sped up, pushing through a swirling curtain of baitfish. I'd never lost a diver, and I was damn well going to do this search correctly, as if my goal were not to lose one now. I made myself imagine bringing up Roux's body, still and pale and open-eyed, unbreathing, laying her out on the deck in front of her son, in front of Maddy. Jesus. My breath hitched, and I worked to even it out. I could not afford the air that emotion cost me.

I was going to do this right. And yet.

I'd sent Winslow west. The kids and I had stayed near the bow, but definitely west. If Roux had gone in, it was more likely she'd done it here, on this side. Even with the limited peripheral vision the scuba mask gave me, I'd have been much more likely to see her if they'd come up on the west. When I chose east, I'd given myself the greater odds of finding her.

I understood then, very deep, deeper than thinking, that I was keeping my options open.

I shook that away, focused on efficient movement and conserving air. If she was findable, I'd find her. She would be alive—or not. Based on my own air gauge, even if she'd gone in hale and hearty, she was out of gas now, or damn close to it.

I came to the first opening in the ship's hull, and I paused. I'd done this dive site fifty times, maybe more. I knew this wreck inside and out. Of the three dangerous entry points on this side, I thought this was least likely. It was a rusty, jagged fissure, just wide enough for a small, lithe woman to slip through. I'd half hoped to find her caught right here, fins waving, arms and head stuck inside, her lower half outside, like Pooh Bear.

But there was nothing. I played my light inside, and it caught movement. My heart stammered, but it was only a goliath grouper, big as Roux. He went gliding away from my light, deeper into the ship's interior. The water inside looked clear. No chance she'd come into this tiny space without disturbing silt.

But I could still go in and search it. If I did it, I'd use the last third of my air on this spot. I'd have to go back for the second tank or surface. If Roux wasn't dead already, she definitely would be by then. She wasn't in this hole. The water was too clear. Except no one knew that but me.

I hovered at the entrance. It was terrible and so tempting all at once. Poor Luca, but lucky me. Lucky Panda. Lucky everyone she'd hurt. Lucky world, lighter with no Roux on it. But Luca . . .

I turned away, swimming for the second opening. She could well be dead already. If I searched the empty hole, I'd have to live with never knowing. Never knowing if it had been an accident or my choice that ended her. I knew, better than anyone, what a weight that was.

I came to the second hull breach, larger and higher up on the side of the boat. It was my favorite point of entry for this wreck. It opened into a wide galley that had a rotted-out doorway that led deep into the interior. I'd once gone all the way to the engine room from here and found it still filled with fascinating artifacts. I played my light inside, and I saw that the silt had been disturbed. It was subsiding, but it was definitely murky.

My heart caught. Through the surging mire, past the galley, in the hallway, I thought I saw a flash of purple. Roux had been wearing purple split fins, the expensive ones that kept their color even in the deeps.

I chased the movement with my light, and through the billowing clouds of silt I saw it again. Neon purple. Definite movement.

She could be alive, kicking. Or it was only the sea, sloshing her still limbs back and forth. I did not decide. My body was already moving, tying my wreck reel off on a jagged metal spire I'd used before, and I knew, for me, there had never really been a choice. I wasn't Roux. I wasn't like her. If there was breath in her, I would not leave her here.

I played out the line as I eased forward, my visibility reduced by darkness and the stirred-up silt. I felt more than saw my way toward that purple flash I'd noticed, pausing to wrap my line around another spire before I took the bend into the hallway. The farther in I went, the less I could see. But I could feel a current of water pushing at me from movement ahead. I swam toward it.

I heard her before I spotted her. Her noisy breath, still going, now in almost zero visibility. I turned toward the sound, blind, and found her with my hands. She went wild at my touch, her limbs becoming ropy bands of panicked muscle, clutching and tearing at me. She was tangled in something, lines or netting. I could feel it winding around me now. Even over the thunder of my own breath, I could hear her scream. I pushed at her hands, seeking her head, her face. One wild hand punched me, dazing me, almost knocking my regulator out. I found her head, though, and I pulled her face to mine. Behind the mask her eyes were crazed, and her hands tore at me, knocking my own mask away. I let it go.

I was doubly blind now, the salt burning my eyes, but I held her head steady, made her look at me. Right then her bubbles stopped. I heard that half suck in, and then the halt of sound, and I knew that she was out of air. She spit her regulator out and screamed at me, a banshee wail, releasing her last bubbles.

She seemed then to understand at least what I was, and her hands came for my face. Her nails scraped at my cheek as she tore at my regulator. She was past human thought, and I knew she would kill us both if I fought her. I let her take my air source and jam it into her own mouth. I heard her panicked, deep inhale, and then she was choking on the water caught inside it. Her body spasmed, coughing, but at least she was no longer fighting me. I kept up a slow and steady exhale, finding the secondary air supply that was built into my BCD. I put the mouthpiece in. Now we were both on my tank, tied together by a frail length of tubing and the twining of something ropelike and binding. I did a quick gauge check. I was down to my last fifth of a tank, and Roux was breathing in great, heaving gulps.

I got her face again, pulled it close to mine, forehead to forehead, my bare eyes peering into hers through the mask. I breathed in and out, slow and steady, calming her by something like osmosis. The netting had me now, too. I could feel it. I waited until she was still, her breath easing, then managed to free one arm and reach my thigh.

She jerked again when she saw the silver flash of my knife near her face. I kept a good grip on it. If I dropped it, we were screwed. She had me so entangled that I doubted I could get to the backup mesh cutter I always stowed in a low pocket on the BCD.

I began cutting the netting away, patient, slow, my movements minimal, preserving air. She hung still, letting me work, and once her hands were free, she reached to see my air gauge. I heard her shuddering cry when she saw it. Not good, but I didn't think about that. I got myself loose and then peered at her through the churning silt. Her BCD and tank were too entangled. I cut some straps and unfastened others, then helped her slide out of it. I'd dropped my light, and I could see its beam slicing through the blackness to our left. Its beam was the only way I knew which direction was down. I left it, reaching instead for the wreck reel clipped to my waist, finding the line. Roux clung to me, slim and trembling in her wet suit, her protective shell removed.

I had to move her hands manually off my arms, putting them on my body. She barnacled onto me, shaking. I followed the reel's line with my hands, working us out of the wreck, foot by foot.

Once we came around the corner, I could see light from my entry point. My air had redlined, and we were seventy feet down. No time to get back to the other air tank. We had to go up. Right then. Still, I took it as slowly as I could, considering the doubled buoyancy, following our shared bubbles up, Roux shuddering and moaning in my arms.

Three minutes later and I would have found only her body. A minute later—thirty seconds, even—she might have drowned me with her, damn her eyes.

We broke the surface, and I dumped the last bit of my air into the BCD, though it wasn't enough to keep us on the surface. I turned her, cradling her with her back to me, floating her in a tired-diver hold. We both dropped our mouthpieces. No point. The tank was dead dry. She took in heaving gulps of fresh air, limp, and I used my free hand to blow more air into my BCD, making it buoyant enough to float us both. I was so exhausted that if the seas had been rougher, we might have drowned right there, with the boat only a hundred yards away.

I unclipped my emergency signal float and unfurled it, and it was a fight to find the breath to get it inflated. The neon tube rose bright and slim from the water like a cheery orange finger, telling them that we were here. They had to retrieve the anchor, but within a couple of minutes the *Miss Behavin'* started her engines and turned our way.

As they got close, I could see Luca and Maddy hanging over the bow, and all three of the Babbages as well, peering across the water at us. Maddy's face was swollen from crying, and Luca looked haggard and terrified.

When the engines cut, Roux lifted one arm in a wave. I think only then did they realize I wasn't holding up a body. Across the water I heard Luca burst into a hail of noisy tears. Maddy grabbed him in a hug, and he turned toward her, wailing in relief.

Jay hit the siren, an alarm that blared down into the water. It would reach Winslow, signaling both where the boat was and that he should come up.

I turned my back and began towing Roux toward the ladder. She'd lost one of her fins, and she lay helpless in my arms. She was craning her neck, trying to see me, but she couldn't see my face in her position.

"This changes nothing," she said. The words rasped out in a fierce and angry whisper, just for me.

Tired as I was, I rose to it. I snarled, "You're welcome," in her ear.

"Fuck you," she said. "Nothing has changed."

Even through my anger, I knew that she was wrong. I knew it before we'd reached the boat and I was shoving her up the ladder, into their waiting arms.

She was dead wrong to say nothing had changed, because I had. I had gone into the water, found her, brought her up alive, against reason and my own dark interests.

The past remained the same, and so, apparently, had she, but I had come up new. I could feel a sea change in me, sure and certain. I was too tired, too blown, to understand it fully. I only knew two things with any certainty: I had changed, and she wasn't going to like it.

17

WE MET AT ROSIE B's near the university. It wasn't my kind of place, much less Roux's. The walls were festooned with neon beer signs, and its mismatched wooden chairs and booths looked pirated from a defunct diner. A warped pool table took up real estate near the bathrooms. This was a student hangout, where Davis's sophomore microeconomics students could coast into Dollar Beer Night on the flimsiest of fake IDs; we would not run into our neighbors here.

The old sound system was playing a grindy R&B song that no one my age had ever heard. Davis had wanted to come with me for moral support, but he thought I was meeting Roux to talk through today's near disaster.

The rest of the weekend's dives had, of course, been canceled, and Maddy and I had told him the whole story in tandem. She'd been breathless, speaking in hyperbole, while I'd tried to downplay the whole event. Davis knew us both well enough to guess that the truth was somewhere in between. He'd been both proud of me and frightened for me, caught in that weird post-event anxiety that sets in when someone dear has a close call. He asked three or four times if I was really okay, and all afternoon he'd unconsciously kept a hand on me. When I'd asked him to take care of Oliver and make us all dinner while I met with Roux, he'd more than agreed. He'd taken Maddy and the baby and gone out to buy filet and fresh, local shrimp for the grill, his go-to celebration meal. We'd left at the same time, me for this ratty bar, them for Publix and Joe Patti's Seafood Market.

It was still a couple of hours before sunset, and Rosie B's was pretty dead. I was sharing the place with only a couple of shaggy-headed beach boys and the bartender. I stopped by the bar and ordered, then staked out a booth in the corner. I wanted the comfort of my back against a wall.

Just as I settled, Roux appeared in the doorway, sheathed in a lime-colored sundress and strappy, elegant sandals. I shivered, as if the old air-conditioning had kicked up a notch. Even so, my inner calm held. I was doing the right thing.

I had found my third road out; it had been there all along. I'd been too scared, too angry, too caught up in Roux's game to see it. It was an ugly, hard road, but I stilled myself and met her eyes, waving her over. I was going to take it.

Roux came and slid in across from me, distaste writ plain across her features.

"Slumming it, are we?" she asked. She'd taken a light tone, but her eyes were guarded.

"You have to go to the bar to order. No waitstaff on yet."

She rolled her eyes, turned, and raised her hand to the bartender. Twenty years ago this guy would have been one of the beach-bum kids he was serving. He was too old to be working here, his sun-kissed curls reced-

JOSHILYN JACKSON

ing to his crown and deep lines scored into his leathery, tanned skin.

Roux called, "What's she having?"

"G&T," he called back.

She held up two fingers, like a peace sign, and he nodded. She turned back to me. The bench seat had us close, too close for comfort. Our knees weren't touching, but I could feel heat coming off hers.

"How are you?" I asked.

"Fine," she said. If she felt any awkwardness, any gratitude, anything at all—none of it was showing.

"Any joint pain? Dizziness or numbness—"

"I don't have decompression sickness," she interrupted. "No symptoms. I had Luca take me to the ER anyway. We were there most of the day, kickin' it with the drug-hunting oxy heads and the loudest child on earth. He'd broken something. Not a classy place, the ER. I really thought that would be today's low point. But look. Here we are."

As if to illustrate, the shaggy boys put quarters in the ancient Playboy pinball machine near the pool table. It burst into sonic beeps and hootings, the ears and tails on the Bunnies lighting up.

"I would have thought almost drowning was the low point," I said, and she did not react. "You're lucky you're not in a hyperbaric chamber right now." *Or dead,* I thought.

"I'm eighteen percent body fat, my resting heart rate is under sixty, and I hydrate like a motherfucker," she said, waving luck away. She was about to say more, but the beach bum appeared with our drinks just then.

"Thanks," I said.

She waited until he walked away before she spoke again.

"Is that why I'm here? So you can make sure I'm not going to fall down dead of the bends? How sweet." Her voice was rich with irony. She reached for her drink and took a large, long swallow. She made a face. "What is that? What gin did you order?"

"I didn't order a specific gin."

"God. This tastes like Lysol." But she drank again. When she set her glass down, it was half empty. It was my only indication that she wasn't as collected as she seemed.

"Why did you go inside?" I said.

She propped her head in her hands, looking up, as if the answer might be written on the ceiling. "I hate fighting with Luca. Earlier, Mark and I looked in that hole, and my light caught something glinting on the floor. Round. Looked like old brass. Maybe a compass or an antique pocket watch. I started to join you, but that fight . . . I was still mad, and I knew Luca was, too. I thought, what if I popped back down and got that compass? For him." I felt my lips compress. It was illegal to steal treasures off wrecks. Either divers left them for the next diver to enjoy or, if an item was unattached and likely to be washed away, we brought them up to donate to museums. But considering every damn thing else Roux had done, pirating a wreck treasure was hardly worth mentioning. "It looked like an easy in and out. I didn't see the netting up in the ceiling." She stopped. I waited, staring her down. She had yet to apologize. She had yet to thank me. Finally she said, "What? What do you expect? Fuck you, Amy. All you did was your job.

I'm glad I'm not dead. Thanks for that. Lucky me, I'm still here. And poor you, nothing's changed."

She was wrong about that.

"Except that I decided not to pay you," I said, easy and cool.

We continued to stare each other down for a few more seconds, and then she picked up her drink and drained it.

"Where's your phone?" she said. I handed it over. I'd already turned it all the way off. She checked, then put it in her pocket and stood, picking up my full drink as she rose. "Ladies' room."

She was stalking off across the bar before I could answer. I got up and followed her. She set my drink down on a different table, right by the women's restroom, then went through the swinging door. I did, too.

The grungy bathroom had avocado-colored floor tile and graffiti in archaeological layers on every inch of the stall doors. She stayed by the chipped sinks, holding her hands out, and I stepped toward her, for once unfazed. I had held her body, racked with shudders, terrified. I had cut it free, carried it up into the air, cradled it until the boat came. My ownership of her body in those moments somehow negated the invasion of her hands now.

She started with my hair again, working her way down as before, talking the whole time. The words came clipped and fast, and I could feel the rising tide of her fury kept in check behind them.

"You aren't noble. Come on. I can read you easy. I can read you, because I am you. You checked the angles, Amy. If you let me drown, you were so fucked. You never saw my certifications. You lied, on paper, to your shop and that crew. That would have come out.

You would have lost your job, maybe faced charges. Probably been sued, and your husband, your neighbors, your coworkers, they all would have wanted to know why you would lie like that for me. Maybe all your secrets would have come out anyway. But you saved me to save your own ass, and oh, now you're supposed to be my hero?" She was being quick but thorough, already crouching to check my legs and feet, her skirt hiked up to keep the pale, pretty fabric of her dress off the filthy tiles. She glared up at me. "While I'm down here, should I rain tears and kisses on your feet, dry them with my hair? Should I say, 'Oh, Amy, thank you for my life, let's call it even'? And just like that you're off the hook."

I shook my head. I'd known that wasn't how this would work right after we broke the surface. Even as she'd floated helpless as a baby in my arms, she'd been rasping at me that nothing had changed. She was too desperate for the money to absolve me now. It was interesting to hear how she tried to justify it, though, and I understood her better. She'd mocked me for living a lie, but she did it, too, exactly the same.

She got up and stomped out of the bathroom, and I went with her, back to the new table. We sat, and she picked up my drink and took a big gulp of it.

"Another round?" the bartender called.

I shook my head. "We're good."

Roux ignored the exchange, her eyes on me, insistent. "Tell me I'm wrong."

I shrugged. There was truth in what she was saying.

"I thought some of those things, but that's not why I saved you," I said.

"Sure," she said, that disbelieving word, but this time it was not enough. She leaned across the table, hands on my drink. "You're such a liar. You're lying to yourself right now." I was looking at her with a kind of pity, because every word she aimed at me was really about her. That story she told Luca, about people needing to pay and her helping them, as if she were the high priest of karma itself, she believed it, too. She had to, to live with herself. It was the largest silent lie I'd ever seen, and I lived with some whoppers. She was trying hard now to find a way to stay karma's agent, the hero, and still take my money. "I see you, Amy. I know you. You've wrapped yourself in a pretty skin so thick it even fools you, but I see you. You can keep that skin on if you want, but you're damn well going to pay me for the privilege."

I shook my head. Maybe so, but how thick does a skin have to be before it's realer than the meat inside? I was already working to undo my steps, rewinding myself to the woman I'd built, reattaching to the family and the home I'd made. I'd started with Tig Simms, sending him a single text.

We missed our window. I love my husband,
Tig. I'm not the kind who'll ever leave him.

I'd hit SEND, and then I'd blocked his number and deleted our text history. I thought it would be enough. We hadn't started anything. Not really. Not yet. We'd only heard the echoes of what might have been, the lives we could have owned if any of a thousand little moments had been different. Tig, with his LOVE/CAKE tats and his easygoing smile, wouldn't pursue me. If I wanted it to happen, I would have to move toward him, and I would not. I couldn't keep Tig as an escape route. I couldn't have a fallback plan. If I was going to fight to keep my family—and I was—I had to be all in.

"I want you to understand," I told her, and my voice was very gentle. "I am a lot like you. I see myself pretty clearly right now. I could fight you, Roux. I could even win."

The Polaroid I'd stolen was tucked away inside my purse. I took it out now and slid it across the table to her. She stared down at this version of herself, her mouth working.

"You've been busy." I could hear the smallest tremble in her voice.

"I've been playing," I told her. "You were right. I was in the game. Deep in. But I'm done now."

She ran her fingers over the image of her own ruined face, and she must have been wondering what else I'd found. I could see wheels spinning behind her eyes, cataloging the secrets hidden in her house; I was under no illusions I'd found everything she had to hide.

"When?" she asked, tapping the photo.

I waved that away. "Doesn't matter. I was there. And I saw what I saw."

Her spine elongated. "Now you're playing poker."

I shook my head. "I'm not playing at all. I'm out," I said. I meant it. "I found a lot of things. Your money, what's left of it. Your fake IDs. Your pot. Your search history; I know you're taking Luca to the Maldives. No extradition there, but I don't think this is about avoiding a warrant. This is about custody. You're going to the Maldives to keep your kid." I was guessing, but I'd guessed right. She blinked in spite of herself, and I knew

I'd scored a direct hit. "I could find the man that did this, Roux. Blackmail you back. If you told my secrets, I could tell him where to find you." I touched the picture.

Roux's gaze dropped to her hands, and that perfect stillness came into her body. She was utterly unreadable, but I knew she was afraid. I could practically smell it, a whiff of something acrid coming off her body. "I decided not to do that. I'm not even looking for him."

She breathed out, like I'd tapped her hard in the stomach.

"I keep underestimating you." Her voice was shaking with some emotion I couldn't read on her carefully blank face.

"Thank Luca. I won't put him in the path of the man who did this to you. And I didn't loiter around waiting for you to die inside that wreck. I could have. I have it in me. You're the one who taught me that. But I decided not to. I chose not to. I stand by that choice, no matter how hard it bounces back on me." I paused, and Roux picked up my drink again. She drained what was left in two long swallows. I went on, "I also can't give you the money. It's not mine. You know that. Charlotte's going to lose something here if you go forward. The money or my friendship. I'm not egotistical enough to think my friendship's worth a quarter of a million. Especially since it is so weighted down with lies on my side. But the money . . . If, God forbid, there's complications with the baby, or if her brother gets sick or in some trouble, the money has to be there."

She started to speak, but I overrode her.

"Plus, Char is sweet, Roux. Sweeter than all the sugar that could be squeezed out of both of us. Even if you tell her the truth, we could end up friends. One day. Eventually. That will be up to her. She would get to decide, and that seems fair. As for Davis, we're strong. I hope we can weather it." I was all in for my marriage. I'd made that decision when I'd blocked Tig. It would be very hard on Davis, and if I had an escape route, our odds of us surviving when the truth came out went down.

She was watching me so closely, waiting now for me to finish before she spoke. Her voice was calm, deliberate.

"Do you understand what it's going to be like? Once everyone knows?"

I swallowed. Of course I did. The idea of it—it felt like getting skinned alive. Every time any of my friends or neighbors looked at me, they would be thinking of it. This thing I did. Not just the accident, the death of Mrs. Shipley, but everything I'd done to Charlotte. I'd killed her mother, and then I'd worked myself so deep into her life that she called me her mom-friend. Leaving the neighborhood wouldn't get me far enough away. The story would follow me as long as I was within a hundred miles of Pensacola. I'd have to move.

Davis loved his job, and he had a teenager who had lived in this town her whole life. No guarantee he would go with me, and if he did, it would mean uprooting his child and losing his tenured position. Davis loved me, but I knew his darkest secret, and it was this: He'd been relieved when Laura left him. If I brought him enough shame and trouble, he might be relieved to lose me, too.

If they did come with me, I would forever be the woman who killed Dana Shipley and stalked her daughter for years. It would be in Davis's eyes, and Maddy's, for the rest of my life. But I had actually done those things. Maybe Roux was right about karma. Maybe I deserved to pay in ways I had not chosen. I just wasn't going to pay her.

"I do understand. But I'm not going to give you Char's money. I also decided, I'm not going to tell her the truth. I'm not telling anyone. If you want it done, you'll have to do it, knowing that I saved your life. Knowing that you owe me. We'll see what your universe makes of you then. I hope, come Monday, you will choose to move along and leave me and my family in peace." I put one deliberate finger on the picture of her battered face. I pushed it toward her. "The way I'm going to leave yours."

Roux started to speak, then stopped. The photo was bothering her. I could see it. After a moment she put a palm over it, covering the gleam of her swollen-almost-shut eyes.

"This is another move," she said at last. "It's called High Road, and it doesn't work on me."

"Okay," I said. I held my hand out. "Can I have my phone back, please?"

She passed it over, and I stood up, reaching for my handbag.

"You're playing chicken," she said. "But you'll blink. I'll see you Monday, noon, and you will do the transfer."

I put my phone away and dug a twenty out of my purse. I set it on the table. "Drinks are on me. Come Monday I hope you walk away. I'm walking away now."

"It's a bluff," she called after me. I wasn't sure if it was a threat or just bravado, but either way I didn't look back. "I'll see you Monday."

She wouldn't, though, and then whatever she decided, I would live with it. Right now I was going to go home and sit down for a celebration dinner with my family. I would eat four ounces of steak and six shrimp and a skewer of grilled vegetables. A sane, regular meal. Maybe afterward I would have a G&T made exactly how I liked it, with Hendrick's and fresh lime. I would tickle the baby, laugh with Maddy and Davis, be happy to be alive. Later I would take my husband up to bed and hope to God that Oliver stayed asleep for half an hour. I'd kiss Davis in a way that let him know I meant business. Whatever happened Monday would happen, but I was done. Roux had an odd sense of right and wrong, but she still had one. She wanted to believe that she was karma's agent, restoring balance to the universe. I thought there was a chance, small but real, that she might simply ghost.

18

AT HOME OLIVER WAS in his bouncy chair, working over a soft teether while Davis loaded cut vegetables and shrimp onto the skewers. The steak was resting on a plate, seasoned, ready for the grill.

I came behind him, tucked my front into his back, and wrapped my arms around him. He leaned into me.

"Are you okay?" He'd asked it fifty times today already.

"Yes, and yes, and yes," I said, but lightly.

He chuckled. "I know. I'm sorry. It's more than the accident. You've had a tough time lately. The Charlotte thing, I guess?"

"I am fine. Davis. We all are. I promise." I spoke into his shirt, my eyes pricking with grateful tears. I was a damn good liar, but he'd still sensed something bubbling around under my surface. His sweetness made me squeeze him tighter, drop a kiss between his shoulder blades. "Where's Mads?"

"Not in the basement, I can tell you that," Davis said, so wry that I knew Luca must be over. "She's there. Where I can see her." He pointed out the window.

I leaned around so I could see. The two of them were sitting in the big hanging swing on the patio, deep in solemn conversation. Luca still looked shaken. His mother really had had a close call today.

I realized I wasn't finished with my reparations tour. I'd put up a wall to block the little line of feeling snaking west toward Tig. I'd opted out of Roux's game. Davis and I might be pointed into a storm, but he loved me. I had never been more sure of that than I was now, listening to him ask if I was all right, telling me he'd somehow seen through me. If the storm came, I had real hope that he'd be willing to weather it with me.

I hadn't yet squared things up with Maddy, though. I'd planned to turn her inside out, make her betray Luca, spill her secrets. I'd been so intent on using what I knew that I hadn't talked to her about what I'd seen, down in the basement. That had not been a healthy, normal teenage make-out thing. I needed to talk to her about her body and her choices. I'd promised Davis that I would.

I let Davis go and went out the back door. Luca started and then stood up when he saw me coming. His eyes were very red around the rims.

"Hey, you're home. I guess I better get going, too." I thought that was probably best. He turned to the door, then paused. "I wanted to say, thank you. I just—" He wiped at his eyes.

"It's okay," I said, and quoted Roux at him. "All I did was my job."

"Well, you're really good at it," he said.

He went out the back gate instead of through the house, heading for home. The grill was on the other side of the long patio, so even if Davis came out, we would still have privacy. I took Luca's place on the other end of the swing.

"Is he your boyfriend?" She flushed pink, shaking her

head. "But he's more than just a friend," I said, careful to make it flat. A statement, not a question. I'd learned long ago not to trap Maddy by asking her if she'd done something I already knew about. She would panic, and lie, and then we'd have dishonesty to deal with on top of the trouble that she was already in.

Her thick, straight brows puzzled up.

"No he's not," she said. I gave her my best skeptical face, and she straightened up, defensive. "I swear we're not. He has a girlfriend."

"Here?" I said. I'd never seen Luca with anyone but Maddy.

"No back in—" She stopped herself. "His old home-town."

If I had still been playing Roux's game . . . God. She really did know where they were from. Maybe even his real name. I pushed that thought away, though. I would not veer off the course I'd chosen. I would not use Roux's methods to squeeze this child.

"Is this a real girlfriend or the kind he 'met at camp,' who lives way up in Canada?"

She shook her head. "No. She texts him all the time, and I've seen pictures. She's, like, got this perfect body, and she's a *senior. . . .*" She trailed off, shrugging.

"So he's not your boyfriend. And he's serious about another girl," I said. This was hard, but there was no way out but through. I spoke softly, firm and calm. "Then I need you to explain to me what you were doing with him in the basement. When I went to get more air tanks."

Maddie's eyes widened, and she searched my face. She swallowed, almost a gulp, and then color rushed her cheeks, washing her crimson.

"Oh, my God. You saw us?"

"I sure did," I said, still calm and soft.

"Oh, my God." She got up off the swing, jouncing me about, but she was too agitated to stay seated.

"Don't run off," I told her.

She walked in a small, spinny circle, saying, "Oh, my God. Oh, my God."

"Maddy. We have to talk about this," I said.

That stopped her, and she wheeled on me. "No we do not! It wasn't anything!"

I put my feet down to still the swing, and I could feel my own cheeks flush. I pushed through it. "He was touching you. Very intimately. That's not what friends do."

She shook her head, desperate and unhappy. "It was nothing. It was a bet. It was a game."

I was sick to death of games. Especially the kind Roux's family seemed to play.

"Your body is not a game. Sit down, Mads."

She did, slumping onto the other end of the swing and tucking her feet up until she was a small, miserable wad. "It didn't mean anything."

"It ought to mean things. Tell me about the game."

She shook her head again. "I'd rather die. For real."

"You're not going to die. Talk to me."

She stared down at her hands. "We play this game. It's called Bet, and he asked me, like, if I had ever . . . If I ever. You know."

"Had sex?" I said.

"No, God. Ugh. If I had ever . . ." She rolled her hands.

"Had an orgasm," I said.

"Ugh, don't say that word." Almost involuntarily, she

scooted another inch away on the swing, pressing her back into the arm.

"Maddy, if you can't say the word 'orgasm' without wanting to die, you've got no business trying to have one with anybody but yourself."

Her face was so red, and a sheen of fine sweat broke out on her forehead.

"Oh, my God! I told him I hadn't ever, you know, had one, and that was the bet. Like, he bet he could get me to. His girlfriend has them, and he said it was easy. I bet that he couldn't, and then we just . . . I don't know. God!" She buried her face in her hands again.

"Okay, okay," I told her. "You were curious. That's normal. And you like this boy. But playing games like that, touching games, will make you like him even more. You don't want that. He doesn't feel for you that way, and you can get seriously hurt. Plus, it is a big, giant step toward having sex, which you are categorically not ready for."

She lifted her chin. "How do you know?"

I said, "Because you are fifteen, and because you can't even hear the word 'orgasm' without dying."

"God, stop!" she said, proving my case. I eased up on her then.

"Was that the only time you played Bet?" I asked, gentle. "Or did you two do other things?"

I could see her considering a lie, weighing her options. In the end she met my eyes. "We played before. But, but not like . . . Like, that was the most—" She stopped.

"Did he make bets to get you to do anything like that for him? Physically?"

She shook her head, adamant. "That was the farthest it ever got. The other bets weren't even about, like, touching stuff," she said, and I believed her. "We never made out. He's not, like, a cheater. He wouldn't do that to his girlfriend."

I thought she was telling the truth, right up until the end. Then she'd started lying, but mostly to herself. I called her on it.

"Do you think his girlfriend would mind him playing that game with you?" I said, and her fading blush came back. "If he were your boyfriend, would you want him to play that game with your friend Shannon?"

She shook her head, and then she peeped up at me through her lashes. "Are you going to tell Duddy?" Her eyes were pleading.

Here was my old road in. I could lie right now, promise not to tell Davis in exchange for Luca's real name, or at least the city where his girlfriend lived, and then I'd have her. Roux was running to keep Luca. She'd inadvertently revealed that back at Rosie B's. I knew her timeline, and if I added Luca's age and description and the city, I could find something on the Internet. There would be an AMBER Alert or a "Have You Seen This Boy?" page. I could get right back in the game. I'd unblock Tig, open up that pathway to another life in case I blew up this one. I pressed my lips together, waited until the wave passed. I was out of it, and I would not step back in and play. Not with Roux. Not with Tig or my marriage. Least of all with Maddy. She'd been played with enough, it sounded like.

"I already told your dad," I said. Her eyes filled instantly with tears, and she clapped both hands over her mouth. "But listen, he didn't want the gory details. Dads do not want to know that stuff about their daughters. I only said that you and Luca got a little physical, nothing that could cause a baby, and that you two need to be more chaperoned. Okay?"

Her hands dropped. "That's really all? You swear?"

"That's all," I said, and there went my leverage. I could not go back now. I was well and truly out.

"Can we never talk about this again?" she said.

I laughed. "Sorry, kid, we're going to be talking about sex and the kinds of choices I hope you'll make quite a bit before we're finished." I wondered if Luca had won his bet, but I didn't know how to ask her, and it was not really my business. If he had, would she need more or less counseling? "I think your feelings for Luca kinda ran away with you."

She smiled a miserable smile. "It doesn't matter. He won't be here much longer."

He really had spilled his guts to her. Maybe he had asked her to play the Bet game because he liked Maddy more than he admitted. For most kids his age, a girl-friend in another state, even a gorgeous senior, didn't have as strong a hold as a cute girl in the room right then.

"I'm sorry," I said. "I know you'll miss him."

"Yeah, but it's good. For him. He says when they move again, he can get back in school. Do regular stuff. At home in Seattle, he played basketball and—" She stopped, realizing she'd said the city.

He'd obviously told her it was a secret. I hadn't asked, and yet this girl I loved had laid a new card down for me to play.

I wasn't going to pick it up. I wasn't. But I couldn't help wondering what else he'd told her. His mother's job? Maybe, but Luca didn't know I was Roux's target.

At least Maddy couldn't know that I was being black-mailed. I wanted to ask, to press, to play. I held myself completely still, like Roux, until the urge subsided.

"I'm getting hungry," I said, as if I hadn't noticed her slip. "Want to help me set the table?"

"Sure," she said, relieved to be out of this conversation. She bounced to her feet, and I went with her.

Dinner wouldn't have seemed like much to an outsider. We sat around the picnic table in the backyard, stuffing ourselves with fresh, hot food from the grill. I spooned sweet potatoes into Oliver between bites of surf and turf and tore up a fluffy roll for him to pincer up and gum. We talked about fall-break plans and the weeds in the back garden, nothing of interest to anyone outside this little circle. But to me every minute was sacred. I wanted to stop time, live inside this meal, this moment, forever.

It had to end eventually. I offered to bathe the dishes if Maddy would bathe her brother, and she laughed at that. Davis, who had shopped and cooked, was absolved of any further chores. He went with Maddy anyway; Oliver loved bath time, and it was fun.

They were all upstairs and I'd just finished loading the dishwasher when the doorbell rang. I felt myself stiffen. I hoped to God it wasn't Roux, back to try some new angle. Not now. Not tonight. Monday was coming, and I hoped she would take the high road in the end, but the odds were against it. I stomped my way to the front door, tense. If this was my last weekend before the storm caught us all, I wanted to enjoy it, Roux-free.

I swung the door open, but I did not find Roux. It was Charlotte, though I hardly recognized her in the weeping woman hunched over Ruby's stroller. Her face was so swollen that her eyes were almost shut, like Roux's in the picture I'd given back. But this was not from bruises. She looked like she'd been crying for hours, and huge tears were still spilling down her face. Ruby looked fraught and tearstained as well, twisting and grunting in her stroller.

"Amy," she said, and stopped. Too choked up to speak. I couldn't speak either. At last she said, "Amy. Your friend. Roux. She came to see me. She told me . . ." she said, and again she was unable to go on. Huge sobs racked her body, and I felt my very heart drop out of me, a sick sinking. Roux hadn't waited. She'd pushed her big red button, stolen my last day.

I wanted to step toward Charlotte, but I knew she would recoil from me. I couldn't bear it. I'd been wrong, I realized. I should have stayed in the game. I should have paid Roux. Anything was better than this, standing naked, all my lies stripped away, while Lolly Shipley's true-blue eyes stared at me like she was drowning.

"Oh, God, Char," I said, my voice breaking.

She shook her head. "I didn't believe her. Not at first. I got so mad and told her to get out of my house, but then I went to talk to him. It was all true. He admitted it. He cheated on me, Amy." She put one protective hand over her rounded belly. "He cheated, and he's leaving us. He slept with goddamn Tate Bonasco."

Then I could move. I came around the stroller, and she fell into my arms.

19

ROUX HAD GONE AFTER CHARLOTTE.

It was unendurable, but I could not respond. Not while Char was weeping herself sick in my arms, telling me the whole sordid story.

"This life, it isn't for me," Phillip had told Char, waving a hand to encompass their tidy home, his toddler, his pregnant wife. "We were so young. I didn't really know myself. I'm so sorry, Charlotte. Turns out I'm not domestic."

It had not been Phillip's first affair, only his most recent. He wasn't in love with Tate. He was actually leaving Charlotte for *Phillip;* he'd been his own one and only all along. My heart was breaking for her, but under my anger and shock and sorrow the part of me that was like Roux was already thinking strategy. Not on my behalf. That would come later. I was thinking about Phillip's next move and how best to protect my friend.

I conferred briefly with Davis, and the strategist that Roux had woken up in me saw with bitter eyes how even this was working in my favor. Davis had sensed how troubled I was, but he had put it down to worry over Char. Now that worry seemed more than justified.

He said Char and Ruby were welcome to stay with

us, but I told him it would be unwise to leave the house standing empty. It was their largest asset, after all, and possession was nine-tenths of the law. Phillip had driven off, telling his devastated, weeping wife that they would talk more when she was "ready to be reasonable," but he could come back at any time. He could squat there. I wouldn't put it past him. Davis agreed, and he knew without being told that of course I'd want to go be with her. He headed to our room to pack an overnight bag for me while I went to coax Char back to her own place.

She balked, saying she couldn't stand to go home, even if I were with her.

"Ruby needs the continuity," I told her, and that was true. I kept my more cold-blooded reasons to myself. "Her whole world has been upended. She needs to be in her own bed, with all her animals."

That worked on Char's soft heart. I left Oliver with Davis and Maddy and took Char and Ruby home. I went in first, but the house was still mercifully empty. Once there, we let Ruby watch one Elmo video after another. Young as she was, she understood that something in her small life had gone very wrong. She was sucking her thumb and asking for her binky, a habit she'd outgrown months ago.

Char sat in a heap on the sofa, her face wan and shiny with exhaustion, too tired to cry anymore. She kept going over the conversation she'd had with Phillip, quietly trying to make sense of it, trying to see what she could have done differently or better. She wasn't blaming Phillip. She didn't even seem angry with him, though that would surely come. Right now she was too blindsided. She wouldn't eat, though I finally convinced her to have a cup of herbal tea, for the baby's sake. When I got up to make it, her face turned toward me, following my every move like a flower following the sun.

"God, Amy, what would I do without you?" she said, and started crying again.

I understood Roux's play then. I hadn't had time or brain space to think of it before, but in that moment understanding came in a flash, immediate and clear. It was brilliant, actually, and thoroughly vicious, and I myself had given her the idea.

Charlotte's going to lose something here. . . . The money or my friendship, I'd told her at Rosie B's. *I'm not egotistical enough to think my friendship's worth a quarter of a million.*

It might be now. Char couldn't take another blow.

I'd told Roux that I was finished playing games with her, and I'd been at peace with it. I wanted to keep my secrets, keep this small, sweet life I loved, but the price Roux demanded was way too high; it stuck Charlotte with my bill. I couldn't accept those terms, and after saving Roux on that ill-fated dive, I'd come to understand that if I sank to her level to win, I'd be killing the very self whose life I was trying to preserve. So I had opted out, on every level. I'd thought I understood the consequences. I'd been both ready and resigned, waiting, eyes open, for her shot to land. I hadn't expected her to set her sights on Charlotte. Not like this.

My body went about the business of putting the kettle on, going to the pantry for a tea bag, but inside, a wild, black fury was surging up my spine from the deeps of me, dark and cold enough to burn. I wished that I had Roux's life balanced in my hands again, right then. I wished I'd never penetrated the wreck. I should have waited five cold minutes, watching for that purple fin to spasm and go still.

But I couldn't linger on that thought. I had to get fluids down Charlotte, hold her shaking body, try to get her to rest. I had to reassure her that she was good and dear and worthy of love and listen as she picked through the rubble of her marriage, looking for a way to make it her fault, so she could fix it. I worried she would keep it up all night, though if she needed to, I'd stay with her and let her do it. But she was pregnant, and she didn't have the physical reserves. By ten she was so tired she was swaying with it. Char wouldn't take one step toward her room, though, much less lie down on the bed she'd shared with her husband.

Ruby had fallen asleep in front of the television. I picked her up and wheeled Char upstairs to tuck them in together. She lay down by her daughter in what Ruby called her "pwincess bed," a four-poster double with a white eyelet canopy.

I turned the lights out and pulled the desk chair over so I could sit close, petting Char's hair. While I waited for sleep to take her, I looked at Ruby's latest pictures, taped in a row over the night-light. Shapes and scribbles, and on each, Char had written down Ruby's descriptions. *Mommy and me if I was a mermaid and she wasn't. A magic cat, he eat up that apple. Daddy stand on the unicorn and dance.* That one made me grit my teeth. As if any self-respecting unicorn would pause to spit on Phillip Baxter. I stayed until Char was as limp and quiet as poor exhausted Ruby, and then I went back downstairs to find my phone. By now, I knew, I'd have heard from Roux.

Sure enough, she had sent a text.

220K. That leaves you enough to pay for her divorce attorney.

It was a greater concession than I had expected. I'd expected a taunt, a reiteration, or maybe only a breezy *See you Monday.*

Instead she was negotiating. She must understand that this, what she had done, could push me too far. It had, actually. I was past an edge I hadn't known existed inside me. Right now it was hard for me to think about Luca, or any other reason that the earth needed Angelica Roux to stay on it, breathing.

I was not without recourse. Maddy had given me a new card to play, no blackmail required. *Seattle,* she'd said. Also, Roux had made this move too early. She should have done it late tomorrow, even Monday morning. She'd given me time to maneuver, and, God help me, I was going to use it. I was going to play her goddamn game down to the bitter end.

I went to Char's breezy blue-and-white kitchen, bringing my phone with me, heading for the built-in desk tucked into the breakfast nook. Char called it her office. I sat down in front of her old desktop, staring down at Roux's text.

The fact that she was negotiating at all proved she knew I'd be close to my breaking point. I couldn't simply agree. I would be lying. She would know it.

Finally I texted, 150. Divorce is pricey.

She must have had her phone with her, because she answered immediately. 200K. Final offer. A penny less and it's not worth it to me.

That left Char around forty thousand, but the math didn't matter. I would see Roux in hell before she saw a dime. I let time pass, as if I were thinking, watching three minutes turn over on my phone. Then I texted, Deal. See you Monday. Noon.

Good girl, she texted back. And that was all. Not a word about Charlotte. Nothing personal. No jabs. Smart of her, but not quite smart enough.

Fuck her generous offer. Her discount blackmail. She'd hit me in exactly the wrong spot. She'd hit me in the Charlotte, and I was going to hit her back. Hard as I could. I waited for the old computer to finish booting, thanking God for Maddy's impulsive nature, her big mouth. Roux didn't think I could find her past before Monday came, but she didn't know that I had Seattle.

I knew what I was looking for; she'd blinked at Rosie B's. She was running from a man. Maybe her husband, maybe Luca's father, I had no way to know. I did know he was dangerous. I did know that I wanted desperately to find him, this man who'd beaten her so savagely. This man who was a loaded gun. I wanted to point him at her, let what happened happen.

Maybe he would kill her.

I hoped that he would kill her.

If he did, he'd be in prison, so Luca would be safe from him.

Thinking the boy's name steadied me, a little. Whoever this man was, he could be a clear and present danger to Luca. I'd need to make sure Luca was out of the way. Of course, he might not be related to the boy at all. I needed to stop projecting. To search now, find out what I could, and then decide best how to use it.

I started putting search terms into Google. *Missing Teenager Male Seattle Custody Dispute.*

I found myself on a website with a database for missing children run by the state government. Even narrowed down to Washington, there were pages and pages of tiny thumbnail pictures of young faces. It paused me, hurt my heart. Every face was someone's missing darling.

I tried to narrow the search further to only Seattle, but the site was counterintuitive and clunky. I couldn't figure out how to home in on a single city.

I went back to Google, thinking through the timeline. I remembered when Roux had first met Tig, but I was tempted to check with him anyway, just to be sure. It had been so very easy to remove him as a contact. Probably because I'd known it would be just as easy to put him back.

I shook my head. I knew the approximate date. I added a month and year to my search, but it didn't help. I tinkered with the terms, and that led me to a national database. It was run by a nonprofit and less tricky to navigate. They even had a page called "Featured Missing Children by State." I used the drop-down to go to Washington, and this time the result looked more manageable. Maybe a hundred young faces looked out at me. There was an interface that let me refine my search, and I went in and checked a box for Male, then checked a second box for Ages 12–17. I hit ENTER, and the page reloaded, slow, the old computer making an audible grinding noise. When it finished, I was looking at only a dozen or so photos.

The third face was Luca's.

Impossible to miss that chiseled jaw, those cheekbones, even though his hair was blond in the picture. My heart rate jacked. I swallowed hard and moved my mouse. I clicked on the picture, and his page opened up.

The first thing I noticed was his birthday. I was

wrong about his age. Luca wasn't sixteen. He was four-teen. Younger than Maddy by almost a year. I felt a flush rise in my cheeks; Roux had let him tool around in that red convertible. He'd driven my girl to school, this kid who wasn't even old enough to have a learner's permit.

The info on the page was sparse, but I learned that Luca's real name was Ezra Wheeler. He'd been miss-ing for over a month now. There was a blurry picture of Roux, clearly cropped from something larger, under his stats. She was turning away from the camera, and she was a blonde as well, but I recognized the high curve of her cheek, the shape of her body. The photo was in the "Last seen in the company of" section. There was a warning that she might be dangerous. "Do not approach," the page advised. Instead anyone who saw them should call the 1-800 number and report it.

I ignored that. I didn't want to talk to a nonprofit, and I definitely did not want to talk to the police.

I went back to Google and entered Luca's real name and birth date. After a moment I added "Seattle" and the word "Missing." The first hit was a website called bringezrahome.com. I found that my hands had left the keyboard to press my heart. It was beating so hard and loud inside my chest, it was as if only the pressure of my palms were keeping it there. I felt warm all over, flushed with an internal heat. I'd been right. It was a custody issue. This page was where I would find the man. The man I believed had beaten her so savagely. Would I re-ally unleash that kind of hell?

On her? No question. But there was Luca to think about.

The page finally finished loading. The top was a

school picture of Luca. He looked so much younger with his fluffy cloud of soft blond hair. Either he was blowing it out these days or the dye had tamped it down. His cheeks looked fuller, too, and the picture didn't show how tall he was. He looked like a baby.

I scrolled down, and it took me a long minute to make sense of what I was seeing.

HAVE YOU SEEN EZRA? asked a huge, scrolling headline. There was a row of smaller pictures of Luca, three in a row. On a bike. Holding a yellow cat. But it was the third one that I could not understand. In it he was hugging a middle-aged woman. She had the same blond hair, cut into a fluffy bob, so similar that hers blurred into his. She was heavyish, her cheeks and jawline rounded, but I could see she had his same full mouth. His deep-set, serious eyes.

I could hardly make sense of the words under the photos. It was a letter, a heartfelt plea. A mother's plea. A mother, asking for her boy back. There was no man. No man pictured on the site at all, though there was a number to call with a 206 area code. This was Luca's mother. No, this was Ezra's mother, and her name was Faith Wheeler.

I shoved myself back from the desk.

"Who are you?" I asked Roux, so shocked that the words came out of me, aloud. "Who the fuck are you?"

Then I was scrambling for my phone, punching in the number on the screen with shaking hands.

It was answered on the second ring.

"Hello?" A woman's voice, urgent. She sounded as if she'd been startled from sleep, though I knew that it was earlier in Seattle. "Hello?" she said again. When I couldn't get my mouth to work, she said, "Ezra?" with such desperate hope in her voice that I unfroze. "Ezra, is it you?"

"No," I said. My voice came out hoarse and graveled. "I'm Amy Whey."

"But you called this number. Did you see him? Is he all right?" she said.

"Are you his mother?" I asked. Because I couldn't get my head around it. Was this woman— Had she been with Roux? A couple? "I mean, are you his only mother?"

"Yes, I— Wait, what?" she said. Her voice became incredulous. "What do you mean, am I his only mother? Of course I am. Do you know where he is?"

I'd risen to my feet. I was walking toward the front door, my steps jerky, pulled almost, as if I were a puppet.

I said, "He's with the woman on the website. The dangerous one. I thought *she* was his mother."

I heard her breath come hissing out of her, as if she'd been struck hard, in the chest. I was at Char's front door now, letting myself out into the night.

"No. No, she is not. Where is he?" she demanded, her voice so raw. "Where are you?"

"Pensacola, Florida," I said.

I closed Char's door softly behind me. I hoped she wouldn't wake up now. I had to get to Roux's. I had to make sure the red car was still in the driveway. I had to know that she hadn't, with her horrifying prescience, sensed something in my text. That she had not already taken him and fled.

On the other end of the line, the woman burst into noisy tears. She tried to talk around her huge, barking sobs, but I could barely understand her. "Is he still there? Is he all right? Is he still with Rose?"

"Yes," I said, not sure which question I was answering. Maybe all of them, assuming Roux's name back in Seattle had been Rose.

I was running now, past the Fenton house, and the red car in Roux's driveway came into sight. I stopped, unsure what to do now. She'd stolen him. Roux had stolen this woman's child.

"God, that bitch, that bitch. She's dangerous. Be careful."

"Should I call the police?" I asked.

The Sprite House was entirely dark, no light shining out from behind the ugly gray blanket tacked up over the picture window.

"No! Let me. This is a dedicated cell line, just for Ezra. I'll call the police from my real phone," Faith Wheeler said. Her sobs had abated, a little, but her urgent words were running all over one another. "There's a detective on the case. Morris. He's good. He never gave up. He can call the locals from here, so they know to be careful. So they know my child is in the house with her. Morris told me to call him, not 911, if I got a tip. I just want Ezra safe. She's dangerous. I don't want Ezra hurt. Where are they?"

Even as I told her the address, I was hurrying on quick and quiet feet up the driveway, past the dark house. Understanding but not understanding. God, I didn't want to understand, but my feet kept moving, taking me back to the tall privacy fence. My fingers lifted the latch.

"They're home," I whispered. "The car is here."

She didn't answer, and a few seconds later I could hear her voice talking to someone else. She must be on the other phone with her detective.

I made my way around to the master-bedroom window. I knew which one it was. No window treatments. No light was on, but the window glowed faintly all the same.

I pushed a quiet path through the high azaleas shielding it. Peered in.

Roux was there. Luca, too. He faced her in profile, wearing only pajama bottoms, his pale, bare chest gleaming in the light from a small spray of candles. She had on even less. Only a bra. She had her hands on his shoulders, and his hands were on her bare hips. She pushed him, down and down, until he was kneeling before her. Then she lifted one leg to wrap over his shoulder, her hand on the back of his head, pressing him in, close.

I turned away so fast the bushes rattled, and then I dropped to my knees. I had seen it, though. I could not unsee it. Now Roux's old words were rattling in my head. *Boys are sweet,* she'd said when I accused her of hating men. I remembered her hands on Oliver, compressing his chest and his hips when he'd woken at her house, crying. He had quieted at her touch, but I could hardly bear the thought of her hands on my tiny boy. *I'm a baby whisperer,* she'd said, and the memories nauseated me. I hadn't understood her. I hadn't understood her game at all.

"Are you there?" Faith Wheeler said. Too loud.

"Shhh," I said, my voice a sick, faint whisper. "They're awake. Inside. I see them."

Her voice dropped to a near whisper. "Is he okay? Detective Morris is calling for help. Keep your eyes on them. Don't let them go. The police will be there very soon."

For the first time since I'd seen the pictures of Ezra

and his mother, I wondered what this meant for me. Nothing good. My life as I knew it was over. My truths were all going to come out. Once I had Roux arrested, revenge would be all that was left to her. She would take it, and I had no way to shield Charlotte.

It didn't matter. This boy—I felt so sick down in the pit of me. I could not stop seeing him, this child, kneeling before her. His fingers clutched tight on her hips, indenting her flesh. I had to get this boy away from her. He must be safely sent back home.

I wanted to peek up over the sill, make sure they hadn't heard me, but I could not make myself look. I could not bear to see that child—I realized I could hear faint music in the room, her janky, discordant jazz, and I had to hope that it had masked my movements.

"How long?" I whispered. "How long until they get here?"

"I don't know. Soon? I hope soon. Oh, God, is he okay?"

"Yes," I lied.

He wasn't. He was being raped. I understood that. The boy in that room was only fourteen years old. I was witnessing a rape. Maybe his fiftieth rape by this time, maybe his hundredth. It didn't matter. It was happening to him now. As I waited for the cops, this woman, who had twice put her hands on my own infant son, was using up a child. If some man had Maddy, if he were using her this way, would I wait here? Would I let it happen one more time, even knowing the police were coming, even knowing how many times it must already have happened?

I was moving, my body answering the question before my mind could.

"I have to hang up," I whispered into the phone.

"Wait—" Faith Wheeler began, but I disconnected. I flicked the button on the side, making sure the ringer was off. Within three seconds the phone was buzzing in my hands. I shoved it into my back pocket.

Then I was at the front door, banging on it. I had no plan beyond getting her hands off that boy. No thought past stopping this final violation.

I banged and banged, and when nobody answered, I reared back and kicked the door with the flat of my foot.

"I know you're home!" I yelled into the door. I kicked it again and then again, making loud, reverberating booms.

Finally Roux snatched it open. I was rearing back to kick again, and it threw me off balance. Her seamless face was furious, and she was wrapped in that spectacular raw silk dressing gown I'd seen before. Alone. Luca, I assumed, was still in her bedroom. Waiting.

"What?" she said, cold and sharp.

"Char's finally asleep," I said. I had no idea what I would say next. "We need to talk."

I pulled a move from her playbook, barging in, pushing past her, letting my fury and my horror carry me. She melted out of my way as I stomped across her den.

She closed the door but stayed beside it, watching me, hands in her pockets, all her weight on one hip, as if perfectly relaxed. The Botox helped her hide her expression, but I could see a little wariness seeping through the lines of her body. Her eyes glistened, wide and bright and glossy.

"Come to bargain?" she asked. "No use. I won't go under two hundred."

I stopped at the fireplace, beside the wrought-iron

stand that held a poker and a miniature broom for sweeping ashes, in front of all the game boxes. I didn't know what was going to happen, but I wanted to be between her and Yahtzee. Between her and the gun.

"A hundred fifty," I said, to be saying something.

She was looking at my face, trying to get a read on me.

In my pocket my phone began vibrating again. We could both hear it, buzzing in my jeans. I should have taken the extra ten seconds and gone into the menu to turn vibrations off.

Roux said, "Better get that. Might be Char."

"A hundred fifty," I said, dogged, ignoring the sound.

She stared me down until the phone went silent. A few seconds, and then it began buzzing again.

The wariness was all over her body now, in the set of her shoulders, the tilt of her head.

"Why are you really here?" she asked.

"To bargain. Like you said," I told her, but I was panting. I couldn't seem to get my breath, and my phone would not stop.

She took her hands out of her pockets then, and I'd been stupid. She already had the gun. It gleamed, black and sleek, in her pale hand. She'd gotten it before she ever opened the door. I was standing between her and an empty box.

"Set that phone down. Kick it over here," she said.

The gun had grown since I'd seen it last. It had looked so small and snub-nosed before. Now, pointed at me, it was a huge thing, almost blotting out the woman who held it. I fished my phone out and knelt carefully to set it down, kicked it across the carpet. Roux bent at the knees to pick it up.

She straightened, then glanced down to check the number lighting up my screen.

"Shit," she said, and dropped it like it was burning her hand.

Either she knew that number by heart or the 206 area code was enough for her to guess. Her eyes came back to mine, the pupils blown wide, as round and black and unfathomable as the eye of the gun itself.

"Luca!" she called, her voice gone harsh. No answer. He must be hiding in her bedroom, wondering why Maddy's nice Monster, his diving teacher, was beating down his front door in the middle of the night. If he hadn't known I was Roux's client before, he did now. Or maybe he was too busy worrying about how much *I* knew. She called again. "Luca! Get in here."

He appeared. He'd been around the corner, listening. He was still only in pajama bottoms. They had Sponge-Bob on them, I saw now, and they hung off his fragile hip bones. His arms were crossed protectively over his narrow, lithe chest. It was nearly hairless. I could hardly bear to look at him, and he couldn't seem to meet my gaze. His cheeks were flushed, a bright, hot red.

Roux said, "Start loading the car. We have to go."

He stared back and forth between us, and then he seemed to notice the gun for the first time.

"Buh," he said, a small, sharp noise, surprised.

"Get the Picasso and the cash. Put a shirt on. And shoes. We're leaving in ninety seconds," she said. He was frozen, still staring at the gun, and she raised her voice and barked, "Now!" at him. He jumped, started moving.

"Ezra," I said. The name made him stop. He turned

to me with such wide eyes. I could see blind panic in them. "Don't. Your mom is on the way."

His hands came up to cover his mouth, and tears started in his eyes.

Roux said to me, "Shut up or I will shut you up. Luca? Go. Now." The gun wavered off me, almost wobbling in his direction as she gestured him toward the stairs. "Get as much as you can in the car. You know what to prioritize. Ninety seconds. I mean it."

He shook his head no, but his body stuttered into action. He turned and ran between us, through the gun's field of vision and her own, headed for the stairs. I should have moved then, but he was by me in a flash. I had missed the moment.

"I can't let you take him," I told Roux.

She laughed outright, a bitter snarl of sound. "You think you're saving that kid? You don't know what you're trying to send him back to. You have no idea. But I do. I know. I know exactly what his life was like." Her eyes closed, hardly more than a long blink, but I believed her. I'd seen the Polaroids. She'd lived with horror, and when her eyes reopened, I could see it reflected in her gaze. "I'll shoot you in your head before I let the boy go back to that."

I nodded, hands up, compliant, but I didn't think she would shoot me. Not yet. Not in front of Luca. Not even with him upstairs. She'd get him out of the house first.

She said, "Jesus, how'd you find out? Your fucking stepchild?"

I shook my head, lying on instinct. "Luca let it slip. He said Seattle." She was staring me down, skeptical, so I kept talking. I didn't want her thinking too hard about Maddy, tucked into bed, reading or texting, only a few blocks away. "I thought I was looking for a man. I thought a man was after you. Someone dangerous. Because of the Polaroids."

"Those are old," Roux said dismissively.

Luca came down, dressed in jeans and a T-shirt now, a half-full duffel in his hands. His eyes darted back and forth between us.

"What are you going to do?" he asked.

"Nothing, baby. Go behind me and get the laptop," Roux told him, moving forward, closer to me. The gun got so much bigger.

He hurried around her to the coffee table and stuffed the computer into the bag.

"Who was he? Mr. Polaroids, I mean," I asked, to keep her talking.

She stared at me over the gun, eyes like ice chips. "My husband. He'll never do it again, though." She let her eyes drift to the gun, then back to mine. "You understand me?"

I did. Perfectly. She was saying I wasn't the only person in the room who had once taken a human life. She was warning me that she'd do it again if she had to. Maybe not even if she had to. Maybe I had made her just angry enough, and she knew she'd never get my money now. I still didn't believe that she would shoot me with Luca in the room, though. I hoped.

"Are you—" Luca said, then stopped.

"It's fine," she told him. "We're just gonna ghost. Get the money."

Luca came over and knelt by me, pulling out the Risk box and dumping the money and the IDs and other papers into the bag. This close, he wouldn't meet my eyes.

Roux said, "Go on out to the car. Start it. I'll be right there."

My mouth went dry. If Luca left, if he was all the way out in the car . . . How loud was a gun? Roux's gaze flicked off me to the sofa, just for a moment, and I knew then that she was going to do it. She would send him out, then wrap the gun in one of the ugly brown couch cushions to muffle the sound. She would shoot me, then coolly grab some clothes and make a run for it. How long would Faith Wheeler's detective take, explaining the situation to the local cops? How long before they came? I heard no sirens in the distance. Nothing. But would they use sirens, given the situation?

Luca stood up and took the Picasso down from the mantel. He got a towel out of the duffel and began wrapping it up.

"You're not going to shoot me," I said to Roux, my voice shaking. "You need me to wire you the money. And I will. You can text me a bank, an account number. I'll wire it anywhere you want, all of it, if you only leave him here."

That paused Luca's hands, and he turned wide eyes to Roux.

She didn't even think about it. "Fuck you. I love him."

He shuddered under the weight of those words, then finished wrapping the Picasso. And maybe she did love him, in some sick and awful way. Loved him like a lioness loves zebra. Loved him like a cannibal. I remembered her disdain for men, how she found boys so sweet. When I reminded her that boys grew up, she'd said, *But at that point don't they also get the hell out of your house?* It made me wonder if there had been boys before Luca. It made me wonder where those boys were now.

"What happens next?" Luca asked her, wavering beside me. He had put the Picasso in the duffel. It was full,
and he was ready to go, if he was going. But he paused,
looking back and forth between us. I could see that he
was panicked.

Roux told him, "We leave. I'm going to tie her ass
up, and then I'll get some clothes on and we'll take off.
Please go load the car."

That reassured him, but she was lying. If he left, she
would put a bullet in me. I laid a hand on him, keeping
him beside me.

"Ezra, wait," I said, as if that name had power to
pause him, and it worked.

"Go start the car," Roux said, calm and sure. Talking
over me. "I'm right behind you."

"Your mom wants to see you so bad." I kept talking
directly to him. He was still looking back and forth between us, his chin trembling. "She's so worried. She
loves you so much."

He hesitated, teetering on some internal cusp.

"Your dad is worried, too, I bet," Roux said, and at
her words he flinched.

He'd refused to talk about his dad, I remembered. But
there was no mention of a father on the website.

"Your father is not with her," I said, trying to stall
him. I could feel momentum gathering in his body. He
pressed his lips together, firming his chin, and now his
gaze was fixed on Roux. Still I kept talking, desperate.
"It's only your mom."

He said, "She picked him. She knows what he's like.
She picked him over me."

He started across the room, bag in hand, obedient but

unthinking. He crossed through the gun's field of vision, and this time I was ready. This time I used it.

I grabbed the poker off the little stand and moved toward her, staying behind him, lifting the poker as I ran.

"Get out of the—" she said, gun swinging wildly, trying to find me. I dodged left, keeping him between us. Then I shoved him, and he got tangled in his own long legs and the bag, falling in slow motion. I ran at her, the poker raised, swinging for the gun hand, the only thing I could reach this fast.

I heard the roar of the shot.

She must have missed, because I was still moving. I brought the poker down, as hard as I could, across her arm. She screamed, and I felt the give of bone under the blow. The gun went flying toward the sofa, thumping to the carpet. I heard Luca screaming, too, high-pitched and terrified, like a child. He was trying to crawl out of the way, the duffel bag abandoned. Roux, her wrist hanging down at an odd angle, was already moving for the gun.

I dropped the poker and leaped for it, too, reaching. I saw without understanding the bright red running down my outstretched arm. I was closer, but Roux spun to me.

She grabbed at me, trying to pull me back with her good arm. We got snarled up in each other, falling. She rolled, banging us both into the coffee table, but it got her on top. She jabbed her good hand down hard at my shoulder. An exquisite kind of pain came then. The world went white at the edges of my vision. Her hand drew back wet with blood, and now I could feel it gushing out of me in beats, so warm. I understood she hadn't missed.

That red, wet hand came clawing at my face, trying to find my eyes, and I hit at her, banging at her other wrist where it hung all kinds of wrongly. She reared back, yelling something. Words. She was telling Luca to get it, to get the gun, but I couldn't see him. I bucked her off, and I scrambled toward the couch on all fours. Then it was in my hands, that cold, black metal, surprisingly heavy. I heaved myself up, sitting on the floor with the gun in my good hand, sweeping back and forth, seeking her. Luca was still on the floor as well, moving away from the bag and both of us, scooting backward toward the front door. He was shaking his head no, and his eyes were huge.

Roux scrambled to her feet, and I saw that she now had the poker in her good hand.

We faced each other in the empty room. She already had the poker raised, but she was four steps away, and I had the gun leveled directly at the center of her chest.

I could feel a worsening pulse of awful pain deep in my shoulder. I felt it as a burning, the slick heat of the blood running out of me. She undulated in my vision, as if she were underwater again. As if I were seeing her magnified, the way things always are beneath the waves. A darkness was closing in at the edges of my eyes.

My phone was ringing again, somewhere, buzzing against the carpet. Luca's mother. But Luca was scooting backward toward the door, crying.

"Luca!" Roux said, but he scrambled to his feet and ran out.

The door slammed behind him, and instantly, outside, I could hear rough male voices yelling. Telling him to get down, get down on the ground, right now. The police? Had they come already?

I could hear Luca yelling back, "Okay, okay, okay! My God, don't shoot!"

"Okay," Roux said, echoing the boy. "Okay."

I thought she would lift the poker and come at me, the way I had with her. But she didn't. She dropped her arm. Let the poker slip out of her hand. It thumped onto the floor.

In mere seconds the police would be in the room with us and all the explanations would begin. Outside, the boy she'd stolen was lying down in wet grass, I hoped unharmed. Two doors over, Char's life was in tatters. Just down the street, my family slept, innocent and trusting, loving me, with no idea of what I was doing now. No idea of all I'd done.

"You know what, Amy?" Roux said, prepping her mouth, curling her lip, readying to say something insouciant. Or sarcastic. Maybe a taunt, or a threat, or a reference to her godforsaken game. She looked me in the face, as if the gun weren't even in my hands. She repeated, "You know what?"

I didn't want to know.

I pulled the trigger.

20

THE BULLET WAS LIKE Roux: It had come for me with all the worst intentions. An inch higher it would have hit my subclavian artery and killed me. As it was, it skated between my ribs and clavicle, barely brushing bone, then buried itself in the wall behind me. It hurt like hell, but then it was gone.

"Lucky," the surgeon told me when he came to check on me just after I woke up.

I was too high to be gracious. I felt like I was floating in my hospital bed, thanks to a machine that pumped me full of morphine when I pressed a button. Instead of answering, I stared at the way the light caught in his gleaming yellow mustache.

"We're all lucky," Davis said. He wasn't only being gracious for me. He meant it. His hand was wrapped strong and tight around mine. He'd already been holding it when I came to, and he hadn't let go yet. He wouldn't. Not ever. I was certain of it now.

I don't think I spoke a word until the surgeon was about to leave. Then I found I had a question after all.

"How long until I can dive?"

Davis told me later that that was the moment he knew I was all right.

And I was. After three weeks I was cleared to go back into the water. My physical therapist warned me, though, if I tried to make my shoulder carry that heavy tank, I could permanently damage myself. I knew a work-around. I waited for a clear, calm day, then jumped off the boat wearing only my wet suit, mask, and fins. Maddy passed my BCD and the heavy air tank down to me, the BCD inflated enough to float the tank. I eased myself into my gear and did my checks while bobbing in the gentle waves, letting the ocean bear the weight for me. I dove like that for almost six weeks, until I could gear up without my shoulder so much as twinging. I did not suffer any lasting damage.

By then the weather had turned colder. Dive charters and classes had slowed to a trickle, so it was mostly me and Maddy, doing walk-ins or paying for the pleasure like a couple of tourists. We went out every weekend that the weather allowed.

Maddy was doing all right, I thought, considering. Her grades hadn't dipped. Her old ebullience remained undimmed. She saw a counselor a couple of times a week for most of fall, but by winter she was tapering off.

We never dove at the English Freighter, though. Neither of us ever suggested it. When the question came up, we always seemed to have another spot in mind. Once a group on our charter asked to go to the English Freighter specifically, but I diverted them to a different wreck, the *Tex Edwards,* telling them that last time, I'd seen a scorpion fish there. I found him for them, too.

I didn't mind winter's lighter work hours. I was busy helping Charlotte navigate her divorce, and I was her partner at prenatal classes. I was with her, telling her to breathe, my hand crushed in her grip, when she pushed baby Esther out into the world. When I held Esther, small and red-faced and so very new, I almost felt sorry for Phillip. He didn't understand or value all he'd lost.

He was going to lose a few things he did value. I was making sure of it. I hired a pit bull of an attorney for Char, though I told her I'd found him through a non-profit that helped women in her exact situation. She was going to end up with the house for sure, though she was afraid she wouldn't be able to afford it. I told her not to worry about that either. The exact same nonprofit also paid off the mortgages of single mothers. It had taken an interest in her case. I was handling all the paperwork with them, so she didn't have to worry. She and Ruby and baby Esther would stay right where they were.

Char was working mornings at Ruby's little pre-school now and designing flyers and other ads for local businesses on the side. She had a talent for it. She was getting by. She was healing, too, getting stronger. She was determined to make a good life for herself and her girls.

She was even keeping up with her book club, which meant I was, too. I was amazed by how fast it became normal again. It helped that the Bonascos moved out of the neighborhood. Last I heard, they were divorcing, and Panda stopped coming when Tate moved away.

Lavonda was rendered cliqueless. She ended up be-friending Lisa Fenton, which put her firmly in my cir-cle. Away from Tate I found I liked her very much. She was funny and sharp and shared my taste in books and movies. Together we even talked Charlotte into picking *Geek Love* for November. Perhaps we should have tried something a little gentler. The next month, God help me,

Char hit us all with Dickens. *Bleak House*. I read all 928 pages of it. It was the least that I could do for Charlotte.

Spring came, and diving began picking up again. I was teaching more, but I made sure to find time for pleasure dives, especially as Maddy weaned herself off therapy completely. In April I booked us both on Captain Jay's boat, and as we got ready to head out, Winslow suggested the English Freighter.

"I haven't been there since . . . in a while," he said. So he'd been avoiding it, too.

I met his eyes, and I found myself saying, "Yeah. The English Freighter sounds good," as Captain Jay pointed us out of the harbor.

Every other diver on board was part of an advanced open-water class that my friend Bev was teaching. Maddy and I were geared and off the boat while the others were still clustered around Bev, listening to her talk them through the dive.

Maddy and I descended, slow and easy, facing each other. When the bow came into view, just under us, I felt a twinge of something like anxiety. Not a feeling I usually experienced underwater. I remembered Luca— Ezra—on this descent. How excited he'd been, watching this very wreck become visible as we sank into the deep. I wondered what Maddy was thinking, but she was looking down. I couldn't catch her eye.

She must have been thinking of him, too, though. They still texted each other, but not, I thought, as frequently as they used to. She had a crush on a trombone player in marching band now, and it seemed to be mutual.

She'd gotten to see Luca again, to say good-bye. Just

once, before his mother took him home. Davis had been anxious about it, but I'd convinced him that it was important for Maddy. For closure, I said, as if I knew what that word meant.

Faith Wheeler brought her son by on the way to the airport. He and Maddy went into the backyard while the adults all sat in the keeping room, me propped up with pillows on the sofa facing the sliding glass door, and Davis right beside me. Oliver was down for his big nap, upstairs. I was a little high on pain meds.

Faith sat catty-corner to us, turning her head every few seconds to make sure Luca—it was so hard to think of him as Ezra—was still on the swing, in plain view. Maddy sat beside him, deep in conversation. Their heads were bent together earnestly. Close, but not quite touching.

He was Seattle-bound in the morning, with his mother. Just his mother. His disappearance had been the final push she needed to leave his father, a surgeon who hadn't been nearly as careful with his hands as he should have been. At night, when he was home and the curtains were closed, his wife and son had both felt those hands, too many times to count.

Faith was living with her sister now, in a much smaller house out in the burbs. She was involved in a divorce that was a thousand times uglier and messier than Charlotte's but that would, she hoped, be a good thing. For her and her son both.

Rose Angier, as Roux had been known in Seattle, had lived in the very wealthy neighborhood where Dr. Wheeler still had a home. Ezra crossed Roux's path when he was barely thirteen, going door-to-door to ask if anyone needed their lawn mowed. Roux had hired him. She'd had more work for him after that: weeding, pool maintenance, planting, trimming hedges. Within six months the boy was spending most of his weekends down at her place. Any excuse to be out of the house, his mother thought. At first.

Faith had eventually become uneasy about the amount of yardwork Ms. Angier seemed to need and how much she overpaid for it. Then she'd gifted the boy some kind of Xbox. Faith had walked down the street to talk about it; it was too expensive a gift. When no one answered the doorbell, she'd gone around to the back and let herself into the yard. She'd found her son there on a chaise lounge by the pool. He was with Roux, doing more than yard work behind her tall privacy fence.

She'd taken her son home, horrified, but too afraid to tell her husband. Ezra had begged her to do nothing, but she'd decided she had to call the police. She was going to, as soon as her husband left for work in the morning. Ezra texted Roux, and the two of them decided to make a run for it that night. They'd set off, following the road that would in the end bring her to me.

The police were still trying to backtrace all Roux's movements. I could have helped them fill in some of the gaps, but I hadn't. I was very good at saying very little. I'd been practicing for decades.

I don't know, I said to most of their questions. My oldest and most favorite lie.

I'd been very clear on one point: Roux had shot me, and then, after I got the gun, she'd come at me with the poker. I'd been in fear for my life, I'd told them more than once, lying the way Roux always had, my body still and quiet and my gaze direct.

My single shot hit her in the center of her chest.

Sometimes, at night, I could still hear the sound of her slight body dropping to the dingy carpet, so fast it was as if she'd gone boneless. I'd heard an odd, windy sucking noise coming from her, but only once. I crawled over just as the police were battering down the door, and her glossy eyes had looked up into mine, open and still and empty of everything.

You know what, Amy? she'd asked me right before I pulled the trigger.

I would never know what. I was fine with it.

Ezra was as cagey with the police as I was, maybe more so. He didn't want to talk about any of it—not his relationship with Roux, not his month as a fugitive, and not the way she'd made her money. We were the most monosyllabic pair of witnesses in the history of Pensacola, I was willing to bet, but in the end it didn't matter. The more the police dug into Roux's past, the more filth they uncovered. She'd been plying her trade for a long, long time. They still didn't know her real name or origin or even her exact age. Rose Angier was as fake as every other name I'd heard. The parts of her life they could track had been very, very busy, and within a few weeks they'd decided that no charges would be filed against me. Self-defense, they said. It was true enough to suit me.

"How did you know?" Faith Wheeler asked me the day she brought Ezra over to say good-bye to Maddy.

Her gaze shifted off me to the yard before I answered, making sure her son was still in sight. Maddy was clutching the boy's shoulders now, telling him something with big, sincere eyes. I could feel Davis shifting uncomfortably beside me. I put a calming hand on his thigh.

"I don't know. Something felt off about her," I said.

"Thank God," Faith said.

"You shouldn't have gone to her place. Not by yourself," Davis said, for about the thousandth time. Thinking about that night, what might have been, it always made him antsy. He rested his hand over mine, twining our fingers together. "I wish you'd called me."

I smiled an apology. "I know. I should have."

Faith was sitting up very straight, clearly wanting to say something else, but it took two false starts before she found the words. "I . . . There was . . ." She shook her head. "This is probably wrong of me. But I don't care. I have to tell you, thank you. Thank you for—" She stopped again, shrugging helplessly, then turned her face to the window to look out at her beautiful son.

"It's all right," Davis said kindly, thinking she was grateful that I'd rescued Luca.

I understood her better. She was thanking me for pulling that trigger. Roux was dead, and she was glad.

I was glad, too. Sometimes. Mostly. I was almost never sorry. But still, there was a hidden corner in my heart that housed regret. I didn't miss Roux, not exactly. Maybe, in some way, what I was missing was the game. Or the woman I'd been when we were playing, the one who could win it; she wasn't in the room with us. She did not belong in this sweet house.

"I understand," I told Faith. She met my eyes, and what happened between us happened in silence. Davis, watching Maddy out the window, wasn't part of it.

"Do you feel . . ." she started, but then she gave me a shaky smile. "Never mind."

I was relieved. I had no good answer. When I thought of Roux, I felt a lot of things. Some I couldn't even name. But I could live with them. I could live with them all. I'd lived with worse.

Faith stood up. "We have a plane to catch."

The kids were leaning in, so close, talking urgently. Maddy's eyes were wide, and I thought she might be crying a little.

I said softly, "Give them another minute."

We waited, and then Luca ducked his head in. He pressed his mouth against hers, just once, and very briefly. It was hardly anything, but Davis rose abruptly. Outside, Maddy's hand fluttered up to her mouth. They both leaned back, blinking at each other.

"Okay. That's it," Davis said, already moving to the door to call them in.

I let him go. It was enough. It had to stop there, because of the ways "Luca" had acted out with Maddy. I recognized in retrospect that what I'd seen on the sofa had been a cry for help, but it hadn't happened in a vacuum. My girl had been pulled sideways into things she'd not been ready to do or see or know. The "girlfriend," it turned out, was Roux herself, sending Luca the same kind of headless selfies she'd sent to Panda Grier. Maddy had seen them. Maddy had seen a lot of things.

Her experience with Luca felt so out of order. I hoped that this sweet, chaste kiss might set some of it to rights. Back in Seattle, Luca would hopefully be having all kinds of therapy, but this good-bye was good for him, too. It was her first kiss, and it was as sweet and fleeting as such a thing should be. Considering his age, it should have been a first for him as well. As it was, I hoped that it would help reset his mouth. I hoped he would remember it.

I knew Maddy would.

Now, hovering over the silty bottom, I signaled to my girl.

You lead, I'll follow.

She gave me an okay, and then she turned us east, down the slope. We were following the side of the barge that I'd searched the day that Roux was missing. Visibility was excellent, at least eighty feet, and as a curtain of baitfish parted around our bubbles, I could see the opening that Roux had penetrated. We paused there, and I looked inside. It was clear. No unsettled silt, no flashing purple fin, only a spotted eel, peeking at us openmouthed from inside a heap of rubble.

We went on past the opening, down to the stern. As we came around the corner, Maddy grasped my arm, hard, her fingers squeezing. I turned to her, and behind her mask her eyes were shining with excitement. She put one flat hand pointed up against her forehead. The sign for shark.

I turned with her to look. It was a bull shark, alone, and it was a big one. At least nine feet, so probably a female. She'd come cruising around from the other side of the wreck. She'd seen us, too. She glided toward us at an angle, curious, giving us side-eye.

We went vertical in the water, hovering side by side and keeping our faces toward her as she did her pass. I checked on Maddy, but she wasn't worried any more than I was. She glanced at me, clearly thrilled, and I heard her noisy, joyous exhale.

The bull shark wheeled, glorious and beautiful and deadly, coming back for another pass, this time a little closer.

Hanging in the deep blue water, even as I turned to keep my face toward the shark, I began imagining all the things that I would leave here. First, and best, and sweetest, there was Tig Simms. Here, down in these deeps, was the only place I ever let myself wonder how he was doing and if he had answered my last text. I'd blocked him. He could have said a thousand things by now, the words waiting for me to change my mind.

Now that I was under, I also thought about Char, the lines of her dear face and the way that I sometimes caught sight of Lolly Shipley's baby features in them these days. My years of practicing not looking had been interrupted.

And I thought about how Maddy sometimes looked at me sideways, with a question in her eyes. I had no way to know what Luca had said to her, out there on the swing. Had he told her more than he told the police? He might have. He'd witnessed most of my last encounter with Roux, heard our conversation. He had to know I'd been a client.

Above the water I did not think about these things at all. I was too busy. Oliver was weaned now, and he was walking, too, unsteady and charming on the fat wads of his feet. I was working hard on eating healthily; I'd even asked my meat-and-potatoes husband to try vegetarian dinners with me three nights a week. It wasn't going perfectly. He only liked it when "vegetarian" meant "swamped in cheese." Maddy was scoping out colleges, and I was helping; she would be a junior in the fall. At work I was planning the dive trip I was going to lead in Belize come June. Plus, I babysat for Charlotte quite a bit as she learned to be a single parent. I did not have time to think about these things.

But now I was under. I kept my eyes on the shark,

and all these things were in me here, down beneath the water.

Last of all I thought of Roux. That winded, sucking noise. Her glossy eyes, gone empty. I wrapped all these thoughts up tight in Roux's dead arms, and then I let her go. She had such weight, and like a weight she sank.

It would all come back, of course. As would Roux herself. I'd done what I had done, and I would have to live with any hauntings it earned me. Honestly, she was a quieter ghost than Mrs. Shipley. But she would come, carrying home to me all the things I'd wrapped up in her arms.

I would only bring them down again. Open my hands. Let them drift deeper to wait, out of sight but present always. As many times as needed, I would bring them here, and I would let them go.

Maddy tucked her arm through mine, squeezing. I checked my gauges. Eighty-eight feet down, and at this depth we didn't have a lot of no-stop dive time. In a few minutes, we would need to turn back, make our slow way up the slope, leaving the shark to keep my secrets company.

The bull shark finished her pass and lost interest. She turned away. We didn't look like anything she ate, and she didn't care for our noisy bubbles. We stayed vertical, watching her sleek, muscular body undulate and surge. She disappeared into the darkness and the blue. The way everything does, eventually.

ACKNOWLEDGMENTS

When I first had the idea for *Never Have I Ever,* the way I thought scuba would work, both technically and thematically, was way off. My first open-water dive changed both me and the book; everything that Amy says about getting under is gospel. It is a meditation, it is peace; it is also unearthly beautiful and hella fun. If you get the chance, go.

Thanks to SeaVentures in Alpharetta, Georgia (especially Claude Smith), and Emerald Coast Scuba in Destin, Florida, for teaching me to dive, taking me down again and again, helping me scout, invent, and amalgamate submerged locations, and answering my endless questions—including the ones about how to commit crime underwater. I've shorthanded some details so as not to bog readers down in the technicalities, but any straight-up errors are my own.

Thank you, Emily Krump, for your enthusiastic response when I handed you the first few chapters and said, *So . . . this is different. Can I do this?* Your wholehearted encouragement allowed me to run full tilt in a new direction, and I am having the best time. Ugly-cry-level gratitude to everyone at Morrow whose passion has both anchored and buoyed this book: Liate Stehlik,

Lynn Grady, Jennifer Hart, Tavia Kowalchuk, Kelly Rudolph, Kathryn Gordon, Maureen Cole, Kate Schafer, Libby Collins, Mary Beth Thomas, Carla Parker, Rachel Levenberg, Tobly McSmith, Ploy Siripant, Mary Ann Petyak, Shelby Peak, Julia Elliott, and Maureen Sugden (aka she who took the word "near" out of every other sentence).

I am grateful to Alison Hennessey and Raven Books for giving *Never Have I Ever* such a perfect home across the pond.

Thank you to my agent, Caryn Karmatz Rudy, for all the things over all the years. I can always count on you for honesty with a support-and-Campari chaser, and I appreciate you more than I can say.

Thank you to the writerly cohort who always has my back: Karen "the rabbit" Abbott, Sara "night whispers" Gruen, Anna Schachner, Reid Jensen, Ginger Eager, Jill James, and Dr. Jake Myers, who speaks fluent lamb. Thanks, Alison Law. Lydia Netzer, you are, in fact, the strongest person of any size.

Deep affection and eternal gratitude to literary agent Jacques de Spoelberch, who pulled my query out of the slush pile and told me I had a voice.

I love you, Scott. I love you, Sam and Maisy Jane. I love you, Betty, Bobby, Julie, Daniel, Claire (our newest Jackson!), Erin Virginia, Jane, and Allison. I love you, Dad. So much. I love you, people of Slanted Sidewalk, small group, and The New Revised Standard Dinner Club. I love you, board members and teachers and students in Reforming Arts, and I believe with you that our voices matter. I love you, STK and First Baptist Church of Decatur, for trying to make the tent a little bigger every day.

Most of all, thank you, person-holding-this-book. Because of you (and the righteous hand-sellers and bookish big-mouths and librarians who helped this book find its way to you), I have the best job in the world. I'll keep writing as long as you keep reading.

Read on for a sneak peek at
Joshilyn Jackson's next addictive novel

MOTHER MAY I

Coming April 2021!

Revenge doesn't wait for permission.

PART I

MOTHERS

I

I WOKE UP TO see a witch peering in my bedroom window.

She was little more than a dark shape with a predator's hungry eyes, razor-wire skinny but somehow female, staring in through the partly open drapes. Sunrise lit up the thin, silvery hair that straggled out from under her hat. I should have leaped up screaming. I should have run at her with any weapon I could find.

Instead I thought, *I hope she's not standing on my basil plants,* hazy and unworried. Even half asleep, I knew that there was no such thing as witches. I'd long forgotten the most important thing the theatre had ever taught me—that the human body can hold two truths at once. Even truths that seem to rule each other out: There's no such things as witches, true. And I was looking at one.

I didn't understand she might be a real person until our eyes met. Hers widened in surprise. She lurched sideways and was gone, leaving me with the impression of a craggy old-lady face with a sour, turned-down mouth.

I bolted upright, heart rate jacking, letting out a strangled sound that wasn't quite a scream. Too soft to disturb the kids, but it woke up my husband.

"Bree?" Trey's voice was thick with sleep.

"I thought I saw someone. Looking through the window at us."

That got his eyes open.

"A person? In the backyard?" He was already climbing out of bed.

There was a careless six-inch gap between the edges of the drapes. Even as he pushed one all the way aside, my rational brain was catching up, trying to dismiss it.

I said, "It was a witch. I mean, I thought I saw a witch. So . . . grain of salt."

Trey was peering out, forehead pressed against the glass, but that turned him back to me, a smile starting. "Big pointy hat?"

The memory was dream-soaked, but when he said it, my brain made it so, snapping my hazy mental picture into focus. Not a cardigan. A tatty robe. Not a knit cap. A pointy witch hat. It made the whole thing ridiculous. Of course there was no witch in our backyard, staring in with hungry, haunted eyes.

"I think so," I admitted. "Her mouth was sunken in, and she was all in black."

I must have been dreaming, I decided. I was prone to postpartum nightmares, though not usually about anything so concrete as witches. My bad dreams after each of the girls had been almost Victorian, all footsteps and fog.

"The gate is closed and locked. Unless your witch looked spry enough to bounce over an eight-foot privacy fence . . ."

That made me laugh, though it was more of a relieved puff of air. "Nope."

Trey let go of the drapes. "Want me to go outside and check?"

"Do I want you to sashay around the backyard in your boxers looking for a witch?" I asked. "No. No, I do not."

He grinned, and I smiled back, even though the animal at the base of my brain was saying that yes, actually, I did want him to He-Man out there and stomp the perimeter, preferably with a golf club cocked up over his shoulder. It was a primal thing, physical and irrational.

There was no witch, obviously, and even if I had seen someone, a flesh-and-blood little old lady was the least threatening type of person on the planet. Only in stories did crones offer poisoned fruit to princesses or snatch up tasty children. But I couldn't think of an innocent reason for *anyone* to watch us as we slept. And her flat, greedy gaze! Not confused or blank, like someone's sweet lost granny. Her hunger was the clearest thing in my memory.

Trey read my doubt. "Seriously. I'll grab some pants and go check. Just to put your mind at ease."

I shook my head. I'd been raised on Grimms' fairy tales by a mother who saw the world as something huge and wild—carnivorous. Her world was *full* of witches. She'd have already called the cops by now, or even snatched one of Trey's hunting rifles out of the gun safe and loaded it. She'd be in the backyard already, making the world safer by accidentally shooting our neighbor's nice old Labradoodle. Or worse, shooting our nice old neighbor.

I wasn't like her. I didn't want to be like her, so I

pushed away that small, wise voice in my head that kept insisting, *You saw something. You saw* someone.

I told my husband, "No. Come back to bed."

Trey tumbled in, and I rolled toward him, running my hand under his T-shirt to feel his heartbeat. It was slow and steady, same as always. Wearing a shirt to bed was new, though. Trey was turning fifty this year. He'd always been built thick, but now he had a bit of a belly, and his chest hair was going gray.

"I hate this stupid shirt," I told him. I wanted the comfort of tucking in close to his bare skin, wrapping my arms around the warm, strong bulk of him.

He pulled me closer. Close enough for me to know he wasn't thinking about witches. "I could ditch the shirt. We are up early."

I glanced back at the clock. "The alarm goes off in twenty minutes. You think you can make it worth my while?" I said it flirty, like a challenge, cocking my eyebrow at him.

His teeth flashed in the dimness. "I can damn sure try."

He kissed my neck, my shoulder. To my surprise I felt a twinge of something good starting. My sex drive had flatlined in my third trimester. I'd assumed it would resurrect in a few months, when Robert started solid food. That's how it had worked after the girls. But here was our familiar magic, already sparking up between us.

Maybe it was the dream. That witch had genuinely spooked me, dumping a ton of adrenaline into my blood. As my husband kissed me, my body arched into him, electric, as if to say, *We could all die! Quick, make more people!* It apparently hadn't gotten the memo about Trey's vasectomy. I kissed him back, serious about it.

"Yeah?" Trey said, surprised.

"Yeah," I said, but I couldn't stop thinking about the window. Of course there was not a witch in the yard. Or anyone. But I added, "Close the drapes all the way and you're on, mister."

He hurried to yank them shut while I started peeling my nightgown off over my head.

That, of course, was the exact moment a soft gurgle came through the baby monitor.

We both froze, our eyes meeting.

"Oh, Bumper, no!" Trey said.

"Oh, *Robert,* no," I corrected automatically. I wasn't going to bend on this. When I was pregnant, we'd all called him Bumper, as in "the bumper crop." That had been cute back when it meant my swelling belly. Trey, who'd grown up in Buckhead with Scooters and Biffs and Muffys, still thought it was cute.

The sound faded. We waited, holding our breath. It could go either way. After ten silent seconds, I lifted a victory fist and Trey started toward me.

Robert started babbling then. He was awake and pleased about it, but if I didn't go get him, he'd start fussing.

"So close!"

"Rain check for tonight?" I asked, pulling my nightgown back on.

Trey shook his head, rueful. "I wish. I fly to Chicago today."

"Ugh, that's right. I must have repressed it." I got up.

He'd be there through the weekend and most of next week, too, thanks to Spencer Shaw. Spence was less than a bosom friend but more than just his partner at the law firm. Their mothers were cousins, so they'd gone to the same schools from the time they were three, even pledging the same frat at UVA. They hadn't gone their separate ways until law school.

Spence had opted out of this Chicago trip because tonight was the firm's annual Spring Gala, and he wasn't one to miss a party. He loved himself a top-shelf open bar and pretty women in cocktail dresses.

Trey wanted me to go to the gala, too. To represent. But I always felt a little out of place at firm events without him. I'd said I would, unless Robert had a cranky afternoon. I had a strong premonition that he would.

"Spence is having a rough time, Bree," Trey said.

Spence was in the middle of an ugly divorce, his second. My husband would carry him through it, just as he'd carried him during his first ugly divorce.

"So are you. You're working crazy hours," I said, shrugging into my robe. "Mostly because of Spence."

"No. It's this client." He and Spence were working with a large Atlanta-based company that was absorbing a family-owned chain of grocery stores. "This is not a marriage of equals we're officiating." He leaned close, as if telling me a dirty little secret. "Our groom is a cannibal."

I let it go. Trey was an equity partner, but Spencer's name was third on the firm's letterhead. His father's name had been first before he died. Also, Robert's babble was getting whiny around the edges.

"I'll plan us a date for next weekend. Dinner, wine, kissing," I promised, then went next door into the nursery.

This room used to be my office, before Robert surprised us. Now the heather-gray walls were covered over in giraffe wallpaper and my desk nook had a changing table in it.

I didn't mind. I didn't need an office now; I'd rolled off the boards of the Alliance Theatre and a statewide literacy nonprofit, promising to roll back on in a year or so. The girls had taught me how brief Robert's babyhood would be. I didn't want to miss it. I'd blinked, and here he was, already ten weeks old.

I bitched about Trey's job sometimes, but I was lucky. When I was growing up, my mom worked full-time as a 911 operator plus waitressed on the weekends to make ends meet. I might not love Trey's long hours, the travel, or the social obligations, but Trey's career meant I got to watch Anna-Claire's voice lessons and rehearsals, go to Peyton's quiz-bowl and robotics meets, and still have time and money to support causes I loved.

I bent over the crib, and Robert kicked his chunky legs, happy to see me. He cooed as I lifted him, trusting that a fresh diaper and a warm bottle were next. I inhaled the crazy perfume of his head. Nothing on earth smelled as delicious as new baby, and this version was particular to him. Not just the scent of baby. This baby. My baby.

I took him to the changing table, and he gave me the goofy grin he'd invented just last week, toothless and so charming. He was easy. A good sleeper, a good eater. Anna-Claire had been trickier, lovely as long as everything went her way but instantly enraged by dirty diapers and late breakfasts. She was so mercurial and demanding that I'd planned a three-year gap before the next one, but she was barely Robert's age when the stick turned blue. Peyton had been born anxious, and she never slept. Even when I was pregnant, my little insomniac kicked and spun inside me all night long.

"You are my sugar baby," I told Robert, tucking his fat potato feet back into his pajamas and refastening the snaps. "You're going to be a nightmare as a toddler to make up for it, aren't you?"

I toted Robert down the hall to the kitchen to warm his bottle, then sat in the great room, holding him close while he pulled greedily at it. By the time he'd taken his five ounces, the sound of squabbling girls was drifting down the stairs. I kept an ear cocked as I marched Robert up and down, trying to thump a second burp out of him. He had one, I knew it, and he'd be colicky if I didn't coax it out. I hoped the fussing upstairs would resolve on its own. Often it did. But late last year Peyton had gotten her period. She'd instantly synced up with Anna-Claire, and right now we were heading into danger week.

"Mo-om!" Peyton hollered in two aggrieved syllables. "She took my . . ." I missed the last word.

I toted Robert to the bottom of the stairs, jouncing and patting as I walked.

"Anna-Claire," I called up.

She poked her face over the banister. She was sleep-rumpled, her masses of dark hair a tumbled mess, and still beautiful enough to take my breath away.

"You always take her side!"

She had a point. I did tend to take Peyton's side. But life had taken Anna-Claire's. She was built like me, tall and slim, and where I was pretty, she was gorgeous. She had my even features, but her true violet eyes tilted like kitten eyes, and her lips had a natural upturn, as if she were holding a delightful secret in her mouth, readying to speak or swallow it. She'd also come with a whopping scoop of Trey's confidence and extroverted charm.

She'd never had an awkward phase, while Peyton was slap in the middle of hers. Right now puppy fat clung to her middle, and her skin had gone a little crazy. She was as cute as a button, with her dad's round face and snub nose, but when she was next to her sister, people overlooked her.

Peyton joined her sister at the banister. "I haven't even gotten to wear it yet!"

"Give it back," I told Anna-Claire, mild but serious, still thumping at Robert.

"Fine. It's in my middle drawer," Anna-Claire told her sister, then gave me the eye roll she'd perfected in third grade. "It's too big for me anyway."

That was straight-up bitchy, but I let it slide with a warning look because Peyton was already off to go get the whatever-it-was. The fight had been derailed.

I felt a sense of relief that was larger than the moment warranted, as if I'd stepped in and diverted a tempest. I shook my head. It was that awful dream. It still felt like a portentous one. The witch's gaze had been so avid. I felt more than I thought, *Something bad is coming for us.*

I shook the little voice warning of doom away. My mother owned it. The voice in her own head must be a stentor. My father by all reports had been a piece of work. I'd never met him, and I was grateful, considering. He was the reason she wouldn't get on an elevator with any man. Not alone. She kept a loaded handgun in a safe by her bed and was always gifting me pepper sprays and safety whistles. I had never once wondered where Peyton came by her anxiety, but I didn't live like that. I refused to see the world that way. And I wasn't going to borrow trouble when I was facing a week of single-parenting two hormone-crazed middle-school girls and a baby.

Anna-Claire stomped down the stairs to the first landing and cocked her hip at me. "Remember you're a snack mom for rehearsal this afternoon."

"I know." Robert let out that last, sneaky burp. It was a whopper.

"Don't bring bananas," Anna-Claire said. "Cara's dad always brings those gross generic fruit-snack things, so you need to bring something edible."

I kept my smile in place, but it went a little stiff when I heard that Marshall Chase was the other "snack mom." They really called it that, as if male parents were incapable of passing out raisin boxes and bottled waters. To be fair, he was the only dad I'd ever seen do it. Marshall was tall and lanky and attractive; the other moms made jokes about *him* being the snack, but a couple of months back, when *Grease, Junior* was cast, Anna-Claire got the alto lead. His own daughter got Marty. It was a good part with a solo, but it wasn't Rizzo. I hadn't ever thought of Marshall as the stage-parent type, but there was no denying that the balmy air between us had gone cool.

I hated it; Marshall and I had both grown up way out in Hurd County, Georgia. His wife, Betsy, had lived across the street from me. She'd been my best friend since before I had concrete memory. She and Marshall dated for most of high school, but they'd broken up when Betsy and I moved into Atlanta to attend Georgia State. Betsy had always been wilder than me, bolder, both more reckless and more fun. By the end of freshman year, she lost her scholarship, and she wasn't even sorry. She went home, got a job, got back with Marshall. They'd gone through the police academy together and gotten married.

Our lives had forked, but Betsy and I had stayed close. We'd been each other's maid of honor, and we'd been pregnant together; Cara was born a month before Anna-Claire. I'd always liked Marshall, though in that best-friend's-husband way that rendered him more Ken doll than man.

When Betsy died in the line of duty, five years back, he'd wanted to move to a safer job, for Cara's sake. Trey had hired him as an investigator. The firm had been thrilled to get him. Marshall was excellent; he'd been one of the youngest cops ever to make detective in Atlanta.

Last year Cara's public school lost its arts funding. No more chorus or drama club, and Cara was distraught. Trey put in a word at St. Alban's, and they'd offered her a scholarship. I'd hoped she and Anna-Claire would bond, like a mini me-and-Betsy, because Anna-Claire was also hip-deep into musical theatre and choir. Instead they were competitors, always up for the same parts and solos.

I couldn't make them love each other, but I could threaten my too-pretty, too-popular daughter with phoneless exile and unending extra chores if she did one single thing to make Cara feel picked on or unwelcome. Cara had quickly found her own friend set, and her grades were excellent, so I considered the transfer a success. For her.

I'd hoped it would finally give me a real friend at the school. I had more in common with Marshall than with any of the other snack moms. At thirty-eight we were a decade younger than the remaining first wives and a decade older than the stepmothers. Most of these women had grown up with ponies and summers in Provence, while Marshall and I had had secondhand bikes and vacation Bible school.

Instead he'd gotten cooler and cooler, until I worried that my daughter was stealth-hazing his. I'd snuck around, eavesdropping at rehearsals, only to find them working well together. Friendly if not friends.

Even so, Marshall got ever more polite, gravely asking me how my day was going in the same professional, cool tone he used on the pampered Gen Two baby-wives of some of the other lawyers at the firm, like the one divorcing Spence right now.

I hadn't hired a full-time nanny and made a career out of yoga class and blowouts. I hadn't gotten into an affair and busted up Trey's first marriage either. He and Maura split up amicably a year before we met, mostly because he wanted children and she didn't. Marshall knew all this. He knew me, knew my family.

It bothered me, and I guess it showed, because Anna-Claire caught my stiffness and added, sly, "You should bring those organic Bunny Fruit Snacks. So Mr. Chase knows not to perpetrate that crap." My eldest had a nose for drama, even when she was offstage.

I shook my head. "All fruit snacks are just tarted-up candy."

"Ho snack!" Anna-Claire said, laughing. "I should tell Cara that you said her dad brought a ho snack. The cheap kind!"

"If you do, rest assured I'll be bringing nothing but

bananas for the rest of the year." She made a face. "Now, scoot. Car pool comes in twenty minutes."

"I'm mostly ready." She came all the way down to pet her brother's head, peeping up at me. "Aw, you look sleepy. Want me to take Bumper so you can get a shower?"

"Robert," I corrected, but I was smiling. Typical Anna-Claire. She'd torment her sister, push boundaries with me, then instaflip to thoughtful. Moments like these I knew she could grow into a lovely, kindhearted woman, as long as Trey and I kept the parenting tight. She was so beautiful that kids and adults alike catered to her in ways that weren't good for her. It was hard to find the balance between pushing back on that while still being a hundred percent on her side. "You're sweet, but I got it. Thank you."

I kissed her and went to check Trey's packing. He was so color-blind that left to himself he could end up looking like a Mardi Gras float. I narrowly averted a green/blue disaster, then got him out the door. The girls' ride showed up soon after, and I fell into my day.

Just errands and e-mails, but I was operating on New Baby Time. Even the simplest things took four times longer than normal. The final bell was ringing as I pulled into the parking lot by the new Performing Arts Center at St. Alban's. Hordes of kids began streaming out of the buildings. I hurried as fast as I could while lugging Robert in his infant carrier, his diaper bag, and a reusable grocery bag full of snacks.

The PAC had a long, narrow greenroom between the chorus's practice room and the orchestra's, furnished in a hodgepodge of donated chairs and sofas. The whole

back wall was windows, facing the parking lot. I saw
Marshall already in there and broke into a trot. He
was dressed for work in a blue suit that was older than
Anna-Claire. I remembered Betsy buying it. It hung
awkwardly on his long frame.

By the time I got inside, he'd already set up the table
and was laying out fruit snacks and Capri Sun pouches
for a steady stream of chattering kids.

"I'm here, sorry!" It came out chirpy and overbright.

"No problem." He didn't look up.

I set Robert's carrier on a nearby sofa and started
putting out milk boxes and Ziploc snack bags of baby
carrots with hummus cups.

Marshall looked at my offering, his eyebrows lifting. "Does every bag have the exact same number of
carrots?"

They did, actually. Ten. I felt a blush beginning, but
I was saved from answering by Cara's entrance. She
looked so much like her mother that it hurt my heart
every time.

"Hey, Sugar Peep," Marshall said.

She shot him a mortified glare at the nickname and
then said, "Hey, Auntie Bree," overly loud and bright.

I said, "Break a leg today, kiddo," and handed her a
milk box.

She hurried out, and I gave Marshall a commiserating look. "Both my girls are in that same stage. Sweet to
me at home, but in public I'm poison."

He smiled, unworried. "I hear that in high school
they stop pretending that they budded off of Rihanna
and will admit to actually having parents."

Just then Anna-Claire bounded through the door in
full sunshine mode, her friend Greer in tow. She re-

leased Greer to hurl her arms around me. "Mom! Hummus! If you'd gotten pita chips, it would almost be a worthy snack!"

"Oh, yeah. I see how it is for you." Marshall sounded good-humored, but not like Marshall. I couldn't explain it, but I'd known him long enough to feel the difference.

Greer ignored the snacks. "Hi, Ms. Cabbat! Did you bring the baby?" As soon as she said it, she saw the car seat and dropped down to her knees in front of Robert. He was awake and beginning to make hungry noises. "Hi, Bumper! Oh, I love his feet! He's so little. I can't stand it!" She pinched his toes, distracting him, making him gurgle.

"We call him Robert," I said.

"That's right, Bumper, we call you Robert," Anna-Claire said, grabbing snacks and then hauling Greer to her feet. They went galloping out in a swirl of plaid uniform skirts.

I turned back to Marshall to say something about adolescent mood swings, but what I saw over his shoulder froze my body, inside and out. It was a blotch of slow-moving darkness on the other side of the big wall of windows. It stopped my words, my very breath. It was *her*. The witch, from my dream. The one I'd seen peering in my window this morning. She was in the parking lot. Right beside my SUV.

2

SHE WAS NOT A witch, of course. Just a little old lady in a baggy black dress and cardigan. She lurched past my car, hurrying across the lot with a limping, pained gait. She did have a hat on, a dark knit cap that came to a sort of peak, but it was not tall or excessively pointy.

"Bree?" Marshall said, concerned. I wasn't sure what my face was doing.

I pushed past him, running to the windows.

He joined me. "Are you okay?"

"I'm fine." I didn't sound fine, even though this woman was the least threatening thing that I had ever seen. She was ancient, and toting an earth-conscious reusable grocery bag much like mine, for God's sake.

But she did resemble my dream witch. Especially her hair, striped gunmetal gray and silver, the thin locks straggling out from under her hat.

I wondered if I should call the headmaster, or even the police, just to get a report on the record. In case the witch hadn't been a dream but a thing my subconscious had made out of this actual woman. In case she really had been lurking in my backyard.

It seemed ridiculous, though. I knew what they would

think of me, a mom with a new baby, overanxious and sleep-deprived. I could perfectly imagine their amused glances if I called them to report seeing a little old lady, maybe twice. It would be worse if I was truthful and mentioned the dream I'd had earlier. *A witch, you say?* They would be polite, but only because we lived in Decatur; we had high property taxes and our own police force. Money bought manners, and Trey made a lot of it. Otherwise I knew how it would go.

I knew because when I was growing up, my mother called the police on the regular. She lived convinced that my father might come back, even after he'd gone to prison. Even after he was dead. She'd hear him creeping around under the house or on the roof at night. And yes, she often thought she saw a figure peering in our windows.

I knew most of our regular beat cops by name. Officer McKenzie would at least shine his light into the crawl space, but his flat gaze and long, slow exhales made it clear he thought my mom was crazy. Officer Loomis was more blunt about it. *There are people in actual trouble. And here I am. With you. Again.* Officer Dobson was the worst, looming over us, anger palpable in the lines of his big body. Once I heard him mutter, *I ought to give you something to be scared about, lady,* as he left. He was only a little less frightening than the imagined man she'd called about.

When I got pregnant with Peyton so soon after Anna-Claire, my mom let us buy her a condo near us. I'd long wanted to evacuate her from the leaky two-bedroom ranch where I'd grown up, but she wouldn't move until she believed she was doing it for me. It *was* wonderful having her close when I had a newborn and a one-year-old, but the best part of the condo was the on-site security. All guests had to sign in and out, and only residents had key cards that would activate the elevators. Mom hadn't called the cops once since she moved in, and yet, as I considered calling them myself, the mingled shame and fear from childhood were churning in me. I'd never learned my born-wealthy husband's ease. In his mind the police worked for him, cruising our neighborhood to keep us safe. Whenever I saw them passing through or parked on our corner, I was swamped with the irrational, anxious feeling that I'd done a crime so secret that even I didn't realize it.

Maybe I should tell Marshall? For all his recent coolness, I still trusted him. If he took my witch sightings seriously, it would be permission for me to as well.

"Did you see that woman?" I asked. She was already out of sight.

"The meemaw?"

"Did she look like a . . . ?" I couldn't bring myself to say the word "witch." Marshall didn't have time for this nonsense any more than the actual police would. "No, it's stupid. Never mind." He was concerned, though, leaning toward me like the old friend that he was. It felt like an opening to fix whatever this breach was, and surely that mattered more than a bad dream. I touched his arm. "Do you have to go straight back to work, or can you stay and watch rehearsal with me?"

He blinked and stepped back. I could almost feel a wall of cool air whoosh back between us. "They let you do that?" There was a slight emphasis on the "you," as if he thought I'd finagled some rare privilege.

"Any parent with a kid in the show can," I assured him. I wasn't sure if this was technically true, but a lot of moms did it. "If we sit up in the balcony, Ms. Taft won't even notice."

Marshall's eyebrows came together. "There's a balcony?"

"Yes. You haven't gone in to see the performance space?" The new PAC had been open for only eight weeks. *Grease, Junior* would be the first middle-school show on the big stage. "It seats five hundred."

"Practically Broadway. That'll be fun for the kids," Marshall said. "And I bet Anna-Claire will be front and center every show."

It sounded like a compliment, but Marshall knew that Trey's family had paid for a good bit of the construction. Trey and his sister were both alumni, and our nieces attended high school here. Was Marshall implying that the Cabbats were buying roles for Anna-Claire?

I felt my cheeks go pink, indignant. Marshall had been at work during auditions, but I'd watched. After Anna-Claire sang "There Are Worse Things I Could Do," I'd heard a mom behind me whisper to her friend, "Wow. Guess we know who'll be Rizzo."

I'd agreed. I was biased, sure, but I'd also majored in theatre. I'd had lead parts in a ton of shows, starting in middle school myself. I still loved theatre, and Trey got the whole family season tickets to the Fox and the Alliance for my birthday every year. I'd taken the girls up to New York for Broadway weekends ever since they were old enough to sit through a show. I'd done and seen enough to know that my talented daughter had beaten out every other kid, including his, that day. By a mile.

I stopped myself before I said any of this to Marshall, though. Anna-Claire had polished her audition for weeks with her vocal coach, Mr. Reggie, who'd been on

Broadway himself. He cost a hundred and fifty bucks an hour.

Cara was as naturally gifted as my kid, but her talent was raw. Early in college I'd lost parts to girls who'd grown up with money for drama camp, acting classes, vocal training. I remembered being eighteen years old and already feeling so behind.

So I only said, "Well, I'm going to watch," and picked up Robert's carrier seat. He made a *pah* noise. "Almost suppertime," I promised him.

To my surprise, Marshall asked, "So where are the stairs?"

I was still smarting, but I gave him the warmest smile I could. "This way."

In the balcony Peyton was already sitting in the back row, reading. I set Robert's carrier down beside her. If he started squalling, I wanted a straight shot out into the stairwell, so we wouldn't disturb rehearsal.

I'd brought his bottle in a warming sleeve, and as I got it out, Peyton asked, "Can I feed Bumper?"

"Robert. Sure." I peeled him out of his chair and settled him in her arms.

Marshall had made his way to the middle of the balcony's front row. I went down to join him, but I sat on the end, still smarting from his insinuation.

The performance was a week away, so they were running full scenes. They were in the park now, and Anna-Claire was singing "Look at Me, I'm Sandra Dee." It was cute, though in this junior version there was no mention of drinking, smoking, or swearing, much less sex. Instead Rizzo mocked Sandy for her good grades and being a "square."

As Anna-Claire vamped across the stage, I realized

the bit about not "coming across" had survived the edits. I don't think Ms. Taft, who was in her twenties, knew it was sexual. And neither did our new young headmaster apparently, because he had approved the script. St. Alban's was Episcopalian, quite liberal for a church-run school—but not that liberal.

I shot an amused smile at Marshall, but he was watching Cara dance with the other Pink Ladies.

Peyton came up and joined me. I glanced back at Robert's carrier seat, still by the back row.

"Asleep?" I asked quietly.

"Dead to the world."

"Did he burp?"

"Twice, Mom." Peyton gave me her mild version of her elder sister's eye roll. "I know how to do Bumper."

"Robert."

"She really is talented," Marshall said in a gruff whisper. He was looking at Anna-Claire now, his face impassive.

If this was an apology, I'd take it. "Cara is, too. Her big number is in the sleepover scene. She kills it."

The director called the kids in for a huddle. I glanced back over my shoulder. The car seat sat sideways to me, so all I saw was Robert's feet in their puppy socks, but this was his biggest nap of the day. I could probably click the carrier into the car and drive home before he woke up.

I told Marshall, "I'm going to clean up the greenroom." I knew from experience the kids would have stuffed fruit-snack wrappers all down in the couch cushions.

He was already rising. "I got it."

"You did the setup," I reminded him.

"Stay. That table's heavy." He turned toward the other aisle so he wouldn't have to climb over my knees.

"Want to help?" I asked Peyton. No response until I put my hand in between her face and the page. "Hey. You coming down?"

"I'm going to read here until it's really time to go. A-C takes forever to peel herself off Greer."

"Anna-Claire," I corrected. Honestly, "A-C" was as bad as "Bumper." "Your sister is not a cooling system."

"She kinda is." Peyton shrugged, jealousy and admiration at war in her expression. "Greer says Anna-Claire makes any room she's in feel cool. Now everyone calls her that."

I glanced after Marshall, already disappearing into the stairwell on the other side. If I didn't hurry, he'd clean up alone. More proof that I was a spoiled second wifey. Still, my middle child needed a moment.

"I think you're cool," I told her.

She snorted. "You're my mom. The fact that you think I'm cool means I'm for sure a dork."

"Well, cool is overrated. And sometimes it's code for a little bit mean. But you? You're smart. A good student. Super cute. Best of all, you have a kind heart."

She shrugged it off, disappearing into her book again, but I could see her fighting a smile.

"Good talk," I said to no one. But it had been.

Peyton went back to reading. Ten seconds later I could have set a bomb off beside her and she wouldn't have heard it. I used to read like that when I was young. Before I was a mother. Now nothing took me that far from reality.

Except maybe watching my children perform. Ms. Taft had decided to run the Sandra Dee song one more time. It was time to clean up, but Marshall had told me I could stay. Anna-Claire came center and began, and the whole world fell away again. It was the same when I was at a robotics match and Peyton was at the controls. At ten weeks all Robert had to do was show his brand-new toothless smile to put me into a trance.

When she finished, I stood and gave her huge, silent thumbs-up, then patted Peyton's oblivious knee. When I turned to go, I didn't see Robert's car seat.

But that wasn't possible. It had been right there.

I hurried up the aisle, caught in a chilly disbelief. Maybe the seat was behind the chairs? But who had moved it? No one else had been up here. I tried to remember the last time I'd looked back to check on him. Not long. I didn't think. But I'd been talking to Peyton, and then Anna-Claire had started singing—

This was scary, but at the same time part of me was sure there was an explanation. Maybe Greer had taken him back down to the greenroom. She was baby crazy.

I was at the row now, and he was gone. Just gone. So was his diaper bag. His empty bottle lay abandoned on the floor. Beside it was a single sheet of white paper, folded in half.

I picked it up, my hands visibly trembling. I opened it. A note. Handwritten in large block print.

IF YOU EVER WANT TO SEE YOUR BABY AGAIN, GO HOME—

The black ink went blurry. The paper rattled in my hands. I couldn't read. I couldn't see or breathe. My spine was glass, and all my blood was water. I found myself sitting on the floor beside his empty bottle. My dazed mind noted there was a little milk in it, maybe half an ounce. I blinked hard, trying to clear my vision. But I didn't need to read more of the note to know what had happened.

I had not dreamed a witch. I'd seen a real person, made of flesh and bone and a secret, dark agenda, peering in my window. I'd seen her again, hurrying through the parking lot toward the fire door that the kids kept propping open. She'd been stalking me.

No. She'd been stalking Robert. And now she had him.